Praise for
Jacey Ford's Partners in Crime novels

"A wonderful edge-of-your-seat read . . . grips you from the first page. I couldn't put it down. Don't miss this one!"

—Christine Feehan

"An entertaining police procedural romance starring two wonderful protagonists. The lead couple is a tremendous twosome . . . fabulous suspense."

—*Midwest Book Review*

"Greed, betrayal, and adventure make for one thrilling read. *Dangerous Curves* hits all the right notes with its combination of romance and danger."

—*Romantic Times Book Club*

"Taut romantic suspense with great mystery."

—*The Best Reviews*

Berkley Sensation titles by Jacey Ford

DANGEROUS CURVES

I SPY

DEAD HEAT

JACEY FORD

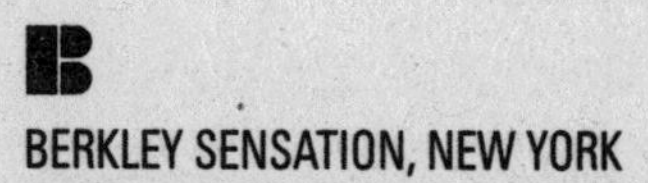

BERKLEY SENSATION, NEW YORK

THE BERKLEY PUBLISHING GROUP
Published by the Penguin Group
Penguin Group (USA) Inc.
375 Hudson Street, New York, New York 10014, USA
Penguin Group (Canada), 90 Eglinton Avenue East, Suite 700, Toronto, Ontario M4P 2Y3, Canada
(a division of Pearson Penguin Canada Inc.)
Penguin Books Ltd., 80 Strand, London WC2R 0RL, England
Penguin Group Ireland, 25 St. Stephen's Green, Dublin 2, Ireland (a division of Penguin Books Ltd.)
Penguin Group (Australia), 250 Camberwell Road, Camberwell, Victoria 3124, Australia
(a division of Pearson Australia Group Pty. Ltd.)
Penguin Books India Pvt. Ltd., 11 Community Centre, Panchsheel Park, New Delhi—110 017, India
Penguin Group (NZ), Cnr. Airborne and Rosedale Roads, Albany, Auckland 1310, New Zealand
(a division of Pearson New Zealand Ltd.)
Penguin Books (South Africa) (Pty.) Ltd., 24 Sturdee Avenue, Rosebank, Johannesburg 2196, South Africa

Penguin Books Ltd., Registered Offices: 80 Strand, London WC2R 0RL, England

DEAD HEAT

A Berkley Sensation Book / published by arrangement with the author

PRINTING HISTORY
Berkley Sensation mass-market edition / March 2006

Interior text design by Kristin del Rosario.

ISBN: 0-425-20461-8

BERKLEY® SENSATION
Berkley Sensation Books are published by The Berkley Publishing Group,
a division of Penguin Group (USA) Inc.,
375 Hudson Street, New York, New York 10014.
BERKLEY SENSATION and the "B" design are trademarks belonging to Penguin Group (USA) Inc.

PRINTED IN THE UNITED STATES OF AMERICA

10 9 8 7 6 5 4 3 2 1

PROLOGUE

2/13/2005

EVERYTHING was perfect.

Jenna Marisol looked up from the red and white birthday cake she was carefully decorating with sugared berries and smiled. Through the wide window over the kitchen sink, she could see the brightly colored waterslide the Parties to Go employees had set up earlier on the back lawn. Painted dolphins, starfish, and other sea creatures adorned the otherwise plain green plastic. With the kitchen window cracked open, Jenna could hear the faint whirring of the motor used to pump water up and over the three slides.

Yvonne and Yvette had always loved waterslides, but Jenna never let the girls have a water-themed party. The weather in February was simply too unpredictable, and Jenna hadn't wanted to chance the other mothers boycotting the twins' celebration out of fear that their own children might catch a cold.

This year, however, she'd decided to throw caution to the wind. Her babies had been born thirteen years ago today and she was going to give them a party no one would ever forget.

Jenna studied the magazine spread out on the counter beside her right hand. It was one of those lifestyle periodicals that showcased the lives of women who had plenty of time—and money—on their hands. This was an older issue, one Jenna had diligently searched for for months. She had known exactly the sort of party she wanted to throw for the twins because she'd attended a similar one at the home of the head of her husband's company a decade ago, and photos of then-thirteen-year-old Nicole Solem's birthday party had been included in this issue. Jenna remembered being as awestruck as her girls as they'd wandered the grounds of the Solems' home in Naples, Florida, that day, stopping first at the mini petting zoo and then taking turns sliding down the waterslides that had been set up for the event.

Jenna had done her best to re-create that long-ago party, cutting back where she had to. Her mother's yard here in Dallas wasn't large enough to accommodate a petting zoo, so Jenna had dropped that from her list. The twins hadn't cared much for the animals, anyway. But the waterslide was something Jenna wouldn't budge on. Yvonne and Yvette deserved that, at least.

She could only hope that her mother didn't make a fuss about the mess the slide would make on her perfectly manicured lawn.

Jenna frowned slightly as she placed another sugared raspberry along the rim of the smallest of the seven cakes she'd made for the girls' party today. Things hadn't been easy since she'd moved in with her mother three years ago.

Mother was too critical, always trying to tell Jenna what she should or shouldn't do. Before her husband, Aaron, had died, Jenna would have found it easy to dismiss her mother's sniping. As her high school sweetheart, Aaron had been Jenna's savior, encouraging her to go to college out of state and get away from her overbearing mother. They'd left Dallas together, she and Aaron. And after graduating from Stanford, they'd married and had the life they always dreamed of—quiet and content with one another. Right out of school, Aaron took a job as a low-level lab assistant with Geon, a pharmaceutical company that specialized in creating antidotes for biological and chemical weapons. In the beginning he had been frustrated, feeling like a faceless drone in such a large company. But at her urging, he'd stuck it out, slowly inching up the corporate ladder while Jenna—a biochemist—took a quicker route to the top at the firm where she worked. Despite a yearlong sabbatical after the twins were born, Jenna had led a seemingly charmed life . . . at work, at least. She'd somehow managed to be assigned to one successful product team after another. The year Aaron had died, her bonus alone had been twice what Aaron earned at Geon.

Jenna had never cared about that, though. She figured the more money she made, the more they could put away for the twins' education and their own early retirement. She hadn't realized that Aaron hadn't felt the same way.

Jenna sighed and shook her head to rid her mind of unpleasant thoughts. Today was supposed to be a happy day. She should be focusing on the good times—on the day her babies had been born and how delighted both she and Aaron were to become parents.

She remembered it all so clearly, her astonishment when her water broke without warning. She'd been in the lab testing a new cancer drug when warm liquid had suddenly flowed down her legs, puddling at her feet. She'd been mortified, had wanted to clean it up before anyone saw what she'd done, but her female coworkers had just laughed it off.

Even now, thirteen years later, Jenna felt her cheeks heat with embarrassment.

But that moment of shame and the hours of painful labor afterward had been a small price to pay for the squirming babies the doctor had placed in her arms when it was all over. The girls were small—Yvonne was five pounds, three ounces, and Yvette was only four and a half pounds—but the nurses assured her that they were actually a very good weight for twins. Jenna remembered beaming when she heard this, as if she were somehow responsible for being able to keep the babies inside her long enough for them to grow to a healthy weight.

Jenna smiled now as she used the rim of a water glass to cut a large circle out of the dark red fondant on the counter. She checked the magazine photo of Nicole Solem's birthday cakes, and then gazed at her own creations with a critical eye. The cakes in the photo were covered with white frosting decorated with dark red and pink circles and then topped with sugared berries. Jenna was certain that Nicole's wealthy parents had hired professional bakers to create their daughter's desserts, but she thought that hers were just as lovely. She stood back and clasped her hands together, admiring her handiwork.

Her cakes were perfect. The twins would have—

"What the hell is going on here?"

Jenna stiffened at her mother's sharp tone, but refused to turn around. Instead, she focused her gaze on the well-tended backyard beyond the kitchen. Her mother had no interest in gardening, but insisted that her gardener keep the hedges and ornamental shrubs neatly trimmed all year round. Jenna, on the other hand, loved being outside with her hands in the dirt. When she was growing up, the gardener, old Tommie Osgood, helped her memorize the scientific names of all the plants, patiently explaining which ones were poisonous, which needed cutting back in the fall if they were to bloom in the spring, which would get spindly if you didn't prune them, and which would only grow so tall, no matter how much fertilizer she heaped on them.

Jenna filled her mind with pleasant memories of old Tommie and tried to drown out the sound of her mother's voice by listening intently to the hum of the waterslide's motor. It was a pleasant day for early February, unseasonably warm at nearly seventy degrees. Last week it had been in the forties, and Jenna had worried that the Parties to Go people might refuse to set up the waterslide if the temperatures remained so low. But she needn't have worried.

"Jenna!" her mother said sharply, and Jenna sighed. She couldn't ignore Mother, not when she was like this.

Slowly, Jenna turned. She knew that she looked like a younger version of her mother—her fair skin still unlined, her light brown hair streaked with blond instead of gray, her green eyes unwrinkled at the edges. But there was something else that differentiated Regina Marisol from her daughter, a hard edge that Jenna had never possessed.

Perhaps that was why the tragedy that had befallen Jenna had left her mother unscathed. Regina had gone on afterward as if nothing affected her, whereas Jenna awoke each day since Aaron's death with such heavy pain in her heart that she felt as if its weight would smother her.

"I thought you were going to be at Mrs. Woolrich's until eight," Jenna said, tracing one of the grout lines in the tile floor with her big toe.

"Nellie got sick and we didn't have a foursome for our bridge game so we cancelled our evening," Regina said, waving one hand imperiously at the cakes on the counter. "But that doesn't explain *this*."

Jenna glanced up at the desserts she had worked so hard on all afternoon. They had turned out so perfectly, exactly like the picture in the magazine. Why did Mother have to come home and ruin everything?

She cleared her throat and chanced a look at her mother, whose face was flushed with—what? Anger? Annoyance? Disgust? Jenna had never understood why her mother was so quick to lose her temper with her only child. Before she'd had the twins, Jenna thought it was typical for parents to be impatient and intolerant with their children. But she'd never felt that way with Yvonne and Yvette. Yes, at times it took them longer to do something than it would have taken her to accomplish the same task, and they weren't always clean or quiet or even obedient. Still, Jenna had found such joy in her daughters that her temper rarely flared with them.

"I just thought I'd do something special today," she said, nervously reaching out to rearrange the sugared berries that graced the top of one of the cakes.

Regina grabbed Jenna's wrist, her grip strong from mornings spent playing tennis at the country club. "It's been nearly three years. This has to stop."

Jenna blinked rapidly, trying to quell the tears that had sprung to her eyes. No. She was *not* going to cry, not in front of her mother. "I didn't realize there was a statute of limitations on grief," she said softly.

"Stop being so melodramatic. I don't expect you to go on as if nothing ever happened, but these grandiose displays are becoming embarrassing. Do you know that Edna Hartman called me last week after she saw you in the junior's department at Macy's? She said you told her that you were buying birthday dresses for the girls. That was bad enough. I can only imagine what the neighbors are going to say about *this*." Regina dropped her daughter's hand and pointed accusingly in the direction of the waterslide in the backyard. The Parties to Go employee who had set it up stood on the far side of the lawn, near a grouping of ornamental shrubs that had small, dark leaves with serrated edges and bright red berries.

Daphne bushes, Jenna thought absently as she watched

the Parties to Go employee glance curiously around the empty yard. When the twins were toddlers, she had asked her mother to get rid of the shrubs because their pretty red berries, which were so appealing to the girls, were highly poisonous. According to old Tommie, just one berry could easily kill a child.

But Mother had refused. She felt that it was Jenna's responsibility to either train her children not to eat things they shouldn't or pay the price for their disobedience by having to watch their every move. Fortunately, neither of her girls were the type to put foreign objects in their mouth and they emerged from toddlerhood without even one poison scare.

"They would have turned thirteen today," Jenna said, surprised to hear herself say the words aloud.

"Yes. If their psychotic father hadn't killed them," her mother countered.

Jenna winced at the harshness of her mother's tone. She was always so hard on Aaron, didn't even try to understand how devastated he'd been when he'd lost not only his job at Geon, but their entire life savings as well.

Jenna hadn't known that Aaron had invested all their money in Geon stock. She'd always left their finances up to him, thinking it would make him feel better about his role as a provider if he was able to take their combined earnings and invest it to increase their net worth. She had no idea that he'd gambled their future on insider information—information that turned out to be as worthless as Geon stock.

If only Geon's CEO hadn't lied to everyone about the fiscal health of the company, none of this would have happened. Nathan Solem, of course, had been divesting his portfolio of Geon stock for months. Meanwhile, assuring employees that the company was fiscally sound, he encouraged them to increase their own holdings.

Until the day it had all fallen apart.

"It wasn't Aaron's fault," Jenna whispered.

Next to her, her mother let out a frustrated sigh and pushed her neatly trimmed graying hair behind her ears. The diamond earrings she'd bought herself for her fiftieth birthday sparkled in the sunshine spilling in through the kitchen window. "Go out there and tell that poor man that there's not going to be any party. And make sure you tip him well. God only knows what he's going to tell people about this. I don't want him saying you're stingy as well as mentally unstable."

Jenna chewed on the inside of her cheek. She didn't want the man to leave, didn't want her fantasy to end. As long as the waterslide was here and there were gaily wrapped packages on the patio waiting to be opened and slices of birthday cake to serve, she could almost believe that her babies were still alive, that her husband hadn't cracked under the pressure of losing everything and drowned them both before turning a gun on himself one night when Jenna was out of town at a conference.

Didn't her mother understand that she just wasn't ready to let go of them yet?

But her mother wouldn't relent. "Then whose fault was it?" Regina asked. "Don't tell me you're now subscribing to some sort of 'grassy knoll' theory. No, it wasn't Aaron who drowned the girls. It was some sort of conspiracy to stop him from selling Geon's high-level secrets to a competitor. Oh, except Aaron didn't know any high-level secrets. If he had, he wouldn't have been stupid enough to put all of your money in Geon stock. Or would he? He wasn't exactly the sharpest tool in the shed, now was he?"

Regina's humorless laugh skittered across Jenna's skin like a chill breeze. She shivered and wrapped her arms around herself. "Stop it, Mother," she said.

"It's not me who needs to stop. It's you. You have to stop moping around this house, stop wasting hour after hour staring at those old photo albums you've kept. The twins are dead. Your husband is gone. It's time for you to move on, start a new life. You can't go on living like this."

She opened a cupboard door and took down a water glass, her neatly manicured fingernails clicking on the crystal. Regina loved her Waterford.

Probably more than she ever loved me, Jenna thought, her gaze following her mother's movements as she poured herself a glass of filtered water from the pitcher on the counter.

It was almost as if her mother believed that Aaron and the girls were replaceable, like crystal glasses that had shattered on the tile floor and all Jenna needed to do in order to get her life back was to go down to Macy's and order a new set.

Jenna squeezed her eyes shut. If only it were that easy.

But Mother was right about one thing—she couldn't go on living like this. Looking at the pictures of her loved ones every day and knowing that the person responsible had never been brought to justice was something she simply couldn't stomach any longer. *He* had had no trouble moving on. As a matter of fact, Jenna wouldn't be surprised to learn that Nathan Solem knew nothing about how his lies had affected someone as insignificant as lowly lab technician Aaron Richardson. Jenna opened her eyes and turned slightly to look at the magazine still spread open on the counter. No, Nicole Solem's father probably had no idea that he was responsible for the murder of Jenna's family. *His* daughter was still alive, had graduated from an Ivy League college and had grown into a lovely young woman. Jenna knew everything about Nicole Solem, had followed her progress ever since she'd managed to claw her way out of the dark pit of despair and pieced together what had really happened to cause Aaron to do what he had done that day.

And now it was time for Jenna to move on.

She let her arms drop from around her waist and turned to face her mother. "I'm sorry if I embarrassed you," she said calmly. "I'll go tell the Parties to Go man that he can leave."

Regina nodded, silently sipping her water as Jenna walked to the French doors that led out onto the patio.

Jenna paused with her hand on the doorknob, intently watching a mockingbird alight on a branch of one of the Daphne bushes near where the party-planning company employee was standing.

"It would be a shame to let all that cake go to waste, though. When I get back, why don't I make some coffee and we can have a taste of the little one. It's lemon with raspberry filling. Your favorite," Jenna added, her grip tightening on the metal knob. It had been Yvonne's favorite, too.

"That would be nice. I'll box the others up and bring them to my canasta club tomorrow," her mother said.

Jenna nodded and let herself out into the backyard.

And as she slowly walked toward the plant with its beautifully poisonous red berries—berries that could easily be hidden in a slice of raspberry-filled birthday cake—she smiled as the mockingbird took flight, heading toward the sunlight as it left the earth behind.

ONE

2/8/2006

"I thought I'd find you here."

Daphne Donovan didn't bother looking up from her dollar-twenty-five cup of coffee as the man slid his stocky frame into the booth across from her. Outwardly she appeared calm and unruffled—uncaring, even—despite the thought that ran through her head: *I'm so busted.* She raised the heavy porcelain cup to her lips, ignoring the heat coming through the too-hot cup and burning her fingertips as she pretended to take a sip.

"I was just following up on a final lead before my meeting with the client," Daphne lied, without so much as a blink or a flicker of her eyes to give her away.

"Yeah? What sort of lead?" her brother, ex–NYPD cop and current *New York Times* bestseller Brooks Madison asked, resting one arm along the top of the booth.

Despite his Ivy League name, Brooks looked more like a

boxer than a member of the Republican Party and he was currently leveling his best don't-give-me-any-shit look directly at her. But it took a lot to intimidate her. Certainly, one dirty look from the guy she'd hero-worshipped since the day her mother had dragged her reluctantly into the Madison household when she was twelve wasn't enough to do it. Maybe it would have worked if Brooks hadn't always been so nice to her, letting her tag along with him even if it meant he had to endure the ridicule of his friends. Daff thought Brooks treated her a bit like a three-legged dog—with mild affection despite the fact that you sometimes had the urge to tie tin cans to its tail just to see it hop around. But maybe that's just what it felt like to be a little sister. Since she'd been an only child until dear old Mom left her at Brooks's dad's house and pulled the Ol' Disappearing Woman act, Daff didn't know if the way she felt about the man she thought of as her brother was normal or not.

Probably not, since nothing in her life had ever been normal.

Daff took a sip of scalding-hot coffee, careful not to let the man across from her know that it was burning her throat as she swallowed.

"I followed Dean down here yesterday and watched him walk into that electronics store over there," she said, indicating a storefront across the street. The windows were brightly painted with red hearts and yellow flowers announcing the upcoming Valentine's Day sale. Daff suspected that on February 15, the hearts and flowers would be replaced with cherry trees and stovepipe hats for an upcoming Presidents' Day sale, while the prices of the merchandise remained unchanged.

"Convenient," Brooks muttered under his breath as the waitress who had brought Daff's coffee sidled up to the table and gave him the once-over about three times.

"What can I get you?" she asked.

"You eaten?" Brooks said with a quirk of one brow.

Daphne swallowed and curled her fingers around her cup of coffee, fighting a sudden wave of nausea. She couldn't eat here. Just the thought of it made her gag.

Brooks looked so sad for a moment that Daphne lowered her head to hide the sudden tears welling up in her eyes. God, she hated that. She was disgusted with both having her brother feel sorry for her and the tears that never seemed far from the surface these days.

"I'll just have coffee," Brooks said, and the waitress disappeared after giving him a disappointed shrug.

Desperate not to talk about what was really on both of their minds, Daphne squeezed her cup tighter and blurted, "Dean bought a cheap clock radio. Nothing fancy. Didn't even have a CD player or anything."

Her brother laid a hand on her arm. "You shouldn't have followed him down here."

Daff blinked rapidly to stop the tears from falling into her coffee. "I'm being paid to find out what he did with my client's money. I can't do that if I don't run down my leads."

"I could have checked this one out for you," Brooks said.

Daphne lifted her head to look out the window beyond her brother's shoulder. The sidewalk outside was filled with the usual array of busy New Yorkers, their eyes straight ahead, hurrying past without looking either right or left. The world was gray, the air filled with a heavy wet dust that seemed to color the people walking past. The occasional car or bus sped by, but traffic seemed lighter, and horns honked almost timidly on this stretch of roadway. Beyond the street stretched the World Trade Center redevelopment site. Progress was slow. From day to day, it was difficult to tell that anything had changed. Yet Daff remembered what it had looked like on September 11, 2001. She remembered the devastation, the heat, the stench. She remembered being overwhelmed by the sheer massiveness of the tragedy. And as one day passed into the next as they searched the rubble, futilely looking for survivors, she remembered thinking that nothing in her world would ever be right again.

"Please tell me you haven't been coming here every day," Brooks said, sliding along the booth until he was sitting sideways, so that he, too, could see the massive construction site. "You promised me that you'd stopped."

Daphne took a swallow of her finally cooled coffee as the waitress arrived with a fresh cup for Brooks. She didn't waste a lot of time placing the cup in front of Daff's brother before disappearing again. The two cups of coffee they'd ordered wouldn't net her more than a buck or two in tips, so why bother?

"I told you, I just came down here to check out what Dean was doing at that electronics shop. I had him figured for a high-end stereo kind of guy and thought maybe he'd be cracking open his secret piggy bank for a new Bang & Olufsen sound system. Turns out he just needed an alarm clock. And since I'm supposed to be meeting with my client on Water Street in"—Daff paused to glance at her watch, even though she knew exactly what time it was—"forty-three minutes, it didn't make sense to hoof it back to the Upper East Side."

This, of course, was a complete lie. Well, maybe not a *complete* lie, because she *was* meeting with her client on Water Street in forty-three minutes. And she *had* followed Joshua Dean to an electronics store yesterday where, as she'd discovered half an hour later after slipping a twenty to the sales guy who had waited on Dean, he'd purchased a plain-Jane alarm clock and nothing else. So what if the electronics store was in Greenwich Village and not downtown? And so what if, yes, okay, she *had* been coming down to Ground Zero every day since taking on her latest assignment? It was her life. She could spend it however she liked.

For the first few days that she'd been back in Manhattan,

she'd been able to stay away. Then, like an alcoholic promising herself that she could stop after just one drink, she'd taken that first sip. Now, six months later, she was addicted again. Her day wasn't complete without a stop at the site of one of the country's greatest tragedies.

A tragedy Daphne could have stopped . . . if only she'd been better at her job.

Suddenly, Brooks sat up, slamming his coffee cup on the table so hard that hot brown liquid sloshed over the rim. "Damn it, Daff—" he began in his best God-damn-it-stop-lying-to-me voice.

Daphne settled back for the lecture she knew was coming and idly looked back across the street at the electronics store. Two men wearing identical black overcoats were entering the store, the taller of the two holding the front door open for the shorter man. She squinted to get a better look at them, grunting when it seemed that Brooks had paused and was waiting for some sort of reaction. Satisfied that she was listening, her brother continued, but Daff's attention was on the men outside. They had paused just inside the store, their backs to the glass door. She couldn't see much through the painted windows, but something—call it a sixth sense or just the voice of experience—made the flesh on the back of her neck tingle.

She held up one finger to get Brooks to stop for a second and scooted out of the booth. She knew that once he got into one of his sermons, he could be hard to shut up. He always seemed to think he knew what was best for her. Even when she was a kid, he hovered over her, questioning her decisions, and always doing it in such a way that she couldn't accuse him of bossiness. It took her years to realize that he was manipulating her. At first, she had thought he was just being protective of his new "little sister."

"Do you really think you should eat that third bowl of ice

cream? Last time, you woke up in the middle of the night with a stomachache," he'd remind her.

And Daff would think, *Oh, yeah. I did get sick, didn't I?* Then she'd put the ice cream back in the freezer, secretly pleased that he cared enough about her to stop her from doing something that would only hurt her in the end.

God knew nobody else in her short life had ever tried to shield her from harm.

But Daff soon discovered that the price you paid for this kind of love was that your business was no longer your own. Brooks was always sticking his nose where it didn't belong—talking her out of running off with Rob Whatsisname at seventeen and convincing her that if Rob really loved her, he'd be waiting for her when she finished college in four years (he didn't, and he wasn't); encouraging her to apply for a job with the FBI even though she was certain she'd never make the cut. Hell, he'd even been the one to force her out of Manhattan and down to Atlanta to form Partners in Crime, a corporate services firm, with her two best friends, Raine Robey and Aimee Devlin, after she'd resigned from the Bureau. For that alone, she probably owed Brooks her life.

Too bad it was worth so pitifully little.

Daff sighed and continued to watch the men across the street as she tossed a five-dollar bill on the table to pay for her coffee. "I'll be right back," she said, ignoring her brother's frustrated glare as she walked out in the middle of his speech.

The cold late-winter air slapped her in the face as she pulled open the coffee shop's door. Inside, the air was warm, almost moist with the heat coming off the grills in the back as the cooks served up hot pancakes and fried eggs. But Mother Nature mocked the humans' pitiful attempt to control their environment—yes, they could heat a few hundred square feet to ward off Her chill, but once outside, She ruled with a frigid fist.

Daff didn't bother pulling her leather coat closed in the front. It wouldn't make much of a difference anyway, and she welcomed the stinging wind that pelted her through the thin jacket. Early on in her career with the Bureau, she'd tailed a child molester who'd left behind a victim who cut thin lines all over her body with a razor blade to release the pain trapped inside her after the attack. At the time, Daff had had a difficult time understanding why the girl—an innocent victim—would harm herself in such a manner.

But now she understood that need for release.

She felt it herself every single day since 9/11/2001, when the terrorist she'd been tailing had helped hijack a plane and drive it into the north tower of the World Trade Center.

Her gaze was drawn inextricably to the reconstruction site as she weaved through the backed-up traffic on Liberty. It didn't look anything like it had after the attacks; the gaping wound had been cleansed by bulldozers and bandaged with fresh concrete. But the scar was still there, if only in the hearts of the people who walked by, their voices hushed by a solemnity that didn't exist anywhere else in the city.

Daphne's coat flapped in the breeze and the chill bit at her exposed ears and fingers as she stepped onto the sidewalk outside the electronics store. Yes, she welcomed the pain because it reminded her of the part she'd played in the tragedy that had happened here.

Without hesitating, she pulled open the door of the store she'd been watching from the diner and stepped inside, intentionally barreling into the man with the long trench coat who was supposed to be guarding the door. He spun around and reached out to grab her, but Daphne had anticipated his move and ducked out of the way before he could take hold of her.

"What the fuck?" he blurted, startled as his hand closed on empty air.

Then he raised the shotgun he'd had trained on the huddled clerks in the far corner, but Daff had anticipated that move, too. She used the would-be thief's momentum to her advantage, diving toward the man's right arm and thrusting upward, bringing the heel of her boot down on his instep at the same time. The man squealed in pain and instinctively loosened his hold on the gun. Daff clasped her hands together and brought them down on the back of the thief's head. Both man and shotgun clattered to the floor.

Daphne picked up the weapon, hurriedly glancing around the store for the second thief. When she didn't see him, she figured he was probably in the back hunting for a safe, though Daff could have told him that most store owners weren't stupid enough to leave cash in their stores overnight. Robbing an electronics store at nine-thirty in the morning was a stupid mistake that only an amateur would make. But that didn't surprise her—she'd had these assholes pegged as newbies as soon as they'd entered the store wearing their identical coats and not even bothering to hide their faces from the surveillance cameras mounted overhead.

She turned to the clerks huddled together on the floor and silently waved toward the door, indicating that they should get out before the second thief returned. One of them, a slim Asian woman with long black hair, hesitated, looking from Daphne to the doorway marked Employees Only and back again. Daff waved once more, this time extending her thumb and pinkie to mimic a phone. The woman nodded sharply and ran out behind her coworkers, who hadn't given Daphne's order to leave a second thought.

Like they said, it sure was hard to get good help these days.

The crook on the floor groaned and Daphne scowled. She

didn't have cuffs on her and, short of shooting the guy, didn't have another way to incapacitate him until help arrived—when and if it ever did. It could take the cops an hour to get here at this time of day, which is why she'd sprinted across the street herself when she realized what was going on. If something had gone wrong during this heist, these two amateurs might have panicked and killed one of their hostages.

When the guy on the ground didn't move again, Daff left him there as she crept to the back of the store.

She positioned herself behind the heavy metal door, the shotgun raised to the point where she guessed the second thief's chest would be when he came out from the back room. He didn't keep her waiting long, obviously having kept one eye on the surveillance monitor in the back and knowing what was waiting for him in the other room.

Great. I'm always up for a challenge, Daff thought as she leaped back out of the way of the door as it was flung open from the other side. It slammed into the wall right where her head had been seconds before. She'd have had a broken nose and a couple of black eyes if she hadn't moved. Not to mention one hell of a headache. That is, if the impact hadn't killed her.

The thief roared as he lunged through the doorway, the sound a cross between a wounded water buffalo and a freight train's whistle.

Daff cringed and ducked as the man fired his shotgun, hitting the wall just above her head. She rolled to the left and pushed herself up to a standing position, her booted feet planted firmly, shoulder-width apart, the barrel of her own weapon aimed at the thief's shaved head.

"Drop your weapon," she ordered, staring into the man's flat gray eyes. He was young, probably no more than sixteen, but unlike his partner, he had the look of someone who had killed before. Something in the eyes gave it away, Daff thought. A deadness that bespoke how little he valued another human life.

He smiled a thin-lipped smile and shook his head. "I don't think so, bitch," he said, his voice full of mockery as he slowly raised the barrel of his own gun to her chest, daring her to shoot him before he got off his next shot.

Daff stared at the dead-eyed criminal—the first of his kind she'd run into since leaving the Bureau after 9/11—and couldn't help thinking that he was no different than the terrorists she'd been tracking before she resigned. Hating indiscriminately, no doubt blaming others for his lot in life, and taking no responsibility for making things better himself. Most likely, he felt subjugated, as if people had nothing better to do than keep him mired in the sewer that was his miserable, pathetic little life.

The trigger felt hot beneath her finger. The smallest bit of pressure was all it would take.

If she fired, so would he. She saw it in his eyes. He wasn't afraid to die as long as he took her down with him.

All she had to do was tighten her grip and her pain would end, the last four and a half years erased.

She hadn't told Brooks this yet, but her case here was finished. Two days ago, she'd discovered where Joshua Dean had hidden the money he'd embezzled; the surveillance she'd done yesterday had simply been a way to pass the time until her final meeting with the client this morning. And Aimee—damn her—had somehow managed to land Daff a new case down in Naples, Florida, starting next week. Trailing some stupid bank president's errant girlfriend, no less. Talk about a meaningless waste of time.

Daphne felt her eyelids growing heavy. But how could she leave here again? Who would tend to her ghosts once she was gone?

It would be so easy to pull the trigger, to let it all end here.

And would she find the absolution she so desperately needed as she lay here, her blood pooling around her on the cold linoleum floor, just yards away from where she'd lost her soul on 9/11/2001? Would she finally find the peace she sought? Or, instead, would the darkness claim her forever, knowing that now she'd never be able to make things right?

She stared into the soulless eyes of the man across from her and wondered if she had the courage to take that chance.

Slowly, she lowered the shotgun until its barrel was pointing at the floor.

The thief snorted, his mouth drawing up into a cruel sneer as he jabbed his shotgun into Daff's sternum, right below her heart. She refused to wince or even to blink.

"You are one dumb bitch," he said, obviously assuming he now had the upper hand.

"What makes you think that?" Daphne asked, leaning one hip nonchalantly against a glass-topped display case containing a wide array of digital cameras. She felt a bit like Bugs Bunny in the old cartoons, leaning against Elmer Fudd's shotgun and munching a carrot while taunting the hunter with his usual, "What's up, Doc?" But, with her name, her talisman wasn't the sarcastic rabbit, but the beleaguered Daffy Duck who, despite his best efforts to deflect hostile fire, always seemed to be the one in the crosshairs.

"You got nothing to fight with," the thief said. "You're stupid you think I won't kill you."

Daphne shrugged and kept her gaze steady on his as she mimicked his words back at him. "Yeah, and you're stupid you think I'd lower my gun if my backup didn't have a bead on your empty head," she said.

The thug jerked around, but he was too late. Brooks was standing behind him, his Sig-Sauer P229 now pressed against the thief's temple.

"Police. Drop your weapon," Brooks ordered, his voice colder and harder than Daphne had ever heard.

Must be doing his bad-cop impression.

It pissed her off that the creep let his shotgun slide to the ground at Brooks's command, whereas he'd virtually ignored her when she'd told him to do the same thing. Fucking discrimination, that's what it was.

She heard sirens coming closer as Brooks cuffed the guy, and she wondered why her brother was wandering around New York City with his gun and his handcuffs as if he'd never quit the force. Maybe he was just trying to get into character. Brooks had written a bestselling thriller series starring alcoholic ex–NYPD cop Jack Richmond. If Brooks was working on a new book, it was possible he had donned the cop gear to get inside Richmond's head again.

When her brother finished cuffing the thief, he turned to face her, and all thoughts of Brooks's writing career fled Daphne's mind. He was pissed. Royally, furiously, looking as if he'd like to shake her until her brains fell out of her head, pissed.

"How the hell did you know I was there?" he growled as the first blue-and-white pulled to a stop outside the electronics store.

And Daphne had to look away because she couldn't bear to see the hurt in his eyes when she answered softly, "I didn't."

TWO

2/13/2006

THIS was what she got for leaving New York.

Daphne grimaced at her reflection in the plate glass windows of the AmTrust building in Naples as she pulled out of the bank's parking lot. Aimee had told her she'd taken care of renting Daff a car, but she hadn't thought to ask what sort of vehicle Aimee had reserved.

"Figures she'd get a freaking convertible," Daphne grumbled, eyeing the hood of the cheerful red car distastefully.

She didn't want a convertible—especially not a *red* convertible. A heavy black SUV would have suited her better. How in the hell was she going to blend in and do surveillance with a car that screamed, "Look at me"?

Daff shook her head and pulled into the slow moving traffic. She hadn't had time to deal with exchanging the car this morning when she'd arrived at the Naples airport. Her plane had arrived barely an hour before she was to meet with her client, Keith Melman. As she'd tossed her duffel bag into the backseat, Daff admonished herself for waiting until the last minute to leave Manhattan. Frankly, if it hadn't been for Brooks's coercion, she'd probably still be in the Northeast, reveling in the marrow-chilling cold rather than in sunny south Florida chasing down a bank president's cheating girlfriend. When she'd tried to go back to sleep after her alarm had buzzed at two o'clock this morning, Brooks had banged on her bedroom door and nearly forced her out of bed and into the shower.

The bastard had even insisted on driving her to the airport.

"Probably didn't want me sleeping in his guest room anymore," she muttered, scowling at the button that would retract the convertible's roof. She'd be damned if she'd drive around like some tourist with the top down in freaking February with her hair whipping in her face.

Daff snorted with disgust, ignoring the fact that her long red hair was up in a ponytail and that it was nearly eighty degrees outside and that she'd fit right in with the residents of Naples if she'd put the top down and enjoy the warm breeze. Instead, she turned the air conditioner on low as she followed the directions the client had given her to the waterfront home where his girlfriend, Nicole Solem, currently resided.

AmTrust Bank's president, Keith Melman, was a forty-three-year-old Cornell grad with one well-alimonied ex-wife and two pre-teenaged children. Mr. Melman, having been married once before to a woman who had not exactly been the most trustworthy of partners, was concerned that history was repeating itself. During their half-hour meeting, her client had mentioned at least three times that he didn't like having to hire someone to trail his twenty-four-year-old girlfriend, but that he wasn't going to get blindsided again like he'd been with Brenda. At the first sign of suspicious activity on his girlfriend's part, he'd called Partners in Crime. Daff had no idea why he couldn't have hired a local P.I. to do the job—it sure as hell would have saved him a bundle—but she also knew that Aimee, smelling a quick buck, would never have suggested such a thing.

Daff glanced down at the address Keith Melman had scribbled on a piece of personalized notepaper and slowed down as she turned right onto a shady, tree-lined street. Wrought iron gates and thick foliage hid most of the homes on this street from the view of interested passersby, but Daff caught the occasional glimpse of red-tiled roofs and tan stucco as she crawled along in her convertible, stalking her prey at the end of the block.

She figured that this case was probably going to take her all of about fifteen minutes to wrap up, but that was fine with her. She'd already proven she wasn't worthy of tackling anything more taxing than tailing dishonest employees and cheating spouses. She didn't need another chance to demonstrate her incompetence.

Daff sighed and shook her head as she spied the two-story faux-Georgian monstrosity up ahead. For a twenty-four-year-old who had never held a job in her young life, Nicole Solem lived pretty well. *Guess that's how it works when Daddy's the former CEO of a Fortune 50 company,* Daff thought as she slowed the car to a stop several feet from the iron gate that had been painted a welcoming shade of green but belied that implied welcome by remaining tightly shut.

According to the research Daff had done after Aimee called with her new assignment, Nathan Solem had retired as CEO of pharmaceutical giant Geon after steering the company through an ugly financial scandal that ended in bankruptcy. After all the investigative dust had settled, Nathan Solem was cleared of any wrongdoing, leaving the company's former CFO to serve her time in the Alderson minimum security prison alone. Solem had come out of the fiasco with his reputation, his finances, and his career intact, and now served on the boards of several of the nation's top corporations.

And when he wasn't playing captain of industry, he could be found relaxing at his gulf-front mansion with his daughter and two standard poodles, a salt-and-pepper pair named, appropriately enough, Salt and Pepper.

From across the street, Daff studied the Solem mansion. Not surprisingly, what she could see of the house and lawns appeared well-maintained. Through gaps in the neatly trimmed hedge that lined the inside perimeter of the fence, she saw snatches of color from the flowerbeds and the green shutters that covered the second-story windows of the house.

This, Daff concluded, was not the sort of place where maintenance was delayed for lack of funds. In this neighborhood, roofs were replaced before the tiles cracked, fresh paint applied before the old coat even thought about chipping. Flower beds were replenished before spring passed into summer, and again just after the hurricane season ended. Here flowers bloomed year-round and the falling leaves of the ancient oaks were scooped up long before they turned dry and crackly on the thick St. Augustine grass.

The Solem compound appeared to have only one entrance and exit—through the green gate in front of her—which made Daff's job even easier. Keith Melman had told her that his girlfriend never left the house before eleven, which meant that Daff had about an hour and fifteen minutes to kill before her job of tailing Nicole Solem began.

Having completed her initial reconnaissance, Daff was about to hang a U-turn and go find a less conspicuous place to park and wait for her subject to appear when a bright blue Lexus convertible appeared on the other side of the gate.

Daff cursed, hunching down in her seat as she hurriedly threw her own car into reverse.

Along with Nicole's usual schedule—get up around nine, nine-thirty; have coffee and breakfast outside on the patio; take a shower and get prepped for a harrowing day at the boutiques; shop; lunch; come home and take a nap; take another shower and get ready for a harrowing evening at some fancy restaurant; go home and go to sleep; lather, rinse and repeat—Keith had given Daff a description of his girlfriend's vehicle, a gift from Daddy on his baby's last birthday. That description matched the car on the other side of the gate, so Daff had to assume that she was about to be "made" by her subject if she didn't get the hell out of sight . . . and fast.

Daphne quickly turned the car around and sped off down the quiet street, then pulled into a side street a few blocks away to sit and wait for the Lexus to pass. She drummed her fingers on the steering wheel as she waited impatiently for Nicole Solem to drive by. This sleepy town was getting to her already. It was too upscale, too sunny, too freaking cheerful. As someone who needed conflict to thrive, Daff found Naples anything but soothing.

Fortunately, she wouldn't be here long.

She watched the blue convertible speed by and waited for a moment to let it get far enough ahead that Nicole wouldn't suspect she was being followed. Then she pulled out and trailed behind at a safe distance, resisting the strange and inexplicable urge to start whistling.

Just another sign of how this place was affecting her, Daff thought as she turned the air conditioner up another notch and squinted at the persistent sunshine pouring in through her windshield. With any luck, Keith's girlfriend was on her way to meet her new lover and Daff could snap a few pictures of the couple in flagrante and be back on a plane to New York by this afternoon.

NICOLE Solem had no way of knowing that the woman sitting next to her on a cold metal folding chair wanted to kill her, or that if Jenna Marisol hadn't been concerned about harming innocent people, she'd already be dead.

It would be much easier, Jenna thought as she contemplated the young blonde listening with rapt attention to the woman standing in the front of the room, if she were a terrorist who didn't care how many lives she took in pursuit of her goal. If that were the case, Jenna's mission would have already been completed, and she would now be at peace.

But targeting one person in the midst of many wasn't easy—not if you wished to avoid what was euphemistically called "collateral damage." And not if you didn't subscribe to the belief that killing innocent people would net you a spot in heaven surrounded by forty virgins.

Jenna had no interest in dying, or in being presented with forty virgins—even if they were men. All she wanted was to get her family back, but since that was not possible, she'd settle for justice instead.

The problem was, after three weeks of attending classes alongside Nicole Solem, Jenna was no closer to her goal than she had been a month ago. It was simply not that easy to kill a person without having access to her food or water supply. One reason why killing her mother had been so easy was that Mother never suspected that Jenna would poison her. It was that trust that made it so simple, and also so easy for Jenna to convince her mother that there was no need for her to see a doctor until it was too late.

No one but Jenna would ever know how her mother had pleaded with her to call 911 while she lay dying. As far as Jenna was concerned, that was only fitting. Her mother had been watching Jenna die a slow death for years and never did anything to help. Jenna had simply returned the favor.

Jenna blinked as the blonde next to her giggled when the speaker standing in the front of the classroom clapped her hands and said, "Repeat after me, ladies: an *engaging* me is an *engaged* me!"

Jenna shared an amused smile with Nicole as they, along with four other women, repeated the mantra. Lillian Bryson, the diminutive owner/president of the marriage preparatory firm Rules of Engagement firmly believed that if the six women in this room followed her advice, they'd have rings on their fingers within a year.

In the three weeks Jenna had been coming to class, she hadn't exactly learned anything earth-shattering. Don't make yourself too available, don't call your intended a thousand times after he announces he wants to break up, don't date married men, don't call him, don't pick up the check on your first date. To Jenna, these things seemed nonsensical. None of this had ever been important to her and Aaron. They'd fallen in love instantly, and Aaron wouldn't have cared if she had called him or if she'd been the one to pick up the tab or if she'd accepted a date at the last minute. With true love, none of this silliness mattered.

But Jenna didn't fault Lillian for making a living by trying to convince these women that if only they would change a few simple things, the men of their dreams would fall for them the way Aaron had fallen for her. What woman didn't want to believe that it was her behavior—not her personality—that was the problem?

"Hey, do you want to grab a cigarette at the break?" Nicole whispered as their instructor launched into an explanation of the anthropological reasons behind why men needed to perceive themselves as the pursuers in relationships.

Jenna tried to contain her excitement. This was the first overture Nicole Solem had made to her, and Jenna didn't want to make Nicole suspicious by acting too eager. She'd never been a smoker, but had taken up the habit after noticing that Nicole headed outside during breaks to puff down a cigarette or two. They were often joined by other smokers who worked in the surrounding buildings, but there had been one or two times when she and Nicole were alone for several minutes. Jenna had also noticed that Nicole had misplaced or forgotten her cigarettes on more than one occasion. Now Jenna just had to figure out a way to use what she'd observed to her advantage.

She shrugged one shoulder nonchalantly. "Sure," she answered, turning her attention back to Lillian Bryson and praying the woman would dismiss them soon. She tried reminding herself to be patient. She had waited a year to put her plan into action. Another few minutes was not going to kill her.

The realization that she needed to seek revenge in order to find peace had come to her that fateful day in her mother's backyard. As she'd plucked the Daphne berries and brought them back into the house, she'd come to understand that her grief was being swallowed up by something else—a rage so icy it was freezing out everything else, including the memory of her girls. That was something Jenna couldn't live with. She owed it to her family to keep their memory alive. In order to do that, she needed to find a way to melt the anger inside her.

At the time, she'd hoped that silencing her mother's ever-critical voice would put an end to the anger. Without her mother telling her to "get over it" all the time, she could spend her days lovingly perusing old photos and family albums, and Aaron and the girls would once again come alive for her. But in the days and weeks following her mother's death, Jenna's grief had not returned. Instead, she felt empty, as if her mother had taken not only the rage, but everything else inside Jenna, when she died.

It had only been later, when Jenna was cleaning the kitchen and happened across that article about Nicole Solem's birthday party—the one Jenna had attempted to re-create for her own daughters that day—that the emotion she had hoped was dead came flooding back, an anger so violent that Jenna's legs had collapsed beneath the weight of it. She sat on the cold tile floor of her mother's kitchen, her head buzzing as if filled with furious wasps.

Why should Nicole Solem continue to live while Jenna's daughters lay in rotting coffins, buried beneath six feet of earth? Perhaps this was why Jenna had been unable to find peace—because some cosmic imbalance needed to be corrected before her grief could be restored. To that end, Nicole would have to die.

Only this time Jenna vowed to move slowly. She had been so certain that killing her mother would fix everything, but it hadn't, and Jenna now realized that it was because she had not been thinking of Yvonne and Yvette when she had taken her mother's life. She hadn't done it for them, but for herself. That's why her grief hadn't returned—because it had been a selfish act and not a selfless one.

She wasn't going to make that mistake again.

She had decided to study her victim this time, to make certain the timing and circumstances were right. Only then would she offer up Nicole's life in memory of her children.

After settling in Naples a month ago, Jenna had begun following her prey, getting to know the younger woman's routine and habits. And when Nicole had enrolled in a class at Rules of Engagement, Jenna had followed. Now, three weeks later, Jenna's plan was coming together.

And, looking at the date—February 13: her girls' birthday—Jenna had to smile.

Yes, this time everything truly was perfect. Very soon, her family would finally rest in peace.

THREE

AFTER six hours of following Nicole Solem around, Daff was convinced that she never wanted to live the life of a socialite. While lunching and shopping and lounging around the pool might sound glamorous—and might even *be* glamorous for a week or two—a life that consisted of nothing more seemed awfully empty.

"Not that trailing cheating spouses is a particularly meaningful way to spend one's days," Daphne muttered to herself as she glanced at the clock on the dashboard of her rented convertible.

5:35 P.M. She had to make a choice: continue sitting outside the Solem mansion waiting to see if Nicole would leave early to meet her lover before her dinner with Keith Melman, or go check out the business where Ms. Solem had spent an hour this morning after she'd first left the house.

Daff craned her neck to look down the empty street leading to the green gates of the Solem compound. What was the likelihood that Nicole would run from the arms of one lover straight into the waiting embrace of another? According to the schedule Daff had received from her client, Nicole was supposed to meet Keith this evening at seven at his home on Egret Avenue. Even if Nicole left now, that didn't give her much time to complete her tryst with her lover and then meet Keith by seven. It seemed unlikely that Nicole would bother rushing things when she could meet her lover later in the week, when she wouldn't have to race from one encounter to the next. Plus, Daff was curious about this Rules of Engagement thing. She couldn't tell what sort of business it was just from its name, and she hadn't wanted to risk getting spotted by going in to poke around while Nicole had been inside.

The hand-painted lettering on the front window said the hours were Monday through Friday, 10 A.M. to 6 P.M., so Daff decided to chance missing Nicole in favor of checking out this mysterious establishment.

She took one last look at Nicole's home with its green-painted shutters and palm trees waving in the breeze as if graciously sending her on her way, and then headed back toward the main part of town.

Traffic here was pretty much nonexistent and Daphne found herself missing the sounds of New York—the constant honking and shouting, the ever-present squeal of sirens. In comparison, Naples was like a graveyard with people talking in hushed tones and walking softly so as not to disturb the dead.

Great, she thought with a self-deprecating snort. She should fit right in here.

Daphne sighed as she slowed the car at the next intersection. She'd never exactly been the peppy cheerleader type, but over the last few years she'd become a walking case of clinical depression. Her partners and friends, Raine and Aimee, were concerned about her. Daff could hardly miss the loaded looks they shot each other behind her back as if she were blind as well as depressed. But as hard as she tried, she couldn't seem to climb out of the dark hole she'd thrown herself into. Even worse, Raine, Aimee, and Brooks kept tossing ladders down into the pit—giving her all the love and support and encouragement they could—but that only made her feel more helpless.

The thing was, they just didn't understand the toll 9/11 had taken on her. It wasn't just that she felt responsible for not convincing her superiors to let her go after the suspected terrorist she was tracking. Mixed in with that guilt was a whole host of other feelings. She felt betrayed by the very system she had worked so hard to uphold. In her pursuit of enemies of the United States, she was forced to play by a set of rules that the other side only used to their advantage. Much of the time, she'd felt ineffectual and frustrated by the restrictions placed on her. And now she was left with the lingering doubt about whether she'd pushed hard enough to get permission to pursue her man. It wasn't like it had been her only case. Had she really given it all the attention she could have? She worked hard, but there were nights she had spent staring at the television or hanging out with friends. If she'd used that time to hunt down leads, could she have prevented the disaster?

In the end, the events 9/11 proved that she hadn't done enough.

And quitting the Bureau had seemed like her only option, but without the job to define her, Daff realized that she had no idea who she was. So now she existed as nothing more than a rudderless being, wandering the earth with nothing but guilt and despair keeping her going.

"You need professional help," Daff muttered to her reflection in the rearview mirror as she realized the direction her thoughts had taken. The blue eyes that peered back at her were so filled with despair that she found herself unable to continue looking at them any longer.

Pretty sad when what you saw in the mirror frightened even yourself.

Daff tried to shrug off her gloom as she parallel-parked the convertible across the street from Rules of Engagement on the aptly named Sunshine Parkway. Traffic here on the main tourist thoroughfare was heavier than in the neighborhood where Nicole Solem lived, and Daff checked over her shoulder to make certain the coast was clear before she opened her door. She could just imagine the look on Aimee's face if Daff submitted a claim to their auto insurance for a ripped-off rental car door. If their rates went up, Aimee would probably dock Daff's pay for the difference.

Unlike Aimee, who wouldn't rest until she was a millionaire several times over, Daff was indifferent toward money. As long as she had enough to pay her rent and cover her meager bills, she was . . . well, not *happy* exactly, but content. That was probably one of the reasons why working for the Bureau had fit so well with Daphne's personality—she wasn't motivated by money, but by the thrill of the hunt.

Which was why she had an eager feeling in the pit of her stomach now as she trotted across the street, a feeling she tried to squelch by reminding herself that this was just some bullshit case that had no bearing on national security or the lives of anyone but some paranoid executive and his nearly-underage bimbo. Still, as she pulled open the door of the business where Nicole Solem had spent her morning, Daff couldn't help but feel a trace of excitement. Tracking people was what she did best.

The bells tied to the front door jingled merrily when Daff pushed it open. She took a second to look around the unremarkable reception area of the business—a circular coffee table flanked with several chairs upholstered in blue fabric one on side and an office with a sliding window like you'd see at the dentist on the other. Daff didn't see anyone in the office, so she took a more leisurely glance around the room, noting the array of bridal magazines on the coffee table, the vase of fresh flowers on the receptionist's desk, and the stack of brochures lying on the counter that separated the office from the outer room. Daff picked up a brochure, idly wondering if Rules of Engagement was a wedding planning operation. If so, why would Nicole, who wasn't even engaged to Keith, have spent an hour here this morning? Daff knew she had jumped to the same conclusion her client had—that his girlfriend's recent odd behavior meant she was cheating on him. But perhaps she was simply helping a friend plan her wedding and was distracted . . . and maybe feeling a bit sad that she herself was not the bride.

Or maybe this business had nothing to do with Nicole Solem's suspicious behavior and she really *was* seeing another guy on the side. Daff wasn't exactly a proponent of the old "innocent until proven guilty" thing these days.

"Good afternoon, and welcome to Rules of Engagement. How can I help you?"

Startled because she hadn't heard anyone approach, Daff spun around to find a trim woman who appeared to be in her early fifties watching her from the hallway beyond the receptionist's office. The older woman had thick, dark brown hair and smooth skin that even a much younger woman would envy. She wore a pair of white slacks with a brightly colored shirt and gold sandals, and her toenails were painted a demure pink. Daff looked down at her own feet, encased in a pair of no-nonsense black boots. Her toes hadn't felt the soothing touch of a pedicurist's hands in years.

Not that she cared. It wasn't like anyone but her ever saw her naked feet anyway.

Daphne cleared her throat, wondering why this petite, obviously harmless woman made her so nervous. "Uh, yes. Hello. I was just here to inquire about your services," she said, suddenly wishing she'd taken the time to research Rules of Engagement before setting foot inside its office. She wasn't usually this careless.

"That's wonderful. I'm Lillian Bryson, the owner. How did you hear about us?"

Daff blinked. "Uh, just, you know, word of mouth," she answered.

Lillian laughed as if Daphne had said something amusing. "Yes, we get a lot of customers that way. Let me lock up and then we can go on back to my office. Maddie—she's my receptionist—is gone for the day, and I like to get through these initial interviews without any interruptions."

As Lillian went to lock the front door, Daphne desperately scanned the brochure in her hands, hoping to figure out an excuse she could give for being here. The brochure had photos of several couples holding hands or gazing adoringly into each other's eyes.

Blech. Daff grimaced.

"Rules of Engagement: Let us help you get from 'I might' to 'I do'," was written in a large script font in the middle of the page. Daff slid the brochure open and read the introductory letter on the left-hand side.

> Sick of the dating scene? Frustrated by an endless stream of first dates that never lead anywhere? In a long-term relationship but having trouble getting that special someone to really commit? Then Rules of Engagement is the place for you!
>
> Let me, owner of Rules of Engagement and a licensed couples therapist, help you put an end to the dating game forever. Rules of Engagement is not a matchmaking service. Instead, we focus on changing the behaviors that are holding you back from having successful, committed relationships.
>
> You've read all the books and tried following the so-called

"rules." Now let Rules of Engagement change your dating life from tragedy to triumph!

Why wait? Call today for your free consultation. A happy, committed relationship could be waiting for you!

Lillian Bryson
President/Owner, Rules of Engagement

Daff frowned at the piece of paper in her hand. She'd never heard of a company like this, although the idea of it certainly made sense. Who didn't know someone who consistently drove away the opposite sex with her clingy or neurotic behavior?

But since the last thing Daff wanted was a committed relationship, she didn't know how she was going to get through this interview without blowing her cover.

"Come on back," Lillian Bryson said, smiling pleasantly.

There was no doubt in Daphne's mind that women listened to Lillian's advice. She seemed so caring, so . . . motherly. Not that Daff had a lot of experience with maternal types. Or with asking for advice, especially not about her love life.

Lillian stopped halfway down the hall in front of the only door on the right. "Can I get you something to drink?" she asked.

"No, thanks." She didn't plan on being here long enough to get thirsty.

"All right, then. Have a seat and we'll get started," Lillian said, ushering Daphne inside her office.

Daff chose a comfortable-looking chair on the opposite side of a large cherry desk, and was surprised when Lillian took the seat next to her rather than sitting behind the desk. But she supposed that made sense. Lillian would want to make prospective clients feel as if they were pals so they would confide their relationship troubles in her and then be made to feel that Lillian really cared.

"Let me tell you a little bit about myself and how Rules of Engagement works," Lillian began. "I'm a licensed couples therapist and have been in business for over fifteen years. We have a great success story here—over fifty percent of our clients have become engaged within a year after completing our program.

The program focuses on three main topics. First, we work to improve or enhance our clients' self-esteem. Many relationship problems—such as a woman who makes herself too available to a man early on in the dating process—can be solved by increasing self-respect and ensuring that our client has a fulfilling life, with or without a partner. Second, we teach our clients the universal truths about men and women. These truths help us to understand why our behavior may be sabotaging our relationships. Third, there are always exceptions to these 'universal truths.' These exceptions are what make each couple unique. In the third area of our training, we focus on the individuals in the relationships, often through role-playing in a group setting. It's amazing the insights our clients come away with when they are forced to act out their own issues in front of others. You will also receive one-on-one sessions with me, where we can explore any concerns you may have about yourself or your relationship in a more private setting.

"The beauty of our three-pronged approach is that you can begin at any time and work at your own pace. All three tracks run simultaneously. There are ten self-esteem sessions, ten classes on the universal truths, and an ongoing group that meets Tuesday and Thursday afternoons to discuss specific relationship issues."

Lillian took a deep breath and leaned back in her chair with a small laugh. "And that's the end of my spiel. Do you have any questions?"

"Um. No. You were quite thorough," Daff answered. So this explained Nicole Solem's change in behavior over the past few weeks. She was trying to get her boyfriend to propose and, obviously, either Lillian or one of the other inmates in this nuthouse had told her that she was sabotaging herself by agreeing to dates with less than forty-eight hours' notice or some stupid crap like that. Daff might not be interested in getting some guy to propose to her—after all, who needed the hassle of having to put the toilet seat down all the time or argue about who had overdrawn the joint checking account—but that didn't mean she was oblivious to this dating stuff. She'd heard about the so-called "rules" that were supposed to increase a woman's chances of having some game-playing asshole put a ring on her finger.

No thanks, Daff thought. If some guy wanted to put a black mark next to her name because she agreed on Thursday to go out on a date with him Friday night, she wouldn't be crying to her pals when he never called for a second date. Not that she could even remember the last time she'd been asked on a first date, much less a second one.

"Well, then, why don't you tell me about your relationship? How long have you been involved with your special someone? And what makes you think it's not progressing as it should?"

Lillian's voice was low and soothing, mesmerizing almost, and Daff had to stop herself from blurting out the truth—that she was only here to ferret out information about one of Lillian's clients. She quickly formulated a story, one about some guy she'd been dating for three years who never seemed to get past the two dates per week point with her, but when she opened her mouth to spill the lie, she was shocked to find herself giving a version of the truth instead.

"I don't have someone special," Daff blurted in a rush. "I think I intimidate men."

Lillian leaned forward and put a soothing hand on Daphne's forearm, and Daff was horrified to feel the sting of tears behind her eyes at the comforting gesture.

God, she was a mess.

"I can sense that you're a very strong woman. I think you just need to find a man who can match your inner strength," Lillian said quietly, the words hanging in the air like rings of smoke from a fragrant cigar.

And then Daphne Donovan—who hadn't cried since that awful day in September 2001 when she'd stood at Ground Zero and been filled with a kind of despair no human being should ever have to face—buried her face in her hands and wept.

FOUR

"I can't go back there," Daphne said, cringing at the desperation she heard in her own voice.

Sitting across from her in his dark-paneled home office, Keith Melman frowned. "Why not?" he asked.

Daff studied the rug covering the hardwood floor in order to avoid meeting her client's eyes. How could she tell him that the owner of Rules of Engagement terrified her? Or, rather, that her reaction to Lillian Bryson terrified her? Daff hadn't known the woman for more than five minutes when she'd lost all control of herself and bawled like a freaking six-year-old girl.

What in the hell had happened to her?

Whatever it was, it had scared her enough to call Keith Melman and insist on meeting this evening after Keith's dinner with his girlfriend. Daff wanted off this case. She figured she'd tell Keith what she'd discovered about his girlfriend and it would all be over.

She never wanted to step foot in Rules of Engagement again.

Only, when she'd told Keith that Nicole was taking classes to learn how to get him to propose, he'd nodded once, his chin resting on the fingers he'd steepled over his desk, and then he'd told Daff he wanted more information about Rules of Engagement.

But she couldn't go back and risk another meltdown. Not to mention the mortification she knew she'd feel if she ever had to face Lillian Bryson again.

There was no way she'd admit that to Keith Melman, however. Instead, Daff took a calming breath and said, "I don't see any reason to go back. Rules of Engagement is a company that teaches women tricks to get their significant other to propose. Your girlfriend is enrolled there, which explains why she's been leaving her house earlier than usual and why her behavior over the past few weeks has changed. She's using what she's learned to get you to put a ring on her finger. What more do you need to know?"

Keith Melman leaned forward, the edge of his mahogany desk digging into the slight paunch at his waist. "I need to know *why* it's suddenly so important to Nicole that I propose. I mean, she's only twenty-four. She has plenty of time to settle down."

He shrugged then and looked away, and Daff suspected that he had something more to say but that, whatever it was, it wasn't easy for him to admit. He took his wire-framed glasses off and set them on top of a stack of papers on one side of his desk. Then he scratched the top of his head through his thinning sandy brown hair.

"I guess I just don't get why she's set her sights on marrying *me*. I'm twenty years older than she is. I've got an ex-wife and two kids who are about to become teenagers. Why does Nicole want me when she could find someone younger, someone without all this baggage?"

Daff fidgeted in her chair. She wasn't accustomed to being asked why her subjects did what they did. Her forte was figuring out the what, not the why. To find out what motivated someone to do what they did meant knowing a lot more about him or her than Daff ever wanted to know.

"Uh, I don't know. Have you asked her?" she asked, feeling a flush creep up her neck. She really didn't want to go here.

Keith snorted and leaned back in his chair. "Yes, I did. She gave me some crap about being an old soul. I don't know where in the world she came up with that."

"Must've heard it on *Oprah* or something."

"Exactly. I . . . uh . . . care a lot about Nicole, but I hardly think she qualifies as an old soul. She still has so much to learn about life and its tough lessons." Keith smiled fondly at a framed picture of his girlfriend that sat perched on the far edge of his desk, and Daff began to wonder why it was that her client seemed so surprised that a woman like Nicole Solem might find him attractive. He wasn't particularly handsome, but he wasn't ugly, either. At forty-three, he was still relatively young. As the president of a large regional bank, he probably made a nice living, even if he had to share a good portion of his earnings with his ex-wife. And although his home wasn't quite as grand as Nicole's father's place, it was still quite nice.

Daff laced her fingers together over her stomach and shrugged. "Maybe that's it. Maybe she's looking for someone who's had a lot more life experience than she has, someone who's already been knocked around a bit. No offense, but Nicole's life seems pretty shallow. Perhaps she hopes that her life will be more meaningful if she's married to someone who has more important things to do every night than go out partying like the guys her own age do."

Keith seemed surprised by her observation, his eyes narrowing thoughtfully as he contemplated her answer. "You may be right," he conceded, and Daff began to hope that he would let her off the hook about going back to Rules of Engagement. That hope was shattered, however, when he added, "I'd still like to know a bit more about these classes she's taking. What sort of advice is she getting? Are they telling her to give up on our relationship if I don't ask her to marry me in some set time frame? I'd like to be prepared if that's the case."

Daff felt her stomach lurch sickeningly at the thought of having to face Lillian Bryson again, but she knew she had to go back. She couldn't very well tell her client that she was scared to return to Rules of Engagement because the owner had made her cry. She'd look like a total wuss. Which she wasn't. She was tough, and determined, and strong . . . and . . . And she felt tears prickling at the back of her eyes again when she thought of how kind Lillian had been and how she had assured Daff that it was okay to be strong, that her problem with men was that she just hadn't found one who could match her strength yet. No one else had ever said that to her.

Even Raine and Aimee had made veiled suggestions about her hair and her clothing, as if all she needed in order to find a guy who would love her was to spend a morning at a good salon or make a trip to the half-yearly sale at Nordstrom. They never suggested that the problem might not be with her, but with the men she dated.

The corner of Daff's mouth twisted in a wry mockery of a smile. She couldn't believe it. Somehow, she'd gotten sucked in by Lillian's psychobabble. All this self-analysis was just a bunch of crap. Daff didn't need some guy to complete her—what she really needed was to get laid so she could stop thinking about men altogether. All this bottled up sexual tension from not having sex in . . . God, how long had it been? Daff frowned, trying to recall the last time she'd been with a man. Then she stood up, disgusted with herself for letting her thoughts take this direction when she should be focusing on the job.

"All right. I'll do some more digging and report back at the end of the week. Also, I haven't ruled out the possibility that Nicole's seeing someone else so I'll work that angle, too. I just thought you might be interested in what I found out today."

Keith got up and rubbed the back of his neck tiredly as he crossed the room to show Daphne out. He seemed to pale a bit at the mention of another man, and Daff suddenly regretted that she'd said anything about it. She reminded herself that it had been Keith who suspected his girlfriend of cheating in the first place, but she still felt bad for bringing it up.

Which was crazy. He'd already indicated that he wasn't interested in marrying the young woman. So why would he be upset if she'd decided to move to more fertile ground?

Daff sighed and rubbed her own neck with frustration as she said good-night to her client and climbed into the convertible for the drive back to the motel where she was staying. She rolled down the window and shivered, surprised to find a chill in the night air.

No matter how long she lived, she'd never understand people. Why was it that they always wanted what they couldn't have and were so quick to reject what was right within their grasp?

FIVE

AT sixteen, Nicole Solem had watched her mother die a slow, lingering death from breast cancer and had been powerless to do anything to stop it. Every morning before school, she would race up the stairs to her parents' room and then stop outside the door, dreading that today would be the day her questioning look would be answered with downcast eyes instead of a faint smile from the nurse who'd been hired to take care of her mom. That day, of course, had come long before Nicole was ready to let her mother go.

Unfortunately, no one had asked for her opinion in the matter.

And, as most people do, she had grieved and "moved on," as people liked to say, although when someone you truly love dies, Nicole believed you never really did move on. What you did was just accept that there would always be a part of you that was missing, a part that had died along with the person you loved.

So, yes, she had learned to accept that her mother was gone, and that she wouldn't be there on special days, like when Chip Roche invited her to the senior prom and Nicole had to find the perfect dress. She had gone shopping with her best friend, Annelise Johnson, and Annelise's mother, who had wiped away tears when her daughter came out of the dressing room swathed in red chiffon. Annelise had rolled her eyes at her mother's sentimentality, but Nicole had had to hide her own tears when her own mother's absence made her heart ache. That day, Nicole had a tiny inkling of what her life would be like without a mom to help her pick out a wedding dress or give her relationship advice or be there for the birth of Nicole's first baby.

It had been in that moment of gaping emptiness that Nicole decided that the empty life looming ahead of her was unacceptable. If she couldn't have a mother like other girls did, then her father would have to do.

And so, Nicole set out to include her dad in everything she would have turned to her mother for, had her mother lived. Initially it felt awkward talking to her father about troubles with the opposite sex and the occasional fight with her girlfriends, but after a while, Nicole began to realize that her dad appreciated their newfound connection as much as she did.

Which was why it troubled her so much now to feel that her father was hurting, but not know exactly what was wrong. Her first thought when he'd started acting so sad had been that he had a terminal disease and was trying to hide it from her. She still wasn't convinced that that wasn't the problem, but as the days passed and he didn't appear to get sick, her mind turned to other possibilities. She'd finally decided—since he wouldn't give her any hints, no matter how often she tried to get him to talk about it—that maybe he was lonely.

And, because she loved him, Nicole had decided it was up to her to do something about it.

"So what are you doing today, Dad?" she asked with faux nonchalance as she entered the yellow-and-white-tiled kitchen that faced the beach out back. Nicole wrinkled her nose at the scent of fresh coffee Dad had brewed as she got a glass from the cupboard and poured herself a healthy measure of orange juice. Then she leaned against the counter and studied the man sitting near one of the open doors that led out onto the terrace.

Her dad was wealthy and attractive, especially for a man his age. He kept himself fit by swimming laps in their pool every morning and he played golf two or three times a week, although, as a golfer herself, Nicole was the first to admit that it wasn't exactly an aerobic activity. Still, it was enough to keep her father in fairly good shape.

His blond hair had long ago succumbed to gray, but at least he hadn't gone bald. Although Keith was ten years her father's junior, his hair was already thinner than her dad's. Not that she minded, Nicole hastened to add, taking a sip of her juice. She felt disloyal even thinking about her boyfriend's receding hairline, as if that was something that even mattered to her.

Her father looked up from the newspapers strewn over the table where they ate most of their meals, a hint of amusement in his eyes as Nicole crossed the room and sat down across from him. "I've got a video conference with the board of directors of AmTrust at ten o'clock, and then I'm having lunch with Dale Feldman at noon. I see you're up and at 'em early again this morning. Where are you rushing off to?"

Nicole glanced out at the turquoise waters of the Gulf of Mexico as she prepared herself to lie to her father. She hadn't told him about Rules of Engagement for several reasons. Mostly because she didn't want to explain why it was so important to her that Keith propose. But she'd also hesitated to talk about it because she didn't want her father to think poorly of Keith for not popping the question yet. Her dad and Keith had a business relationship and Nicole didn't want to jeopardize that by making her father feel that he had to pressure Keith into it. That would be the worst—having her dad force someone to marry her.

Nicole put down her cup. It would be so much easier if people would just fall into step with her plans.

"I'm meeting a friend downtown for breakfast. She's going through a rough time with her boyfriend," she lied.

"You remember that we have an engagement this evening?" her father asked.

Nicole nodded. Daddy was hosting a small party tonight on his yacht. She was bringing Keith, but her father—as usual—would be alone. "Yes, I remember," she answered, and tried not to smile with glee when she realized this would be the perfect opportunity to try to set her father up with someone. She clasped her hands together tightly to keep from clapping with glee as she continued. "I have a fundraising meeting for the Naples Art Museum this afternoon, so I'll just meet you at the marina."

By the time Daddy realized what she had done, it would be too late for him to do anything but be gracious about it.

"Good. Well, I've got to get ready for my conference call. Have a good day," her father said, gathering his newspapers up before bending down to kiss her on the forehead.

It took all of her willpower not to throw her arms around her father's neck and hug him tight, as she had when she was a girl. Soon they were both going to be happier than they'd been in years. Because soon they would both have new families to love.

DAFF could not believe she'd let herself get suckered into coming back to this place. She wiped her sweaty palms on her jeans and stared at the entrance of Rules of Engagement as if willing the business to disappear.

This was ridiculous. She didn't belong at some stupid dating or marriage prep or *whatever* kind of business. She didn't even *want* to know more about snagging a guy.

She rubbed her forehead and closed her eyes against the relentless glare of the sun.

She should just cancel this stupid appointment and tell Keith Melman that if he wanted to save his relationship with his girlfriend, he should learn to talk to her about his concerns instead of hiring people to tail her. What relationship could survive this sort of breach of trust anyway?

"Daphne, there you are! I was hoping you'd be back today."

Daff squinched her eyes closed even more tightly and pulled the brim of her baseball cap down low over her forehead, but it was no use. She'd been spotted.

With a sigh, she looked up into the smiling face of Lillian Bryson. Now why had the woman just happened to come outside while Daff was sitting here debating whether or not to blow off her appointment? Had Lillian been lying in wait to pounce on her the minute she drove up? Did she like to make grown women cry? Was that it?

Daff pushed open the car door. She might as well get this over with.

"Hey, Lillian," she said, slamming the door behind her.

In a gesture that would have seemed presumptuous with anyone else, but that seemed perfectly natural for her, Lillian looped her arm around Daphne's in a friendly fashion. "I was afraid you might not show," she admitted as she half-dragged Daff across the sidewalk toward Rules of Engagement.

"That makes two of us," Daff muttered darkly, which only made Lillian chuckle.

"You'll have fun this afternoon. Today we're covering

things women should and should not do early on in dating if they want the relationships to continue. We'll even do a little role-playing. I think you'll enjoy it."

Yeah, like she'd enjoy a tonsillectomy.

Daff just grunted while Lillian all but shoved her inside, as if afraid Daff might bolt. Which, when Lillian showed her into a roomful of giggling women, was exactly what Daff was tempted to do.

Instinctively, she tried to take a step back, away from these shiny, happy people who had so much hope for their own futures. Daff felt like she was suffocating and struggled to take a breath while Lillian kept a firm hand on her arm.

"It's going to be all right," she whispered, as if sensing Daphne's panic.

Daff had no idea why she was reacting this way. These women certainly posed no threat to her, yet Daff found herself in full flight-or-fight mode.

"Good afternoon, everyone. This is Daphne. She's going to be joining us today," Lillian said cheerfully, depositing Daff in a chair after closing the door behind them and making certain the only exit was blocked.

Daff tried to conjure up a smile as the five women in the classroom welcomed her in a seemingly genuine manner.

But why shouldn't they be genuine? It wasn't like she was competition for them, Daff thought as she slouched in her chair and attempted to smooth the wrinkles out of her well-worn T-shirt. She hadn't exactly packed her most glamorous attire to come to Naples. Surveillance work usually meant long hours sitting in a car, so she'd brought comfortable clothes—mostly jeans and T-shirts that hadn't fared all that well during their long stay in her duffel bag.

Unlike her, the women sitting in a circle around her were well dressed. There were two brunettes, a blonde, and a redhead, who all looked to be in their late twenties or early thirties, and an older woman with the most beautiful head of silver hair that Daff had ever seen. One brunette and the blonde looked as if they'd come from work, both wearing pantyhose and mid thigh–length skirts with expensive-looking blouses and high heels. The redhead had on a pair of slinky black pants and a sleeveless black-and-white silk tank top with lots of silver jewelry that clinked together whenever she moved. The other brunette looked as if she had stopped in on the way to her job as a stripper. Or, rather, *exotic dancer,* Daff amended silently as her gaze skimmed her classmates. The woman didn't look sleazy. Just sexy in a very blatant way.

The older woman had on one of the flowing long-shirt-and-matching-pants outfits that women over a certain age favored. Daff figured that with age came the intelligence that told women to skip the damn strangling nylons and go for whatever felt most comfortable instead—which probably explained why most older men went for younger women. Men were visual creatures and liked to see the wares on display when they went shopping for a mate.

"Okay, so let's get started," Lillian said from her seat within the circle. "I hope you're all ready to have some fun, because today we're going to be talking about those pesky rules of dating. We'll go over the rules that are meant to be broken and the ones you should never break, no matter what. I think this will be more meaningful if I demonstrate how to apply each rule. Daphne, would you like to come up here and help me?"

Lillian pushed her chair away from the circle.

Daff stared at her, frozen in shock. No way was she going to get up there and make a fool of herself.

"Aw, come on, do it. This role-playing stuff is fun," a man drawled from the back of the room.

Wide-eyed, Daff spun around to find a stocky man of about six feet tall standing in the doorway, his arms crossed over his wide chest and his dark brown eyes sparkling as he watched her.

"Sam! What are you doing here?" Lillian asked, sounding delighted to see the intruder lounging there. She hurried to the door and grabbed the man's beefy arm to steady herself as she raised up on her tiptoes to plant a kiss on his cheek.

Daff began to revise her opinion of Rules of Engagement. If the hunky Sam was Lillian Bryson's squeeze, she obviously knew a hell of a lot more about men than Daff had given her credit for. She could almost smell the pheromone level in the room quadrupling as all five of her classmates preened for their visitor.

It's like watching a damn show on the Discovery Channel about the mating habits of animals, Daff thought as she gauged the reactions of the other women.

The businesslike brunette leaned back in her chair and puffed out her chest, while the blonde's lips seemed to swell and pucker right before Daff's eyes. The redhead did one of those hair-toss thingies that Daff had never quite figured out how to master. Not that she spent any time working at it, just that the few times she'd tried it out in front of her mirror, she looked as if she were going into some sort of epileptic seizure or something.

Even the older woman with the silver hair seemed affected, her eyelashes fluttering as she smiled up at the man in the doorway.

The stripper, however, had them all beat. She slithered out of her chair and was across the room in the amount of time it took Daff to squelch the urge to smooth her own dark red hair, even though it was poking out the back of her baseball cap in its usual ponytail.

Daff admired the redhead's initiative as she introduced herself to the newcomer. She'd always been a big believer in going after what you wanted, herself.

Lillian pulled the man into the room and closed the door behind him, then turned to face her class, her eyes lit with excitement. "Everyone, this is Sam Bryson. My son."

Ah. So he wasn't Lillian's boy toy. Bummer. *Someone* around here should be gettin' some. Though from the signals the redhead was sending with her swaying hips and tittering laugh, it looked like Sam Bryson might be getting lucky sometime in the very near future. Stripper Barbie looked as if she'd be happy to give it up right there in the middle of the room if he wanted.

What Daff couldn't figure out was why this annoyed her. It wasn't like she was in the market for sex these days. A shrink, yes. A lover, not so much.

Lillian quickly introduced everyone and then said, "Let's get back to where we were, class." She clapped her hands as if that might dissipate the hormones weighing down the air in the room. Daphne frowned at the maniacal glint she saw in Lillian's eyes and wondered what the older woman was up to.

It didn't take long to find out.

"I've got a great idea," Lillian continued in that cheerful, soccer-mom-on-speed way. "Sam, Daphne was just coming up to help me with a little role-playing thing I like to do. Why don't you stay and play the part of the man?"

Daff blinked. What? No way was she—

Sam Bryson's gaze slammed into hers, chasing all thoughts from Daphne's brain. She sat there, staring at him dumbly, glued to her seat by a force stronger than anything she'd ever felt before. She didn't know what the feeling was, but it wasn't unpleasant. It was as if all the air had been squeezed from her lungs and she couldn't breathe, but that was okay. Who needed oxygen, anyway?

Then Sam smiled at her, his eyes full of an equal mix of challenge and laughter, and the life slammed back into Daff's lungs. She gasped from the strength of it, then felt her face go red with embarrassment when she realized that everyone was staring at her.

She felt the overwhelming urge to run and was halfway out of her chair when Sam reached her. He planted his booted feet six inches from hers, so close that she could see the lines etched around his eyes that told her he was a bit older than she had first thought, and could smell a faint trace of soap as if he'd recently showered.

His teeth gleamed white against his tanned skin as he stood there, wordlessly smiling down at her as if he alone knew the punchline to some cosmic joke. Then he reached out and laid a heavy hand on the top of her shoulder, as if to make sure she couldn't bolt like some frightened colt.

Daff shivered, although she certainly wasn't cold, and found herself licking her lips when he leaned into her, ever so slightly, and said, "I think I can tackle the role of a man. How good are you at being a woman?"

SIX

"I think we should wait until we know each other a little better before we have sex," Daphne mumbled, her cheeks so flushed that Sam was surprised her hair didn't burst into flames.

He had to bite the inside of his cheek to keep from laughing at the mortified look Daphne shot his mother for making her do this. He, on the other hand, was having a ball.

"Very good, Daphne. Now, Sam, you respond the way you think a man normally would in this situation," his mother encouraged.

Sam choked back an unholy grin. Could this *be* any more amusing?

Okay, he had to act serious here or his mom would kick him out of class. What would he do if he wanted to have sex with a woman on a first date? Well, to begin with, he sure as hell wouldn't be expecting to get any if he hadn't at least kissed the woman first to gauge her level of interest.

He reached out and took the brim of Daphne's cap between his thumb and index finger and slowly slipped it off her head so that he could see into her pretty blue eyes. He had no idea why she hid her best feature under the brim of a worn New York Yankees ball cap, but guessed that she used it to keep some distance between herself and the rest of the world.

Sam took a step closer and heard Daphne's sharply indrawn breath when he slid his hand up her arm. He couldn't stop a self-satisfied smile from creeping across his mouth when he felt her shiver beneath his fingers.

Then, telling himself he was just following his mother's instructions, he softly said, "Well, here's what I'd do," and then lowered his lips to Daphne's.

He half expected her to pull back, to roll her eyes and laugh at his joke, but she didn't. Instead, she astonished him by actually leaning forward, into his kiss.

And Sam, who was no fool, was happy to play along.

Still holding her cap, he slid his arms around her waist as their lips met. She tasted sweet, like lemon-lime soda, though any thoughts he might have about her being all sweetness and light vanished the instant she opened her mouth beneath his. Sam realized at that instant that the joke was on him. She made this sound that was half purr and half moan and he went hard. Bam. Just like that, he felt his cock go erect, pressing against the zipper of his jeans as if to say, "Hey! Let me out of here!"

"I guess that's one way to convince a woman to sleep with you on the first date."

It took a moment for it to register in Sam's passion-fogged brain that the class was laughing at his mother's dryly-uttered comment, and it took him another moment to decide that what he wanted to do right now would best be done *without* an audience.

He raised his head and looked down into Daphne's bemused blue eyes. She seemed as stunned as he was by their reaction to each other. Sam tried to remind himself that he knew nothing about this woman, but that didn't seem to matter to his libido. He'd gone from zero to let's-get-naked-right-here-and-now in less than a second. That had to be some sort of record.

Sam cleared his throat and took a step away from Daphne. Trying to lighten the mood, he conjured up a wiseass smile and said, "So. Are you sure you don't want to have sex with me tonight? I promise I'll respect you in the morning."

He flinched when his mother punched him on the shoulder.

"See, gals. This is exactly why you must wait to sleep with a man you're dating. First, you need to make sure that he has a chance to get to know you and see what a wonderful, valuable person you are. If you have sex with him on the first date, he doesn't have any incentive to ask you out again. He may believe that he's already seen everything you have to offer. Secondly, you haven't given yourself time to find out if *he's* a complete jackass."

"Hey," Sam protested, rubbing his arm after his mother smacked him again as she said the word *jackass*.

"Wait a second," Daphne interrupted. "But what if I *want* to have sex with him? What if I don't care if he asks me out again?"

Surprised, Sam turned to look at her. Was she kidding?

"But—" Lillian sputtered. "Of course you care! If you didn't, why would you be here?" she asked, clearly befuddled by this turn of events.

Sam watched as Daphne's eyes filled with amusement. Her lips twitched, but she didn't smile, and Sam found himself contemplating the baseball cap he had gripped between his fingers. Maybe that was why she wore the damn thing, because her eyes gave away too much of what she was thinking. With the hat on she could hide her feelings, but without it she was completely exposed.

"That's a good question," he heard Daphne mutter under

her breath. Then she reached into the back pocket of her jeans, pulled out a scrap of paper, and handed it to him.

Bemused, Sam turned the paper over in his hand and realized that she'd given him her business card. He was about to ask why she'd handed her card to him, but he was interrupted by his mother, who had obviously had enough of him and started shooing him out the door.

But it seemed that Daphne wasn't the type to leave anything up to luck, because, before his mother managed to shove him out into the hall, he heard Daphne say, "It's not your respect I'm interested in, Sam. I'd settle for a cold beer and a burger and some really hot sex."

Sam tried to turn around, to tell Daphne that he'd be happy to start with just the beer and the burger, but his mother slammed the door in his face and locked it before he could get his hand on the knob.

He pounded on the door a couple of times, but his mother ignored him. She raised her voice to drown out the noise and, even from this side of the door, Sam heard her sigh loudly and say, "It's clear we have a lot of work to do here. Daphne, let's start over at the beginning. I can tell we're going to need to schedule some extra sessions."

Then Sam laughed and backed away from the room when Daphne meekly said, "All right. What was rule number one again? Something about never making the first move with a guy?" before shouting through the door, "Call me, Sam."

JENNA Marisol carefully held the pipette in one gloved hand as she released the tube's contents into the filter of the cigarette she held steady with her other hand. The bone-colored ash was barely visible to the naked eye—no larger than a single dot typed on the middle of a blank page. But even this small amount was enough to kill Nicole Solem.

And she wouldn't even know she'd been poisoned until

days later, when the first symptoms appeared. Even then, she'd most likely assume she was coming down with a cold or the flu. She'd experience a stuffy nose. Fatigue. Perhaps some twinges of pain in her joints and a dry, persistent cough. Nothing that would prompt her to seek medical care or, even if she did, nothing that would make a doctor suspect she'd been exposed to a deadly bacteria. Typically, if anthrax exposure was suspected at this stage of the disease, the victim could be treated with antibiotics and could expect a full recovery.

That is, if the bacteria wasn't from a strain that had been engineered to resist all known vaccines.

Even before the bacteria began to proliferate inside Nicole's body, she'd be dying.

The disease would engulf her lymph nodes. Within a matter of hours after the disease took hold, her entire lymphatic system would be overrun with bacteria. Next, the bacteria would enter her bloodstream, multiplying at a furious pace in the warm, moist environment rich with nutrients the bacteria so desperately needed to survive.

This, however, would not be what caused her death. Instead, it would be the toxin that the mature bacteria released—a toxin that attacked the body's organs and lungs, filling them with liquid and cutting off their oxygen supply. Nicole's skin would take on a bluish tinge. Every breath would be more painful than the last. Death would come suddenly, perhaps in the midst of a convulsion or even while Nicole was in the middle of a conversation, trying to explain what was happening to her or begging for someone to save her.

The thought of Nicole's skin turning blue was what gave Jenna the most comfort. She couldn't help but remember the pale blue lips of her own girls as they lay, deprived of life-giving air, in the oversized tub in her bathroom.

Jenna dropped the pipette into a bowl of bleach. Then she carefully slid the anthrax-laced cigarette into the pack she had placed near the door of the airtight cabinet. With her hands still inside the gloves attached to the side of the cabinet, she put a stopper in the top of the vial of bacteria, and then carefully wiped down the inside of the cabinet, including the gloves.

It would have been better to complete this process inside a biosafety level 3 lab, but it wasn't as if she could just show up at the Centers for Disease Control and ask to borrow one of their labs for an hour or so.

So she would just have to take the chance that she, herself, might get infected. This method of killing Nicole was too perfect to pass up. The anthrax contained in the filter of the cigarette would go directly into Nicole's lungs, with an extremely low risk of it escaping into the air where it might infect anyone standing nearby. If Jenna did not become infected, there would be no way to tie Nicole's death to her. And if Jenna did start to see symptoms in the next few days . . . Well, she'd think about that when and if she saw the first signs that something was amiss.

Jenna glanced at the clock on the wall in the kitchen adjoining the sunroom.

She was late for her class at Rules of Engagement this morning, but what she was doing couldn't be rushed. Jenna chuckled at that thought. What was that saying? Revenge was a dish best served cold? Yes. It shouldn't be rushed. That only led to sloppiness.

But she had been patient long enough.

It was time for Nicole to die.

Jenna was filled with a mixture of elation and sorrow as she pulled on a pair of latex gloves and approached the sealed door of the cabinet. She was happy that her journey was finally nearing an end, but sad, too, because her plan had given her a purpose. Once Nicole was gone, what reason did she have for getting out of bed every morning?

Jenna frowned at the latch.

No. She couldn't start thinking like that. This was not

about her, it was about Yvonne and Yvette. Once she'd avenged their deaths, the rage she felt inside would be gone, allowing her daughters' memories to come alive again. That would be enough for her.

Praying that she'd safely contained the deadly bacteria, Jenna opened the door to the cabinet and removed first the pack of cigarettes and then the vial containing the anthrax. Carefully, she transported the vial back to her refrigerator, which was empty but for the other vials containing bacteria and other toxins she had brought with her when she'd moved to Naples.

There was a small refrigerator outside, on her patio, which was filled with bottled water and whatever small stock of food she happened to have on hand at the time. Food had ceased to interest her. She ate only when her body demanded it, and, even then, did so reluctantly. But even if she had needed a well-stocked fridge, she wouldn't have stored her vials in the smaller outside refrigerator since she had no way of securing it. The interior of her house was another matter entirely. She'd paid dearly to be able to lock down her home with the tap of a button.

Which meant that her home was the one place where Jenna felt completely safe.

But now she had to leave her haven. Jenna tried to wrap herself in the serenity she felt here as she eased the pack of cigarettes into the nesting place she'd prepared for it inside her purse. When she was certain it was secure, she snapped her purse shut.

Jenna nestled her pocketbook carefully against her side like a mother hen protecting her egg. After she'd backed her car out of the garage, she pressed and held a button on her keychain for three seconds until a green light came on. She smiled as she drove away, knowing her home was once again secure.

The drive to Rules of Engagement was short. The few

traffic lights she came to seemed to magically change from red to green as Jenna approached them. Then, just as she was about to pass Rules of Engagement to find a parking spot on the street farther down the block, a large black pickup truck pulled out of a space right across from Rules' front door.

"This must be my lucky day," Jenna said to herself as she maneuvered her tan Honda into the spot the truck had just vacated.

She eased the strap of her purse over her shoulder and rehearsed her plan once more as she locked her car and crossed the sidewalk to Rules of Engagement. Jenna waved to the receptionist as she stepped into the building, carrying her precious cargo. She hurried down the hallway and quietly opened the door to slip inside the classroom. Lillian Bryson was speaking—some nonsense about men and what stage they were in in their careers making a difference in whether or not they were ready to settle down—and Jenna took her regular seat in the back row next to Nicole, who was nodding in agreement with every word Lillian said.

Jenna forced herself to feign interest, but it seemed as if time were conspiring against her as the second hand on her watch dragged itself slowly from one number to the next. By the time the break was called, she shuddered with the effort it had taken to remain still.

As soon as Lillian excused them, Jenna turned to Nicole and said, in as casual a tone as she could muster, "Hey, want to go get a cigarette?"

Nicole smiled a funny sort of half-smile, and it was all Jenna could do not to race out the door leading to the back patio where all the neighborhood smokers congregated.

"Where's the fire?" Nicole teased from behind her in the hallway.

Jenna chuckled and paused for a moment so the younger

woman could catch up. "Sorry, I guess I'm feeling kind of rushed today."

Jenna was momentarily blinded by the sunlight as she stepped outside, so she put a hand up to shade her eyes as she turned to face Nicole. She half expected the heel of one of her sandals to get stuck in a crack or for someone to bump into her so that some cosmic force could look on in amusement as she fumbled with the pack of cigarettes. If she dropped them, the tainted cigarette would no doubt fall on the ground and Nicole would refuse to take it, even if that meant she had to go without a smoke during their break.

Jenna was certain that whatever sadist was running the world these days would find that hilarious.

But she didn't trip or even stumble, and Jenna started to think that maybe her luck had truly turned this day, especially when she managed to get the pack of cigarettes out of her purse before Nicole even had the chance to undo the heavy buckle of her own designer handbag.

Jenna shook the anthrax-laced cigarette out of the otherwise-empty pack and held it out to Nicole. "Here, take this. I need to open a new pack anyway."

Nicole seemed to hesitate, the rectangular pack of plastic hovering between them like something alive. Jenna nudged the cigarette toward the younger woman, silently willing her to take it.

Slowly, Nicole raised her hand as Jenna fought the urge to scream with impatience, but she relaxed when Nicole's fingers closed around the tan paper of the filter.

Yes, yes, yes. She was so close.

The empty plastic pack crinkled loudly as Jenna stuffed it back inside her purse and reached for her lighter. Once she had lit Nicole's cigarette, she'd open a new pack for herself to make the illusion complete that they were just two pals sharing a smoke break.

But when she finished fumbling around in her purse, she

found the young woman staring at the cigarette as if it had just grown legs.

"What?" Jenna wanted to shout, but was cut off before she could express her frustration.

"I think I may be pregnant," Nicole blurted.

Jenna inhaled so sharply that she choked. She felt her air supply being cut off and wheezed in a gasping breath, trying to fill her air with lungs. It did not escape her that this was how Nicole would have felt right before she died, if only she'd smoked that damn cigarette.

One day too late.

Her plan had been off by just twenty-four hours.

Jenna placed her hands on her knees and hunched over, both to get her breath back and also to hide her rage from Nicole. She couldn't blow it now, not when she was so close to success. She'd just have to come up with another plan.

But what? a petulant voice inside her wailed.

Jenna tried to ignore the question, but she couldn't. Coming up with this plan to taint Nicole's cigarette hadn't been easy. It wasn't as if she could just hand Nicole a toxin and expect her to ingest it.

"Are you all right?" Nicole asked from beside her, patting her back as if that would help get air back into her lungs.

Jenna nodded and sucked in a deep breath. "I'm fine. So . . . what makes you think you're pregnant?"

Nicole wrapped her arms around her waist and smiled a mysterious sort of smile. "Well, the home pregnancy test I took this morning that came out positive, for one thing," she answered with a chuckle.

Jenna was tempted to slump to the ground and wail. "Have you made an appointment with your doctor yet? I understand those home tests aren't one-hundred-percent reliable."

"I know, but I'm certain I'm pregnant. I got sick for the first time this morning and . . . I can just feel it, you know?"

Slowly, Jenna closed her eyes. Yes. She did know. She

had felt the changes in her own body almost immediately after conceiving the twins. For one thing, she had acquired a voracious craving for milk, which she had never really cared for before getting pregnant. She also became so tired every afternoon around three that she had started locking her office door and taking a nap. She remembered being so happy back then—she and Aaron had struggled to conceive for years, but the fertility specialists they saw warned them that with Aaron's low sperm count, it would be difficult for Jenna to get pregnant. They'd almost resigned themselves to remaining childless when Jenna finally felt those first stirrings of life inside her womb. It was a time in her life she'd never forget.

"Of course, I made an appointment with my OB-GYN anyway," Nicole continued, oblivious to Jenna's painful recollections. "I know I need to start taking better care of myself right away. That's why I've got to stop smoking, even if kills me."

Jenna did her best to chuckle along with Nicole, all the while prodding her numbed mind to come up with another plan of how to eliminate the blonde.

"I wanted to ask you something," Nicole said as two bright spots of color appeared on her lightly tanned cheeks.

"Yes?" Jenna responded absently.

Nicole reached up to fiddle with the leather strap of the wide purse nestled just under her armpit. "Um. I know you told me you're not dating anyone special right now. So, I was wondering . . . Would you like to maybe go out with my dad tonight?"

Jenna blinked wordlessly, shock striking her dumb.

No. Life couldn't be handing this gift to her. Not now. Not after all she'd been through. She had become convinced that the powers that be were punishing her for something awful she must have done in another lifetime. To have them suddenly turn into a benign force was just too strange to contemplate.

That didn't mean she wouldn't accept their offering, however. To get to know—even slightly—the man who was responsible for killing her family before she took his loved one from him . . . Oh, the thought was too tempting, too sweet.

She couldn't stop the smile from spreading across her face. "I would love to," Jenna said softly, her joy so great that she felt as if her heart might burst with it.

"Great. We're going out on Daddy's yacht this evening. It should be a nice night to be on the water, and the food will be excellent. We're leaving from the Gulfside Yacht Club marina at 6:30. Do you know how to get there?"

"Yes. It's down near the LaPlaya Hotel, right?" Jenna asked, just to make sure she knew where it was. She was certain there was more than one yacht club in this town.

"That's the one," Nicole said, and then reached out to squeeze Jenna's forearm. "I'm so glad you can come. My dad is a great guy. He doesn't know I'm pregnant yet, so I'd appreciate it if you didn't say anything about it. It should be a fun evening, though. I have this feeling that you and my father will get along famously."

I doubt that, Jenna thought as she patted Nicole's hand and felt for the first time in four long years that she was finally close to being able to lay her babies' souls to rest.

And as she turned to follow Nicole back inside, she realized that the blonde must have slipped the tainted cigarette into her purse. Maybe Nicole would succumb to the urge to have just one more smoke before giving it up for the duration of her pregnancy. If she did, Jenna's initial plan would work out perfectly after all.

SEVEN

DAFF did not expect Sam Bryson to call. Yeah, when she'd first pulled her business card out of her back pocket, she hoped that he would. He was the first guy in a long time who could turn her on with just one touch, and she didn't like to let men like that get away without at least giving them a chance to prove they were as hot in bed as they promised to be. After a few hours had passed, though, she realized that she'd made the fatal error of acting like a woman who might enjoy sex in front of Sam's mother.

She'd found that guys were really into that whole Madonna/whore thing. On Saturday night, they wanted you wearing black latex and swinging from a trapeze, but come Sunday morning, by God, you'd better have your inner Sheena the Sex Goddess locked away.

Daff lowered the binoculars and snorted at that thought.

Where had she come up with that? Inner Sheena, indeed. She was obviously spending way too much time in the sun.

She drummed her fingers on the steering wheel of her rental car and stared at the two-story pink stucco building in front of her. Nicole Solem was inside, having met her boyfriend—Keith, not the imaginary one that Daff was beginning to suspect her client had conjured up in his low self-esteem-inspired imagination—in the parking lot five minutes ago.

Nicole had arrived first, the top down on her cheery blue Lexus convertible, her silky blond hair streaming in the wind. She'd run a quick comb through her hair before stepping out of the car and looking around the parking lot, obviously searching for someone. Parked three rows away, Daff scooted down low in her seat, glad for the tinted windows that made it difficult for anyone to see inside her vehicle. She'd straightened up in her seat when Nicole leaned against her car, folding her arms across her chest as she waited for whoever she was meeting to arrive.

Daff didn't know why Nicole didn't just go inside the yacht club to wait, but maybe she was simply enjoying the view.

A few minutes later, Daff was surprised when Keith pulled up. She checked the schedule that Keith had provided her with when they'd first met. He wasn't supposed to be there until 6:30.

Not that there was anything suspicious in that. Maybe Nicole had asked him to meet her earlier for a drink.

Daff watched Keith get out of his car and lock it with the button on his keychain. When Nicole saw Keith pull into the lot, she uncrossed her arms and pushed away from her car, smiling as she watched her boyfriend approach. Then they embraced, and Daff couldn't help thinking that they looked like the perfect couple dressed in their matching blue-and-white nautical attire.

They were outside on the patio now, sipping drinks under an umbrella that kept the early evening sun out of their eyes.

And Daff's job, at least for now, was done. Keith had indicated that their date would last until eleven or eleven-thirty and that most likely Nicole would go home with him afterward. If Daff actually thought this case had any merit, she'd stick around to make sure, no matter how many hours that meant she'd be stuck in the car.

But she was convinced this whole affair thing was total bullshit.

Daff sighed and looked out at the boats bobbing gently in the harbor. She should just go back to her motel room, but the thought of sitting on her bed all night staring at the pastel paintings of seashells on the wall made her skin itch. If she were back in Atlanta with her partners, Aimee would most likely drag her out to some bar where all the cute businessmen would hit on Aimee and ignore Daff. Or maybe not. Last time Daff had talked to Aimee, she seemed to be eschewing the business types in favor of a certain CIA agent who'd staked a claim to Aimee's bed . . . and her heart. Plus, with a newly adopted teenager to handle, Aimee wasn't getting out as much as she used to.

Her other partner, Raine, was deep into another case—something to do with Internet fraud, Daff thought, though she hadn't paid much attention to the details Raine had e-mailed, other than to note that her blond hacker pal was still holding off saying "yes" to her ex-boss and current lover, Calder Preston. Still punishing him for having a hand in getting Raine fired from the FBI, Daff figured, though the couple was living together and Raine seemed happier than Daff had ever seen her.

She laughed halfheartedly. So maybe if she were back in Atlanta, she'd be staring at the walls there, too.

Looked like it was another night of mind-numbing television and dinner from a sack.

Daff turned the key in the ignition and then jumped about four feet when her cell phone buzzed.

"Jesus, that scared me," she muttered, one hand clasped to her racing heart.

She picked the phone up off the passenger seat and pressed the talk button. "Hello," she said.

"So, I'm sure my mother has told you about her silly forty-eight-hour rule already, but I promise I won't hold it against you if you agree to go out with me tonight," a husky voice that even *sounded* like hot sex crooned softly in her ear.

Daff squirmed in her seat, the inner seam of her jeans rubbing against a part of her that had gone instantly warm and wet. Okay, she *really* needed to get laid.

"Who is this?" she asked, just so she wouldn't seem too easy.

She half-expected him to be insulted, but instead, Sam laughed. She noticed, however, that he didn't answer her question.

"I'm sorry for the late notice," he said. "I had an errand to run and was out of cell service range for most of the afternoon. So how about it? I can't promise you a burger, but there will definitely be beer."

Daff looked down at what she was wearing. Standard blue jeans, rumpled black T-shirt, and black boots. Not exactly sexy first date attire. She could stop by her motel room, but she didn't have any sexy first date attire there, either. "Uh, I'm not really dressed for a date," she said.

"Oh? What are you wearing?"

Daphne couldn't help but laugh at the suggestive tone of his voice. "Uh uh. I am not going there. I've only been to one class, but I can just imagine what your mother would have to say about having *phone* sex on a first date."

Sam laughed, a deep, throaty rumble that made Daff smile. "Okay. Sorry. But you can rest assured that I don't tell my mother what goes on in my love life. Whatever happens between us, stays between us."

"That's nice to know. I wouldn't want her to give me detention or anything," Daff said dryly.

"Look, I'd really like to see you again. I don't care what you're wearing. It's just going to be the two of us," Sam said, then paused before beginning again. "Well, sort of. I hope you don't think this is weird, but I'm actually working tonight. I captain a yacht and my boss planned a cruise for this evening. But it's an easy cruise—just out into the Gulf and back—so we'll have plenty of time to talk. The food will be great and I checked with the chef to make sure he's all stocked up on cold beer. So, what do you say?"

Hmm. Go back to her motel room alone and ease her sexual itch with fantasies of the man on the other end of the line, or spend the evening with him and get her itch scratched in person?

Tough decision.

"What time and where shall I meet you?" Daff asked, hoping she at least had time to go get a hairbrush and do something with her hair.

"We're sailing at 6:30. Do you think you could make it down to the Gulfside Yacht Club by then? That's where the boat is moored."

Daff glanced down at her watch. It was 6:10. So much for her hair.

She reached up, took off her Yankees cap, and groaned inwardly. Major case of hat hair. She put the cap back on.

"Yeah, I can be there," she said.

"Good." Sam sounded genuinely pleased, and Daff hoped he still felt that way when he saw that she looked exactly the same as when they'd first met.

"When you get to the yacht club, walk straight through to the back. I've already let the security guard know to expect you. We're in slip T-7. I'll be watching for you."

It was only after Daff hung up that it occurred to her that

Sam must have been pretty sure she would come if he'd already given her name to the guard.

She rolled her eyes at herself in the rearview mirror before pushing open the car door. She was making this entirely too easy for him. Maybe she should take heed of Lillian Bryson's rules of engagement after all.

EIGHT

DAFF pulled the brim of her cap low over her forehead to shade her face as she hurried through the quiet yacht club. She passed an elderly couple dressed as if they were on their way to a presidential inauguration and they both gave her the required you-obviously-don't-belong-here look down their noses. Daphne ignored them.

She followed the signs to the rear exit and made certain Keith and Nicole couldn't see her from where they sat on the patio as she gave her name to the security guard sitting in his booth outside the marina. He buzzed her through after dutifully checking her name off of a list.

The heavy chain-link gate clanked back into place after Daphne slipped through. She paused for a moment, looking over the marina to figure out where she was supposed to go. It didn't take her long to find the piling with a black T painted on it, and she headed that way. The air was filled with the sounds of water slapping the undersides of the floating wooden docks, sailboat rigging clinking against metal masts as the boats rocked gently in the harbor, and inflated plastic bumpers being squeezed against the docks.

Daff hadn't spent a lot of time around boats, but she guessed that the specimens moored here were on the large side of the scale. This wasn't the sort of marina that harbored twenty-foot fishing boats or small pleasure craft—not unless they were being carried onboard sixty-foot yachts.

As she approached slip T-7, Daff eyed the vessel tied up there. The thing had to be at least seventy feet long. It had a black hull and white decking, with smoked glass windows hiding the interior from prying eyes.

Daff looked up to the top deck, where two men stood with their backs to her. The taller of the two men wore a loose-fitting gray silk shirt tucked into black dress slacks. His gray hair glistened in the sunlight. The other man had on a white uniform that clung to his broad shoulders and showed off his nice, firm ass.

Yummy, Daff thought, shielding her eyes from the sun as the glare got to be too much for her.

She blinked and looked back up to find that the men had turned around. As she'd suspected, the man in the uniform was Sam, who waved at her and then said something to the man next to him before climbing down a staircase on the left—or would that be, port?—side of the yacht.

"I'm really glad you could make it," Sam said as he stepped onto the teak swim platform at the rear of the boat near where Daff was standing. He held out a hand to help her onboard and she let her fingers be engulfed in his. His grip was firm and sure, and Daff was certain that if she suddenly slipped and plunged headfirst into the water, he would pull her back to safety. He was a man a woman could trust not to let her go.

Daff shook her head at her silliness. What a strange thought. She didn't even know this guy.

"Thank you for inviting me," she said politely, feeling awkward all of a sudden.

"You're welcome." Sam kept her hand grasped firmly in his own as he led her up a short flight of stairs that opened up onto an outside bar area, complete with a sink and small refrigerator.

"Have you been onboard a yacht before?" he asked.

"No. I haven't spent a lot of time hobnobbing with the rich and famous," Daff admitted.

"You should try it sometime. They have the best toys." Sam grinned and squeezed her fingers to let her know he was teasing and Daff started to relax.

"We have time for a quick tour, if you'd like," Sam offered. "I'll have to stay up on the bridge while we're underway, but, of course, you're free to roam around. It's a fairly small party this evening. Only nine or ten couples; some people around town that my boss occasionally does business with."

"What business is your boss in?" Daff asked, then gasped as Sam stepped aside and she got a glimpse into the yacht's interior.

Highly polished teak gleamed under the glow of can lights set into the high ceiling. A built-in black leather couch flanked one wall and wrapped around a circular, granite-topped coffee table. In the center of the room was a kitchen that Emeril Lagasse himself would have been proud to cook in. Stainless steel double ovens and a six-burner gas stovetop were framed in the rectangular opening between a gleaming countertop and a set of cabinets attached to the ceiling. Four tan-and-chrome barstools were bolted to the floor overlooking the kitchen, where a man in a spotless white chef's coat appeared to be rearranging an already perfectly arranged tray of hors d'oeuvres.

"This place is gorgeous," Daff breathed.

Sam looked around the salon and nodded. "Yeah. Like I said, the rich have the best toys." He smiled down at her and tugged her farther into the room. "Come and meet the chef. If you're nice, he might even make you a burger."

Daff noticed the array of fancy food set out on the counter and doubted that the cook was too familiar with ground beef. He seemed more like the filet mignon type to her.

"Alain Duprese, this is Daphne Donovan. She's taking a class with my mother. Daphne, Alain owned his own restaurant here in Naples before chucking it all to become a personal chef."

"Nice to meet you," Daff said as she held out her hand.

"You, too," Alain drawled, surprising her with his strong grip and his Texas twang. Maybe he'd know how to whip up a burger and fries after all.

Beside her, Sam glanced at his watch and frowned as the sound of raised voices reached them. "Damn," he muttered. "I've got to get upstairs and prepare to get underway. Daphne, why don't you come up with me? I can give you the grand tour a little later."

Daff nodded and obediently followed Sam through the dining area and up a tight staircase that opened up onto the bridge. Two dark gray leather captain's chairs faced a wall of electronics that would have made NASA proud. Behind the captain's chairs was a cream-colored leather banquette that could easily seat twelve, with a small stainless steel sink and granite-topped counter off to one side. Beyond the darkened windows, Daff saw a large black Zodiac and a crane that was used to raise and lower the smaller watercraft from the upper deck.

"Impressive," Daff said.

"Yeah, it's amazing what several million dollars will buy you, isn't it?" Sam said, patting one of the captain's chairs.

"Make yourself comfortable. Would you like something to drink? Beer? Wine? Soda? There's a head—that's a bathroom to you landlubbers—right there if you need it." He waved toward a door behind him.

Daff hopped up onto the chair and propped her feet up on the footrest. "A beer would be great," she said. She spun around in the swivel chair to watch Sam's progress as he walked back to the area near the banquette and opened the door of yet another small refrigerator. He bent down to pull a brown bottle off the bottom shelf and Daff couldn't help but admire the way his uniform stretched across his taut thighs and well-muscled backside.

He twisted the top off her beer and handed her the chilled bottle just as his cell phone chirped.

Sam pressed a button on his phone. "Ready to get underway?"

As Sam gave the thumbs-up signal to someone down below, Daff slowly sipped her cold beer and watched him expertly pull the yacht away from the dock and pilot it out of the harbor.

They headed directly into the setting sun, the wispy clouds catching the sun's last kiss and blushing bright pink. The turquoise waters of the Gulf of Mexico shimmered before them as if strewn with millions of twinkling lights. From below, Daphne could hear the muffled sounds of a party getting underway, the tinkling of glassware, the strains of some soft, unobtrusive music, the raised voices of people who hadn't seen each other in ages renewing their acquaintance.

"So, did you grow up in Naples?" Daff asked, leaning back in her chair.

"No. We moved here when I was in high school. My dad was in the Navy and we moved around a lot until he retired. Mom never complained, but it's obvious that moving wasn't her choice. She's lived in Naples for almost twenty years now."

Daff could understand that need to put down roots. She wasn't even sure she knew how many places her own mother had dragged her to before dumping her with Brooks's dad and splitting when Daff was twelve. After getting assigned to the New York office of the FBI, she'd decided to stay there forever. And she would have, too, if Brooks hadn't kicked her out a year ago and insisted she move down to Atlanta to start up Partners in Crime with Aimee and Raine.

"I grew up in New York," she volunteered, without getting into details she was certain he wouldn't want to hear—especially not on a first date. "My dad was a cop with the NYPD. He loved being a policeman." Daff smiled at the memory of the only man she'd ever considered her father. Jack Madison, Brooks's father. A short, barrel-chested bear of a man who never once complained about getting stuck with Mary Catherine Donovan's illegitimate kid when their one-month "relationship" ended and Mary Catherine took off, leaving Daff to fend for herself.

Jack had been so kind to her in those first days after her mother disappeared. She had tried to act as if her mother's leaving didn't bother her. She had the tough-kid-who-isn't-gonna-let-the-world-beat-her act down pat, even at twelve years old. But having your mom just up and leave one day was pretty traumatic, even for a tough kid who wasn't gonna let the world beat her.

She'd gotten over it, though. And realized, after a few years, that Ma had actually done her a favor by disappearing. For once, Daff had some stability in her life.

That hadn't stopped her from searching for her mother, though . . .

But that was another story.

"What about your mother? What did she do?" Sam asked.

"She died when I was twelve," Daff lied, the words rolling easily off her tongue. They should. She'd certainly had enough years to practice them.

"I'm sorry. It's tough to lose a parent at any age. My dad passed away when I was twenty-two and I still miss him."

Daff took another swallow of her beer. That was one lie she could never manage to choke out. She didn't miss her mother. Not at all. She cleared her throat and changed the subject. "So, have you always been a boat captain? I've never known anyone who did that for a living."

"No, I—" Sam began, but was interrupted by the sound of footsteps on the stairs followed by a loud voice.

". . . got to see the bridge and my new GPS," said the voice in the stairwell.

Sam turned to her and smiled. "Ah, here's my boss. He owns the *Long Shot*."

Daff slid down off the captain's chair and set her beer in one of the cupholders, then smoothed her palms down over her jeans. She chastised herself for being nervous. Yeah, so what if this guy had more money than Bill Gates? That didn't mean anything. Hell, she didn't get rattled facing down ruthless armed robbers or terrorists. One aging millionaire shouldn't bug her.

The thing was, she *knew* how to handle creeps and thugs. But aside from her brother, she had no experience with the rich and famous.

Either sensing her discomfort or just feeling the need to touch her, Sam slipped his arm around her shoulders just as a man with a graying but full head of hair appeared.

"Hey, Sam. I've got a tour group for you," the man announced.

Daff stepped away from the crowded stairway, intending to do her best to blend in with the woodwork while Sam gave his guided tour. Instead, she inhaled sharply and nearly choked on her own saliva when Sam's boss stepped aside to reveal Nicole Solem standing on the steps behind him.

With a strangled sound, Daff jerked around and lunged for the door of the bathroom that Sam had pointed out earlier. She managed to gargle out a mumbled, "Excuse me," before throwing herself into the head and slamming the door shut behind her.

She slid the lock in place and closed her eyes, resting her head against the cool wooden door. How the hell was she going to get out of this mess without blowing her cover?

She was so screwed.

Daff sat down on the toilet seat and put her head in her hands, trying to think of how she could possibly avoid coming face-to-face with Nicole Solem tonight. Spend the evening locked in the bathroom? Pretend she'd just come down with some hideous facial disfigurement and wrap her head in a towel? Try to escape out the tiny porthole window, jump overboard, and brave prime feeding time with the bull sharks in the Gulf as she attempted to swim back to Naples?

The last option began to appeal to her when she heard Sam's concerned voice on the other side of the door say, "I didn't think to ask if she had trouble with seasickness."

NINE

"NATHAN, you old capitalist bastard! What are you up to these days? Manipulate any stock prices recently?"

Jenna clamped her mouth shut and struggled to breathe in through her nostrils as the man beside her tensed. She'd been surprised to discover that Nathan Solem was as handsome today as he'd been when she first met him eleven years ago. Somehow, she'd expected the evil inside him to have warped and twisted his outward appearance as much as it had destroyed his soul, but apparently it didn't work like that.

It hadn't affected his manners at all, either. Nathan had been nothing but solicitous since the moment his daughter had introduced them. He'd put a steadying hand beneath her elbow when helping her onto the yacht half an hour earlier, made certain she had a drink, and seemed happy to make small talk with her while Nicole and her boyfriend remained up on the bridge.

Too bad for him that Jenna knew what wickedness lay beneath his gentlemanly manners.

"Better watch what you say, Rollie. You never know when the Feds might be listening," Nathan said lightly as he stepped forward to greet the tall man with a thick shock of white hair.

Jenna narrowed her eyes as she watched them clap each other on the back, hoping the disgust she felt couldn't be easily read on her face. They were all alike, these aging captains of industry. Almost without exception they were male, white, and arrogant, acting as if their positions of power excused them from responsibility for their own actions.

It was evident in the flip, uncaring way they joked about the economy, about jobs, about stock prices. It was like a game to them, and why not? When the companies they ran into the ground were bankrupted, they laughed and walked away with millions of dollars, while those who toiled in the trenches or invested their life savings were left with nothing.

"Jenna Marisol, I'd like you to meet Rollie Parker. Rollie and I worked together years ago. He's running up an investment banking firm up in New York, but took a few weeks off to enjoy our mild winters here in Naples. Jenna's a friend of my daughter's, and is a newcomer to our fair city." Nathan turned to Jenna and smiled, his teeth perfectly straight and whitened.

Rollie Parker. Jenna recognized the name. He had been Geon's chief operating officer during the scandal that cost Aaron his life. Jenna hid her hatred behind her most charming smile as she held out her hand for Rollie Parker to shake. "Nice to meet you," she murmured.

Rollie's handshake was firm, if a bit sweaty, and Jenna had to force herself not to wipe her palm on her skirt after he released her. She kept a smile pasted on her face as the men chitchatted about nothing—the weather, their latest golf scores, how Rollie's wife, Trisha, enjoyed the shopping in Manhattan—and it was all Jenna could do not to ask them how it felt to be responsible for the deaths of three innocent people.

"So how are the plans for the CEO summit coming along?" Rollie asked, then turned to Jenna and added, "Nathan's hosting a meeting for some of the country's top CEOs the weekend after next. He's got some fabulous events lined up."

"I'm fortunate to have an excellent assistant. She's the one who keeps everything running," Nathan said, deflecting the praise.

But Jenna wasn't listening. Instead, she cocked her head at Rollie Parker. "It sounds fabulous. Will you be attending?" she asked.

Rollie nodded. "Wouldn't miss it for the world."

The men continued talking while Jenna's mind raced. Wouldn't it be wonderful if she could figure out a way to sabotage this event, to get revenge not just for her own family's tragedy, but for others who had been harmed by these greedy heads of industry as well?

Jenna tried to contain her excitement as the party around her buzzed. She was fairly certain she managed to smile and nod and say all the appropriate things, but her mind was so busy elsewhere that she looked up, startled, when she felt the touch of Nathan's hand on her back.

"Jenna, I'd like you to meet Jahia and Adnan al-Sayed, who have come to Naples from Saudi Arabia. Mr. al-Sayed is the new CEO of one of the largest real estate development firms in Florida."

Jenna wasn't certain exactly what to do and cursed herself for not paying more attention while other introductions were taking place. Was she supposed to bow? Hold out her hand for the Saudi couple to take?

Mr. al-Sayed solved the dilemma by offering her his hand, which was as firm and cold as the look in his obsidian eyes. Jenna suppressed a shiver and wondered why she felt this sudden onslaught of fear. Was it that since 9/11, all Middle Eastern men were considered suspected terrorists, or was it Adnan al-Sayed's harsh features and unfathomable expression specifically that made her nervous?

Whatever it was, Jenna was glad when al-Sayed dropped her hand and turned his attention back to the men in their widening circle. Jenna turned to greet Mrs. al-Sayed and had to stop from wrinkling her nose at the almost overpowering scent of the woman's strong perfume. Like her husband, Jahia al-Sayed had dark, unreadable eyes and smooth brown skin. But Mrs. al-Sayed had none of her husband's frightening charisma. She bowed shyly to Jenna and then stepped back, happy to remain in the shadows. She lowered her gaze to the tile floor and interlaced her small-boned fingers over her belly, which Jenna realized was bulging under her loose-fitting dress. Either Jahia al-Sayed was pregnant or she had acquired a fondness for American food since arriving in the States. Jenna guessed it was the former, but soon forgot all about the Saudi couple when Nathan stepped to the head of the room and raised his glass in a toast, wishing a happy and profitable year on all of his guests.

DAFF remained in the bathroom as long as she felt she could without arousing suspicion. As the voices outside on the bridge continued to drone on and on, she knew she was going to have to risk blowing her cover. Nicole Solem would be much more likely to remember her if Sam broke down the bathroom door and dragged Daphne out.

With a sigh, Daff flushed the toilet she had not even used and made a big show out of washing her hands, just in case anyone was listening at the door. Then she lowered her head, hunched her shoulders, and unlocked the door. As she stepped back out onto the bridge, she glanced around and had to bite back a triumphant grin.

Yes! Nicole was finally leaving the bridge.

Daff watched the woman's long blond hair swirling around her back as she descended the staircase. Then she looked up to see that her client, Keith Melman, was staring at her in open-mouthed surprise. For the time being, all Daff could do was shrug apologetically. She certainly didn't want to explain what she was doing here in front of Sam.

"Are you all right? Can I get you some Dramamine?" Sam asked, eyeing her with concern.

Daphne cleared her throat. "No, I'm fine, thank you. I'm usually okay after the first half hour or so." At least, she hoped so. She'd never been on a boat long enough to know whether or not she was prone to seasickness.

Sam continued studying her as if he knew something didn't add up. Daff blinked up at him innocently and pushed her hat back so he could see her eyes. She'd always been good at hiding her feelings, at seeming unconcerned even when her world was falling apart, and she figured she might as well use that skill to her advantage now.

But instead of smiling back at her as she'd expected, Sam raised his eyebrows and continued watching her as Keith followed Nicole down the stairs.

"So," he said, casually crossing his arms over his broad chest. "Are you going to tell me what's going on here, or do I get to guess?"

Daff hopped up on the chair she'd vacated earlier and grabbed her less-than-cold beer. Then she swiveled around to face Sam and took a swallow of her drink before raising the bottle and grinning. "I've always loved guessing games," she answered.

Her grin faltered as Sam uncoiled from his position and stalked toward her, a dangerous glint in his eyes. She swallowed again as he put one hand on either side of her, trapping her where she sat, but she refused to back down. Instead, she raised her chin, as if daring him to take his best shot. Sam came closer, stopping only when his taut abdomen was pressed firmly against her knees. Daphne had the sudden and wholly irrational urge to open her legs and scoot forward on the chair, as if Sam were some sort of snake charmer weaving his spell on her. Without realizing what she was doing, she nervously licked her bottom lip and squirmed in her seat as Sam lowered his face until his mouth was just inches from hers.

She looked into his eyes, expecting to see annoyance or irritation, and was surprised when she saw only desire mixed with amusement. Then she didn't see anything at all when Sam said softly, "I'm a really good player," right before he closed the gap between them and claimed her mouth with his.

When Sam finally came up for air, Daff felt as if he had sucked her brain right out of her head. She had trouble forming any coherent thought aside from, *Damn, he's a good kisser.*

Sam stepped back and flashed her a self-satisfied grin. "I say we continue this later. I'm still working out the rules of engagement."

Daff swallowed and tried to think of something amusing to say back, but . . . No, her brain still wasn't working. Maybe another beer would help.

Sam's chuckle followed her across the bridge, but Daff chose to ignore it as she extracted a chilled bottle from the small fridge located near the door leading out to the upper deck. Feeling as if she needed to put some distance between herself and this man who was able to fluster her like some preteen with a crush on her older brother's best friend, Daff waved her bottle toward the Zodiac and mumbled, "If you don't mind, I'm going to go take a look around."

Without waiting for Sam's answer, Daff pushed the door

open and let herself outside. She walked to the far side of the deck and hugged the railing as she walked past the Zodiac. A large white crane hovered over the smaller boat. Daff hid behind the crane, using its bulk to shield herself in case Sam was watching from inside the bridge. She needed to get her equilibrium back, and she couldn't do that if he was staring at her.

She'd never met a man who could rattle her so easily, and she didn't understand why this one did. He was a boat captain, for God's sake. He wasn't dangerous or powerful or wealthy. So why the hell was she so jumpy around him?

Daff rested her forearms on the chrome railing and took a sip of beer as she stared unseeingly out into the Gulf of Mexico and listened to the clink and clatter of party noises coming from the deck below.

Maybe she was just nervous because she hadn't been this attracted to someone in a long, long time. Perhaps that was what made her feel like her skin was a little too tight, making her wish she could rub herself against a rock and shed the dry outer hide to expose the more sensitive layer underneath.

Or maybe she just needed to get laid.

Daff snorted and took another drink of her beer, then straightened up when she heard footsteps on the stairway that opened up on the other side of the Zodiac. Whoever it was paused on the steps as if peering inside the lighted bridge, looking for something. Daff remained hidden behind the crane, but had nowhere to go when the man—Daff assumed it was a man by the heavy sound of the footsteps—began walking toward the bow of the smaller boat.

Reminding herself that she had no reason to hide, she leaned back against the railing and relaxed. The only person she didn't want to run into this evening was Nicole Solem, and the squeak of the rubberized soles coming toward her hardly sounded like the clack of inch-high heels Daff had seen the other woman wearing earlier in the evening.

"Hello, Daphne. I was surprised to see you here tonight," Keith Melman said as he stopped a few feet away. The breeze from the moving yacht ruffled his sandy hair and he instinctively raised a hand to push it out of his eyes, but by the next second, it had flopped back over his forehead again.

"I wish I could say it was the result of my superior investigative skills, but the truth is, I got invited to come along by the ship's captain. I had no idea you and Nicole would be here tonight," Daff said wryly. No use lying to the guy, especially since he'd told her to take the night off.

Keith nodded and shoved his hands into the pockets of his navy blue slacks. "That's all right. Nicole didn't see you. She still has no idea I'm having her tailed."

He sounded unhappy, and for the first time, Daff wondered why he couldn't just accept that his young girlfriend loved him and wanted to marry him, as simple as that. Why did people always have to complicate things?

"I haven't found out anything else about Rules of Engagement or noted any suspicious behavior on Nicole's part," Daff said dispassionately. Which was as it should be. She wasn't being paid to judge either her subject *or* her client. She was being paid to gather information. That was all. She made it a point not to get involved with any of her cases anymore, and this one wasn't going to be any different.

"Keep tailing her. I know something's up." Keith's shoulders slumped as he leaned his hip against the railing alongside her. "She's been really affectionate lately, like she's trying to atone for something she's done."

Daff took a deep breath and reminded herself to stay out of it. Her client certainly didn't need relationship advice from her. Besides, Aimee would be thrilled the longer this case continued. Aimee was a big fan of billable hours.

"All right, I—" Daff began, then snapped her mouth shut

when the sound of raised voices drifted up to them from the outdoor deck below.

She leaned out over the railing and saw the colorful flash of a woman's silk dress flapping in the breeze. Keith also squinted down into the darkness as the angry words punctured the steady hum of the yacht's engines.

"You would risk everything for this mission of yours?" the woman tearfully asked.

A man's answering voice was low and gruff, uncaring. "We have to think about more than just ourselves. Has your courage deserted you? I never expected to be married to a coward."

"And I never expected to be married to a man who would sacrifice his own child for a cause which he cannot win."

"I must do what I must." The man's voice was even harder than before, bordering on cruel. "What I do, I do in the name of Allah."

The sound of the man's heavy footsteps was followed by the faint sob of the woman left standing alone on the lower deck. The strong scent of heavy perfume wafted up from below as Daff turned to look at Keith, whose eyes had narrowed on the bright fabric still fluttering in the wind. They remained silent until the soft sound of the woman's footfalls faded away.

Cautiously, Daff crept out from behind the Zodiac and walked toward the staircase leading downstairs. She crouched down and peered into the opening to make certain the couple had gone.

When she straightened up, she was surprised to see the dark look on Keith Melman's face.

"Who was that?" she asked.

"Adnan and Jahia al-Sayed. They're new to Naples, but are very well connected," he answered. "Mr. al-Sayed came highly recommended by someone I trust. He has dealings with my bank."

"Hmm," Daff said. She wasn't going to jump to any conclusions. As a matter of fact, she wasn't going to do anything at all. If the al-Sayeds were involved in some nefarious doings, it was up to the proper authorities to take them down. Tracking suspected terrorists was no longer her job. Besides, she could hardly slap the "terrorist" label on the couple based solely on a heated conversation and their permanently tanned skin.

"I lost a friend on 9/11," Keith Melman muttered absently, staring into the darkness below them where the al-Sayeds had stood moments before.

As Daff turned away, she couldn't help but think, *And I lost my soul.*

TEN

BY the end of the cruise, Daff had pushed all thoughts of unpleasantness out of her mind. Or, rather, Sam's constant and successful efforts to rub against her, to trail his fingers down her arms, to touch her at every freaking opportunity had pushed everything but lust out of her head.

She leaned against the railing and turned her face up to the night sky, hoping the wind would help to cool her ardor, but the weather would not cooperate. Now that the yacht was snugly moored back in the harbor, the air had gone still and sultry, without even a wisp of breeze to cool her heated skin.

Sam had gone below a few minutes ago with the promise that he'd return soon, and Daff was tempted to jump to the dock below and get away while she still had a smidgen of sense left. Unfortunately, that ounce of sense was not accompanied by even a pinch of willpower. She willed her feet to move, but they remained stubbornly rooted to the spot, waiting obediently for Sam's return.

She shivered, but not from cold. She was honest enough with herself to admit that she was anticipating Sam's next move. He'd spent all night priming her and done a damn good job of it, too.

She turned when she heard his footsteps on the stairs and did her best to look nonchalant as Sam stalked toward her. His knowing smile was less of an arrogant smirk than the teasing grin of a guy who knew exactly what he'd been doing to her all night and how well it had worked.

Just to screw with him, Daff smiled and stuck out her right hand. "I had a great time tonight. You sure know how to impress a girl on a first date."

Sam's throaty chuckle was like the low purr of a lion. He took her hand in both of his and Daff felt her entire body shudder as his skin touched hers.

Shit. She hoped he hadn't felt that.

Daff realized then that she had made a tactical error. She was cornered between the railing to her right and the wall surrounding the bridge to her left, and as she pressed her back against the warm fiberglass, Sam just kept coming. He didn't stop until the toes of his black boots were touching hers. Annoyed at being crowded, Daff looked up into his eyes and saw the laughter there.

"Didn't your mother tell you that full body contact isn't appropriate on a first date?" she asked crossly.

Sam insinuated his right foot between hers and stepped closer, until the last half inch separating them had disappeared. Daff could feel the cool metal buckle of his belt digging into her stomach and felt her nipples harden as her breasts came into contact with the hard muscles of his chest.

"Do you really want me to end tonight with a kiss on your nose and the promise to call you tomorrow? Because if that's what you want, that's what I'll do," Sam said.

Daff took a deep swallow of night air and slowly curled one leg around Sam's, watching his eyes darken as she rubbed against him. "If you even *think* about saying good-bye to me right now, I'll kill you," she said softly. And she wasn't even sure if she was kidding.

Sam didn't wait for any more encouragement from her. He lowered his head until he was blocking out the moon-light, the stars, and everything else but the sound of Daff's wildly beating heart. His mouth claimed hers, their lips open, searching. Daphne slid her hands up Sam's hard chest, her fingers tingling as they caressed the rough fabric of his crisply pressed uniform.

She wound her arms around his neck as Sam sucked her tongue into his mouth and bit down lightly. In retaliation, Daff raised her knee until she was wrapped around Sam's muscled thigh and she was pressed against the hard ridge of his erection. Sensation rocked through her as the seam of her jeans rubbed against her clitoris.

God, it felt good to want a man this badly.

Daff felt a frisson of pleasure slide over her skin when Sam groaned and pulsed his hips into hers. It felt even bet-ter to have him want her back.

Sam lifted his head and looked down at her, the look in his eyes intense. "Okay," he said. "We have a decision to make. Years from now, when we think back on the first time we made love, do we want to remember it as an intense wall-banger on the top deck of a yacht, or a more leisurely exploration on the silk-covered sheets of a king-sized bed as the water laps against the sides of the boat?"

Daphne's heart stopped as she thought about what Sam was saying. What the hell was he talking about? This wasn't a "years from now" sort of thing to her. This was an "if you don't scratch this itch, I'm gonna go take care of it myself right fucking now."

But the idea of solo sex versus doing it with the hard,

horny, living, breathing man standing in front of her made Daff wince. She'd been going solo way too often over the past few years. She wanted some dual action tonight.

So, rather than telling Sam this was a short-term thing for her, she answered breathlessly, "Let's just start out here and see how far we get, shall we?"

Sam stared down at her for a long moment, the steady thump of his heartbeat ticking away the seconds as Daff began to wonder if she'd unintentionally made the wrong choice. But then Sam nodded, and she turned away as some unrecognizable emotion—or some emotion she chose not to interpret—flickered in the depths of his dark eyes.

Then, tenderly, Sam tugged the hat from her head and slowly pulled the band holding her long red hair from its ponytail. Daff self-consciously raised her hands and ran them through her hair to fluff it out. She could only imagine how awful it looked after being stuffed up under a hat all day.

Sam stopped her with his hands on her wrists, tugging her arms down. "You're beautiful just the way you are," he said, and Daff just stared at him, mesmerized by that snake-charmer's voice of his.

He fisted his hands in her hair, his fingers caressing her scalp until Daff wanted to close her eyes and hum in ecstasy. Sam closed in on her again, pressing her back against the wall and fitting his body to hers as if they had been poured into interlocking molds that fit perfectly together. She felt the now-familiar edge of his belt buckle pressing into her stomach, his muscled thigh between her legs, rubbing so gently that she wondered if he even knew he was driving her mad.

He tilted her head back and laid her neck open to his hot, moist mouth.

Daff groaned and pressed herself even closer as he licked the sensitive skin just below her earlobe. Suddenly, she needed to feel him, to see if his skin was as hot as hers was. She greedily slid her hands beneath the waistband of his slacks and untucked his shirt. He wore a T-shirt beneath his uniform shirt, and Daff slipped her hands between the soft cotton and Sam's smooth skin, tugging his shirt free as her hands roamed up toward his shoulders. She felt the hard ridge of a scar on the left side of his back, but didn't allow her fingers to linger there. Tonight wasn't about questions or lengthy history lessons, it was about sex. Pure animal attraction and lust. No more and no less.

Frustrated with Sam's unhurried pace, Daphne decided to take things into her own hands. Literally.

With a wicked grin, she moved her hands around to the front of Sam's shirt, untucking as she went. Her eyelids lowered to half-mast, she again rubbed her hips against Sam's as she lazily went about unbuckling his belt. She felt Sam's erection pulse against her, but he did nothing more than stand and watch her, his eyes hooded and unreadable.

Daff slowly popped open the top button of Sam's pants and then, one inch at a time, she lowered his zipper. But before she could reach in for what she liked to call the moment of truth, Sam disabused her of the notion that she was in charge by swooping her up in his arms and growling, "We can do it your way next time. Right now, I want a nice, comfortable bed to stretch out on."

Daphne squealed and then cringed when she realized that that sound had actually come out of her mouth. The whole Neanderthal/caveman/knight-in-shining-armor effect was ruined, however, when Sam stopped at the top of the stairway leading down to the next floor. The opening was too narrow for him to fit through with her in his arms. He set her down and grabbed her left hand as he started downstairs with a grumbled, "Follow me."

He didn't say anything more as he nearly dragged her through the sliding glass doors into the living room of the yacht. He headed for another staircase—this one with narrow spiral stairs that opened up into a small foyer. Sam pushed open a set of double doors and pulled Daphne inside a spacious stateroom before closing the doors behind them.

The room was dominated by a king-sized bed with three sets of pillows and a chenille throw draped artfully at the bottom as if a designer had arranged it just so. The bedspread was patterned with large rectangles in muted shades of yellow, tan, and lavender, and the walls were paneled with glossy teak.

"This is nice," Daff admitted reluctantly.

Sam grunted his agreement as he pulled her with him toward the bed.

For some reason, now that they were in this room with the bed looming between them, Daff felt nervous. Which was ridiculous. Two minutes before, she'd been ready to slap skin out in the open where any lucky passerby could see them. So why did she now have the sudden urge to flee?

Daff tugged her hand out of Sam's grasp. She wasn't going to chicken out now.

She sat down on the edge of the bed, crossed her right ankle over her left knee, and reached down to tug off her boot, but Sam put his hand over hers and stopped her.

"We don't have to do this," he said.

Daff raised her eyebrows at him. "Are you kidding? You spend all night getting me revved up and *now* you've got performance anxieties?"

Sam crouched down before her and he gently moved her right foot back to the floor. He put his hands on her knees and slowly, slowly, ran them up her thighs, his strong fingers caressing her through the fabric of her jeans. Daphne was glad she was sitting down, because as his hands reached the juncture of her thighs, he lightly ran his thumbs over her and she felt her bones turn to Jell-O.

"I do not have performance anxieties," Sam assured her softly.

Daff believed him.

She resisted the urge to scoot to the edge of the bed to follow his magic hands as Sam ran them back toward her knees. Still crouching on the floor, he picked up her left foot and gently pulled off her boot. He took his time removing her sock and lightly massaging her toes, as if he were trying to memorize everything about her.

Daphne pulled her bottom lip into her mouth. She'd never felt so thoroughly pleasured before and the guy had only touched her foot. She couldn't imagine what it was going to feel like when the main event was over.

She felt guilty just sitting there enjoying the sensation as Sam tugged off her right boot and started in on that foot, so she summoned a heroic amount of willpower and managed to move her toes down the hard line of Sam's thigh, getting ever closer to the bull's-eye without actually touching him there.

Sam slid his hands up inside her jeans and rubbed the backs of her calves, pulling her closer until her feet were in his lap. She could feel him under her toes now, hard and eager as he pulsed against her, their breathing becoming labored as the seconds ticked by.

Daff felt as if every part of her body had somehow become an erogenous zone. How could he turn her on so much just by rubbing her freaking ankles?

Sam ran his hands up her thighs again, and this time he followed with the rest of his body, pushing her back onto the bed as he came to lie next to her. He caressed her shoulders through the fabric of her T-shirt, sliding his hand slowly down her side and over her hip to the back of her knee. He drew her leg up and over the firm muscles of his thighs, resting it over his hips, and Daff groaned when she realized that, in this position, she could feel his erection at the juncture of her thighs.

She reached up and trailed her fingers lightly down the side of Sam's face. "I feel like we're in high school, making out in my bedroom and being quiet so my dad won't hear," she said with a wry smile.

Sam smiled back and rolled his hips into hers, and Daff felt a wave of pleasure roll through her body. "I didn't want to rush it. Not our first time," he said, the words tumbling lazily out of his mouth.

"Umm," Daff answered as she tightened her grip on him in an effort to have him hit that magic spot again.

Sam chuckled and obliged, rubbing his erect penis against her until Daff found it difficult to think about anything but the driving need have him touch her again. She didn't realize how close she was to the finish line until she felt the rough skin of Sam's hands slide under her bra. The pads of his thumbs touched her aroused nipples at the same time his erection rubbed against her equally aroused clitoris, and without being able to stop it, her orgasm ripped through her, making her muscles tense as if she'd been struck by lightning.

Her mind went blank, thought and reason replaced by pure, unadulterated sensation.

And then she relaxed. And kept her eyes closed, mortified that she'd just managed to come while both she and Sam were still fully clothed.

She opened her eyes and scowled when Sam had the audacity to laugh. She would have said something scathing then, but Sam rolled her over on her back, covered her body with his own heavier one, and silenced her with a kiss. Daff resisted at first—she didn't want him getting too cocky—but gave up sometime during Sam's onslaught and ended up with her legs wrapped around his waist and her hands tangled under his T-shirt.

Finally, Sam raised his head and grinned down at her.

If she'd have been able to get her hands free, she would have punched him when he winked at her wickedly and said, "No, performance anxiety is definitely not a problem for me."

ELEVEN

KEITH Melman quietly raised himself up on one elbow to look at the woman whose blond hair was spread out on the pillow next to him. She lay curled up like a kitten, her knees tucked up to her chest and her hands resting under her chin.

She was young, wealthy, and beautiful, and, for the life of him, Keith couldn't figure out what the hell she was doing with *him.*

As if she were trying to provide him with an answer, Nicole mumbled something in her sleep. But the words were unintelligible so Keith was left to ponder the mystery while she snuggled into her pillow and dreamed on.

Keith released a troubled breath and slid out from beneath the covers. He had been better off when he thought Nicole just saw him as a short-term fling, the older guy she had to sleep with before settling down with someone her own age. Instead, she kept getting more and more serious about him. Which was why he had half-hoped that her odd behavior lately could be attributed to an affair.

He eased the bedroom door closed behind him as he stepped out into the hallway leading to the kitchen. Keith wearily rubbed his forehead as he reached for a tumbler and the bottle of bourbon he kept in the cabinet above his fridge. He wasn't typically a heavy drinker, but tonight's party had put him on edge.

Nicole had been at her most charming this evening, constantly smiling up at him with a serene look that clearly said, "Don't you think I'd make a great corporate wife?"

And, of course, she would. For someone who wasn't twenty years her senior with an ex-wife and two kids about to enter their dreaded teens.

Keith half-filled his glass with liquor and left the bottle on the counter as he wandered into his study. He pushed his laptop to the corner of his desk and sat down, his elbows propped up on the dark wood with the tumbler between them.

God, he wanted a cigarette. The nicotine craving always got to him when he drank. And the alcohol craving always got to him whenever he started thinking about a long-term relationship with the daughter of one of his most powerful clients.

The prudent thing to do would be to break up with Nicole now, before she invested any more time in him. This relationship could only end in disaster. She just didn't realize it because she was still young and hopeful. Life hadn't had a chance to knock her around and show her that it wasn't always hearts and flowers, even for someone like her.

He picked up his bourbon. Maybe he was just feeling grumpy about staring middle age in its wrinkled old face and his pessimism would pass if he'd let himself believe that someone like Nicole could really be in love with him—second mortgages and alimony and all.

Keith took a swallow of his drink and closed his eyes as it burned its way down his throat. Funny. "Feel the burn" used to mean a whole different thing entirely.

But Nicole's infatuation with him wasn't the only thing that had troubled him this evening. Overhearing the al-Sayeds' argument had also set him on edge. He wasn't a racist—at least, he didn't think he was—but hearing the enigmatic Middle Eastern man use religion as justification for whatever he was doing that had his wife upset had made Keith wary. He couldn't help but think that if only regular Americans such as himself had been a little more suspicious of those hijackers, 9/11 might never had happened. Part of the problem, he believed, was that there were so many laws to protect innocent people from invasion of privacy or unreasonable search and seizure that it was too easy for those with nefarious intent to hide behind the system.

Prior to 9/11, Keith had religiously adhered to that system. He would have required any official who asked about a client's banking information to show him a warrant before releasing any information.

But that was before the FBI had come knocking on his door after the tragedy had occurred and informed him that one of his clients had helped fund the terrorists. Even worse, Keith had had his suspicions about the man's banking history, but had told himself that unless the amount of any one transaction was greater than the federally mandated threshold, he had no duty to turn the man's name over to the authorities.

If only he hadn't allowed federal regulations to lull him into a false sense of security. If only he hadn't assumed that "the government" knew what it was doing. "The government," he later realized, was made up of people who did the best they could, but were not all-seeing, all-knowing, infallible entities.

He was not going to make the same mistake again.

Keith set his drink aside and reached for his laptop, then noticed Nicole's purse lying on its side near the door to his office. Peeking out of the top was a little piece of tobacco temptation.

He got up and surreptitiously looked out in the hall, as if afraid he was about to get busted. He'd been after Nicole to quit and didn't want her to find him sneaking a smoke while nagging her about the dangers of her nicotine addiction. But all was quiet, so he reached down and snagged the cigarette out of Nicole's purse. As he walked back to his desk, he sniffed the slim cigarette, pulling the sweet smell of tobacco into his lungs and wishing that would be enough to satisfy his craving.

It wasn't, of course.

Keith put the cigarette between his lips and pushed his chair back so he could open the middle drawer of his desk. He rummaged around for a moment, searching for the book of matches that had been there the last time he'd looked. When he didn't find what he was looking for, he took the cigarette out of his mouth with his right hand and tilted his head to look inside the drawer.

There they were, wedged in the back of the drawer next to a pad of yellow Post-it notes. He straightened up and put the cigarette back in his mouth. The flame flickered for a moment and then flared to life. He held the fire to the tip of the cigarette and inhaled deeply.

Content, Keith opened the lid of his laptop and pressed the power button to get it out of sleep mode, then entered his password to access the bank's network.

"What did we ever do before wireless networking?" he muttered around the cigarette in his mouth as all the programs that were available to him at work flashed on his screen at home. He was old enough to remember management's resistance to allowing people to work at home in the days when the words "home office" conjured up images of employees lollygagging around in their pajamas and using the excuse that they were "working at home" to squeeze in yet another mental health day.

In fact, quite the opposite was true. Now that most everyone in America had at least some sort of home office, they'd become a nation of workaholics—logging on to check e-mail at midnight or finishing up that vital report during the weekend while the kids splashed around in the pool out back.

For Keith, the ability to work at home was a godsend. On the weeks when he had his kids over, he could stay connected to the office while still running them around to soccer and gymnastics and the million other activities their mother insisted they needed in order to become well-rounded adults.

Exhausted, was more like it.

Keith clicked on a magnifying glass icon that represented AmTrust's tracking program. With this tool, he could put watches on transactions coming to or from a certain person or organization, get notified of any deposits or withdrawals that fell outside a specific dollar range, or check for repeating patterns of transactions that seemed suspicious.

In less than five minutes, he had requested a nightly report on the al-Sayeds business and personal accounts that would list any transaction in excess of $100. For most people—even wealthy people like the al-Sayeds—the number of hundred-dollar transactions a day should be fairly low.

Keith leaned back in his chair, the leather beneath him creaking like an old man's bones in cold weather. He took a deep drag on his cigarette and then removed it to tap the ash into the trashcan before picking up his tumbler and draining the remainder of his drink. He sat in the dark for a long time, long after his cigarette burned down to nothing and the stars outside the window began to fade.

If the al-Sayeds were up to something, he would find out about it and alert the authorities. Never again would he trust that the U.S. government was one step ahead of the bad guys.

And as he slipped back into bed beside his still-slumbering lover, Keith closed his eyes and tried to assure himself that everything would turn out all right in the end.

THEY didn't do it her way the next time. Or even the next.

Daphne squinted at the alarm clock on the nightstand, but it was difficult to read the glowing red numbers from her side of the bed. She hadn't remembered Sam stripping her of her watch last night, but he obviously had because she wasn't wearing it—or anything else, for that matter.

5:14 A.M.

She had to get out of here.

Every time she'd attempted to escape, waiting until Sam's breathing had become deep and even, he'd grabbed her and pulled her back under the covers before she could evade him. Of course, she could have insisted he let her go. It wasn't like she couldn't get away from one naked man—even one as fit as Sam obviously was.

The problem was, she hadn't really wanted to leave. At least, not until now.

Daff grimaced and slowly inched her way toward the edge of the bed so as not to disturb the sleeping man beside her. Her thigh muscles protested the movement, apparently feeling that they deserved a few more hours of rest after their unaccustomed workout the night before.

Clearly, she needed to do this more often.

Daff slid her left leg out of bed and quietly eased her foot to the floor. God, she hated morning afters. Why hadn't Sam just let her go last night, when she could have escaped into the darkness? Now, she'd have to slink off the yacht, ducking the curious stares of any early-morning workers going about their business around the docks.

She listened to Sam's deep and even breathing as she slipped out from under the covers and awkwardly crouched on the thick carpeting as she tugged on her panties and reached out to grab the T-shirt that Sam had flung carelessly to the floor when they'd started in on round two.

Not that she'd been complaining about his lack of neatness at the time.

Daff felt a flush creep up her cheeks at the remembrance of just how eager she'd been to get both of them free of their clothes at the time. It had to have been plain to Sam just how desperate she was.

She would have straightened her shoulders and told herself to knock it off—that no man would complain about getting laid two or three times in one night—but since she was crawling around on the floor looking for her jeans, that sort of posturing was impossible.

Her jeans and bra were at the foot of the bed, along with her boots and her socks. Daff gathered her clothes in her arms and crept toward the bedroom door.

She just wanted to get out of here; didn't want to be forced to watch Sam lie when he told her he'd call her back. She refused to be someone's booty call, and that's all she'd be to Sam after last night. And that was fine. She'd gotten what she wanted from him. It wasn't like she was looking for love or commitment or even a nice dinner out. Her life was as complicated as she wanted it to be these days . . . which was not complicated at all. She came and went as she pleased and didn't have to answer to anybody. It didn't get much better than that.

The hinges squeaked slightly as Daff eased the door open. She paused and cocked her head, listening to hear if Sam's breathing had changed. When she decided it was safe, she cracked the door open another inch and slipped through.

Early morning sunlight flooded the foyer with its cheerful rays, but Daff just grunted at the intrusion as she steadied herself with one hand on the railing of the stairs and bent down to pull on her jeans.

Then she gasped and nearly fell over onto her face when Sam asked, "So, do you have any interest in going for a run?"

His voice was completely neutral, as if he didn't even suspect she was trying to slip out without him noticing. But when Daff looked up to find him leaning against the doorjamb, she couldn't miss the flash of amusement in his eyes. She also couldn't miss the way her own heart started banging against her chest at the sight of him standing there, shirtless, wearing a pair of navy blue sweatpants that he must have pulled on in the two seconds since she'd left the bedroom.

She cleared her throat and continued tugging on her jeans. "How did you know I was a runner?" she asked.

"Just a guess," Sam answered. Then he uncurled himself from the doorway and lazily stalked toward her, his bare feet silent on the hardwood floor of the foyer. When he got within arms' reach, he startled her even further by reaching out and smoothing a lock of hair behind her ear. "Let me at least make you some breakfast."

Something in his voice scared the shit out of her. Without realizing what she was doing, Daff took a step back, away from him.

"I'm not hungry," she said. Of course, her stomach chose that moment to growl like a ravenous beast awakened from a long winter slumber.

Sam raised one eyebrow at her. "I make an excellent omelet."

"I'm sure you do," Daff mumbled under her breath.

"We've got a juicer. I'll even make you some fresh-squeezed orange juice," he cajoled.

Because she was frightened at how tempted she was to let

him pamper her, Daff felt she had no other choice but to lie. "I can't. I've got to get to work."

Sam studied her silently for a long moment and Daff forced herself not to fidget. Finally, he nodded. Once. Abruptly. As if to say he knew she was lying but was going to let her get away with it. This time.

"You never did tell me what you do for a living," Sam said easily, though Daphne got the impression that he wasn't going to let her get away with another vague answer . . . or outright lie.

Which was fine. She didn't really have any reason to prevaricate. It wasn't like her investigation involved him. "I'm a private investigator," she said as she bent down to put on her socks.

"Hmm," Sam said, still studying her with an intense look.

"I used to work for the FBI," she blurted, without knowing why. She never admitted that to anyone she had only just met. It usually made people look at her as if she'd suddenly sprouted a third eye in the middle of her forehead.

Sam yawned. "Oh? What division?"

Daff frowned. He made it sound like she'd just said she was a kindergarten teacher. Not that there was anything wrong with that. But most people acted a bit more surprised that she used to be a special agent. Or at least a bit more interested.

"Antiterrorism," she announced flatly. There. That ought to get his attention.

She pulled her boots on and waited for him to sound impressed. Instead, he just yawned again and asked, "Why'd you quit? Big difference going from being a Fee-bee to a P.I."

She crossed her arms in front of her chest and scowled at him. "The paperwork drove me nuts," she answered, exasperated without realizing exactly why she felt that way.

"Yeah. Government jobs can do that to a person," Sam

said as he nudged his way past her and started up the stairs. "I retired from the Navy, myself, so I can understand."

Daphne blinked up at Sam's retreating back. What? He'd been in the military? And was already retired? She'd guessed that he wasn't over forty, which meant he would have had to enlist when he was fresh out of high school.

"I went straight from graduation to boot camp," Sam said, as if she'd voiced her thoughts aloud.

Slowly, she turned and followed him upstairs. "Is that where you learned to drive boats? In the Navy, I mean. Not boot camp."

"Pilot," Sam corrected as he walked to the kitchen and retrieved something out of a cupboard.

"You were a pilot?" Daff asked, impressed despite herself.

Sam plunked a juicer down on the black granite countertop and plugged it in, then turned toward the stainless steel fridge with glass doors. The doors made a whooshing sound when Sam pulled them open. He grabbed a plastic bag full of oranges out of a drawer and turned back to Daphne with an amused look in his eyes. "No, although I'd probably do better with women if I lied and said I had been a pilot. Why do women think pilots are so great? Not that most of them aren't. But us boat guys aren't so bad, either."

Daff guessed this was all rhetorical, so she sat down on one of the barstools overlooking the kitchen and remained silent as Sam cut several oranges in half and fed them into the juicer.

"I mean, you don't *drive* a yacht. You *pilot* it. And, yes, I learned that in the Navy. Among other things," he added with an enigmatic grin.

He slid a glass of orange juice in front of her and she automatically picked it up and drank without recalling that just a moment ago she'd insisted that she had to get to work.

Hmm. It was as if he had tossed that last bit out to her on

purpose, knowing she'd pounce on it like a kitten on a piece of string. But he was wrong. He didn't know her at all.

Daff hid her smile behind the glass of juice. He had no idea who he was dealing with here. He couldn't know that she prided herself on being able to find out anything about anybody, anytime she wanted. Hell, hadn't she found her very own mother at the age of sixteen, even though Mary Catherine had moved nine times, had no permanent address, and had married and divorced twice more since dumping her daughter off with Brooks and his dad?

It was only later—as she unlocked her car in the yacht club parking lot where she had left it overnight and reflected that Sam's cheese, bacon, and chive omelet had been as good as he'd promised—that Daphne realized he'd used that morsel of mystery to sucker her into having breakfast with him when all she'd really wanted was to be left alone.

TWELVE

"NICOLE, are you okay?"

Nicole Solem released the hair she'd been holding back in a makeshift ponytail and swallowed a silent groan.

Ugh. She hoped Keith hadn't heard her throwing up.

She flushed the toilet a third time and looked around for some scented spray or a candle or something that would mask the scent of vomit.

"Figures, he doesn't have anything like that," she mumbled. Bachelors never did.

She coughed and straightened up, grimacing at herself in the mirror above the sink as she saw how pale she looked.

"I'm fine," she called through the closed—and firmly locked—bathroom door. She rinsed her mouth out with Listerine and dabbed at her already made-up face with a damp washcloth before figuring she might as well stop hiding. There was nothing she could do if Keith *had* heard her.

She'd just have to let him assume she'd had too much to drink last night. No way was she going to tell him the real reason she was sick. Not yet.

Nicole put a hand on her flat stomach and wished she could feel unconditionally happy about the new life growing in there.

But she couldn't.

She would have to keep the baby's existence a secret as long as she could. She was not going to be one of those women who pressured a guy into marrying her because she was pregnant. If Keith didn't propose before she started showing, she would break it off with him. Once he found out about the baby, he'd feel obligated to marry her—both because she knew he genuinely cared for her, but also because he valued his professional relationship with her father. Daddy would expect Keith to propose, and Keith would.

But Nicole didn't want a marriage based on guilt and obligation. She wanted Keith to realize that he loved her.

Which was why she was determined not to miss her class at Rules of Engagement, even though she'd rather go home and curl up in her bed until the nearly constant nausea went away.

Nicole took a deep breath and pulled open the bathroom door, bracing herself for the wave of queasiness she knew would come as soon as the smell of the sausage Keith had made for breakfast hit her nostrils. She felt herself start to retch and swallowed hard, trying to make it stop.

It was so much better at her father's house, where there was nothing more offensive than coffee and fresh fruit for breakfast.

She did her best to breathe in and out through her mouth as she hurried toward the kitchen. She was going to have to make a quick escape if she didn't want to hurl all over Keith's Spanish tile floor.

"Good morning," she said as breezily as she could, giving Keith a quick peck on the cheek as she passed him on her way to the fridge. She pulled out a bottled water and resisted the urge to roll the cool bottle over her face. Instead, she twisted off the cap and took a healthy swig.

Oddly enough, she didn't even miss drinking coffee in the morning. Nicole liked to believe that her body instinctively knew what was and wasn't good for the baby. For the last week, she'd craved things she never wanted before—steak, bananas, and peanut butter ice cream were on the top of her list. She hadn't realized until yesterday morning, when she'd seen that pink plus sign on the home pregnancy test, that her changing tastes were not the result of aging, but the first signs that she was pregnant.

Keith looked up from where he sat at the kitchen table with a breakfast of heart-attack-on-a-plate in front of him and gave her a concerned look. "Are you sure you're okay?" he asked.

Nicole tried to look casual as she backed as far away from the sausage and fried eggs as she could get. "I'm fine, but I'm running a bit late. Got another of my volunteer meetings this morning. Would you like to come have dinner with me and my father this evening?"

Please say yes, Nicole prayed silently. He almost always said no, and Nicole took it as a sign that he didn't want to get any closer to her and her family than he already was.

"No. I've got to work late tonight," Keith said, but his gaze slid to the floor and Nicole knew he was lying.

She smiled to hide her disappointment. This was one area that Lillian Bryson had been coaching her on since she'd started her classes at Rules of Engagement last month. Trying to pressure Keith into doing something he wasn't ready for was not going to get him to the altar, Lillian had said. Nicole was supposed to learn to give him a choice and then accept whatever decision he made. The hope was that Keith would stop resenting being pressured into spending time with her and realize that he actually *wanted* to be with her more.

At least, that's what Lillian assured her would happen. Nicole wasn't quite so sure.

"All right, then. I'll see you . . . hmm. When are we scheduled to see each other again?" Nicole asked, as if she really didn't know the answer.

Keith took a bite of sausage and slowly chewed it. "Friday night. Your father is hosting a dinner party at eight. Remember?"

"Oh, yes. That's right. Friday at eight, it is." Then, because she was irritated that he always seemed to have the upper hand when she was accustomed to being the one in charge where men were concerned, she gave him a nonchalant shrug, turned on her heel, and stormed out of the kitchen to go find the purse she'd tossed in his office last night before going to bed. She left Keith's house without even kissing him good-bye and felt like crying as she roared out of his driveway.

"He probably doesn't even care that I didn't say good-bye," she said to her reflection in the mirror, viciously stabbing the on button of her stereo and half-watching the road while she turned on her iPod and scrolled to the "Angry Women" playlist she'd programmed in a while back.

She drummed her fingers on the steering wheel as Jann Arden belted out "Insensitve."

"That's it. If this doesn't work out, I'm turning lesbian," she muttered. Men were such exasperating creatures. Why couldn't they just do what you wanted them to do when you wanted them to do it?

Aside from her mother dying, which was a pretty big exception, her life up until now had been relatively free of frustration. She had always gotten what she wanted without having to work all that hard for it.

That was all going to change once she had the baby.

She eased back on the accelerator and turned down the volume on her stereo. She had acted like a spoiled brat, stomping out of Keith's house like a two-year-old having a tantrum.

Nicole sighed.

She eyed her reflection in the mirror, clucking her tongue at herself with disapproval. It was time she grew up and stopped behaving as if the world should revolve around her. If Keith truly did have to work late tonight, perhaps the mature thing to do would be to make him dinner and then leave so that he could get a good night's sleep. She knew he didn't sleep well when she spent the night. Neither of them was used to sharing a bed and it would take more than the occasional sleepover for them to get used to sleeping together.

Or maybe it would be best if they didn't see each other at all this evening. Lillian had tried to tell her that the more needy a woman acted, the more likely her man was to pull away. He was conditioned by thousands of years of breeding to be the pursuer, and, while the overall "rule" may not apply in all situations, Lillian generally believed that the less available a woman was, the harder a man would work to win her over.

Nicole may just as well have hung a bright red "Free" sign around her neck where Keith was concerned.

She laughed a little at herself. No wonder Keith still hadn't proposed, even after all these weeks she'd been going to class. Obviously, she hadn't learned a thing.

Nicole was still smiling as she entered Rules of Engagement and waved to the receptionist, who seemed surprised that she was actually a few minutes early. Usually, Nicole was at least fifteen minutes late.

It was a nice change to not have to slink into class and hide apologetically in the back row.

She slipped into the open seat next to Jenna Marisol, who seemed as surprised to see her as the receptionist had been.

Note to self: stop being late all the time, Nicole thought to herself.

"Good morning," she said aloud, setting her purse down on the floor near her feet. "Did you have a good time last night?"

She and Keith had left Jenna and Daddy talking companionably in the parking lot near Jenna's nondescript beige sedan. While she didn't want to pump Jenna for all the gory details, Nicole couldn't help but be curious as to how the night had ended for them.

"I did, thank you," Jenna answered, then snuck a glance at her watch. "We've got a few minutes before class starts and I'm dying for a smoke. Want to come out and keep me company?"

Nicole put a protective hand over her stomach. Would the secondhand smoke hurt the baby? Then she rolled her eyes heavenward and chuckled at herself. She was not going to turn into one of *those* kinds of people—the ones who plugged their noses whenever a smoker walked by as if one whiff of smoke might give them lung cancer.

"Sure," she said, slinging her purse over her shoulder as she stood up and followed Jenna outside.

"I had a really good time last night," Jenna said as they stepped out onto the patio that was crowded with several other smokers out getting their morning fix.

"That's great." Nicole hoped her father felt the same way. It would be so cool if her matchmaking effort led to something more than just a few dates. Dad deserved a little happiness.

Beside her, Jenna rummaged around in her pocketbook for a moment before looking up at Nicole, a small frown creasing her forehead. "I must have forgotten my cigarettes at home," she said.

Nicole squinted against the sunshine that was making her eyes water. She had tossed out a nearly full pack yesterday morning when she'd gotten her first real proof that she was pregnant. No sense in carrying them around anymore—they'd just tempt her to start smoking again. "Oh, sorry. I got rid of all of mine yesterday morning before coming to class."

"How about that one you borrowed from me yesterday? I noticed you didn't smoke it," Jenna said.

Nicole frowned. Wow, Jenna must be really desperate for a cigarette to be this persistent. "I forgot about that," she said as she released the clasp on her purse. It was her turn to poke around amid the contents of her handbag—the barely-used, forty-dollar lipsticks from Lancôme, the bulky key-chain that held an assortment of charms in addition to her car and house keys, a tin of mints, a pen or two—but she didn't find what she was looking for. She shrugged and shot Jenna a rueful smile. "Keith must have taken it. He thinks I don't know that he smokes on those nights when he stays up brooding in his office."

NICOLE continued babbling about Keith and his nocturnal habits, but Jenna tuned her out as her mind started to race.

There was no way that whoever smoked that cigarette wouldn't be infected with anthrax. Keith Melman would be dead within a week. In a day or two, he'd start feeling unusually tired. Just getting out of bed would become a chore. He'd start feeling better after another few days, but then breathing would become a struggle. He'd begin having convulsions. It would be obvious at the end that his death was not from natural causes.

And that could cause enough alarm that Nicole's father might call off his CEO summit. Her fledgling plans to expand her circle of revenge could die right along with her unintended victim.

Jenna couldn't let that happen. She had to think of some way to make Keith's death appear natural.

But how?

She shaded her eyes as Nicole's gold watch caught the sun's rays when she twisted her wrist to check the time.

"Well, we'd better get back. I'm going to have to leave a

few minutes early to make my appointment with my OB-GYN at noon."

Jenna froze as an idea flashed into her mind. "Are you going to tell Keith about the baby tonight?" she asked, feigning nonchalance.

Nicole shook her head. "I don't want him to know about it yet. If I tell him and he ends up proposing, I'll always wonder if he did it for the baby's sake and not because he loves me."

"That's just your pride talking," Jenna said. "He wouldn't propose if he didn't love you. I think he'd respect you more for telling him about the baby than if you kept the information from him as if you were playing some sort of game."

"That's not what I'm doing," Nicole protested, though Jenna could tell that she wasn't as certain as she sounded.

"Telling him would be the adult thing to do. It's a sign of maturity when someone faces difficult situations head-on." Jenna patted the younger woman's shoulder sagely. She knew that the age difference between Nicole and Keith was a big issue for them. Nicole had said as much in their sessions over the past three weeks, and Jenna knew that Nicole was trying hard to prove to her boyfriend that she was a mature, responsible adult.

Come on, take the bait, she urged silently, her eyes narrowing to slits as Nicole hesitated.

Then a slow smile spread across her face as Nicole sighed, turned toward the door, and said, "I guess you're right. I should tell him."

THIS was all Tom Selleck's fault.

Daff sat in her rented convertible with the top up, hunched over the steering wheel as she cursed the star of the old television hit, *Magnum, P.I.* On the show, he had made investigative work look exciting and dangerous. The truth was, most times it was downright boring.

Like now, for instance.

Parked across the street from Rules of Engagement, Daff had a clear view of the business's front entrance. She expected Nicole Solem to emerge in about ten minutes and then—joy of joys—she'd spend the day traipsing along behind the wealthy socialite as she wasted her time shopping or getting a pedicure or lying around Daddy's pool working on her tan.

Daff tried unsuccessfully to stifle a yawn and told herself this was what she got for using her talents to trail cheating spouses and thieving employees. She'd had her chance at danger and excitement and proven she wasn't up to the task. This mind-numbing boredom was only what she deserved.

"At least you know she's not going to give you the slip and go kill thousands of innocent people," Daff muttered under her breath, then scowled when the cell phone on the seat next to her started to vibrate.

She looked at the caller ID display and frowned at the unfamiliar number.

"Hello?" she answered, wondering if it might be her client calling for a progress report.

"So I was sitting here wondering if it was too early to call you for a second date," Sam Bryson said, his deep voice sending a shiver down Daff's spine.

She could imagine him standing on the bridge of the yacht, staring out into the Gulf of Mexico with a half-smile hovering around his lips. She wondered briefly if he was always this amused or if he was laughing at her. Though she couldn't imagine why. Daff did not consider herself the least bit funny. Tragic, perhaps. Comical, definitely not.

She leaned back in her seat and pushed her sunglasses up the bridge of her nose, continuing to stare at the door across the street. "Didn't your mother ever tell you that you're not supposed to call a woman again if she sleeps with you on the first date?"

"Is that why you slept with me? So I *wouldn't* call you?"

Yes. He was definitely laughing at her.

Daff ran her tongue along the backs of her bottom teeth. "Well, that *is* one of the rules, you know."

"I've always liked breaking the rules," Sam said.

"I can imagine," Daff countered dryly, refusing to be drawn in by his easygoing manner. He had proven this morning how easy it was to manipulate her. She wasn't going to be suckered again.

"How about it? Want to have dinner with me tonight? It'll be just the two of us this time."

And just like that, Daff was tempted to say yes. She reached up to rub her forehead and admonished herself for being so weak. Why was she so eager to see him again? She couldn't blame it on her libido this time. Last night, Sam had done a stellar job of scratching her desperate-to-get-laid itch.

"Come on," Sam cajoled, obviously sensing her hesitation. "Let me prove that I know how to take a girl on a real date."

Daff gazed out at the busy sidewalk and asked the question that had puzzled her since yesterday evening. "Why *did* you invite me on that cruise last night? I mean, if you wanted to go out, it could have waited until tonight."

"Because," Sam said, "I knew the moment we met that you were going to need a lot of convincing. I didn't want to waste any time getting started."

Daff frowned as the front door of Rules of Engagement opened and Nicole Solem stepped out, her shiny blond hair gleaming in the sun as she pointed her keychain at her fancy car and unlocked the driver's-side door.

"What do you mean? Convince me of what?" Daff asked, confused. What the hell was he talking about? Had she missed something in their conversation while she'd been watching for Nicole to come out?

When Sam answered, it was as if his voice were licking her ear, making her shudder as she remembered just how good it had felt when he really had been touching her. She forgot all about Nicole and everything else but Sam, however, as he all but purred, "Convince you that you're mine."

THIRTEEN

HALF an hour later, as Daff pulled into the three-story parking garage behind Nicole Solem's sporty blue convertible, she still felt stunned by what Sam had said.

Convince you that you're mine.

It was either the cheesiest line ever invented by a man to get a woman to sleep with him again or . . . or Daff was in real freaking trouble here.

She was not the sentimental type. Nor was she in the market for a husband. Or even a long-term relationship. Even so, her heart had literally stopped beating when Sam had uttered those words.

She kept waiting to feel insulted, like she was some fire hydrant that he'd just peed all over to mark his territory or something. But she couldn't seem to summon up any outrage. Or anything else except this odd sort of tightness in her chest that wouldn't go away.

Daff struggled to take a deep breath and lowered her chin so Nicole couldn't make out her face in the darkened garage attached to a medical center across the street by a glassed-in breezeway.

"Good thing we're near a hospital, because I think I must be sick," Daphne mumbled to herself. There had to be something wrong with her for thinking for even a second that Sam might be sincere. Even more troubling was the niggling worry that she might actually *want* him to be.

She shook her head, as if that would clear all thoughts of Sam Bryson from her mind. She needed to concentrate on this case—no matter how trivial it was—not sit here mooning over some guy who had somehow discovered the perfect thing to say to her.

Hurriedly, Daff parked her car and stepped out into the cloying warmth of exhaust fumes trapped in the stuffy garage. She tossed her hat into the backseat of the convertible and hung her head upside down to fluff out her hair while at the same time reaching into the car to grab a pair of wire-framed glasses and a retainer fitted with plastic tubes that made her cheeks seem chubbier than they actually were.

Finally, she looked around to make sure no one was watching (although, if this had been a "real" case, she would have also scanned for hidden cameras before putting on her disguise) and then slipped on an ankle-length floral skirt over her jeans. In another two seconds, she had stripped off her jeans and tossed them in the backseat next to her hat.

Her disguise complete, she slammed the door of the rental car and trotted off in the direction she had seen Nicole go.

She made it to the elevator just in time to watch the blonde disappear inside. Daff hung back, figuring it was best not to put her disguise to the test if she didn't need to. She took the stairs two at a time, easily beating the slower elevator to the third floor where the breezeway was located, and was halfway across by the time she felt the presence of someone behind her.

Daff tilted her head down and to the right until she could see the feet of the person following her. It was Nicole Solem all right, with her impractical three-inch-high platform sandals and perfectly pedicured toes.

The breezeway opened up onto a foyer where a directory hung on one wall, listing the doctors with their corresponding office numbers. Daff paused and pretended to look at the directory while Nicole clomped past her and went down the hall.

Daff sighed. This had to be the easiest case she had ever worked.

She followed Nicole down the hall, which led to an open waiting room where half a dozen women sat. Several were reading magazines and didn't even look up when Daff entered the waiting area. One woman who was reading a book with a bat on the cover to a little girl of about three glanced up, but her words didn't falter. Daff assumed that the mother had read the book to her child so many times she had it memorized.

She smiled wistfully at the woman, who had dropped her gaze back to the illustrated book.

Yet another thing her own mother had never done for her.

But, hey, she should be grateful—her mother's hands-off approach to child rearing had taught Daphne to be self-sufficient. Besides, she'd realized long ago that the world was full of broken people who had even worse pasts to overcome than she did.

She slid into a chair where she could see the one entrance and exit to the exam rooms beyond the reception area.

Her own childhood could have been a lot worse. Like if her mom hadn't left her with Jack. It would definitely have been worse then.

"How far along are you?"

Lost in her thoughts, Daphne's head jerked up in surprise when she realized that the woman who had been reading to her daughter was talking to her.

Daff blinked several times. "Pardon me?" she asked.

The woman gasped and covered her mouth with her hand. She looked horrified as she quickly backpedaled. "I'm so sorry. You don't look pregnant or anything. It's just that most people who come to see Dr. Thomas are, and I assumed . . ."

Suddenly, Daphne realized why all the patients here were women. She swiftly scanned the waiting room, taking in the posters about prenatal vitamins, breastfeeding, and the importance of giving up smoking and drinking during pregnancy.

She shot Nicole a calculating look from under her lashes and then turned her attention back to the woman across from her. Giving her best impression of maternal serenity, Daff put a hand to her flat—thanks to hours of exercise and a complete disinterest in food lately—stomach like she'd seen other pregnant women do.

"No, you were right. It's just that this is my first appointment and I'm not used to people being able to tell that I'm pregnant. I'm probably only a month or two along."

The woman frowned. "A month or two? You don't know how many weeks you are yet?"

Daff's serenity faltered. Shit. She should have just kept her mouth shut. What the hell did she know about being pregnant? Neither Raine or Aimee—her two closest female friends—had ever been pregnant. And, truthfully, Daff had mostly hung out with guys all her life. They didn't talk about crap like that.

"The doctor is supposed to tell me how far along I am today." Then, because she didn't know how else to stop this conversation, Daff leaned forward conspiratorially and whispered in such a way that anyone in a ten-foot radius could easily overhear, "My boyfriend and I have sex so often that it's impossible for me to pin down the exact date he knocked me up. It could pretty much be any time in the last three months since we first started going out. I know you're not supposed to have sex with a guy on the first date, but I just couldn't stop myself. He had the cutest butt. And, whew, I tell you, when he dropped his pants for the first time, I nearly fainted right there on the spot. You should have seen how big his—"

The woman's eyes had widened to twice their original size as she held up her hand to make Daphne stop. Her daughter had lost all interest in her book and had turned her rapt attention to Daphne. The woman quickly stood up, grabbing her daughter's arm and tugging her along behind her.

"Sorry, they're calling my name," the woman lied, and Daff had to force herself not to laugh at the horrified look on her face.

You're evil, she admonished herself as the woman hastily retreated.

Then she sat back, thankful to be left alone as she contemplated whether or not she should tell her client that it was very likely that his girlfriend had been acting strange lately not because she was cheating on him, but because she was pregnant.

FOURTEEN

SHE was late.

Daff sat in the driveway outside of Keith's house and drummed her fingers on the steering wheel of her rental car. Those words could have an entirely different meaning depending on the circumstances. In Nicole Solem's case, they meant she was pregnant. In Daff's case, they meant she was sitting out here procrastinating about knocking on the door because she wasn't sure whether she was about to do the right thing.

Yes, Keith was her client and he had hired her to find out what was making his girlfriend act so odd lately. And that's what she had done, but was it her place to spring the news on him? Wasn't that up to Nicole? And what if the baby wasn't Keith's? What if that's why Nicole was trying to keep it a secret?

Daff sighed. This was becoming way too complicated.

She had to take her emotions out of this. It wasn't her place to judge the information she had uncovered. All she was supposed to do was to present the facts as she knew them. What her client did with the information was none of her business.

"Stay out of other people's lives," she mumbled as she pushed open the car door, wondering why she seemed to have forgotten her motto in the last few days. She didn't even know these people. So why was she so concerned about how her investigation might impact their lives? Besides, it wasn't like she was delivering news that was really so shocking. Women got pregnant all the time. Every day, in fact. That's why Daff always got a chuckle out of people saying that childbirth was such a miracle. How could something that happened virtually every second of every day be a miracle? She thought miracles were saved for things that never happened, like water being turned to wine or seas parting down the middle.

Daff chuckled to herself as she headed up the walkway leading to Keith's front door. She'd told him she would be here half an hour ago and she hoped he wasn't annoyed that she was late.

When he answered the door, he seemed more distracted than irritated, leading her into his home office after vaguely offering her something to drink as they passed the kitchen. Daff declined. She just wanted to get this over with.

She knew that once she told Keith what she'd discovered, her work was through. She'd be free to go back to Atlanta, or to New York, if her brother would have her.

The thought of moving back in with Aimee, who had a full house with her newly adopted daughter, Josie, and quietly handsome boyfriend, Race, made Daff more than a little uneasy. She would feel like an intruder, even though Aimee had assured her that Daff's room was ready whenever she was ready to come back.

What troubled her the most, though, was how much it suddenly bothered her to feel like she had no roots. Since when had that been a problem? She didn't have roots and never had. For someone who had never really belonged anywhere, Daff had gotten used to feeling like an outsider. Frankly, she found it comforting to know she wasn't expected to pick out drapes or make her own personal mark anywhere she lived. It gave her digs a temporary look that Daff found strangely reassuring.

Why, then, did knowing that she wasn't wanted anywhere after she finished this job make her feel like crying?

"So, what is it that you've discovered?" Keith asked, sounding defeated as he sat down across from her behind his mahogany desk.

Without quite knowing why, Daphne hesitated, and then admonished herself once again for not just doing her job in her usual disinterested manner. "I believe I've discovered why Nicole is pressuring you so hard to get married," she announced, stripping all emotion from her voice.

Keith leaned forward and rested his elbows on the desk. "Yes?"

"Yes. Now, I just want to warn you first that I don't have any hard proof of this yet, so this information can only be considered preliminary at this point."

"Understood," Keith agreed with an impatient wave of his hand.

"It's likely that your girlfriend is pregnant."

Keith blinked once. Twice. And then a third time.

Then he buried his head in his hands. "Oh, God," he mumbled. "So that's why she wants to marry me."

Before she could stop herself, Daphne blurted, "Have you considered the possibility that maybe she loves you? I mean, it's not like she couldn't have her pick of men."

Surprised by her own outburst, Daff stood up and agitatedly paced to the door and back. What the hell was wrong with her? Since when had she turned into a romantic? Besides, she had no evidence that Nicole Solem was in love—if such a thing even existed—with her boyfriend. All she really knew was that the young woman was taking lessons in how to get a man to the altar and that there was a good chance she was pregnant. It was very probable that Keith's conclusion was correct, that Nicole had accidentally gotten knocked up and now wanted Keith to marry her and make it all legitimate. Not that anyone cared about that sort of thing these days—an attitude shift that had happened about thirty years too late for Daphne, whose mother didn't even bother to name Daff's father on her birth certificate, much less marry the bastard.

Keith had lifted his head and was watching her with narrowed eyes. "Do you really think a woman like Nicole could fall for a guy like me?" he asked skeptically.

"Stranger things have happened," Daff said with a shrug, not meaning to be rude.

But Keith was already shaking his head, his shoulders slumped in defeat. "No. I think it's just that she got pregnant by accident and sees this as her only way out. She'd never have an abortion, she's been clear about wanting children ever since we met. And, despite what you might think, Nicole's pretty old-fashioned. She believes in marriage and family and all that happily ever after crap." Keith put his head in his hands again and sighed. "I can't believe this is happening to me again."

Daff assumed this meant the first ex–Mrs. Melman had presented Keith with a similar situation a decade earlier. She was tempted to suggest he might want to think about starting to use condoms from now on, but since the horses were already out of the barn, so to speak, she figured she'd be better off just keeping her mouth shut about the subject of birth control.

"So what are you going to do?" she asked instead. She

knew it was none of her business, but for some reason, she felt compelled to ask.

Keith didn't even bother raising his head as he answered despondently, "I'm going to marry her, of course. What choice do I have?"

DAFF was not surprised to find Sam leaning up against a black pickup truck in the parking lot outside her motel room. Unmoving, he watched her drive into the spot next to him, looking as if he were patient enough to stand and wait for her forever.

So much for her indecision about whether or not to go out with him again.

As she put the convertible in park, she felt her resolve crumble like cotton candy melting in the rain. An apt metaphor, Daff thought with a snort, since her resolve had been about as strong as spun sugar to begin with.

She got out of the car and pushed the door shut behind her. "You do know that stalking is against the law, don't you?" she asked, not bothering to glance at him as she started toward her room.

Sam wouldn't have come this far to turn tail and run now.

She had the key in the lock when Sam's hand covered hers, his front pressed up against her back, so close that she was trapped between his hard body and the door. Daff stiffened and then relaxed into him. Damn. She hadn't even heard him move.

Sam lowered his head and nuzzled her neck. "Do you really want me to go?" he asked.

Daphne closed her eyes and let the pleasurable sensations evoked by Sam's touch wash over her. She had forgotten how good it felt to be wanted.

And what was so wrong with that? To have someone be attracted to her and to feel the same way in return.

Nothing, that's what. So why was she so quick to push Sam away instead of enjoying whatever time they had together?

"No. I don't want you to go," Daff said, pressing herself against him and gasping when, instead of pushing open the motel room door so they could finish this inside, Sam pulled the key out of the lock and stepped away from her.

"Come on, I promised you dinner," he said, tugging her back toward the parking lot with one firm hand around her wrist.

Daff dug her heels into the pavement, unaccustomed to being dragged anywhere against her will. "Hey, stop man-handling me," she protested, then squeaked with surprise when Sam spun on her with a grin that would have made Satan proud.

"Don't make me have to kidnap you," he said, his eyes gleaming with amusement.

If her hands had been free, she would have crossed her arms over her chest in a way that shouted, "Hands off." But since Sam still held her tightly by the wrist, all Daff could do was glare and do her best to look ferocious.

If anything, Sam's grin just widened as he leaned forward and planted an avuncular kiss on the end of her nose. "I love it when you look at me like that."

Daff scowled. "Look at you like what?"

"Like you'd like nothing more than to spank me," Sam said. Then he winked at her and added, "But you're going to have to wait until later. I'm taking you out to dinner first."

And so it was that Daff found herself hustled off to a casual burger joint on the beach where several people greeted Sam by name and eyed her curiously as the pair made their way to a table near the back.

"So, do you come here often?" Daff asked, feeling suddenly awkward after a tiny-waisted waitress who only had eyes for Sam took their order for a couple of beers and left.

Sam leaned back in his chair and nodded. "Yeah, I do. After spending so many years traveling with the Navy, I made it a point when I retired to put down some roots."

The pixielike waitress returned carrying glasses of beer that were bigger than her tiny little head. She absently set Daff's glass down in front of her and smiled at Sam, who smiled back politely and thanked her. Daff wondered if Sam realized she was sending him pretty strong "buy" vibes and he just wasn't interested, or if he was clueless as to the woman's feelings.

"She's not my type," Sam said after the waitress had gone, raising one eyebrow at Daff as he picked up his beer.

Daff coughed. Geez, since when had she become so easy to read? "So . . . you never did tell me what you did in the Navy," she said to change the subject. Expecting another evasive answer, she took a swig of her own beer and cast about in her head to think up her next question. That's what people did on dates, right? Fished around in each other's past, trying to see if they had anything in common?

"I was in spec ops," Sam answered evenly, as if announcing he'd been a janitor or a cook.

Daff inhaled sharply and choked on her beer. Had he really just admitted to being a SEAL?

Sam ignored her coughing and took another drink of his beer. "I don't usually tell people that, but it's something about me that I thought you should know. Plus," he added with a grin, "if you still have friends in the Bureau, you'd find out anyway. This way, I figured I'd win some points for telling you right up front."

She sat there blinking dumbly at him. Good Lord. And she'd thought he'd be intimidated by her former job with the FBI.

"Shit," she mumbled, feeling like an idiot as she nursed her beer. The heavy glass was sweating, condensation rolling down and pooling onto the damp napkin the waitress had set under it.

"I should have known you wouldn't be impressed," Sam said, sounding more amused than disappointed.

Slowly, Daphne raised her gaze to meet his deceptively soft brown eyes and a shiver of something very much like dread rolled through her body. Now she knew why she'd found him so irresistible. Underneath all that lighthearted banter was someone who *understood,* someone who had faced evil and death, someone who knew the frustration of fighting for a government that played by rules that often didn't make any sense in the real world.

She felt the dark past she'd done her best to hold at bay crushing in on her, the voices of the dead talking to her, whispering in her ear, pleading with her to save them. Bile rose in her throat as she remembered the unholy stench of burned flesh, the sight of human bodies crushed to tissue-paper thinness between slabs of concrete.

Sam knew this kind of horror, too. He would have had to with twenty years as a SEAL.

Which was why she had to get away. With someone who couldn't understand, there was no danger. Daff would never be tempted to talk about what had happened on 9/11 with someone who hadn't seen death for himself. She was safe with people like that because they would never be able to get close enough to really know what was in her heart.

But Sam could. If she ever let her guard down, ever once looked up at him with vulnerability in her eyes, he would know.

And knowing her weak spots would give him the power to destroy her.

Daff clenched her teeth and drew in a labored breath. She shivered again and tried to swallow the sick taste in her mouth. Her gaze slid away from Sam's as she cleared her throat and pushed her chair back on the scuffed hardwood floor.

"I've got to go. To the ladies' room," she added and then walked unseeingly toward what she hoped was the bathroom. Behind her, she heard Sam's chair scrape the floor. She didn't know if he was just being a gentleman by standing up when she did or if he was concerned and intended to follow her to the bathroom, so she hurried toward a door marked "Women" and hastily pushed the door closed behind her.

Surely, he wouldn't follow her in here.

Daff held her breath as she spied the shadow of someone's shoes on the other side of the bathroom door. *Move on,* she silently urged, then let out her breath as the shadow finally disappeared.

Desperate to escape, she looked around the bathroom, and couldn't believe her luck when she saw a window about eight feet up. She had to get out of here and away from Sam. Now. Before she caved in to the urge to unburden herself, seeking the salvation she craved but knew she didn't deserve.

She shoved open the door to the last stall and balanced her weight on the tank of the toilet. The window was small and the sill had been painted over, but Daff wouldn't give up. She hopped down off the toilet and grabbed an extra roll of toilet paper that had been left on the dispenser. Then she got back up on the tank and used the roll to protect her hand as she jabbed at the glass, trying to get it to budge.

Just as she was beginning to think she was going to have to come up with another plan, the window cracked. She pushed at it again and it flew open, the pane falling to the ground and shattering loudly as it came loose from its rusted frame.

Daff looked back toward the bathroom door, squinting to see if the shadow beneath the door had returned. Assured that she was alone, she put her hands on the windowsill and jumped up. Her stomach scraped over the sill as Daff pulled herself through. She wiggled her hips until she was balanced halfway in and halfway out of the window.

Now came the tricky part.

If she pulled herself forward any farther without being properly braced, she'd end up landing headfirst on the concrete. Instead, she cocked her toes outward and, glad she was wearing boots and not sandals, let her body slide forward until her feet were braced along the sides of the window. She was still about three feet from the ground, but that wasn't very far to fall.

She reached her arms down and then let go, wincing when her full weight came down on her wrists. Quickly, she flipped her feet behind her in an effective—if inelegant—backflip. Once she had righted herself, she carefully dusted the shards of glass from her palms, ignoring the few places where she had started to bleed.

Then, without another look toward the restaurant, she squared her shoulders and started running. And, while Daff might have preferred to think she was running toward her motel and freedom, the man silently watching her from the shadows was deadly determined to discover why she was running away.

FIFTEEN

"NATHAN, I'm telling you, a determined twelve-year-old could blow this so-called security plan to hell." Sam pushed the folder across the desk as if it were filled with ten-day-old sweaty gym shorts. He wasn't in the mood for this today, not after Daphne had run out on him last night. He hadn't been hired on as Nathan Solem's security consultant or to do anything more dangerous than to scrape barnacles off the bottom of the *Long Shot*. That was the deal he'd made with himself when he got out of the Navy. There'd be no more nights when he'd wonder if he'd still be alive come morning, no more staring down the wrong end of a weapon or knowing that one bad move could get him killed. He'd put his life on hold for twenty years and that was enough. He wanted nothing more to do with criminals, lunatics, despots, and thugs. He was ready to settle down, and the last thing he wanted to do was to put his wife through hell every day wondering where he was or if he'd make it home in one piece.

No, that life was over. Sam just wanted to go about his business of ferrying his boss and his rich friends and work associates around on one of the Solems' many watercraft. That was enough of a challenge these days.

Too bad he hadn't yet learned to keep his mouth shut.

Nathan frowned and flipped open the file that contained the details of the security plan for the upcoming CEO summit. "What do you mean? What's wrong with it?" he asked.

Sam sighed and wished like hell he could just mind his own damn business. He should be out working on Solem's thirty-eight-foot cabin cruiser. Nathan wanted the Sea Ray in tip-top condition for the first day of the summit, when attendees and their families would have their choice of hanging out by the pool, playing on the jet skis, or cruising the Gulf. And while making sure the Sea Ray was clean and seaworthy, Sam could figure out his next move with Daphne. He figured she at least owed him an explanation for why she'd run out on him last night. He had no idea why the news that he was a retired SEAL had freaked her out like that . . . but he intended to find out.

If he thought she was just a flake, he wouldn't bother. After all, he was a relatively attractive guy with a decent job and a minimum amount of emotional baggage. It wasn't like he had any trouble getting dates. But something about Daphne intrigued him, something he couldn't explain. His mother would probably call it chemistry, but it felt deeper than that to him. It was more of a . . . connection. As if his soul recognized hers.

Like he'd said, he couldn't really explain it. All he knew was that if he gave up on her now, he'd be making the biggest mistake of his life.

But before he could hunt Daphne down again, it looked like he was going to have to point out the holes in Nathan's security plan. This is what you got for relying on a firm whose founder was featured on *E! Hollywood Weekly* and whose claim to fame was finding an explosive that had been sculpted into the shape of an Oscar statue by one of the dancers at last year's Academy Awards.

From what Sam had read about the incident, the guy had been nervously eyeing the exit and sweating profusely even before the dancing Oscar skit began. When the security team made a routine walkthrough of the backstage area, the kid had lost his nerve and darted for the door. The burly security guys made quick work of tackling the dancer before he could escape, and that's when Lance Muldoon—founder of On Guard Security Services—arrived on the scene, just in time to milk the moment for all the publicity it was worth.

Sam was willing to admit that the risk of Nathan Solem's CEO summit becoming a terrorist target was fairly low. There were only twenty CEOs attending, so it wasn't like taking them all out would cause the U.S. economy to collapse or anything. Plus, unlike Bill Gates's big summit held every year in Seattle, Nathan's event was very low-key.

Still, that didn't mean there was no threat at all. Plenty of people knew about the summit—it wasn't being publicized, but that didn't mean it was a secret, either. A gathering of this sort would make a good terrorist target, simply because it would be expected to be less secure than a larger event of the same type. Plus, the people attending were high profile, so taking them all out in one fell swoop would achieve terrorism's prime goal, that of proving that no one was safe.

And that meant that figuring out what to do about Daphne would have to wait.

Sam leaned forward in his chair and rested his elbows on his knees. Might as well get this over with.

"Well," he began, "to start with, On Guard's not planning to do any background checks. Not on the attendees or on the employees who'll be working the event."

Nathan seemed horrified at the suggestion. "The attendees? Why in the world would we need to check them out?"

"Can you be certain that no one on your guest list is susceptible to blackmail? Or might have some other motive—perhaps religious or political—to disrupt an event like this?" Sam asked, knowing that Nathan would never believe that one of his peers might throw in with a terrorist group. In Sam's opinion, that was the terrorists' main source of power—the average American's inability to comprehend that there were people in the world who felt no compunction about killing others who didn't conform to their own beliefs.

Not that Sam was simpleminded enough to believe that things were always so black and white. He'd been involved in enough conflicts over his twenty-year stint in the military to have had cause to question his own government's motives a time or two. Overall, however, he steadfastly believed that the U.S. government was mostly made up of good people who tried to do the right thing. The same could not be said of many other governments he'd become intimately involved with over the years. Nor could it be said of the people in certain countries around the world who had been brainwashed to think that their skin color or religion or family tree made them gods while others around them were disposable, like so much human Kleenex.

Sam had learned early on in his military service that you didn't always know a person the way you might think you did. Running background checks on the attendees would at least give them a clearer picture of the people who would be attending the summit.

Only Nathan was still shaking his head. "I just don't believe that's necessary. I've known these men and women for years. It would be an invasion of their privacy to do what you're suggesting."

Sam clamped his teeth together to keep from saying what he wanted to say. He reminded himself that security was not his job. All he could do was offer advice which his boss could either use or not as he saw fit.

It wasn't his responsibility to keep the world safe from harm any longer.

All he had to do was protect the people in his own world. Everyone else was on their own.

"Okay," he said. "Then what about the employees working the event? I assume you'll have caterers, a clean-up crew, valets, extra staff on hand to take care of guests?"

"Yes, of course. But we're using firms we've used for years. We've never had any sort of trouble with them before," Nathan protested.

Sam sighed so deeply that he was surprised the papers on Nathan's desk didn't blow off. He figured he had nothing to lose by stating his mind. He'd never been big on blindly following orders or ignoring a bad situation. He wasn't about to start now. "Look, Nathan, I'm the first to admit that my background tends to make me a little suspicious. Paranoid, even, at times. But just because someone's paranoid doesn't mean he's not being followed, if you know what I mean. Now, you've hired this company to keep you and your business associates safe during this summit. I'm just telling you, they're not giving you the level of security you're paying for. You don't want them spying on your peers? Okay, I understand that. But the least they should be doing is checking out the people you *don't* know, the ones you can't vouch for personally. That's not so much to ask.

"You may not think these people are a threat, but you have to remember, they're the ones with unlimited access to your food, to your vehicles, to your home. All it would take is one person with an ax to grind with anyone attending this event and . . ." Sam shrugged and let Nathan complete that last thought himself. Maybe he was being overly pessimistic, but better that than to pretend nothing could go wrong simply because his boss didn't want to believe it could.

The silence between them lengthened, but Sam remained still, perched on the edge of a chair in Nathan's large home office with his hands clasped between his knees. He had nothing to gain here. It wasn't his job or his life on the line. He'd just always been a stickler for doing the right thing. And that meant not backing down from a fight, even when it would be easier to walk away.

Finally, Nathan leaned back in his own chair. "Fine. We'll do background checks on the employees," he said.

Sam's bubble of satisfaction burst when Nathan tapped his fingers on his desk and added, "But I want *you* to do them. I don't want it getting out that we pried into people's lives like this. Lance Muldoon would sell his own jock-strap size if it meant some extra publicity for his company, and I wouldn't want this leaked to the press. I trust that you'll keep this to yourself."

Great. Just what he needed—another job. And a thankless one at that.

Sam squeezed his hands together as a thought occurred to him. In order to do these searches, he'd need to get in touch with some people he knew—people who knew how to get information that wasn't accessible to the general public.

Which meant he could find out just about anything on just about anyone. Including the woman who'd made like a gazelle being chased by a hungry lion last night after he'd told her about his former career.

WHEN Keith's alarm rang, he groaned and rolled over in bed to shut the damn thing off. God, he was tired this morning.

He coughed and reached for the glass of water sitting on the nightstand beside his king-sized bed. The tepid drink did little to ease the dry scratchiness in the back of this throat, and Keith wondered for a moment if he was coming down with a cold.

Great. That's just what he needed—another sign of weakness to show his healthy young girlfriend just before he proposed.

Maybe he should rent a fucking wheelchair and get it over with.

He flopped back on the pillows and stared up at the white-painted ceiling. He knew he was being irrational. Forty-three was not old. His own father was still alive and in good health at sixty-three. There was no reason for Keith to feel the way he did. Yet, he did.

And knowing that he was about to become a father again just made it worse.

He didn't want *more* responsibility; he wanted less. His entire adult life had been filled with obligations—a wife who expected to be supported, then one child, and then two.

Maybe he'd like to take some time off, enjoy his life for a change. Maybe travel and lie around on the beach counting the grains of sand between his toes for a while. Instead, he was about to get saddled with yet another wife who had no intention of ever finding a job and another baby to raise for the next twenty years.

Keith shuddered. He'd be about his own father's age by the time the kid was out of the house.

Not that he didn't love his children or that he'd want Nicole to have an abortion. It was just that . . . he felt sometimes like his own biological clock was ticking, that pretty soon his life would be over and all he'd have to show for it would be a nice gold watch from the bank and a healthy inheritance for his children.

Wasn't life supposed to be a little more fulfilling than that?

He pulled himself up into a sitting position, grimacing at the ache in his shoulders. He rolled his arms a couple of times, but that didn't help ease the tightness.

"Maybe it's the flu," he muttered as he reached out and pulled open the top drawer of his nightstand.

A midnight blue velvet box stared back up at him.

Nicole's engagement ring.

He'd bought it months ago, but it never seemed the right time to give it to her. It wasn't her fault. She was a beautiful, caring person and, if he were being honest with himself, he would have to admit that he loved her.

He just wished she were a little older, a little less interested in starting a family and settling down. He was already settled enough. Any more settled and he might as well be dead.

Keith sighed and reached for the phone. He might as well call Nicole and get this over with. By eight o'clock tonight, he'd be an engaged man.

AS soon as the client signed off on her time sheet, Daff was free to go.

She sat in her rented convertible with the top up and the engine running, across the street from Keith Melman's house. In her desperation to get out of Naples as soon as possible, she'd tried calling Keith's home and his office several times already this morning, but he hadn't answered at either number.

All she needed was to get his signature on one little slip of paper and then she could escape this relentlessly cheerful little town. She'd checked out the Weather Channel this morning before leaving her motel room. It was thirty-four degrees and raining in New York today. People bundled in their gray winter coats dodged each other on the sidewalk as they hurried to get inside the warm, equally gray buildings where they worked.

Daff couldn't wait to get back.

But first she had to get that signature on her time sheet so Aimee could send Keith a bill.

Her cell phone rang and Daphne glanced at the caller ID. The number that flashed on the screen was no longer unfamiliar.

Sam Bryson. The guy sure didn't know how to take a hint.

Daphne had been prepared for that, however. That's why she'd checked out of her motel first thing this morning and planned to spend all day in her car if she had to. If Sam couldn't find her, he couldn't talk to her. And if he couldn't talk to her, she wouldn't have to try to come up with an explanation about why she'd given him the slip last night.

Really, it would be so much easier on them both this way.

Anyway, wasn't that the perfect male fantasy? A little no-strings-attached sex and then—bam!—the woman disappears? No messy discussions about what feminine hygiene products she preferred or her complicated feelings about her mother. He'd never have to know if she wanted kids (she wasn't sure) or whether she was a cat person or a dog person (dog person, hands down—she wasn't sure why, but cats gave her the creeps).

"Damn. What's *she* doing here?" Daff muttered to herself as Nicole Solem's sporty blue convertible pulled into Keith's driveway. Daphne hunkered down in her seat as the blonde exited her vehicle and, without a glance in Daff's direction, headed toward the front door.

Daff glared at the digital clock on her dashboard. Nicole could be in there for hours.

So much for a quick getaway.

She noticed a movement out of the corner of her eye and looked up to see a suspicious shadow behind one of the upstairs windows of a neighbor's house. Great. That'd be just what she needed—to get tagged as a stalker and hauled in by the Naples police.

Obviously, she couldn't sit here all day. But where could she go?

Daff saw the curtain across the street flicker again and figured she'd better get out of here before Mrs. Kravitz up there called the cops. With no particular destination in mind, she meandered through the winding streets of Keith's neighborhood, wondering what it would have been like to have grown up someplace like this. She'd spent all her life—up until the time she left for the FBI Academy in Virginia—within five miles of Manhattan, where there were no such things as acre lots and tiled roofs.

That didn't mean she hadn't been pretty impressed with Brooks's dad's place when Mary Catherine had brought her over to spend the night at Jack's house while they went out and did whatever it was a New York City cop and a failed actress would have done in those days. To Daff, Jack's place had seemed enormous. She and good ol' mom most often shared a couch or an empty spot of floor at the apartments of Mary Catherine's numerous friends and acquaintances. That was one thing about Mary Catherine—she seemed to have a lot of friends who didn't mind her bumming off them . . . as long as they didn't stay more than a night or two.

Daff was willing to bet that the kids who lived in the houses in Keith's neighborhood hadn't spent many nights sleeping on someone else's dirty linoleum floor.

She snorted to herself as she pulled out of the housing development and headed downtown. She might as well get something to eat. It could be hours before she boarded a flight for New York, and she'd learned never to get on a plane with an empty stomach or a full bladder.

Street parking was amazingly easy to find on the main tourist drag, another thing Daff found hard to believe after living in Manhattan for so long, where empty parking spots were like faithful men with good jobs and a full head of hair.

Daphne pocketed the keys to the Mustang as she stepped out onto the pavement. A passing car stopped, its driver waiting patiently for her to close her door and move around the front of her car before continuing on his way. Daff waved at the man to thank him for not running her down, even though he'd had plenty of room to pass and hadn't really needed to stop. No way would any self-respecting New Yorker have done the same thing. It was a point of pride in the city to know that your life was in your own hands at all times. You go out into Central Park at 1 A.M., you'd better not expect anyone to come running when some mugger sticks a gun in your face and demands that you hand over your valuables. In New York, you had to take care of yourself.

Apparently, the same cutthroat rules didn't apply here in Naples.

Daff pressed the button on her keychain to lock the Mustang and glanced down the street to see what her dining choices were. Then she flinched when someone tapped her on the shoulder and she heard a familiar voice say, "Well, if it isn't Daphne Donovan. I wondered if I'd ever see you again."

SIXTEEN

NICOLE could hear Keith coughing as she unlocked the front door and stepped inside his tidy, five-bedroom, four-and-a-half-bath house. She'd always liked it here. His place was so much cozier than her father's house, although the view from her room at Daddy's was nothing to complain about.

The thing was, she could afford a place on the Gulf by herself. Her maternal grandparents had left all their money to her when they'd died ten years ago, and the millions she'd inherited had been sitting in the bank earning interest year after year. She and Keith had never talked about her financial situation. She figured he assumed she lived off of whatever her father gave her. But she was wealthy in her own right.

So if Keith wanted to move to a house on the water after they were married, she could make that happen. That is, if he ever proposed.

She wished she knew how he was going to take the news that she was pregnant. Would he suggest an abortion? She sensed that he wouldn't be overjoyed about the baby, but she didn't think he'd go so far as to want her to get rid of it. If he did . . .

Nicole shrugged and tossed her purse on the living room couch before heading to the kitchen.

If he did, then at least she'd know where she stood with him.

He came into the kitchen wearing the purple-and-green silk robe she'd bought him for Christmas last year. His sandy brown hair was mussed, as if he'd run a towel over it after getting out of the shower. She had expected him to be dressed for work already. When he'd called her an hour ago to invite her to dinner that night, she figured he'd already been up and in the shower.

Keith was one of those dreaded morning people.

He coughed again and Nicole frowned slightly. "Are you all right? You sound sick."

Keith covered his mouth with his hand and coughed one more time. "I think I may be coming down with something," he admitted.

Nicole reached out to rub his shoulders. "Poor baby. Why don't you sit down and I'll make you some breakfast. How about some fruit and yogurt? That'll get some vitamins in you." Plus, she couldn't stomach the thought of frying up sausage and eggs.

"That would be great. Thanks."

She turned to the fridge and heard one of the heavy dining room chairs scrape across the Spanish tile as Keith pulled it out and sat down heavily. Maybe this wasn't the best time for her to tell him about the baby . . .

Nicole pulled a carton of strawberries and a banana out of the fridge and sighed. Who was she kidding? It was never going to be a good time.

"So what was so important that it couldn't wait until tonight?" Keith asked, sounding weary.

Nicole took a deep breath and began slicing the banana into a bowl. This was *so* not going to be easy.

She reminded herself of what Jenna had said yesterday. Facing this thing head-on was a sign of maturity. And that wasn't just Jenna's opinion. Nicole had asked Lillian Bryson for a private session yesterday and the owner of Rules of Engagement had agreed. Keith had a right to know the truth, no matter how difficult it was for Nicole to tell him.

She licked her lips and turned to find Keith watching her with an odd look on his face. He must have suspected something was wrong. Usually, she had no problem chatting away, even this early in the morning.

Nicole set down the knife and the banana.

"I'm pregnant," she said quietly. "I've suspected it for a few days, and the doctor confirmed it yesterday. I'm probably about three or four weeks along."

Keith nodded but didn't seem surprised.

He must've heard me throwing up yesterday morning, Nicole thought.

And at least he didn't insult her by asking if she knew it was his.

"I wish I could say I was happy," Keith said.

Nicole slowly crossed the room and pulled out a chair across from her boyfriend. She sat down and folded her hands primly together on top of the wooden table. "I didn't plan for this to happen."

Keith reached out and covered her hands with his. His fingers were smooth, his nails neatly trimmed. "I know you didn't. I'm not upset with you. I mean, it takes two to tango and all that," he said with a shrug.

"I think once you get used to the idea, you might enjoy having a baby around again," Nicole suggested.

Keith laughed wryly and removed his hands. "Nicole,

honey, I did the baby thing over a decade ago. Yeah, they can be fun, but they're also noisy and messy and take a hell of a lot of energy that I just don't have anymore. I'm not trying to be a downer. I know you've always wanted to have a family of your own. It's just . . . You only know the fantasy of having children—the hugs and the laughter and the good times. The reality is a bit more challenging."

Nicole blinked back tears and bit her bottom lip to keep from crying. "That's not true. I'm not romanticizing it. I know it's going to be a lot of hard work."

Keith rolled his eyes heavenward. "Believe me, you have no idea."

"Well, it's not like people don't manage to raise kids every day. I'm not helpless, you know. Besides, it doesn't matter. I'm not going to get rid of this baby, even if you want me to."

Keith stood up and had started walking toward her when a coughing fit made him stop. Irritated, Nicole stomped into the bathroom to find some cough syrup. Damn men anyway. Why was it they didn't take medicine like normal people when they were sick?

They might be able to run entire companies, but give them a cold and they turned into big babies.

She stormed back into the kitchen with a bottle of orange liquid in her hands. "Here, drink this," she said, handing Keith a plastic cup full of medicine.

Keith tipped his head back and swallowed the sweet liquid with a grimace. "God, that tastes awful," he complained.

"It's good for you," Nicole said, taking the cup from him so she could rinse it out in the sink.

While she held the cup under the water, Keith came up behind her and wrapped his arms around her. "I'm sorry, babe. Maybe you're right. Maybe I just need a little time to get used to the idea of having another baby. This cold just has me feeling old and tired. I'm sorry to rain on your parade."

Nicole dropped the cup into the sink, leaned back into Keith's embrace, and closed her eyes as the tears slipped down her cheeks.

See, she thought as Keith's hold on her tightened, *everything's going to turn out all right, after all.*

DAFF straightened her shoulders and pulled herself up to her full height before turning around. Despite the fact that she was at least three inches taller than Lillian Bryson, she still felt like an awkward twelve-year-old who had been caught checking out her older brother's hidden porn collection.

"Lillian. How are you?" she said after swallowing to clear her throat.

"I'm good, thank you. And you?"

Daphne shuffled her feet, her boots making a scratching noise on the sidewalk. "I'm fine."

Lillian looped her arm through Daphne's and started pulling her toward the front door of Rules of Engagement. "That's good. So were you coming to see me? You know, the package you bought includes three one-hour counseling sessions. My schedule is open if you'd like to get started."

Daphne felt herself being pulled along as if she'd been caught up in a force much greater than her own. Now she knew what it must feel like to be a minnow staring down the gaping mouth of a whale.

"No, I—" Daff tried to protest as Lillian pulled open the door.

"Oh? Do you have somewhere you need to be?" Lillian asked.

A blush heated Daff's cheeks as she thought about lying and quickly discarded the idea. Lillian would see right through her. "No," she admitted.

"That's wonderful. Come on back," Lillian said, pausing briefly to ask her assistant to hold her calls for the next hour.

As Lillian shepherded her into her office and closed the door behind them, Daff knew she was in trouble. For whatever reason, all Lillian had to do was to give her one of those maternal hugs and Daff would find herself spilling her guts all over the carpeted floor.

"So," Lillian began after seating herself in the plump chair next to Daphne. "How are things going with you and Sam?"

Daphne squeezed her eyes shut. She *so* did not want to talk about this. "I'm going back to New York today," she blurted. "Sam and I . . . we were just a fling."

"Oh?" was all Lillian said, in a patient tone that suggested she had all the time in the world to sit there and wait for Daphne to say more.

"Yes."

"Is someone waiting for you there?" Lillian asked, and Daff considered saying yes. She guessed that all she'd have to do to get rid of Sam for good was to tell his mother that she had another man waiting for her back in New York. And it wouldn't even be a lie. Not really, because if she called Brooks and told him she was on her way, he'd be waiting at LaGuardia to pick her up.

She opened her mouth to say the words that would end any hope that this thing with Sam might go any further. Just one little word and it would be over.

Yes.

"No," she said, her gaze shifting to the floor beneath her feet.

"Do you want to talk about why you resigned from the FBI?" Lillian asked quietly, the words seeming to echo in the interior of the office.

Daff's entire body froze. Her toes and fingers went instantly numb, and a strange buzzing noise started in her head. Even her breathing stopped, her lungs seeming not to care that she'd deprived them of oxygen.

"I noticed on your application that you used to work for them," Lillian continued. "I just wondered why you quit. I mean, Sam's told me that he got out of the Navy because he wanted to settle down and he didn't want to put anyone he loved through the hell of not knowing where he was or if he'd ever come back. I thought maybe you were at the same point in your life. But then, if you are, why is it that you seem so resistant to the idea of a relationship? I could tell from the class you took that you really weren't interested in learning how to keep a mate."

Daphne's lungs finally forced her to take a breath and she shuddered as her body came back to life. She wasn't going to talk about why she'd resigned. Not with Lillian. Not with anyone.

She'd tried. In the beginning, right after 9/11, she'd actually talked to a priest about her role in the tragedy. She'd told him about her rage, her feelings of helplessness, the sense of responsibility for all those lives that would no longer be lived. He'd listened and nodded and then told her to find comfort that this was all God's plan.

Frankly, that had just pissed her off.

How could it be "God's plan" to allow thousands of innocent people to die at the hands of these terrorists? If the God he worshipped could stand by and let such a thing happen, she wanted no part of Him.

Time had only made things worse. The anger, the hopelessness, the despair—those she could handle. But what she couldn't take—what she had never admitted to another living soul—was the horror she felt when she started to heal, when she woke up one morning and realized that she hadn't dreamed of people jumping out of eightieth-story windows or of scraping blood off of concrete for DNA tests. She had started to forget, and *that* she couldn't live with. So she started going back to Ground Zero again, to make certain she would remember. To continue punishing herself for not being good enough to prevent what had happened.

"I probably shouldn't tell you this, but Sam once had the opportunity to kill bin Laden and he didn't take the shot." Lillian's softly uttered words cut through Daphne's pain like a surgeon's scalpel against a layer of skin.

Daphne jerked her head up to find Lillian staring at her.

"His friend Tony told me the story one night when he and Sam had come home to Naples on leave. Tony . . ." Lillian shook her head sadly before continuing. "He'd had too much to drink and it was obvious that he was pretty shaken up. He stayed up long after Sam had gone to bed and I just watched him while he talked. His head was bowed, as if he were praying, his shoulders stooped forward like a man struggling beneath a terrible burden.

"In 1994, they were sent into Afghanistan to take out a Taliban chief who had planned a bombing that killed thirty-seven people—four U.S. citizens and the rest innocent women and children who were on their way to the market that morning. Anyway, they had orders to retaliate, so that's what they planned to do. Sam's team was in a country where most people couldn't even afford food, and they'd arrived at this man's mountain retreat where there were palm trees and a marble palace and seven swimming pools.

"The team split up and Sam and Tony went around the back to check out the pools. They followed the sounds of splashing and found that there was some sort of child's birthday party going on. There were men and children in the pool, while women hidden beneath heavy burkas walked around fetching and serving like slaves.

"At one point, a slender man with a long beard who had to be well over six feet tall snapped his fingers at one of the women, who hurried over with some sort of drink. That was when Sam realized that the man was Osama bin Laden. He was surrounded by children, but Sam and Tony were fairly certain they could get to him without hurting anyone else if they could just wait until the time was right. They stood there, hidden in the thick brush, and waited to make their move, knowing that their chance of escaping unharmed was going to be slim once they shot bin Laden and gave away their position. Finally, the children moved away. Sam was about to take the shot when his team leader signaled that they had the primary target and had to get out of there.

"Sam and Tony looked back at bin Laden, who by now had a child on his shoulders who was squealing with laughter. They could have taken the shot, but they would have killed that child. After another second, another child swam in front of bin Laden. The team leader was signaling for them to get out now before the target's absence was noted and the entire team would be at risk of getting caught. Their mission had been accomplished," Lillian added.

"But they didn't take the shot," Daphne whispered.

"No. They didn't," Lillian agreed. "And my heart aches knowing that my son will have to carry that around with him for the rest of his life. He did the right thing at the time, but . . ."

Daff squinched her eyes shut and felt her own heart start to ache for what she knew Sam must feel. "How does he live with it?" she asked, hot tears scalding her closed eyelids as she waited for the answer about how to cope with her own living hell.

Lillian's warm hand squeezed her arm as she answered softly, "I don't know, Daphne. You'll have to ask him."

SEVENTEEN

"SO, did you tell him?" Jenna asked eagerly as soon as Nicole appeared in the doorway of their classroom.

Nicole dropped her purse on the floor and slid heavily into the chair next to her. "Yes," she sighed. "And he wasn't very happy."

Perfect. Jenna had to sit on her hands in order to resist the urge to clap her hands with glee. "Did he propose?" she asked.

"No." Nicole picked at the cuticle of her right thumb. "I probably won't see him again for a few days. We were supposed to go to dinner tonight, but he's not feeling well. At least that's the excuse he gave me. I'm sure my telling him I'm pregnant had something to do with it."

This was wonderful. Unlike Nicole, Jenna believed that Keith really wasn't feeling well. He was experiencing the first symptoms of anthrax poisoning.

Jenna had to kill him now, before the spores released their toxins into his bloodstream. At this point, she could easily make it look as if he'd died from other causes.

Even better, because Nicole had told him she was pregnant—just as Jenna had encouraged her to do—and because—just as Jenna had suspected—Keith wasn't exactly thrilled at the prospect of becoming a daddy again, it would be easy to make it look like Keith's death was a suicide. The police would see evidence that Keith took his own life. Nicole would admit that her news had upset her boyfriend. When the autopsy was performed, there might be some evidence of respiratory distress, but the cause of death would be . . . Hmm. What would the cause of death be?

Jenna would have to give that some thought.

But it clearly wouldn't be anthrax poisoning or anything that might cause Nathan Solem to call off his CEO summit or to increase the security around his daughter.

"I'm sure that once the baby comes, Keith will forget that he ever thought about not wanting another child," Nicole said from beside her.

Jenna patted the younger woman's arm comfortingly. "Yes," she said. "I'm sure you're right."

JENNA Marisol knew from firsthand experience that men often commit suicide by shooting themselves.

In the first moments after she'd discovered her husband's body, she'd allowed herself to feel anger that Aaron had done this knowing full well that she would be the one to find him. She thought at the time that there was nothing more awful than seeing your husband's blood and brain matter splattered all over the bedroom wall—dripping down the family portrait that she'd had taken the year before and drying all over the faces of their children. But then she'd gone into the bathroom and seen the girls lying motionless in the tub, and she'd known then that there was, indeed, something worse than that.

Even so, she was not going to shoot Keith Melman and try to make it appear like a suicide. For one, she had no experience with guns or forensic evidence, and knew there was no way she could stage it correctly. But also, she wouldn't subject Nicole to finding her boyfriend the way Jenna had found Aaron. She wouldn't do that—even to her worst enemy. And she didn't even dislike Nicole. As a matter of fact, she'd actually grown quite fond of the younger woman during the weeks they'd been in class together.

It was such a shame she was going to have to die for her father's sins.

Jenna simply couldn't think of another way to get her revenge. The fact that Nicole was pregnant made it that much more poignant. Nathan Solem would lose not only his daughter, but his only chance at a grandchild as well.

Jenna shrugged and quickly palmed the bottle of Valium she'd discovered in Nicole's purse earlier that day as she got out of her car. She'd parked on a busy street two blocks from Keith's house, just in case he had nosy neighbors who kept track of vehicles coming into and out of their neighborhood. She'd also changed into a pair of shorts and a T-shirt, to make it look like she was just a jogger out for an evening run.

After looking both ways to make sure the coast was clear, she jogged across the street and headed into the quiet, tree-lined development where Keith lived. She passed well-manicured lawns with expensive landscaping and driveways with the occasional Lexus or Mercedes parked outside. The homes were large and ranged from Mediterranean to Moorish to Georgian-style with large white columns out in front. The lots were fairly small—probably no more than three-quarters of an acre—barely big enough to contain the three-thousand-plus-square-feet homes that were built on them.

Jenna waved at a woman wearing a navy blue power suit

and sensible pumps who was struggling to get her toddler out of the backseat of a BMW sedan. The woman smiled and nodded in that way of women everywhere united by the trials of raising children in a busy world.

She ran past Keith's house first, slowly making a U-turn in the cul-de-sac and watching to see if anyone happened to be peering out of any second-floor windows. Satisfied that no one was watching, she jogged back toward the house second from the corner. She kept an even pace as she ran up the driveway, trying to make it appear as if this had been her intended destination all along.

She paused for a moment outside the front door and willed her heartbeat to return to normal. Then she raised her arm and pressed her elbow to the doorbell. No sense leaving a nice clear fingerprint for the police to find.

From inside, she could hear the sound of Westminster chimes playing. She'd always hated that tune, much preferring the sound of regular bells to that overused chime.

She shifted her weight from one foot to the other while she waited. She hadn't considered the possibility that Keith might not answer his door.

What would she do if he didn't? She couldn't afford to wait much longer. He seemed to be on an accelerated schedule with the anthrax poisoning. A normal incubation period was one to five days, and he'd started showing symptoms by day two. He should start feeling better within the next two or three days. If he ended up proposing to Nicole then, people might not be as willing to believe that he'd committed suicide. Plus, finding the Valium in Nicole's purse had been a godsend. Nicole didn't often leave her purse unattended, but she'd done so briefly that morning in class—and Jenna had taken the opportunity to rifle through the other woman's belongings.

Jenna planned to leave the bottle here at Keith's house to make it seem as though Keith had premeditated his own death by taking the drugs from his girlfriend's purse when he'd last seen her. But if he didn't answer the door, Jenna was going to have to risk slipping the pills back into Nicole's purse . . . and pray their disappearance had not been noticed.

But she needn't have worried.

She saw Keith squinting at her through the etched-glass front door, a slight frown on his face. He had on a rumpled T-shirt and shorts and looked every bit as sick as he sounded when he pulled open the door and said, "Ms. Marisol? What are you doing here?"

Jenna was tempted to step back when he started coughing, even though she knew he wasn't contagious. Still, knowing the person standing a foot away from you was infected with a deadly bacteria was a little frightening. Had Jenna used a virus like smallpox, just the little bit of contact they'd had already would have been enough to kill her.

"Oh, am I disturbing you? I'm so sorry. When I told Nathan Solem where I lived, he said I should make sure to drop by and say hello. Since we're neighbors and all," Jenna added with a friendly smile. This was a total lie, of course. First of all, her house was several miles from here. Secondly, she doubted that Nathan would encourage anyone—especially not a virtual stranger—to drop in on his banker unannounced.

Too bad Keith Melman wouldn't live long enough to be able to check out her story.

For the same reason that most people do not simply hang up on telemarketers who interrupt their evening meals, Keith did not slam the door in Jenna's face. Instead, he hastened to assure her that she wasn't interrupting him as he pulled the door open wider and invited her to come in.

Jenna bit back a smile.

"You sound a little hoarse. Can I fix you some tea?" she offered, as if she had been to his house a thousand times.

Behind her, Keith laughed somewhat wryly. "Actually, I was thinking more along the lines of a bourbon. I've had a tough day," he admitted.

Perfect. The alcohol would magnify the effect of the Valium and make Keith's death seem even more like a suicide.

"Why don't you point me in the direction of your liquor cabinet, and then go put your feet up," Jenna suggested.

She didn't know if it was the effects of the anthrax that were making Keith so agreeable or if he was simply the easygoing sort, but he did exactly as she had suggested, waving toward a cabinet next to the refrigerator before sitting down on the overstuffed couch in the family room. He had a clear view of the kitchen from where he was seated, so Jenna was careful to keep the brown bottle of drugs out of sight as she pretended to search for a glass.

She shook a handful of blue dust out of the bottle—she'd already crushed up the thirty-plus pills, knowing there was no way she'd be able to get Keith to swallow them whole—and smiled when she spied an Insta-Hot next to the kitchen sink. The near-boiling water might help to dissolve the powder while Jenna stirred it into Keith's drink.

"Do you like Norah Jones?" Keith asked, briefly turning away to hunt for the remote for his stereo.

Jenna used that opportunity to quietly slide the Valium into the bottom of a tumbler and fill it with about an inch of hot water. Then she hurriedly shoved the glass under the ice-maker in the freezer door when Keith stood up and started toward the kitchen.

Had he seen her dump the drug into his drink?

Jenna felt her face flush as her heart rate immediately quadrupled.

If Keith looked at the glass in her hand, he'd see the powder halfway dissolved in the bottom. The dozen or so ice cubes did nothing to hide the telltale blue and white flecks suspended in the water.

Keith plucked the remote control from the top of the counter that separated the kitchen from the family room and pointed it at the stereo. As the strains of "Come Away With Me" filled the room, Jenna took a deep breath and turned to see Keith walk back to the couch and sit down.

She closed her eyes.

That was close.

She picked up the bottle of bourbon and filled Keith's glass halfway full of golden-brown liquid. As quietly as possible, she opened the drawer next to the sink, praying that he kept his silverware there and sending up a silent thank you when she discovered that he did. She pulled out a long-handled spoon and gave the drink a quick stir. The Valium hadn't dissolved completely, and the clear bourbon had turned cloudy with the addition of the drug. Jenna would just have to hope that he wasn't that observant, but she added more liquor to the glass to try to dilute the cloudy mixture. Then she added a few more ice cubes, poured herself a drink, and brought both glasses into the other room, where she held out the larger tumbler to Keith.

"Wow. That's quite a drink," he said.

"I figured I'd save you from having to go in for a refill for a while," Jenna said easily as she took a seat in the leather wingback chair next to Keith.

"So, you live in this area?" Keith leaned back into the soft pillows lining the couch and took a sip of his bourbon. Jenna watched closely to see if he could taste the addition of something foreign in his drink. He wrinkled his nose the tiniest bit, and then coughed.

Jenna crossed her legs and swallowed a mouthful of her own drink. "Yes," she lied. "Over in the Sandpiper development across the way."

Keith nodded and took another drink.

They chatted about nothing for several minutes—the weather, how long Jenna had lived in Naples, the awful hot summers in South Florida. Jenna could sense that Keith would rather be alone, but she wasn't going to leave this to chance. In the movies, the villain always left the scene of the crime too early, assuming that the poison or the acid or the winch holding the hero over the pool of starving alligators would do its job, and surprised when, in the next scene, the resourceful hero and his trusty sidekick showed up to foil the villain's plans to take over the world.

Jenna wasn't that stupid.

She wasn't going anywhere until Keith Melman drew his last breath.

EIGHTEEN

DAFF sat outside her client's house, feeling like a limp dishrag.

After she had left Lillian's office, she had done what she always did when she felt overwhelmed: she'd gone for a run. Miles and miles of white sand had passed beneath her feet as she ran south along Vanderbilt Beach until she'd finally turned around and headed north as far as she could go. For hours, she'd pounded up and down the beach, punishing herself for what, she didn't know. Or perhaps she was just trying to outrun the sound of Lillian's voice telling that awful story.

She wondered if Sam was searching for the same thing she was, something she would never get—absolution from those who had died on 9/11, from those she couldn't save.

It was damn hard to get mercy from the dead.

Daff turned the air conditioner on high and rested her forehead on the steering wheel of her rented convertible.

Cool air chilled her cheeks and ears and Daff shivered from the cold. She'd changed out of her soaked shorts and T-shirt and into a pair of jeans and a long-sleeved white shirt, but her skin was still damp with sweat, and the a/c blasting at full power quickly dried the moisture and raised goose bumps on her arms.

But turning it down would have taken too much energy.

Daff opened her eyes and stared at the speedometer, its red arrow unmoving in the glow of the early evening sun. The engine was purring, the air conditioner running cold. Daff absently checked all the indicator lights. Battery fully charged, oil pressure medium, gas tank two-thirds full. The odometer sat halfway between 16,123 and 16,124 miles and she had the sudden and inexplicable urge to drive around the block until it hit an even 16,125.

But she had business to attend to, and driving aimlessly around the block wouldn't increase her billable hours.

Daff had come back from her run to find two messages waiting on her voice mail. One was from Keith Melman. He'd missed her call that morning while he was in the shower, and he'd called in sick to work so hadn't gotten her message there until after noon. He was happy to sign off on her time sheet but wondered if she had another case lined up, because he had another job he'd like her to do. Something about checking the background of someone who'd attended the party on Nathan Solem's yacht the other night.

The second message was from Sam, asking her to meet him at the yacht club that evening at seven.

Daff sighed and rubbed her finger across the odometer.

It would be so much easier if she could just give up, just stop getting up out of bed every morning, and not have to face herself in the mirror every day. It would be so easy to lie and tell her client that she had to leave Naples now that the case was over. No one would ever know.

That's not true. Sam would know.

Daff stared at the numbers on the dashboard until they all ran together like one of those Magic Eye puzzles that had been so popular years ago—the ones where, when you stared at them long enough, a 3-D image magically appeared. Only, it had never worked for Daff. She stared and stared at the puzzles, but no images ever appeared.

A coworker once told her she couldn't see the solution because she was concentrating too hard.

She had always wondered if he'd been talking about the puzzle.

The digital clock on the dashboard clicked over to 6:00. Keith's message had said to meet him at his house at six. It was time for her to decide whether she was going to take his case or not.

If she did, she had no doubt she'd see Sam again. Her resistance to him was about as high as the average number of feet above sea level in Florida.

But if she left now, she'd be free of him forever.

Was that what she really wanted? To run away from the first man in a long time who wasn't ready to give up on her after the first date?

Daff raised her head and scowled at her reflection in the rearview mirror.

"For God's sake, Daphne," she muttered to herself as she turned off the ignition. "You're not making a fucking lifelong commitment here. Get in there and take the goddamn case."

JENNA sprayed the paper towel in her hand with a cleanser that contained bleach. Bleach was an amazing product. It killed everything from the deadly Ebola virus to more common threats like anthrax. She figured if bleach didn't obscure her fingerprints, nothing would.

She carefully wiped off the bottom of Keith's glass, then

set it back on the coaster to wipe down the sides. Her own glass was already in the dishwasher, halfway through a sanitizing rinse.

Not that it would matter if the police *did* find her fingerprints. They'd have to identify her as a suspect in order to get a match. Even though she'd been fingerprinted as a university employee, those prints didn't exist anywhere outside the school system's records. That was a fallacy too many viewers of popular television were led to believe—that police had immediate electronic access to anyone who had ever been fingerprinted, and that all a detective had to do to solve a crime was to run the prints though the system. That was only true if the perpetrator of the crime was a repeat offender. Other citizens who had been fingerprinted—insurance agents, teachers, and the like—their records lived on paper, filed away with hundreds, perhaps thousands of others. No one would find her prints unless they knew exactly where to look.

Jenna smiled up at Keith, who gazed back at her with lifeless bluish-gray eyes.

"Of course, that doesn't mean I can be sloppy," she said to him and then paused, as if waiting for him to respond. When he didn't, she continued. "The police are still going to check your glass for prints, and they'd find it awfully suspicious if *your* fingerprints weren't there."

She reached out to take his hand, which lay limply in his lap, and felt a moment of regret. He had died so easily, with so little fuss. Near the end, he'd looked into her concerned face and wheezed out a request for her to call 911. She'd obediently gone to the phone—which she had since wiped down with bleach—and pretended to call for help while Keith lay on the couch, wheezing in short gasps of air.

By the time she'd come back, he'd slipped quietly into a coma.

Poor man.

If only he'd learned to play with women his own age.

Jenna clucked her tongue as she took Keith's hand in her own. This was the last thing she had to do before leaving. Everything else was all set—the bottle of Valium lying open, tipped over on the table. She'd dumped the bourbon with the Valium sediment still floating in the bottom of it into the toilet and flushed it several times. Then she'd poured another drink, a short one this time, to make it look like Keith had died while drowning his sorrows in liquor.

Now she'd wiped down every surface she had touched, and it was time to go.

"Just one more thing and the illusion will be complete," she said, reaching out to place Keith's hand over the glass.

Her entire body jerked when the doorbell rang.

She knocked the tumbler over with Keith's limp hand, and bourbon and melting ice cubes spilled onto the coffee table and dripped onto the carpet. Some of it splattered on Jenna's bare legs, but she barely noticed the cool liquid dripping down her skin as her mind started to race.

She had to get out of here.

She shoved the bottle of cleanser beneath the couch as she glanced into the backyard with its six-foot-high wooden fence. Keith's home was bordered on every side by other large homes, their second-story windows giving the neighbors a clear view into Keith's backyard.

Even if Jenna were willing to risk getting spotted by the neighbors, that left her only two possible exits—the gates she assumed would be at either side of the house. But what if the person at the front door got curious and came back to check if Keith was hanging out by the pool? That's what she'd do if someone was expecting her and didn't answer the doorbell. That meant Jenna had a fifty-fifty chance of escaping out of the right gate without getting caught.

She didn't like those odds.

But she couldn't stay here. The family room and kitchen

both opened up onto the back patio and pool area via large sliding glass doors that gave anyone outside a clear view inside the house. If whoever was at the front door did go around the back, he'd see Keith lying here and know that something was wrong.

Desperate, Jenna quickly scanned the room. In order to move to another part of the house, she'd have to cross the center hall, which was visible from the etched-glass front door. She'd have to wait until the front stoop was clear before making her move. Although, she didn't really know where she could go from here. Leaving the house while someone was lurking around outside seemed risky. But staying put while Keith's body was discovered wasn't exactly the safest move, either.

Jenna slowly backed toward the kitchen as the doorbell pealed again.

She hunkered down in a blind spot that couldn't be seen from either the back patio or the front hall, and tried to think.

Jenna forced herself to slow her breathing. Panicking wouldn't help.

She nibbled her thumbnail and squinted, as if that might help her to focus. Then, staring at the creases in her thumb, she gasped and looked up at the couch.

Keith's fingerprints! She hadn't gotten them on the glass.

She scrabbled forward on her hands and knees, her heart racing so hard she feared she might have a heart attack right here.

Peering out from behind the end of the couch, she saw Keith's right hand flopped down over the edge of the cushions. The tumbler she'd knocked over still lay on its side on the table.

Jenna looked behind her as whoever was at the front door pounded on the glass.

She had to move. Now.

She scooted out from behind the couch and grabbed

Keith's hand in her own. She wasn't going to have time to clean up after herself, so she had to make this look good.

Keith's skin felt clammy beneath hers as she reached his hand out to take the glass. As she pressed his fingers against the cool tumbler, she caught a flash of movement out of the corner of her eye.

She let Keith's hand fall and the glass fell to the carpet with a thud.

Jenna pressed her back into the side of the couch and curled herself into the smallest ball she could manage as the first rattle of someone trying to open the sliding glass doors hit her ears.

Please let them be locked, she prayed.

She knew her luck had run out when she heard one of the oversized doors slide open.

NINETEEN

"DAD, can we talk for a minute?" Nicole Solem said, poking her head into her father's home office. His assistant was set up in the room next door, which wasn't exactly small but seemed crowded with copy machines, computers, and filing cabinets that held Nathan Solem's contributions to America's top companies over the last forty years.

Nathan put down the voice recorder he'd been talking into. He knew that the younger execs these days typed their own correspondence, but he'd come of age during a time when managers—especially men—didn't type. He'd never gotten the hang of it. The placement of the keys made no sense to him.

Besides, he needed a secretary—No, strike that. An *executive assistant*—for much more than just typing letters. His current assistant, an efficient woman in her midforties, made travel arrangements, kept his office equipment running, organized him to within an inch of his life, and was a whiz at event planning. At this moment, she had her hands full checking off the million and one details that needed to be taken care of for the CEO summit he was hosting next week. The summit would bring together managers of twenty of the top companies in the country, and would be kicked off with a pool party for his guests and their families.

Nathan had debated whether or not to include the attendees' children in the summit's opening event, but decided it would be a nice change from the typical cocktail party scene. Plus, the weather in Naples this time of year was extraordinary—midseventies without a hint of the humidity that would come during the summer. While most people were digging out from under four-foot-high drifts of snow, they were enjoying balmy weather and warm gulf breezes. Might as well let the kids enjoy it.

He looked up and smiled at his daughter, who was hovering in the doorway.

She'd actually been the one to suggest the pool party to him. God knew, she'd been thrust off on nannies and hotel baby-sitters often enough herself at events like these. She thought it might be nice to make people's children feel welcome.

Nathan thought she was right.

"What's up?" he asked, setting the recorder down on his desk and waving at one of the chairs across from his desk as an invitation for her to come in and sit down.

Nicole pushed open the door to his office and came into the room, rubbing her hands together as if she were nervous. She looked tired today, the normally clear skin under her eyes marked by faint green and purple bruises. He had no idea what she could be stressed out about. Maybe one of her volunteer positions wasn't going well.

Nathan felt a stirring of concern when Nicole sat down and buried her face in her hands.

This seemed a lot more serious than some issue down at the Museum of Fine Arts. He stood up and walked around the desk.

"What's wrong, honey?" he asked, putting a comforting hand on her shoulder.

He felt her shoulders move beneath his hand as she took a deep breath. When she raised her head to look at him, he frowned at the sight of tears coursing down her cheeks.

"Tell me and let's see what we can do to fix it. There's always a solution if you just look hard enough," he said.

"I'm pregnant," Nicole said, struggling to blink back her tears.

Nathan swallowed and slowly sat down in the chair next to his daughter. "It's Keith's?" he asked.

Nicole's perfectly arched eyebrows drew together in a frown. "Of course."

He closed his eyes and sighed, realizing then what an insult the question had been. "I'm sorry, baby. I didn't mean to imply anything. I just . . . had to ask."

"Yes, it's Keith's. And I'm keeping it, just so you know."

Nathan sighed again and slumped back in his chair. "Well, I figured you wouldn't have told me if that wasn't the case," he said. At least, he hoped she wouldn't. There were just some things a father didn't need to know.

God, he wished her mother were still alive. She would have known the right thing to say, whereas he felt like a . . . a man who had been suddenly thrust into the role of a mother without knowing what the hell he was doing. Which is exactly what he was.

"Does Keith know?" he asked.

"Yes. I told him this morning. I don't know whether or not he plans to ask me to marry him. I'm not even sure that I want him to. He wasn't exactly overjoyed by the news," she admitted, staring down at her hands in a dejected manner.

Nathan tilted his head and studied his daughter as if seeing her for the first time. She was a lovely young woman who had never flaunted her wealth or acted like a spoiled brat or taken advantage of her social position to do anything but good for the communities where they had lived. She remained close to her childhood friends, honored her commitments, and loved her father with all her heart.

So, didn't she deserve to be happy about this, even if her boyfriend wasn't?

"How do you feel about it?" he asked slowly, seriously, because he knew that this was a serious matter.

Nicole kept her head bowed for a long time, as if considering the question from all angles. Then, as if of its own accord, her right hand crept over and cradled her stomach. She glanced up at him then, her green eyes, so like his, peeking out through her bangs.

"I couldn't be happier. Even without a ring on my finger," she said.

Nathan reached out and put his right hand over her left one, covering up the fact that she wasn't wearing an engagement ring. He studied his only child, his only reason for getting up in the morning after Sarah had died, the little girl who had brought him back to life and made it impossible for him to retreat back into work.

"You have everything you need right here to make the perfect family," he said.

Then he smiled and thought, *And if that asshole doesn't marry you, I'm going to kill him.*

"NO. No. Fuck!" Daphne shouted as the glass door opened four inches and then jammed to a stop. Desperate to get inside, she tried shoving her way through the opening, even though logically she knew she couldn't squeeze through such a small space.

Keith had one of those goddamned burglar deterrents—the acrylic kind that flipped up to stop the door from opening any wider—stuck onto his door. Why, Daff thought, was an alarm system not sufficient in this neighborhood?

She yanked her leg out of the doorway and spun around to grab one of the heavy metal patio chairs. Keith hadn't even flinched when she yelled, and her quick glance into the room revealed a bottle of some sort of prescription medication and a mostly-empty bottle of something that looked like Scotch on the table, as well as a puddle that was dripping from the coffee table and onto the carpet. If Keith had passed out, it had been fairly recently. The liquid hadn't even had time to stop dripping.

Which meant that if he'd OD'd, there was still time to save him.

Daff hurled the chair at the sliding-glass door, right in the middle where it would be the weakest. The tempered glass cracked, but didn't shatter.

She picked up the chair and threw it again. It bounced off the door and landed on the patio with a crash.

This time, Daff didn't waste time with the chair. Instead, she tucked her head into her chest, folded her arms together at her waist, and aimed her right shoulder at the weakened glass. She could hear the glass splintering as she fell through it, and braced herself, knowing her momentum would send her hurtling forward.

She threw her hands out to catch her fall as she lost her balance.

Her shoulder made a sickening crack as it came into contact with the arm of the couch, but Daff didn't have time to feel the pain. She rolled to her side and pushed up off the carpet, lurching toward Keith, who still hadn't moved.

Daff unclipped her cell phone from her waist with one hand and used the other to feel for a pulse at Keith's neck.

Nothing.

She dialed 911 as she tipped Keith's head back to clear his airway.

"Hurry up." She urged the emergency operator to pick up the call. She needed both hands to do CPR. Raine was always after her to get a hands-free unit. That would be the first thing Daphne did when this was all over.

The 911 call took less than thirty seconds. Daff tossed her cell phone onto the coffee table and started compressions. Five compressions to the chest. Plug the nose, tilt the head back. Five puffs of breath into the airway. God, she hoped she was doing this right.

"Come on, Keith," she encouraged as she repeated the process again.

She tried not to think about why Keith might have done something like this, tried to remain focused on getting his heart beating again.

You shouldn't have told him about Nicole.

"Shut up," Daff muttered to that inner voice. Keith couldn't possibly have tried to commit suicide because his girlfriend was pregnant.

Could he?

"Stop. Just stop." She shook her head and focused all of her attention on her routine. Do compressions. Breathe. Don't think.

By the time the paramedics showed up four minutes later, Daff's arms were aching from the effort of trying to bring her client back to life.

They rang the doorbell, which Daff thought was odd. But what were they supposed to do? Break down the door?

She hurried to the front door and jerked it open, then stepped aside to let in the two men wearing white short-sleeved uniform shirts and navy blue pants.

"He's back here," she said, and led the way to the room adjoining the kitchen.

When the doorbell rang again, Daff reluctantly left the

paramedics to answer the insistent summons. Not that her help was needed. Even before the two men had exchanged glances, Daff knew it was over.

Keith Melman was dead.

Her footsteps echoed in the empty hallway as she walked toward the front door. She paused for a second with her hand on the doorknob. Funny, she didn't recall closing the door after letting the paramedics in.

Daff shook her head and pulled the door open. She must have closed the door without realizing it.

A tall, slender man with light brown hair and kind brown eyes stood on the front stoop. He flashed her his badge.

"I'm Lieutenant Danny Agar from the Naples PD. I understand we have an attempted suicide here?"

Daff nodded and retreated into the hallway. "I'm sad to report that the attempt was successful," she said as she and the police detective entered the family room, where the paramedics were preparing to leave. The room had just been transformed from a makeshift emergency room into a crime scene.

While Lieutenant Agar talked with the paramedics, Daff retreated to the rustic wooden kitchen table to wait. She knew that she'd be treated both as a critical witness as well as a potential suspect.

Fortunately, she was good at waiting. Years of boring surveillance work had honed that trait. So much of investigative work was following leads that dead-ended, searching through overwhelming volumes of data to find that one clue needed to solve a case, or simply waiting and watching, ever patient, for someone to slip up.

So Daff sat there, staring out into the backyard and absently toying with an empty blue box that had been sitting on the table. She didn't want to think about Keith, lying dead on the couch, possibly because of the news she had delivered to him last night. But it was impossible not to keep returning to that thought.

Before finding out that his girlfriend was pregnant, her client had seemed fine. Resigned to the possibility that Nicole was cheating on him, yes. Unable to believe that she might actually love him, yes. That, too. But not despondent or filled with despair.

As a matter of fact, he'd seemed rather . . . businesslike about the whole thing. Like he'd been analyzing his relationship on a spreadsheet or something.

The news about Nicole being pregnant had bothered him, though. Daff remembered what he'd said when she asked him what he was going to do about it.

Marry her, of course. What else can I do?

Well, he could take his own life, for one. It was a rather dramatic—not to mention, final—option, but it was an alternative.

Daff turned the box over in her hand and wearily rubbed her eyes with the back of her hands. If she had kept her mouth shut about Nicole, would Keith be alive right now?

"Now that that's over with, would you like to tell me who you are and what you were doing in the home of the deceased?" Lieutenant Agar said as he pulled out a chair and sat down across from her.

Daphne winced. It hadn't taken long for Keith Melman to go from a living person with an identity of his own to becoming "the deceased." Depersonalization was critical in the law enforcement business, she knew. You'd never last a year if you grieved for every victim of a crime.

"I'm a private investigator and I was working a case for Mr. Melman." Daphne pulled her ID and P.I. credentials from the back pocket of her jeans and laid them in front of the detective. "I don't know who his next of kin would be, but I do know he's dating the daughter of a prominent local businessman. Nicole Solem."

Lieutenant Agar raised his eyebrows when she mentioned Nicole's name. Daff figured that a guy who had a yacht as large as Nathan Solem's would be fairly well known in a town this size. Hell, he'd probably be fairly well known even in Manhattan.

"I'll stop by the Solems' after we get done here," the detective said.

Daff waited for him to ask her a question or say something more, but he didn't. Instead, the silence between them lengthened, the only sound that of a clock in the kitchen counting off the seconds. She couldn't get Keith's last words to her out of her head.

What else can I do? he had asked.

She'd said nothing in return, not really wanting to get involved with this man and his messy personal life. She hadn't wanted to get to know him or his girlfriend, to learn what was important to them or what they feared. She simply wanted to hand over the facts and release herself from any responsibility for what her client might do with the information she had given him. She didn't want to know what happened after she walked away. It was so much easier that way.

If only she had left Naples this morning. She could have gone on with her life the way she had been living it the past five years, not responsible for anyone's actions but her own.

And now, because she had stayed, she had another man's death on her hands.

Daff looked up at the detective, who sat across from her, watching her intently as if he knew she had something she wanted to confess.

"I may have killed him," she was about to blurt when a steady voice cut through the silence surrounding them.

"What's going on here? Who are you?"

Both Daphne and Lieutenant Agar jumped at the sound of the young woman's voice coming from the hallway. Daff turned to find Nicole Solem watching them with narrowed green eyes. Her cell phone was out and in her hand, and Daff wondered if she had thought to call the police before barging into her boyfriend's house with no other weapon other than her Prada handbag. She couldn't have missed seeing the broken glass on the floor and the mess that the paramedics had made trying to bring Keith back to life. Plus, two complete strangers were sitting in plain sight. Nicole could just as well have interrupted a burglary in process as anything.

Some people had no survival skills whatsoever. Daff guessed that Nicole Solem was one of those people. But then, she'd probably never been in danger in her entire life. Pretty tough to hone your survival skills when the biggest threat you'd ever faced was from a pair of nail scissors during your twice-monthly manicure.

Detective Agar pushed his chair back from the table and stood up, holding out his right hand in a nonthreatening manner. "I'm Lieutenant Agar from the Naples Police Department. You're Nicole Solem, right? I've seen your picture in the paper from time to time."

Nicole stepped forward, her high heels clicking on the Spanish tile floor. She was dressed to kill, her slim, twenty-four-year-old body sheathed in an expensive-looking midnight blue cocktail dress that ended halfway down her thighs. Daff didn't know how far along Nicole was, but she certainly wasn't showing even a hint of her pregnancy, even in the curve-hugging dress.

"Yes, I'm Nicole. It's nice to meet you," she said, obviously by rote. It was never nice to meet a cop. Not unless you were at the annual policemen's ball.

Daff slunk down in her chair, hoping that Nicole would forget that she was there. But, of course, she didn't. Instead, she turned from the detective and asked, "And you are?"

"Daphne Donovan," she answered, without elaborating.

Lieutenant Agar pulled out a chair and indicated that

Nicole should sit. She did so obediently, crossing her legs in a graceful manner that Daff had never been able to duplicate. It seemed that some women were born with the whole short skirt/high heels thing, but Daff was not one of those women. During her teenage years, she'd tried to master it, but it had never worked for her. She always felt like a little girl playing dress-up with her mother's clothes.

"I'm afraid I have some bad news, Ms. Solem," the detective said in his best "I'm afraid I have some bad news" voice.

Daphne shifted her gaze away from the young woman sitting across from her, a young woman whose life was about to be changed forever.

"Your . . . boyfriend?" Lieutenant Agar waited for Nicole to confirm that that had been the status of their relationship before he continued. "I'm afraid he's dead. It appears that he committed suicide but, of course, I'll be conducting a thorough review of the evidence before an official cause of death is determined. Ms. Donovan was the one who found him and called 911. I'm sorry, but the paramedics were not able to revive him."

Daff heard the gentle music of metal upon metal and it took her a moment to realize that it was the sound of Nicole's bracelets clinking together as her entire body started to shake. She closed her eyes and shivered, trying to drown out the sound of another person slowly coming apart.

"No," Nicole whispered.

"I'm sorry," the detective repeated. "Is there someone I can call for you? Your father perhaps?"

Nicole's bracelets continued their merry tune and Daff had to fight the urge to cover up her ears.

"Who are you? Why were you here?" Nicole turned on her and asked sharply, as if she could read the guilt etched clearly on Daff's soul.

Daphne cleared her throat and then swallowed, forcing

herself to meet Nicole's clear gaze. "I'm a private investigator. I was working for Keith on a . . . a case."

"What sort of a case?" Nicole asked.

"I was following you," Daff answered. No use trying to hide it. Lieutenant Agar would need to know what reason she had for being here anyway, and if she refused to tell him, he could subpoena Partners in Crime's records. Her gaze slid to the detective, who was leaning against the back of the couch with his arms crossed over his chest. "Keith felt that you had been acting strange lately and he wanted to know why. I followed you to Rules of Engagement and told him that you were taking classes to learn how to get him to the altar." Daphne shrugged and turned away, hoping Nicole wouldn't ask any more questions.

Of course, she wasn't that lucky.

Nicole's hand flew to her throat, her bracelets clanking together like cymbals at the end of a discordant symphony. "Did he know I was pregnant?" she whispered. "I told him this morning but . . . did he already know?"

Here it was. The moment where Daff could lie and leave here without anyone placing the blame for Keith's death on her. No one had to know that she'd followed Nicole to the OB-GYN yesterday. Her findings had never been put in writing. Not even Aimee or Raine knew.

Her secret could go to the grave with her . . . and with Keith.

But then Nicole might believe that she had caused Keith to take his own life. Who knows, maybe if Keith had heard the news from Nicole and not some stranger, he would have handled it better. Perhaps that was what had pushed him over the edge.

"Yes," Daphne answered clearly, raising her head so that she was once again looking into Nicole's eyes. "He knew because I told him."

Nicole blinked and two fat tears raced down her face, making twin tracks in the perfectly applied makeup. "When?" she asked.

"Yesterday evening." Daff refused to look away even as the accusations started.

"You had no right to tell him," Nicole said.

"I know."

"It was between me and Keith. It had nothing to do with you."

"I know," Daphne repeated.

"I wondered why he seemed so despondent this morning. He told me he wasn't feeling well, but . . . that was before I told him about the baby. He'd already called in sick to work before I arrived." Nicole pushed herself out of her chair and stalked toward Daphne with a menacing look on her face, but Daff didn't move.

"He must have been planning this since last night," Nicole accused.

Daff nodded sadly. She feared that Nicole was right.

"You killed him," Nicole hissed, raising her hand.

Daff didn't move, didn't flinch, even as the younger woman's perfectly manicured hand came toward her.

"Yes, I did," she agreed just at Lieutenant Agar grabbed Nicole's wrist and stopped her blow from connecting with Daphne's cheek.

TWENTY

"SHE was on a plane on the morning of September 11, on her way to arrest one of the terrorists involved in the attack, when all the flights were grounded. If she'd been even two hours earlier, she might have been able to prevent the towers from coming down."

Sam sat on a barstool next to his friend Tony Maggiore, former teammate and ferreter of information *extraordinaire*, and listened to a modern horror story that did not have a happy ending.

"Jesus," he breathed, rubbing his forehead with the fingers of his left hand.

"Yeah," Tony agreed. "According to my source, she'd been trying for months to get the powers that be to allow her to arrest the guy, but they kept shooting her down. She didn't have enough evidence, and they were afraid to piss off Saudi Arabia by hauling their citizens off to jail on nothing but a hunch."

"There was nothing more she could have done," Sam said. He was intimately acquainted with how the government worked, knew that those same laws that were put in effect to save the innocent more often sheltered the guilty. Even in his world, in spec ops, politics and public relations played a part.

"Well, I'm sure she doesn't see it that way. She resigned from the Bureau that day. I've got photos of her at Ground Zero on the twelfth. She must have driven all day to get to New York that quickly."

Tony turned his laptop on the bar so that Sam could see the screen. At first, he thought the photo was in black-and-white, but he realized after a moment that everything in the picture had been covered by a blanket of gray dust. He pulled the computer toward him and clicked the mouse to enlarge the bottom right-hand section.

It looked like a war zone, with giant steel girders lying like broken bones pointing up to the sky, concrete and debris piled hundreds of feet high, and that awful gray dust everywhere. Daphne stood on top of the rubble, her mouth and nose shielded by a surgical mask. Her face was red and she was sweating, and Sam remembered reading about the heat, about the rubber boots the rescue workers wore that literally melted right off their feet.

In the next frame, she had turned toward the photographer and the look in her eyes made Sam want to weep.

He'd seen the same look before on the faces of people who had lost so much during their lives that they no longer had hope. He'd always thought of them as the walking dead because they didn't seem to care whether they lived or died.

"You want me to get you a full background report on her?" Tony asked as he chewed the swizzle stick that had come with his fruity drink.

Sam had always been amazed by Tony's ability to gather information about people seemingly at the push of a button. Even after retiring here to Naples, Tony stayed connected to his information sources. Sam didn't know how Tony did it . . . but at times like these, he appreciated his friend's unique abilities.

"No. I think I'd rather learn the rest the old-fashioned way," he said. He may have only known Daphne Donovan for a few days, but he guessed she was the type who liked to keep her emotional scars well hidden until she trusted that you wouldn't poke at them to hurt her. Besides, just knowing about the role she'd played in 9/11 told him a lot about why she'd run last night after finding out he'd been a SEAL.

He probably scared the hell out of her because he could give her the one thing she feared the most: forgiveness.

SHE couldn't live with the guilt anymore.

The hinges of the patio chair creaked when Daphne rocked forward to stare into the deep end of Keith Melman's swimming pool. At one o'clock in the morning, the neighborhood was silent, all the people in their expensive houses safely snuggled into bed for the night. Daff sat outside Keith's darkened home and tried to ignore the irony that she was right back where she had started, spending her life haunting the dead.

Because of her, Keith would never see his children grow up to become adults. He'd miss the big things—the high school graduations, the marriages, and the grandchildren—but it was the smaller, day-to-day moments where his kids would miss him the most. It would be the rituals, the silly jokes, the times when they'd think, "Dad always took care of that," when they'd most feel his absence.

She had doomed Keith's children to the same fate she'd had, of knowing that a parent had chosen to leave her.

That was the worst part, knowing that there must have been a moment when her own mother had decided to go. It wasn't as if she had been taken from Daphne involuntarily. No. She had consciously chosen to leave, and in doing so, had left Daff with the knowledge that if only she'd been better, Mary Catherine might not have gone. Irrational as it may be, Daphne knew Keith's children would feel the same way, as if they could have swayed his decision to take his own life if only they'd behaved better, fought less, helped out more around the house, spent more time with him, said "I love you" more often, and on and on.

Daphne understood because she'd lived her entire life knowing she wasn't good enough.

The chair squeaked again as she leaned back, one hand resting on the gun in her lap.

She wasn't afraid to die. She was competent enough with a handgun to know where to shoot to make death relatively painless and instantaneous. There were only three people in the world who would miss her, and only one of them would truly mourn her passing. Raine and Aimee would cry at her funeral, of course, and they might even wish for her glum company every once in a while, but Brooks would be pissed that she'd taken what he considered to be the coward's way out.

Easy for him to say. He didn't have nearly three thousand deaths on his conscience.

Daff inhaled a shaky breath and realized that she was crying. She wasn't sure who the tears were for—Keith, his children, or herself. Not that it mattered. Tears never helped anything. They couldn't bring the dead back to life, and they couldn't heal a wounded soul.

She only wished she knew what could.

Daff wrapped her palm around the butt of her pistol, her index finger sliding over the trigger. The gun felt like a part of her, an extension of her hand, its heaviness comforting in the silence of the night.

With her thumb, she flicked the safety to the off position. The pistol was fully loaded—no self-respecting law enforcement officer carried an unloaded weapon—and ready to fire.

She sat still for a long moment, admiring the play of moonlight along the matte black barrel in the cloudless night.

"That's not the answer, you know."

Daff didn't look away from the gun in her lap as Sam's voice reached her ears. She thought for a split-second that maybe she was just imagining that he was here, but when she heard the tap of his boots against the concrete patio, she knew that she had not just conjured him up in her mind.

He crouched down before her but didn't make a move to try to take away her weapon.

"How did you find me?" she asked. She'd parked half a mile away in the Publix grocery store parking lot so the neighbors wouldn't see her car and call the cops. She'd already been interrogated once in the past twelve hours. That was enough.

"I looked," Sam answered simply.

Daphne turned away from the compassion she read in his eyes. She didn't deserve the comfort he offered.

"I know about Keith," Sam said. "And I know that you probably think you're to blame because you told him about Nicole's pregnancy before she had a chance to do it herself. You do know that's bullshit, right? That if Keith took his own life, that's his responsibility and his alone?"

"Sure," Daff lied.

"Yeah. I always struggled with that, too," Sam said as he settled himself more comfortably at her feet. He turned so that he was also facing Keith's house, his back resting against her legs. Daff was tempted to reach out to him, to touch his shoulder and feel the warmth of his skin beneath her fingers, but she remained still as Sam continued to speak.

"I used to wish that there was some sort of magic pill I

could take that would wipe away my memory. If I couldn't remember the decisions I've had to make, it wouldn't be so hard to live with the consequences."

His voice was full of sadness and Daphne wondered if he was thinking about the opportunity he'd missed to kill bin Laden. She squeezed her eyes shut.

"Of course, there *are* drugs that do that. I just couldn't stand the thought of wiping away the good memories as well as the bad. Seemed like I'd be left with a pretty empty life that way."

"And you have a full life now?" Daff asked and felt Sam's shrug against her knees.

"I'm working on it."

She wasn't. Instead of trying to fill her life, she was doing her best to empty it—to remain disconnected from everything and everyone around her. And it was a good thing, too. Look at what happened when she *did* interact with others.

Daphne stared unseeingly at a crack in the patio. It all came back to this. She was a destructive force in people's lives. They were better off never knowing her at all.

"I wish there was something I could say that would give you peace, but there isn't. It can only come from inside yourself, when you accept that you're a flawed human being who is only doing her best to do what's right."

"How very Zen of you," Daff said, shifting in her seat so that her shins were no longer touching Sam's back.

"The answer will come to you when you're ready to hear it," Sam insisted.

"Yeah, well, I'm ready. So where is it?"

Daff was surprised when Sam turned to her abruptly and laid one hand over the one she was using to cradle the gun in her lap. "It's right in front of you, Daphne. You just have to be willing to see it."

TWENTY-ONE

JENNA knew she was taking a risk, but with Keith out of the way, Nicole Solem no longer had any reason to attend classes at Rules of Engagement. That meant Jenna had to find another way to remain in the younger woman's life long enough to exact her revenge.

And how ironic that Keith's death provided the perfect excuse.

Jenna cradled the bouquet of flowers in her arms as she stood on the front porch of the Solem mansion and waited patiently for someone to answer the doorbell's summons. The front gates had been open when she arrived, so she had driven straight through and parked her nondescript sedan on the circular drive.

"Jenna, what a surprise. What can I do for you?"

She tried for the perfect mix of friendliness mixed with compassion as she smiled sadly at Nathan Solem. "I brought these for Nicole," she said, holding out the flowers. "When she missed class today, I asked our instructor if she knew what was wrong. She told me about what happened. I am so sorry."

Nathan automatically took the flowers she offered and stepped back to invite her into the marble foyer of the mansion. "Thank you. It has been a . . . difficult time for my daughter. I'm sure she'll appreciate these." He nodded toward the bouquet, his eyes troubled.

Jenna wanted to ask if she could see Nicole but she didn't want to arouse Nathan's suspicions by being too pushy. Instead, she laid a hand on Nathan's arm and said, "She'll get through this. I lost my husband four years ago, and at first it seemed like my life was over, too. At least Nicole has her baby to live for." Jenna nearly choked on the words. Nicole had more than Jenna had been granted.

Nathan sighed. "I just wish . . . I wish I knew how to help her process this. She hasn't stopped crying all day and I'm worried about her. Her mother would have known what to do, but I . . ." Nathan shook his head with frustration, and Jenna saw her opening.

"Maybe I could help?" she offered. "Sometimes a woman just needs another woman's shoulder to cry on."

"Would you mind trying? I would appreciate it."

"I wouldn't mind at all. Nicole has become a friend to me over the past few weeks. I'll do whatever I can to help." *And to stay close enough to kill her when the opportunity arose.* Jenna shot Nathan her most innocent smile.

"Let me show you to her room then," Nathan said, turning toward the wide staircase that flanked the left side of the foyer.

Jenna followed him up the marble stairs, absently wondering if rich people's children didn't have the same sorts of accidents that other kids did. Yvonne and Yvette would never have made it past the toddler stage if she and Aaron had bought a home with marble stairs.

They crossed a hallway at the top of the stairs and stopped at the first of several doors in what Jenna guessed would be termed the east wing. Nathan tapped lightly on the door and said, "Nicole? Honey, there's someone here to see you."

There was a muffled sound from inside the room, which Nathan took as an invitation to open the door. Then he stepped back into the hallway, clearly thankful to let Jenna take over from here.

Jenna inhaled deeply to calm herself before moving into the room. She had to be careful here, to show just enough compassion without giving away too much about herself. She wasn't sure what her next step would be, but it was important that Nicole continue to see her as an ally and not a threat. And that meant, as difficult as it was to feign sympathy and understanding when what she wanted most was to scream at this spoiled girl that she knew nothing yet of how tragic life could really be, she had to continue this charade for a while longer—just long enough for her to come up with another plan and put it into action.

She forced herself to focus on Nicole and the young woman's grief. That was how she would get through these next few hours, by allowing her own pain to bubble to the surface without boiling over.

Jenna took another deep breath and stepped into the doorway, then gasped with horror at what she saw lying in the middle of Nicole Solem's neatly made bed.

THE answer was right in front of her nose.

Daphne pressed her cheek against the cool glass of the sliding door that led into Keith Melman's family room. Someone had boarded up the one beside it—the one she'd broken in her attempt to save the man who had already taken his last breath. From her hiding place behind a row of hibiscus bushes, Daff had watched the workmen come that afternoon. They hadn't gone into the house or even bothered to sweep up the stray shards of glass still lying on the patio. Instead, they had simply hauled a piece of plywood into the backyard, stood it on end, and used duct tape to hold it in place, presumably just to keep the rain and any stray animals out of the house until a replacement door arrived.

Without knowing why she did it, Daff reached out and rubbed her hand across the surface of the rough wood. Perhaps she hoped that the sting of a few splinters might help alleviate the guilt crushing the air from her lungs.

It didn't.

She feared that nothing short of death would make it stop.

She closed her eyes and kept her face pressed against the smooth glass, longing for the comfort of Sam's arms around her but knowing she didn't deserve to be comforted. Keith's death was her fault, and her punishment was to live alone with the guilt.

She didn't understand how Sam had found peace. She didn't blame him for not taking bin Laden out when he'd had the chance—he couldn't have known what was going to happen nearly a decade in the future—but how had Sam forgiven himself? Surely, it hadn't been as simple as just accepting that he wasn't infallible and moving on from there.

But she couldn't ask him. When he'd left her that morning, Daphne had known the next move was up to her. Short of dragging her by the hair back to his cave, Sam had done everything he could to convince her to stay with him. Now she had to decide: was she going to stay with the dead or reenter the land of the living?

Daff rubbed her eyes on the arm of her T-shirt. The tears seemed to have become a constant companion since she'd come to Naples. Maybe because no one knew her here, so it didn't matter if they saw her fall apart.

That was exactly what she was doing here. Falling apart.

She felt stuck here in Keith Melman's backyard, like a spirit that couldn't move to heaven or hell, trapped in purgatory until some lesson she had failed to learn while alive had finally been driven home.

And didn't it figure? Other ghosts haunted brooding Southern mansions and Daff was stuck in this sunny fucking Yuppieville. Some happy family with a stay-at-home soccer mom and 2.5 kids would probably move in next and she'd be trapped trying to haunt them.

She shivered. Yeah, that's when she'd know she'd gone to hell.

She turned and leaned back against the sliding glass door. As much as she might like to, she couldn't stay here forever. For one thing, she needed a shower. She'd checked out of the motel yesterday morning, before coming to Keith's, and by tomorrow, she'd be positively ripe.

She supposed she could break into Keith's house and use his shower. Wasn't like anyone else was availing himself of the facilities. But it didn't seem respectful of the dead. Besides, she had no way of knowing whether someone had set the burglar alarm and, since Lieutenant Agar had her pegged as his number-one murder suspect if the evidence came back leaning toward a homicide instead of a suicide, she didn't figure getting caught at the scene of the crime made a lot of sense.

Daff narrowed her eyes at the inviting waters of the swimming pool.

Hmm. She wasn't going to risk breaking into Keith's house, but a dip in his pool couldn't hurt.

She stepped away from the door and scanned the backyard. The landscaping around the perimeter of the fence did a commendable job of shielding the pool from the neighbors, whether by design or luck, Daff didn't know. Afternoon had already given way to evening, and without any lights on outside, it would be difficult for anyone to see her.

As long as she didn't splash or make a lot of noise, she should be able to at least rinse off some of the last two days' dirt unmolested.

Without hesitating, she stripped down to her plain white cotton bra and panties. Unlike her partners, Victoria's Secret had never separated her from any of *her* hard-earned money. The water seemed cold at first, but Daff forced herself to keep walking toward the deep end until her toes were balanced right on the point where a nudge in the right direction would send her underwater.

Daphne was a competent—but not comfortable—swimmer. She hadn't grown up in a world of swimming pools or watering holes. She could get around Manhattan alone by the time she was six, but hadn't learned to swim until she was twenty-one. She'd only learned then because she'd had a dream where she was drowning and she hated waking up with the taste of fear in her mouth. She'd signed up for lessons at the Y that day, but she'd never learned to love the water like other people did.

She let her feet slide out from under her, feeling the water suck her down beneath the surface as she freed her hair from its ponytail. She shook her head underwater to fan her hair out around her face. One of these days, she'd get it cut. It was always in her way, and she didn't even know why she bothered letting it get so long.

Liar. You know why.

Daff kicked toward the surface and scowled at the voice in her head.

Yeah. All right. She knew why she never cut her hair. She remembered her mother brushing it one night, saying in a surprised-sounding voice, as if she'd never noticed it before, "You have such pretty hair." The unaccustomed praise had come as such a shock that the memory of it was still burned into Daphne brain. Or maybe it wasn't the praise that made it as memorable as the fact that Mary Catherine had vanished before the next morning, abandoning her daughter to a virtual stranger.

Daff paddled into the deep end and rested her elbows along the edge of the pool.

Gotta love those fond childhood memories.

She sighed and laid her head down upon her arms, staring unseeingly into another set of sliding glass doors that Daff presumed led into the master bedroom. As the evening darkened, a faint light from inside glowed eerily.

"Must be a night-light," Daphne muttered to herself. It was too faint to be a lamp, although she supposed that someone may have left a light on somewhere in the house and that was what was casting the glow into the bedroom.

Her eyes soon became unfocused and Daff blinked several times to clear them. When she squinted toward the door again, she noticed something lying on the carpet, just inside the sliding glass doors. It looked like one of those rubber dog toys shaped like a bone, but Daff knew Keith didn't have a dog. Curious, she hauled herself out of the pool and padded toward the bedroom, leaving a trail of water in her wake.

Crouching down, she pushed her wet hair away from her face and peered into the room.

It did appear to be Keith's bedroom. In the faint glow of light given off by the night-light—it was plugged in over by the large bed that dominated the room—Daphne saw beige-colored carpeting, the open door to a walk-in closet, and the glint of a mirror from what was most likely the master bath. She was looking into a small sitting room that was off to the side of the bedroom. The walls bowed out into a semicircular shape, built, no doubt, to add some extra square footage and architectural interest to the Mediterranean-style house. Two chairs and a small table had been placed in the sitting room, facing the swimming pool.

One of the chairs had a child's carseat on it, which Daff found odd. Neither of Keith's children was young enough to need a carseat. But she ignored that as she tried to figure out what was lying on the floor. When she realized it was a baby's rattle, she frowned and looked back up at the carseat, which had a large green bow taped to the handle.

Had Nicole brought this over as a way to tell Keith she was pregnant?

Daff squinted at the envelope that had been taped next to the bow.

Wait a second. Something wasn't right here. The name spelled out in heavy black letters wasn't *Keith.* It was *Nicole.*

That didn't make sense. Not unless Keith planned the carseat to be a giant F— you to blame Nicole for his death. But that didn't seem to fit with Keith's reaction after Daff had told him that his girlfriend was pregnant. He certainly hadn't been overjoyed, but he wasn't angry, either.

Daff shook her head and shivered as water dripped from her hair and down her back. She straightened from her crouch and wrung out her hair, still eyeing the gift on the other side of the glass.

She had to know what that card said.

She pulled her clothes on over her still-damp skin, her jeans not exactly cooperating when she tried tugging them up her thighs. When she was dressed again, she contemplated her options—look for an open window or an unlocked door, or pull the plywood down from the broken sliding glass door.

Daff opted for the plywood. With any luck, if someone *had* set Keith's alarm, they'd armed it only for a crook who opened a window or door.

She struggled to move the unwieldy piece of plywood out of her way and grimaced when a large sliver embedded itself in the palm of her hand. Gingerly, she picked at it as she stepped into the family room, studiously avoiding looking at the couch where Keith Melman had died. She had to hurry.

If the motion detectors perched up in the corners of the room were working, the cops would be here within minutes.

Daff jogged through the kitchen and down the hall toward the master bedroom. She passed a home office on her left, barely sparing a glance at the laptop computer and various papers strewn across the top of the desk as she passed.

The bedroom was large—easily five times as big as her room at Brooks's townhouse back in Manhattan. One of those giant plasma TVs that cost more than Daff used to earn in six months dominated one wall. The furniture was black lacquer—what Daff liked to term "early bachelor"—and was covered with framed photos of smiling kids.

She hurried to the sitting area and kneeled down in front of the chair with the carseat crammed full of baby stuff. Daff plucked the card from the carseat and a stuffed bear fell from the top of the pile of treasures and onto the carpet.

She picked it up and put it back.

The flap of the envelope had been tucked inside instead of glued shut, so it didn't take long for Daphne to get the card out. On the front was a cartoon drawing of a baby carriage with cute little animals peering in. Frankly, Daff thought that was a little creepy. If she found a baby carriage with a bunch of animals hovering around it, the first thing she'd wonder was how long the poor thing had been dead.

But that was just her. And, of course, she *was* aware of how sick that made her.

She opened the card and skimmed the verse about the miracle of childbirth, and then skipped over to the handwritten message on the blank side of the card.

Dear Nicole,

I'm so sorry I wasn't more enthusiastic when you told me that we're going to have a child. I have no excuse other than to say that I'm a selfish bastard and

I'd hoped to have you all to myself for a while longer before we started a family of our own. Please accept my apologies, and know that I will love this baby every bit as much as I love you.

Keith
P.S.—Will you marry me?

Daff swallowed hard as she put the card back inside the envelope. Then, without intending to, she reached out to touch a tiny terry-cloth outfit dyed seafoam green with a turtle embroidered on the front. Very few women could resist thinking how sweet such a thing would look on a newborn baby, even one with a heart as hard as Daff liked to pretend to have.

That Keith had bought all this stuff was an enormous gesture of goodwill. Especially since Daff wasn't sure she believed that the sentiment he'd written in the card was how he had really felt. Maybe in a month or two, he would have become accustomed to the idea and have been able to be happy about it, but when she'd left him two nights ago, he had most assuredly not attributed his reaction to selfishness on his own part.

Whether it was true or not, however, there was one thing Daphne knew after reading Keith's message.

No way had the guy who had written that note turned around a few hours later and killed himself.

Which could only mean that Keith Melman had been murdered.

TWENTY-TWO

JENNA stared at the spotted stuffed elephant Nicole had clutched to her chest and nearly collapsed under the force of her grief.

Eleven years ago, Aaron had asked her to pick up a gift for Nicole Solem's thirteenth birthday party. Jenna had brought the twins with her to help her pick something out. She had no idea what a thirteen-year-old might want—probably cash or expensive electronics, but Jenna wanted to get the girl a more personal gift. As they'd walked the aisles of Toys "R" Us, Yvonne and Yvette suggested just about every toy they passed.

Easy-Bake oven? No, girls, that's for someone a little younger.

Candyland game? Maybe something a little more grown-up.

Barbie Dream House? She *lives* in the Barbie Dream House.

And then the girls had spotted it—the perfect gift. A pink stuffed elephant with purple polka dots and eyes that looked so kind you could almost believe they were real. The twins loved the thing so much that they cried when they boxed up the gift. Jenna felt so bad that she went back to the store a few days later and tried to get one for each of them, but by then the store was sold out.

A few weeks after the party, they had received a handwritten thank-you note from Nicole saying that she would cherish "Ellie" forever.

The girls had moved on to other toys, to other well-loved stuffed animals, but seeing their gift now—the one they'd wanted so much to keep for themselves—being held so tightly by the daughter of the man who had killed them, made Jenna want to weep with despair.

And it was that memory, that sharp burst of remembering her girls' laughter and the silly game they had started playing at the toy store, that made Jenna realize that she had been right all along. Seeking revenge *was* helping to bring her family back. Because she was so focused on doing this for them, it was as if they were alive again. She would do anything to make that feeling last.

Jenna reached out and gently stroked Nicole's hair. "I'm so sorry," she whispered. "I know how much it hurts to lose someone you love."

Nicole clutched the stuffed animal even closer to her chest but didn't say anything, so Jenna slowly lowered herself onto the bed, keeping one foot on the floor as she turned toward the younger woman.

She tried to think of something to say that Nicole would find comforting, and found herself remembering a time when Yvette had come home from school, heartbroken because a girl in her class didn't like Yvonne. Jenna didn't know if it was normal for sisters to feel such hurt for each other or if Yvonne and Yvette were so close just because they were twins, but whatever the reason, Yvette had cried as if her heart was breaking when someone snubbed her sister.

Jenna had tried consoling Yvette with the usual platitudes—there will always be people in the world who don't like you; this girl doesn't know how special Yvonne is; just try to ignore her—but nothing worked. Yvette just cried harder until Jenna finally held her daughter in her arms and said, "There is nothing you can do to make this better. It's wrong, and it hurts, and sometimes the only thing you can do in the face of a bad situation is to cry and then pick yourself up and wipe yourself off when it's all over."

She had no idea why that made Yvette calm down. Maybe it was simply admitting that there were situations over which one had no power, no control, and when one was faced with such a circumstance, it was best to just give in to it until it had passed.

She didn't know if it would work now with Nicole, but figured it was worth a try. When she was done repeating what she'd said to her own daughter so many years ago, Nicole finally lifted her head. Her cheeks were stained with tears, her normally smooth skin red and blotchy. Jenna prepared herself for the worst, for Nicole to scream that she didn't know what the hell she was talking about and to get out of her room, but she didn't.

Instead, she held out one hand, grabbing Jenna's with surprising strength. "Thank you," she said softly.

"Uh, thank you. What for?" Jenna asked.

"For not saying I'm young and I'll find someone else. For not telling me to stop crying or I'll hurt the baby. For understanding."

Jenna squeezed Nicole's hand and chanced a look back toward the hall, where Nathan Solem was still standing. He bowed his head sheepishly and gave a sharp nod before disappearing from his daughter's doorway. Jenna shook her head. Men. They could be so stupid sometimes.

She turned back to Nicole and gave her a slight smile. "You're welcome," she said. "I've never heard of anyone blaming a miscarriage on too much crying. I don't think you need to worry about that. As for finding someone else, well . . ." Jenna shrugged. She didn't want to depress Nicole further, but there were no guarantees in life. If Keith had been Nicole's soul mate as Aaron had been hers, then there was no hope that she would find somebody else. But she didn't want to say the words, so she let her shrug speak for itself.

She was about to make up something about understanding how powerless Nicole must feel right now, but was interrupted by the sound of a commotion from downstairs. Nathan had left the bedroom door open when he left and the sound of voices echoed in the marble foyer and wafted upstairs.

"—didn't kill himself. He was murdered. If you'll just listen to me—"

"Is this your idea of a joke?" Jenna heard Nathan say.

She didn't recognize the first voice, but when she looked over at Nicole, she saw that the younger woman's face had turned a ghastly shade of white. Afraid that Nicole was going to faint, Jenna tugged on her hand and asked, "Are you all right?"

Nicole didn't answer. Instead, she leaped up off the bed and raced out of her room, dropping the stuffed animal on the floor as she headed downstairs.

Jenna stooped down and picked up the elephant as she followed at a slightly slower pace. When she reached the top of the stairs, she held back, keeping out of sight of the drama unfolding in the entryway. She peered down over the railing to see a slender woman with dark red hair pulled up in a ponytail holding a child's carseat. When Nicole slid to a stop at the bottom of the stairs, the redhead held out the bright blue seat.

"Keith bought this for you. For the baby. Don't you see, he wouldn't have done that if he planned to kill himself." The redhead turned back to Nathan and held one hand out beseechingly. "Go to the police. You have clout with them. They'll treat this case as a homicide if you ask them to."

"Get out of my house!" Nathan roared as he pushed past his daughter and grabbed the redhead by her arm and started dragging her toward the front door.

Nicole seemed frozen to the spot, staring at the other woman with such hatred that Jenna took another step back. She didn't know why, but some instinct told her to stay well out of sight of the redhead, whoever she was.

"He didn't do it," the woman said, holding her ground with admirable strength against the taller, heavier man who was trying to throw her out.

"What's going on here?"

A man wearing navy slacks and a short-sleeved starched white shirt dashed into the foyer, doing his best to make it sound as if he had control of the situation. A few seconds later, it became painfully obvious that he did not. He turned his back on Nicole, and Jenna watched from above, her eyes wide with surprise, as Nicole calmly stepped forward and yanked the man's gun from where he'd tucked it into the waistband of his slacks at the small of his back. Then she stepped to the side of the foyer, raised the weapon with both hands, aimed it at the other woman, and said, "You killed Keith. Now it's your turn to die."

THIS was his punishment for sticking his nose where it didn't belong.

Sam glanced at the clock on the wall, then at his silent

cell phone, and then back at the computer screen in front of him. He wasn't getting paid to put in all these extra hours doing background checks on people, but since he'd "volunteered" to do so, the list had grown like a two-bellied tapeworm.

Why hadn't he kept his mouth shut about the half-assed security plan for Solem's upcoming CEO summit?

Sam grunted and shook his head as he keyed in the next social security number and hit enter. Of course, he knew why he'd butted in. You couldn't turn off that protective gene just because it was no longer convenient to have it.

Besides, what the hell else was he going to spend the night doing?

Until Daphne called, he—

Sam was on his feet instantly when he heard the unmistakable *blam* of a gunshot.

He ran toward the front of the house, where the noise had come from, his steps faltering when Daphne's voice reached his ears.

"Nicole, I know that grief makes people do crazy things, but you do not want to shoot me . . . or anyone else. Now put down the gun."

What? Nicole had a gun?

Sam cautiously approached the foyer by a side hallway that led to what had formerly been the servant's quarters but now housed several offices for Nathan's staff. He stayed in the shadows as he assessed the situation. From his vantage point he could see Nathan and Daphne, but nothing else. Nathan stood by the massive front door, staring straight ahead as if in shock. Daphne had her back toward Sam, and he could clearly see the outline of a pistol nestled in the small of her back. Why wasn't she using it to defend herself?

He didn't know what the hell was going on here, but he couldn't just stand here and do nothing, so he put his hands in the air and calmly announced, "Nicole, it's Sam Bryson. I'm coming out. Don't shoot."

Then he stepped into the well-lit foyer, his gaze taking in the shattered vase lying on the marble floor, the stricken look on Nicole's face as the gun in her hands started to wobble, and the way Nathan's head of security—the idiot who had suggested they hire Lance Muldoon to help with the CEO summit—had slunk back behind a giant potted palm and was hiding among the fronds.

He walked over to Nicole and took the weapon from her shaking hands. Then he turned to face Nathan and Daphne.

"Is everyone all right?" he asked.

"This woman showed up here with this . . . this sick excuse for a joke," Nathan said, waving toward a child's carseat sitting near Daphne's feet. "Nicole was just— Just—" He stopped, his breathing ragged as if he were trying not to cry.

"Everyone's fine," Daphne said quietly.

"I'll call the police." Solem's head of security came out from behind the plant and officiously unclipped his cell phone from his belt.

"That won't be necessary," Sam said.

"But what about this intruder?" Nathan sputtered.

Sam leveled a hard look at his boss. "And what about your daughter? Last time I checked, assault with a deadly weapon was a felony offense. Do you really want to get the police involved in this?"

Nathan was silent for a long moment before he answered, "No. You're right."

"Good. Now, if you'll excuse me, I'll take care of *her*," Sam said. Without looking at Daphne, he reached out and took her by the upper arm. She didn't protest—and neither did anyone else—as Sam half-dragged her out the front door and into the cool evening air.

* * *

IN the silence that followed the departure of Sam and that horrible woman, Nicole found herself replaying the last ten minutes of her life over again in her head. Like someone in a movie theater, she watched herself grab the gun, point it at another human, and squeeze the trigger. She could clearly read the emotions on her own face, the flash of rage turning to disbelief and then horror when she realized what she had just done.

Nicole felt her knees give out and she sank to the floor in a puddle of shock.

She had almost killed someone.

Nicole wrapped her arms around herself to try to stop the shaking.

"Excuse me, do we have the correct evening?" As if watching through a smokescreen, Nicole saw her father turn toward the couple standing in the wide-open doorway. It was that Middle Eastern couple who had recently moved to Naples. Nicole had met them last week on Daddy's yacht. The man frightened her for some reason—it was something in his eyes that didn't seem quite alive, like a shark that might suddenly turn on a diver and take a bite with its razor-sharp teeth. The wife seemed nice enough, though she had remained a few steps behind her husband, like a well-trained dog that was afraid of being choked by its leash. She wore a brightly colored silk dress that did nothing to conceal her pregnant state.

"I'm sorry. Didn't you get the message? We canceled the dinner party this evening," her father said, his cheeks reddening.

Nicole knew he must be embarrassed by the scene the al-Sayeds had inadvertently stepped into. His daughter, collapsed into a heap on the floor, a broken vase nearby hinting that some sort of violence had recently taken place.

But it could have been so much worse. Nicole could have

killed that woman, and then their home would have been swarming with police.

It could still happen. What had Sam said she could be charged with? Assault with a deadly weapon?

Nicole made a noise that was a sort of half-choke and half-laugh before she slid the rest of the way to the floor, her cheek resting against the cool marble as she started to cry.

Her father abandoned the couple at the door and dropped down beside her on the floor. "Nicole? Are you all right? Is it the baby?"

"She is pregnant?" Jahia al-Sayed asked in a tentative voice as she too crouched down on the floor and smoothed Nicole's hair away from her face in a maternal fashion.

"Yes. She's not far along," Nathan answered.

Nicole wanted to tell them that she was fine, but she couldn't seem to summon the energy to do anything but cry. As Jahia leaned toward her, a wave of her sweet perfume wafted over Nicole. The smell made her stomach protest, and Nicole realized she hadn't had anything to eat since lunch. Nibbling on oyster crackers seemed to be the only thing that kept her from getting sick these days.

Nicole swallowed against her gag reflex. She couldn't get sick here, not in front of everyone.

She tried to push herself up off the floor, but her father's firm hands held her down. "Shh, baby. Stay there until you feel better."

"I . . . I have something that might help," Jahia offered.

Nathan nodded over his daughter's prone form. He'd do anything to make this better for her.

Jahia slipped a large woven handbag off her shoulder and rummaged around in it while she explained, "All of the women in my family use this. They say it helps to keep the baby calm and happy inside the mother's womb."

She pulled out a spray bottle and released a cloud of cloyingly sweet perfume before Nathan could stop her. He had thought that perhaps she had some sort of medication that would calm his daughter, not some voodoo remedy from "the old country."

Nicole inhaled the perfume and gagged, closing her mouth to try to keep from vomiting. She coughed and fought the urge to retch, but the impulse was too strong. She barely managed to turn her head as the contents of her stomach spewed onto the marble floor at her father's feet.

TWENTY-THREE

SAM didn't say a word as he hauled Daff behind him past her rental car and toward his truck, which was parked down near the entrance to the Solem mansion. He was glad she didn't try to talk, because with every step he took the pressure in his head mounted. By the time he reached his old black Ford, he was ready to explode.

He unlocked the driver's-side door the old-fashioned way—with a key. The ten-plus-year-old truck didn't have an electronic clicker to open his doors or his trunk or brew him a fresh cup of coffee like the new vehicles did. But Sam wouldn't give up on this heap of metal until it gave up on him.

"Get in," he ordered, holding the door open for Daphne and half expecting her to argue with him. He found himself almost wishing she would. He was goddamn good and ready for a fight.

She slid into the front seat without protest and Sam slid in next to her.

The engine revved when Sam gunned the accelerator with more force than was necessary and the truck leaped forward like a cat whose tail had been stepped on when he shoved the transmission into drive.

A muscle in Sam's jaw twitched as his fury mounted with each passing second. He wasn't even aware he had a destination in mind until he turned toward the beach.

Daphne stared out the passenger-side window and remained silent, her arms wrapped around her waist as if she, too, were angry. Sam didn't know what the hell she had to be upset about—it was he who had just watched the woman he loved nearly get gunned down right in front of his eyes.

Sam barely tapped on the brakes as he jerked the steering wheel to the right. The tires of the truck sank into the soft white sand and Sam kept his foot on the gas until he was sure they were well out of sight of the road. He didn't want an audience for this.

Satisfied that they were alone, Sam shoved the truck in park, pulled the keys from the ignition, and tossed them onto the dashboard with a loud clang.

Then he turned toward Daphne, who gave every appearance of having turned to stone during the last twenty minutes.

"All right. What the fuck was that all about?" Sam knew he was shouting, and he didn't care. He was through being Mr. Patient, Mr. I'll Give You All the Time and Space You Need Because I Think You're the One for Me. Fuck that.

"Keith didn't kill himself," Daphne said.

Sam jerked his door open and stalked around the front of the truck to pull open the passenger-side door. The cab of his truck was too small, too contained. He needed an entire fucking ocean to rail at right now.

"I don't care about Keith. Don't you get it? You just stood

there while someone took a shot at you! Nicole could have killed you."

"Nicole couldn't hit the side of a barn with a bazooka."

Daphne rested her arm along the back of the seat and watched him as he paced the sand in front of her. Sam wanted to reach in and haul her out of the truck, but he was afraid he might be tempted to throttle her once he had his hands on her.

"People get lucky sometimes, Daphne. You didn't even try to defend yourself."

"I'm not afraid to die." She said it casually. As if she were telling him she wasn't afraid of spiders.

"No, but you're sure afraid to live."

Daphne's teeth snapped together so hard that Sam heard the clack from where he was standing. She jumped down from the truck and stalked toward him, her blue eyes flashing with ice. "That's not true."

"Yes, it is. You're fine as long as nothing touches you emotionally. You can just keep on pretending to be this aloof, uncaring person who can look death in the eye and laugh."

"That's bullshit."

"Is it?" Sam said with a dangerous glint in his eyes. "You sit alone in the dark, refusing to let anyone know about the shit that's going on inside your head. You want to believe it's because no one else could possibly understand, but that's a lie. The real problem is, you don't want anyone to know too much about you. You'd rather isolate yourself from everyone around you than take a chance that you might actually start caring enough for someone to let yourself get hurt.

"That's why you ran away from the FBI. Yes, I know about what happened," he said when Daphne gasped, but continued before she could interrupt. "You damn sure did cared about all those people who died on 9/11. Now you're wasting your talents on these bullshit cases so you don't have to give a shit anymore. Your client's girlfriend is cheating on him? You hang around for a few days, snap a few photos, collect your thousand dollars, and you're off to the next case. You don't get involved, you don't have to see what happens next, and you escape life unscathed. Is that how it works in your world? Because in my world, people get hurt *every day,* and you know what? They survive. They pick themselves up and dust themselves off and go on with living and loving and hating and dying. They don't just fucking give up and walk away. They stay and fight."

During Sam's tirade, Daff slowly backed up until she was trapped against the bed of his truck. With each step she had retreated, Sam followed her. Now they stood toe-to-toe, with no place left for Daphne to retreat.

"I have to go," she said quietly.

"No, Daphne. You don't *have* to go. You're *choosing* to leave. There's a big difference."

"This case is over. I've done everything I can do."

"Have you? I missed the first part of your little tête-à-tête tonight, but I did get that you don't think Keith killed himself. Can you really just walk away, knowing that an innocent man may have been murdered?"

Daphne put her palms on his chest and tried to push him away, but Sam wasn't going anywhere. Instead, he leaned into her, pinning her even more tightly to the side of his truck. She could have tried to hurt him, to dig her fingers into his flesh or try to knee him in the groin, but she didn't.

"Yes, Sam. I can walk away. I've had a lot of practice in my life."

They stood together for a long moment, neither of them speaking, just looking into each other's eyes as though seeing each other for the very first time.

Sam finally broke the silence, stepping back to free them

both. "Then you're not the woman I thought you were," he said.

Daphne looked away so he wouldn't see her wince. "Oh, really? Who did you think I was? Despite this silly tattoo, I'm no superhero." Daff flashed him the tattoo on her right buttock that depicted Daffy Duck in a green SuperDaff cape.

"No," Sam answered quietly as he took another step away from her and stared out into the dark waters of the Gulf. "But I'll bet you used to be."

NOW was her chance to leap in and play the part of the hero.

Jenna hurried into Nicole's bedroom and grabbed several towels from a cupboard in the adjoining bathroom. She wet one in the garden tub that could easily have accommodated four people and then made her way down the stairs to where Nicole lay groaning in a pool of vomit.

"Everything's going to be all right," Jenna soothed as she gently lifted up Nicole's head and spread the warm, wet towel over the mess. "Nathan, could you find the number for her doctor? Mrs. al-Sayed, thank you for trying to help. We'll take it from here."

Jahia al-Sayed nodded and held out the perfume that had made Nicole so ill. "Would you like to keep this? It will ensure that she does not lose the baby," she assured Jenna.

Jenna forced herself not to roll her eyes. Someone had obviously convinced her that this stuff really worked. "Thank you," Jenna said as she took the perfume. No sense insulting the woman. Nicole could just throw it away after Mrs. al-Sayed left.

Nathan apologized again to the al-Sayeds as he politely ushered them out the front door, and Jenna gathered that there was supposed to have been a dinner party here at the Solems' this evening. Keith's untimely death appeared to have caused a change of plans.

"I'll go get that phone number," Nathan said and disappeared down a hallway.

Jenna used one of the dry towels to wipe Nicole's face as the young woman began crying again.

Jenna moved so that she was positioned between Nicole and the carseat the redhead had brought in earlier, the one that had caused Nicole to become so distraught.

"Could you get rid of that, please?" She jerked her chin in the direction of the carseat and the uniformed man who had been hovering uncomfortably near a potted plant nodded.

"What should I do with it?" he asked.

Jenna's eyes narrowed on the offending object. She wasn't stupid, and even the snippet of conversation she had overheard led her to believe that the redhead had found the carseat at Keith's house and believed it contained evidence that his death was not a suicide.

"Take it off the premises and dispose of it. It's upsetting Miss Solem," Jenna said. Then, because she wasn't one to take chances, she plucked the card from the handle. She would take care of *this*.

"I'll be right back, Nicole. I'm just going to get you a glass of water." Jenna clutched the card in her hand as she hurried down a hallway that she assumed would lead to the kitchen. She would have liked to have read the card, but no way was she going to risk it. Only a dead man and that redhead would ever know what it said.

Jenna easily found the kitchen near the back of the mansion. She tore the card, still in its envelope, into several strips and stuffed it into the garbage disposal in one of the two large sinks. With the cold water running, she turned on the disposal, watching intently as the paper disappeared. Even when it was safe to assume that it had all been shredded, Jenna wasn't satisfied. She left the disposal's motor running as she turned to find a glass in the enormous, cheerily painted kitchen.

After she filled a tall water glass, she finally turned off the disposal and peered into the sink to make sure the envelope was gone. She had a phobia about sticking her hand into the disposal, so instead she pushed back the black rubber guards and squinted into the darkness to be certain no flecks of paper remained.

Only then did she return to the front of the house, where Nicole had finally managed to pull herself into a sitting position.

Jenna handed her the glass of water and sat down next to her on the floor.

"Are you all right?" she asked after Nicole had emptied half of the glass.

Nicole inhaled a shaky breath and turned away from her. "I think so. I don't feel . . . sick or . . . anything."

"No cramps or other pain?"

"No. Just . . ." She wiped away a tear and couldn't seem to continue.

Jenna put a hand on the younger woman's knee and squeezed in what she hoped was a comforting manner. "It will be okay. Nothing happened here tonight that can't be fixed."

Nicole's shoulders started to shake. "I almost killed that woman," she said on a hiccupping sob.

Jenna was quiet for a moment, wanting to frame her question the right way. "Who was she? Why did she make you so upset?"

"Her name is Daphne Donovan. She's a private investigator that Keith hired to tail me. He thought I was cheating on him." Nicole shook her head and delicately dabbed at her nose as if that might stop it from running. Not wanting to interrupt their conversation so she could get a tissue,

Jenna handed her one of the dry towels from off of the floor.

"No way," she said, feigning incredulity.

"I know. It's just so ridiculous. He thought that's why my behavior had changed. He didn't know it was because of our classes at Rules of Engagement."

Jenna just shook her head, as if to say that the conclusion Keith had drawn was incomprehensible to her, too.

"This woman—this investigator—found out I was pregnant and she told Keith before I had a chance to. If he'd heard it from me and not from some stranger first . . ." Nicole lowered her head and Jenna watched as two tears dripped onto the thick white towel resting in her lap.

"That's awful. I mean, to hear something so personal, so . . . life-altering, like that."

"Exactly." Nicole sighed.

"How did you find out about this woman, this Daphne Donovan, you said her name was?"

"Yes. She was there when I showed up to meet Keith for dinner. She—" Nicole stopped and swallowed loudly before beginning again. "She was the one who found Keith's body."

Jenna's eyes narrowed on the shattered vase lying on the floor on the other side of the foyer. This investigator could make trouble for her if she went to the police and tried to convince them to look further into Keith's death. Jenna wasn't arrogant enough to believe she had made no mistakes when cleaning up the crime scene. Had she had more time, she might have felt more confident about it, but as it was, it wouldn't surprise her to discover that she'd left a fingerprint or two behind that the police might question if this Daphne Donovan was able to convince them to treat the case as a homicide instead of a suicide.

And that would mean more police presence around the Solems, especially Nicole, who knew the most about

Keith's habits and the people he came into contact with every day.

Jenna couldn't have that, because if the police were hovering around Nicole, their attention might just land on Jenna. And although she had done her best to cover her tracks, a savvy detective would be able to connect the dots between Jenna Marisol, Aaron Richardson, and the former CEO of Geon.

Which meant she needed to make sure this private investigator kept her nose out of it until Jenna had a chance to come up with a new plan to get her revenge.

But what could she do without arousing anyone's suspicions?

"I have that phone number," Nathan said as he returned to the entryway and studied his daughter with concern.

Beside her, Nicole pushed a hand through her hair and stood up. "I'm so sorry about this, Daddy," she said with a wave toward the broken glass on the floor.

"Don't worry about it. I'll have Anna clean it up."

Nicole nodded, but looked to be back on the verge of tears, so Jenna once again took charge. "I think everything will look better after a good night's sleep. Nathan, Nicole seems to be fine but I'd keep her doctor's phone number handy just in case. I guess I'd best be off," she said. There was nothing more she could do here, and she wanted to be alone to contemplate her next move.

Nathan put a hand under Nicole's elbow, presumably to help her upstairs. "Would you mind waiting here for a moment?" he asked. "I'll be right back."

"Certainly," Jenna answered, frowning at their retreating backs. She wanted to be prepared in case she had to make a hurried exit—one should always plan for the worst—so she glanced around the foyer for her purse. Hadn't she left it down here when Nathan invited her in?

Her gaze stopped on a blue leather pocketbook that had

been tossed carelessly onto a wrought iron bench with a padded ivory seat that sat near the door. She was certain she'd seen Nicole carrying it during their classes at Rules of Engagement. A set of keys lay next to the purse, and it was those keys that got Jenna thinking about a way to make sure Daphne Donovan stayed out of her hair.

She didn't have time to think it all through right now. Nathan could appear at the top of the stairs at any moment.

Without hesitating, Jenna walked across the foyer and picked up Nicole's keys. She didn't have any pockets in her white silk slacks or anywhere else to hide the jangling key-chain with its multiple charms dangling among the keys. Jenna turned. Where had she left her own purse?

She spotted it on the other side of the entryway just as Nathan appeared on the top step.

Damn it, Jenna cursed under her breath.

She palmed the keys in her left hand, doing her best to keep them quiet and shield them from Nathan's view as he hurried down the stairs. Her own pocketbook was a rich caramel-colored leather that she had left zipped on a table that held a large bouquet of fat red roses and the bottle of perfume that Jahia al-Sayed had left behind. She reached out with her right hand and grabbed the strap.

"I'd like to talk to you," Nathan said from behind her.

Jenna could feel the sweat beading on her upper lip as she nonchalantly pushed open the zipper of her purse and turned around. "Oh?" she said.

"Yes. I—" Nathan stopped. Cleared his throat. Looked down at the intricate pattern inlaid in marble on the floor of the foyer. "I want to thank you for tonight. For being so kind to Nicole."

Jenna's shoulders slumped with relief as she slipped the keys into her purse and slid the strap over her arm. "You're welcome. I'm glad I was able to help." She paused for a moment and then said, "You might want to warn the police about that woman. You know, just in case she tries to contact Nicole again."

Nathan raised his gaze to hers and wearily rubbed a spot on his forehead. "Yes. You're right. I'll call the chief of police tonight."

"Good. It's so nice to have people around to protect you," she said. Too bad the super-rich were the only ones who were that lucky.

She turned toward the door, then stopped as if something else had just occurred to her. "By the way, you might want to ask them to keep an eye on Keith's house. Just in case she tries to break in or something," Jenna added.

"I can't believe that it's come to this."

"It's an ugly world out there sometimes," Jenna agreed.

Nathan nodded and started walking toward the door. "Yes. Well, I appreciate that some kindness still exists." He smiled warmly at her as he put a hand on the small of her back to usher her to the door.

Jenna smiled back, but her steps faltered as she slipped on a wet patch of marble. She would have pitched forward and fallen if Nathan hadn't been right there to stop her fall, but the movement jostled her purse and Jenna watched in horrified silence as the contents of her unzipped bag—including Nicole's easily identifiable keychain—clattered to the floor.

"Are you all right?" Nathan asked.

Jenna dropped to the floor, her hand snaking out to cover Nicole's keys.

"I'm fine. I'm such a klutz."

"No, this marble is terrible when it gets wet. I don't know what possessed the original owner to put it on the floor. Not with the rains we get here in Florida." Nathan crouched down and gathered a handful of her things.

As he held them out to her, Jenna tried to hide Nicole's keys while holding her purse open for Nathan to drop the stuff in. She felt the keys slipping out of her hand and nearly screamed with frustration as they fell, once again, to the marble floor.

Then she bit her lip and closed her eyes when Nathan bent down to retrieve them, scowled, and asked, "What are you doing with this?"

TWENTY-FOUR

DAPHNE was old enough to remember when cartoons only ran on Saturday mornings. When she was growing up, there was no cable, no satellite TV with its thousands of channels running twenty-four/seven. There was no Disney Channel. No Cartoon Network. No Nick at Nite. And she wasn't even that old.

There was something wrong with being able to watch everything and anything at any time of day. She didn't have a lot of happy memories from the time before good ol' Mom had ditched her with Jack Madison, but one of the things she'd loved about Jack was their Sunday night television ritual. Every Sunday at 7 P.M., *Wild Kingdom with Marlin Perkins* would air, followed by the Disney hour at eight. Jack popped a giant bowl of popcorn for the three of them—Jack, Brooks, and Daphne—and then he'd make root beer floats.

Even the popcorn was different back then. Instead of the microwave popcorn everyone made these days, Jack had this popcorn maker that actually stirred the kernels as the griddle below heated up. You'd put oil in the griddle, lay out a single layer of unpopped kernels, then turn it on and put on the plastic lid. The stirrers would keep the oil from burning as the corn started to pop. When the plastic lid looked like it was about to explode with the pressure of the popped corn building up inside it, you turned the popper off, turned it upside down, and unlocked the lid. You could eat the popcorn right out of the lid/bowl if you wanted to, but the three of them ate so much of it that Jack always made two or three batches, dumping each one into a huge yellow bowl that could have held enough food to feed a family of ten for an entire week.

Saturday morning cartoons were different, but they held their own memories. She and Brooks—who was four years older than Daff, but still watched cartoons—were under direct orders not to wake Jack unless death was imminent. He worked Friday and Saturday nights in the pre-Giuliani days when New York's streets weren't safe, even for the criminals, after dark. After spending ten hours with pimps, prostitutes, drug dealers, addicts, and thieves, Jack wanted to be left alone with his dreams.

So, Daff and Brooks would get up and make themselves pancakes or cinnamon toast (one of Daff's all-time favorites, with enough butter to clog her arteries for years), and the Saturday morning cartoonfest would begin. As long as they kept the volume low, they could laze around in front of the television for hours uninterrupted by a grumpy adult threatening them with chores.

On this particular Saturday morning, Daff lay in her motel room bed, surrounded by cheap, unfamiliar furniture and wondering why it was that she sought a nomadic existence when the happiest memories of her life were from the period when she'd been able to put down roots for the first time.

Yeah, like she'd told Sam last night, she had a lot of practice walking away. But just because she was good at it, did that mean it was her only choice? What if she was tired of running away? What if she had finally found someone who was worth staying for?

Daphne squinted against the sun's rays trying to accost her from the slit between the motel's thin curtains. She and Sam had ridden back to the Solems' last night in silence. The anger oozing from him was so thick, Daff had been surprised not to find a trail of green slime dripping off him when he'd gotten out of his truck to watch her walk to her rental car.

Or, rather, Daff corrected, to watch her walk away. From him and from all that he had so freely offered to her.

How arrogant of her, to be handed such easy affection and understanding and to throw it back in his face as if it meant nothing. The truth was, it meant a lot to her. She was just too damn afraid to accept it. Too scared that once she'd let Sam into her life, she'd be devastated when he left. And, inevitably, he would leave. People always did, even those you loved so much that the grief nearly killed you when they were gone.

She dashed the tears from her eyes and told herself it was the sun's glare that was making her cry, but even she didn't believe it.

This fucking town was turning her into a crybaby.

She grabbed the remote control and punched the on button.

"It's rabbit hunting season," Daffy Duck sputtered in that too-much-saliva way he had.

Daff somehow felt comforted by the appearance of Saturday morning cartoons. And, silly as it was, since she'd been saddled with the Daffy Duck thing, she'd actually grown to kind of like the silly character.

"Duck," Bugs Bunny countered, leaning on Elmer Fudd's rifle as he chowed down on a carrot.

"Rabbit."

"Rabbit," Bugs agreed.

"Duck," Daffy said, not realizing he'd been hoodwinked.

"Rabbit."

"It's duck, I tell you. Duck, duck, duck." Daffy jumped up and down to emphasize his point.

Bugs shrugged and stepped back to let Elmer Fudd do his thing.

Blam. The shotgun went off. And there was Daffy, his face blackened, his bill on upside down as he got hammered with yet another of life's series of blows.

"I hate you," he spat as he pulled his bill off and righted it, then waddled away, presumably to get cleaned up so he could come back and get his head blown off again another day.

Daff supposed that this was why she liked Daffy Duck so much. Bugs never got hurt, never lost a fight, so it was easy for him to keep coming back. But Daffy? He was the one with courage. He *knew* the odds were not in his favor, knew that chances were he was going to get his bill blown off every time he had to face the enemy. Still, he did it anyway.

So maybe . . . maybe he *was* a superhero after all.

Daphne sniffled and turned off the TV. Jesus, she was falling apart here.

She wiped her eyes with the back of her hand and then threw back the covers of her bed. She needed to get in the shower and figure out where to go from here.

The way she saw it, it was time to move on. She'd presented the evidence that Keith's death wasn't as cut and dried as it may seem to the two people who a) had clout in this town to make the detectives pay attention and b) had a vested interest in knowing the truth about how Keith had died. If the Solems chose to believe Keith's death was a suicide, then what concern was it of hers? Nobody was going to pay her to investigate the matter. She should just let it be.

Yeah. Right after her shower, she'd check into flights to Atlanta.

Daff grabbed a clean pair of underwear out of her duffel bag and headed into the four-by-four room that served as the motel's bathroom, but took a detour past the nightstand when her cell phone rang. She glanced down at the caller ID display. She didn't recognize the number, but it began with the local area code.

Which meant it was either a telemarketer based in Naples—not likely—or something that had to do with Keith Melman or the Solems.

Okay. So after this call, she'd check into flights to Atlanta.

"Hello," she answered, pressing the phone to her ear.

"Is this Daphne Donovan?" a woman asked.

Daff didn't recognize the voice, which wasn't surprising. She didn't exactly have a lot of close friends here in Naples. "Yes," she said, and then sat down on the bed, laying her white cotton panties on the bedspread beside her.

"This is Nicole. Nicole Solem." The woman on the other end of the line coughed. It sounded as if she were holding the phone away from her mouth when she continued, "I'm sorry. I woke up with a bit of a cold this morning."

Daphne didn't know what to say to that, so she just kept silent. Yesterday, this woman had tried to kill her, and today she was apologizing for sneezing in her ear?

"Look, I wanted to apologize for last night. I . . . I don't know what came over me. Keith's . . . death . . ." She seemed to be floundering for the right words before summing it up by saying, "I've just never had to deal with anything like this."

Recalling her own frantic rage on 9/11, Daff could understand how finding out her boyfriend was dead and then having some stranger show up with baby toys and the accusation that Keith had been murdered might have thrown Nicole for a loop. "Grief makes people do strange things," she said.

"Yes, it does. I hope you'll forgive me."

Alone in her motel room, Daff shrugged. Sure. What was a little attempted murder between friends? She cleared her throat. "Of course."

"Good. Then that's settled. Now, I'd like to ask you a favor."

"A favor?" Daff repeated.

"Yes. It has to do with what you were saying yesterday. Now that I've had some time to think about it, I believe you may be right. I don't want to go to the police without having a few more facts, so I wondered if you wouldn't mind meeting me at Keith's house this afternoon. Say around two? I could use your help in looking for clues."

Daphne pulled the phone away from her ear and looked at it as if it had just sprouted legs and started to dance. "Um," she said.

"I'll pay you, of course." Nicole sweetened the pot.

Daff opened her mouth to say no, to tell Nicole that she appreciated the offer but that she was on her way back to Atlanta on the next flight out. Keith Melman's death was none of her business. It was a police matter. As Sam had said yesterday, she didn't want to get involved, didn't want to care about Keith or Nicole or their unborn child, and she certainly didn't want to risk running into Sam again.

"Two o'clock is fine." She heard herself say the words and actually gaped at her own reflection in the mirror hanging above the bed. No. She had *not* just agreed to meet with the woman who'd used her for target practice last night. No way was she that stupid.

Or was she?

"Great. Look, if I don't answer the doorbell, just come on in. I've got to meet with a contractor about getting the back door fixed so I may be outside and won't hear you knock."

As Daff stepped into the shower a few minutes later, she couldn't recall what her response had been. All she could remember was digging herself deeper into this mess when all she really wanted was to give up and go home.

Right.

"Okay. So after you meet with your dead client's girlfriend, then you can check into flights to Atlanta," she muttered as the warm shower rained down on her back.

GETTING into Keith's house was easy since Jenna had a key.

She smiled as she surreptitiously scanned the neighborhood, looking for anyone who might be watching. As she had the first time she'd come here, she'd parked in a public place and jogged back to Keith's neighborhood, not wanting to leave a car where some nosy neighbor might note the make and model or take down the license plate number.

Satisfied that she wasn't being watched, Jenna casually jogged to the front door and inserted the first key that looked like it belonged to a door into the brass lock. When it didn't fit, she tried the next, her smile widening when it easily slid into place and unlocked the deadbolt with a satisfying thunk.

She checked for a second lock, but didn't find anything other than the deadbolt. She didn't want to risk opening the door for fear that the remote control on Nicole's keychain wouldn't work on Keith's security system. If the system were armed, the alarm would go off before Daphne Donovan arrived, and the police might arrive before the private investigator showed up for her supposed meeting with Nicole Solem.

Jenna figured that even if Ms. Donovan opened Keith's

door to the shrieking alarm, it would already be too late. As soon as the investigator pulled into Keith's driveway, Jenna would be on the phone to the police. And if Nathan had done as promised and asked them to be on guard, they'd be primed to hurry to the scene of an attempted break-in.

She pocketed the heavy keys and turned to dash back out onto the sidewalk, just your average jogger on her daily run. Her gaze scanned the cul-de-sac as she felt a flutter of unease in her gut. Call it a sixth sense or intuition or whatever, but Jenna had the feeling she had been spotted.

She lowered her head and ran down the street toward the stop sign at the intersection, forcing her feet not to slow when a red Mustang turned into the cul-de-sac. Jenna glanced at her watch. Eight minutes till two.

Ms. Donovan was early.

She pulled her cell phone from her pocket and crossed the street. Using a prepaid calling card so the call couldn't be traced, she dialed the number for the Naples police.

"What is the nature of your emergency?" the operator asked.

"I'd like to report a break-in. My neighbor died two days ago and there's a strange woman going into his house."

The operator asked for the address and then asked her name. "Allison Posner. I'm just across the street." Jenna believed in doing her homework, and coming up with the name and telephone number of one of Keith's stay-at-home neighbors had been easy. All she'd had to do was to drive by earlier and make a note of the children playing out in the yards. Then she went on the Internet and matched the addresses with phone numbers. Surfing through the county's real estate records to figure out who owned the homes at each address was easy. Even if one spouse didn't contribute financially to the purchase of the home, both were typically listed on the paperwork.

When she'd spied Allison Posner out getting her mail half

an hour ago, Jenna figured she'd use her name and phone number if the police asked for contact information. She knew, however, that if they caught the intruder Mrs. Posner had called about, there would be no need to contact her.

And Jenna intended for Daphne Donovan to get caught.

She choked back a smile as the first police car sped by. Since this was the only road leading into and out of Keith Melman's neighborhood, Jenna would be able to tell if Ms. Donovan somehow managed to escape. She had slowed to a walk, not wanting to leave until she saw the private investigator handcuffed in the back of a cop car. Jenna didn't know how long it would take, so she meandered along the sidewalk, Nicole's keys jingling in her pocket with every step.

With a snort, she recalled how close she had come to getting caught with them last night. When Nathan had asked, "What are you doing with this?" she'd been certain he'd seen her holding onto his daughter's keys. Instead, he'd picked up the perfume Jahia al-Sayed had given to Nicole. It had been sitting on the table next to Jenna's purse and she'd absently slipped it inside after thinking it might come in handy.

"Oh, that stuff made Nicole sick, so I figured I'd take it. I have a couple of nieces who love to get castoff makeup and perfume," she had lied. "Of course, if you think Nicole wants it, I'll leave it here."

Nathan had apologized and told her she was welcome to it, and the evening had ended with him thanking her again for her help. Jenna had hoped for an invitation to come back, but she hadn't received one, so now she was back to trying to come up with a plan to get close to Nicole again without seeming suspicious.

She knew she'd think of something.

Jenna snapped back to reality with a start when a happy-but-tired-looking mother who appeared to be in her early thirties stopped a two-seater, side-by-side stroller in the middle of the sidewalk. She couldn't get past Jenna, who had been walking straight toward her, as if in a trance.

"I'm sorry," Jenna mumbled as she stepped off the sidewalk.

"No, I'm sorry," the woman replied with a laugh. "I should get one of those strollers with one seat behind the other, but every time I put them into one, the girls throw a fit about who gets to sit in front."

For the first time, Jenna glanced down at the children and felt her heart start to pound in her chest. The two girls, obviously twins, were about three years old and looked just like Yvonne and Yvette had at that age. Their impossibly long blond locks were held up into two ponytails by pink butterfly clips. The girls were playing some sort of game together, completely absorbed in their own world as everyone else went about their business.

"They're beautiful," Jenna breathed, one hand unconsciously fluttering to her heart.

"Thank you." The mother beamed as if she had had something to do with it other than having had the good fortune to pick a mate with the right gene pool.

"How old are they?"

"Almost three. Their birthday is tomorrow. We're having a big party. Aren't we girls?" She leaned over the top of the stroller to smile at the twins, who continued playing their game as if they hadn't heard her.

Her girls had often done the same thing, but Jenna never took it personally. She didn't think it was intentional—sometimes the twins were just too wrapped up in each other to notice anyone else.

"Do they like water slides?" Jenna asked. She couldn't seem to take her eyes away from the children. They were just beautiful, so like her own daughters.

"Oh, yes. They're definitely water babies. I had them swimming before they were one. I've never understood those parents who didn't teach their kids to swim right away. Not living here in Florida, where everyone has pools. I would have just died if they'd drowned."

Jenna's hand tightened on her chest. "Yes. You would have," she whispered.

The woman obviously sensed a change in the atmosphere, because her smile dimmed as she eyed Jenna sharply. "Pardon me?" she asked.

Jenna shook her head and forced herself to take a step back, away from woman and her perfect twins. "Nothing. I hope you have a wonderful party tomorrow."

The wheels of the stroller creaked as the woman started down the sidewalk, back toward her happy home, her happy life. Jenna clasped her hands together in front of her to stop them from shaking. God, how she wished she could go back to the time when she'd been happy, too.

She missed her family so much. It was true what the woman said. You just died when your children were gone. No matter what you tried, no matter how much therapy you went through or what you did to try to get on with your life, you could never get back to the person you were before. That old you ceased to exist, and the new you carried around such a burden of grief that it consumed your every waking moment.

Jenna was so lost in her thoughts that it wasn't until she'd passed the entrance to the housing development and started up the busy road toward her car that she realized she had stopped watching for police cars. Chances were that Daphne Donovan was now under arrest, but Jenna had been so preoccupied with the past that the present had ceased to exist.

TWENTY-FIVE

WHEN Daphne pulled into Keith Melman's driveway, she was surprised that Nicole Solem's car wasn't already there. Of course, she could have pulled it into the garage, Daff thought as she pulled her keys out of the ignition of her own car. Or she could be running late.

Or, correction, make that running on time, since Daff was actually a few minutes early.

Figuring she'd try the door in case Nicole had parked in the garage, Daff slammed the door of the Mustang and proceeded up the walkway to Keith's front door.

She rang the bell and waited a moment to see if anyone answered. She peered through the glass, but didn't see anything moving inside the house, so she tried the door. It was unlocked, so she pushed it open and stuck her head inside.

"Nicole?" she called. "It's Daphne Donovan."

When there was no answer, Daff stepped into the front

hallway. Maybe Nicole was out back, like she said she might be.

A quick glance into the family room proved that was not the case, so she headed back toward the front door. Only, as she passed a door to her right, she made the mistake of peering into the room.

Daff pursed her lips. It was Keith's home office. His laptop sat to one side of the desk, and the top of the desk was strewn with loose papers and several manila folders.

The message Keith had left the day he died said he wanted to talk with her about checking out someone who had been on Nathan Solem's yacht the night Sam and Daphne had first met. Before she'd found Keith's gift to Nicole, Daff had assumed that Keith had left that message just so Daphne would be the one to find his body, as a way of telling her from beyond the grave that his death was her fault.

But if Keith had not committed suicide—if he'd been murdered, instead—then that would mean he'd been serious about having her take on another case. What if it had been Keith's interest in this person that had put him in the killer's crosshairs? If so, then knowing the identity of the person Keith wanted tailed might help lead Daff to his killer.

She glanced at the front door to make sure Nicole wasn't heading down the walkway. Then she stepped into Keith's office and hurriedly rifled through the papers on his desk. Pushing aside what appeared to be a personal bank statement, she flipped through some sort of credit report for a company called Jackson Ventures, LLC. Since that name didn't mean anything to her, she moved it out of the way and kept digging.

Daphne hit the jackpot just as she heard the front door creak open. There, on the top of one of the piles of paper on Keith's desk, was a yellow Post-it with her name written on it. The Post-it was stuck to a stapled report about five pages long.

Daff grabbed the report, quickly rolled it up, and shoved it into her purse. Nicole may be here to apologize, but Daff wasn't going to chance her having another meltdown and ordering her out of the house.

"I'm in here," Daphne called as she turned around, expecting to hear the tap of Nicole's high heels on the tiled hallway.

Instead, she was greeted by the clomp of heavy boots right before a uniformed police officer struck the classic shooter's pose in the doorway, his 9mm aimed at her chest as he commanded, "Put your hands behind your head and slowly turn around. You're under arrest."

Daff sighed and did as she was told.

Looked like there was one more thing she was going to have to do before she could check into flights to Atlanta: get out of jail.

I'LL *never have another child.*

Jenna Marisol wiped away the tears that had dripped onto the framed picture of her daughters that was balanced on her lap. She sat at the edge of the indoor side of her indoor/outdoor swimming pool, her bare feet dangling in the heated water. Outside, the comfortable day had turned to cool night as Jenna sat on the other side of the six-inch wall of Plexiglas and thought about what she had lost.

Seeing those twins today, the girls who looked so much like her own babies, had nearly ripped out her heart.

She didn't understand how could it be that the evil ones who manipulated stock prices and ruined others' lives while feathering their own nests could enjoy happiness when their actions caused unthinkable pain to others.

Two more tears dropped from Jenna's eyes and splattered onto the smiling faces of Yvonne and Yvette.

Her babies. They looked so happy. So innocent.

The photo had been taken at Christmas, the year before their death. They wore matching red velvet dresses with green ribbons in their hair. They looked exactly alike, but Jenna had always been able to tell them apart. Yvette had a mischievous glint in her eyes as she grinned into the camera, while Yvonne's smile was more solemn and pure. Yvette had always had more of a devilish streak than her older sister, who had been born less than five minutes before Yvette but who had exhibited the classic take-charge attitude of an older sibling.

They had been her entire life.

Nicole's pregnancy only drove home the fact that Jenna would never again experience the miracle of childbirth. She'd never again hold a squalling infant, still warm and pink from the womb; never marvel at the tiny perfection of each finger and toe or feel the wonder that this new life had come from her.

Conceiving hadn't been easy for her. She and Aaron had tried for years to become pregnant, and with each passing month, it seemed to become more of a chore than the month before. And, of course, it had seemed that everyone around her was pregnant at that time, which only made Jenna feel even more inadequate and hopeless.

Even worse were the supposed "remedies" that were offered by well-meaning friends and even strangers Jenna would meet at her OB-GYN's office.

Douche with green tea before you have sex. Wear a jade rabbit around your neck. Lie with your hips elevated so no sperm will escape after Aaron's orgasm.

Near the end, Jenna had gotten so desperate that she'd tried every one. In a roundabout way, they had actually worked. Not because of any magical healing properties in anything she'd tried, but because one night after Aaron had come home and found her bathing in a tub full of warm milk (yet another tip from a well-meaning friend), she'd finally realized how utterly ridiculous she had become.

That was the night she and Aaron had really talked about how desperately she wanted children. She had fallen in love with her husband all over again when he had cradled her face in his hands and said, "Don't worry, Jenna. Your babies are out there waiting for you. I just know it."

With Aaron's reassurances shoring up her flagging confidence, Jenna had finally been able to relax. And when that hadn't worked, they went in for fertility testing and learned that Jenna couldn't conceive because Aaron wasn't producing enough healthy sperm.

That's when Jenna discovered the lengths her husband would go to in order to make her happy.

At first, when her doctor had proposed that Jenna be inseminated with sperm from an anonymous donor, Jenna had balked at how Aaron might take the suggestion. Would he somehow feel like less of a man if his wife was impregnated using another man's sperm? Would he love her child anyway, even knowing that, biologically, it wasn't his? But even with her concerns about Aaron's feelings, she had to try. Artificial insemination was her best hope at getting pregnant.

When Jenna had broached the subject, Aaron had gone pale and retreated into himself for days. As Jenna had feared, her husband looked at his inability to procreate as a sign that he was inadequate as a man.

After days of feeling as if she were living with a shadow of her former husband, Aaron had come to her in bed one night and told her to go ahead with the procedure. Jenna knew it wasn't easy for him to accept this solution, and she loved him even more for putting her needs ahead of his ego.

He had even seemed happy when she conceived after the very first insemination attempt.

Jenna closed her eyes and hugged the photo of her girls tightly to her chest. God, she missed them so much.

The corners of the frame dug into her upper arms as she hugged it to her, wishing it were the girls' soft bodies that she was holding instead. She inhaled deeply and could almost smell the sweetness of the shampoo they used every night to wash their long honey-wheat colored hair. She remembered everything about them—from their smell to their smiles, their favorite foods, how they both loved kittens but were a bit put off by dogs, the way they giggled, and how they were each other's best friend.

And these two miracles had come into the world because of her. Jenna had always felt a sort of wonder in that. She had put her mind and heart into getting pregnant, and in the end she had learned that when you tried hard enough, there was always a solution to any problem.

Which was why, she thought as she dangled her toes in her swimming pool and felt a wave of emptiness wash over her again, she would never give up. She would figure out a way to avenge the death of her children if it was the last thing she ever did.

TWENTY-SIX

"JUST do me a favor and keep her away from the Solems."

Daphne was tempted to roll her eyes at the man standing next to Sam, but she resisted the urge and concentrated on neatly signing her name on the property release form instead. She slid the signed form back to the desk sergeant, who gave her a manila envelope that contained her belongings in exchange.

She opened her bag to make sure the report she'd taken from Keith's office was still inside. Not that the cops would have had any reason to confiscate it, but she had to check. After seeing the paper stuffed amidst her sunglasses, cell phone, and pack of chewing gum, she nodded, satisfied. Then she turned to Sam, gave a phony smile to the police chief, and said, "Am I free to go?"

"If she gets into trouble, I'm holding you responsible," the officer said to Sam, completely ignoring Daphne.

"Understood." Sam completely ignored her, too.

"What is this, the 1950s?" Daff muttered under her breath. Like she was just some silly girl who was too simpleminded to be held accountable for her own actions.

Sam shot her an empty look that was full of meaning and Daff clamped her teeth shut. He had done her a huge favor by convincing the police that this was all a mistake.

So Daff did her best to look meek and harmless as Sam and the police chief finished up their small talk. When the chief finally waved good-bye, Sam put his hand against the small of Daphne's back and ushered her out into the cool evening. It had been six hours since she was supposed to have met Nicole Solem at Keith's house—four of which she'd spent in an interrogation room insisting that Nicole had told her to make herself at home. Nicole, of course, denied Daphne's claim.

It was obvious to Daff that Nicole Solem had set her up, and she knew that without Sam's intervention, she'd still be in jail right now.

"Thank you," she said as Sam unlocked the passenger door of his truck and held it open for her. "I mean, for getting me out of there," she amended, lest he think she was merely thanking him for the ride.

Sam closed the door in answer, remaining silent as he walked around the hood of the truck to the driver's-side door.

"You're welcome, Daphne. Any time you need someone to bail your ass out of jail, you just give me a call." She did a lousy job of mimicking Sam's voice.

Sam gave her another one of those looks before pulling out of the police station parking lot.

Daphne sighed loudly and rolled down her window. She was at a loss as to where to go from here. Calling Sam had seemed a good idea two hours ago when the cops made it clear they weren't buying her story. And Sam had performed some sort of miracle in getting them to release her. But now what?

For starters, it might be a good time to drop the smartass attitude, her conscience suggested in that superior way it had of talking to her.

Wearily, she rested her head against the palm of her hand. Yeah. That wasn't a bad idea.

"I'm not leaving Naples," she announced. "You were right. I can't just abandon this case."

"And what about us, Daphne? Will you abandon our relationship when things get tough?" Sam asked, a muscle in his jaw twitching.

"No, I—"

"You think I'm just some guy you can call to bail you out of jail or have sex with whenever the whim strikes?" he interrupted before she could answer. "You've done everything you could to push me away. Well, congratulations, it worked."

Daff shivered at the coldness in Sam's voice. Her first instinct was to withdraw, to say, "To hell with it," and let him take her back to her motel and never see him again. It would be so much easier, so much less emotionally messy, that way. And with anyone else, she would have done it.

But she couldn't walk away from Sam. As much as the cowardly part of her—the part that feared rejection worse than it feared death—wanted her to give up, she couldn't. She needed him too much.

Daphne unbuckled her seatbelt and slid across the seat of Sam's truck until their thighs were touching. "Okay, I deserve that. What if I . . ." she began, but she didn't know what it was she should offer. She swallowed and tried again. "Look, I know that if I asked your mother, she'd probably tell me the best way to get you back would be to let you go. You know, that whole 'if you love something, set it free' crap. But I'm not into rules, and I'm not playing games here.

I realize I'm not the easiest person to get to know. I have . . . issues. But I'm doing the best I can, and I . . . I really like you, Sam. A lot.

"The truth is, I'm scared to death here," she admitted, knowing the only chance she had of getting Sam back by being honest, truly honest, with him. And with herself

"You make me feel—" *God, was she really going to tell him this?* What if he laughed?

Daff closed her eyes so she wouldn't have to see Sam's reflection mocking her when she continued. "Hopeful. You make me feel hopeful. About the future. About *my* future. I'm not used to allowing myself that luxury. I mean, what happens when everything turns to shit? When you realize I'm not the woman you thought I was?" She clenched her teeth against the all-too-familiar feeling of hot tears welling in her eyes, and then whispered the question she feared the most. "How will I cope when you leave me?"

Sam remained silent for so long that Daphne knew her instincts had been wrong. Obviously, opening a vein and bleeding all over him was not the way to Sam's heart.

She took a deep, shuddering breath and was about to scoot back over to the window when Sam's softly uttered words stopped her.

"Well. Fuck me," he said, sounding nonplussed.

Daphne let out the breath she'd been holding and attempted a wobbly smile. "If that's what it takes to win you back . . ."

She put a hand high up on Sam's thigh. Then she looked up as he pulled the truck into a parking lot and killed the engine, surprised to find that they were at the yacht club and not at her motel.

"Come on," Sam ordered gruffly as he opened his door and tugged at her hand to pull her out behind him. He nodded to the security guard as they passed through the gate, but didn't say anything more to her until they were standing on the dock outside of Nathan Solem's yacht.

"Are you sure I should be here? I don't want to get you in trouble with your boss," Daff said.

"I'll take my chances." Sam hopped onboard the yacht and turned to hold a hand out to her.

Daphne placed her palm on top of his, expecting him to pull her aboard. Instead, they stood there like that for a long moment—their hands touching, him on the water and her on land, separated only by the dark Gulf between them.

Then, without any effort at all, Sam leaned forward, scooped her up in his arms, brought her close to his heart, and said, "You're not the woman I thought you were, Daphne. You're more."

IT was the perfume that did it.

Jenna shot bolt upright in bed, staring into the darkness as her subconscious served up the solution she'd been seeking for days.

Jahia al-Sayed believed that the perfume she was wearing would help her keep her baby to term. So why not exploit the woman's fears to further Jenna's cause?

Revenge could be had for the cost of an ordinary perfume atomizer. No doubt security at the CEO summit would be tight, but a perfume bottle carried in a woman's purse wouldn't set off any metal detectors or other alarms. She could store the anthrax spores in the pump and put a harmless scented mixture in the bottle, and with one spray, tens of thousands of spores would be released into the air.

She only needed a small amount—she wanted to make certain the atomizer would be empty by the time the CEO summit was over so no one outside the event would be harmed.

And although Nicole, with her sensitivity to fragrance,

wouldn't be the one spreading the disease, there would be enough anthrax in the air to kill her . . . and her unborn child.

Jenna's mind raced as she pushed herself up out of bed and padded down the hall toward the kitchen in her bare feet.

Yes. This could work.

She sat down at the kitchen table and began scribbling notes about the supplies she would need. The best thing was that this plan, if she could pull it off, meant that further contact with Nicole was unnecessary. She would be even further removed from the woman's death than she would have been before.

TWENTY-SEVEN

BY Sunday evening, Daphne knew the amount of the al-Sayeds' mortgage, where they took their cars to have them repaired, the name of their favorite Thai restaurant, and that they'd recently purchased a five-thousand-dollar security system from All Secure Home Services. She knew that they were leasing their brand-new Mercedes 560 SL. She knew that they were higher-than-average energy users. She knew that it cost $56.48 to fill up their gas tank, that they paid forty dollars a week to have their lawn mowed, and that they had just had their spring landscaping done.

But what she didn't know—even after twelve hours of running down every item on the five-page list of banking transactions—was why Keith Melman had wanted her to see this report.

What was she missing?

Daff stared at the computer screen in front of her as if it might suddenly tell her the answer.

Of course, it remained silent. Technology only helped when you knew what to look for.

"Nothing?" Sam asked as he came up behind her and put his hands on her shoulders.

She leaned back into his touch. "Nope. How about you?"

While she'd been analyzing each transaction—tracing it to its source and then researching every company al-Sayed had funded—Sam had been busy doing background checks on the employees hired to make the upcoming weekend's CEO summit run smoothly. She'd raised her eyebrows at some of his sources, sources most private citizens were not allowed to access, but Sam had just grinned at her and shrugged.

Apparently it was true that everyone had a price.

"Nothing major," Sam answered. "Got a few people arrested for possession of marijuana and the like who lied about it on their employment applications, but no one with ties to antigovernment or terrorist organizations."

"Me, neither," Daphne said, shaking her head with frustration. "I just don't get it. Why did Keith want me to see this if there's nothing here?"

"Have you tried looking for patterns? Like frequent cash withdrawals or . . . I don't know."

"I've analyzed everything. I looked for suspicious time stamps—like restaurant bills that were paid at 3 A.M.—or transactions that were logistically impossible, like a lawn service in Chicago when all the companies here are local. Either I need more data in order to spot a trend or—" Daff waved away the rest of the sentence, but Sam understood what she meant. The alternative was, there was no trend to spot. It was possible that Keith had been paranoid because he'd overheard an out-of-context snippet of conversation from a Middle Eastern man and leaped to the conclusion that al-Sayed must be a terrorist.

But then how did that help explain Keith's murder?

The answer was simple. It didn't. Right now, Adnan al-Sayed was the only lead Daphne had in this case, and she wasn't going to give up on it. Maybe al-Sayed had nothing to do with Keith's death, but maybe he did.

All Daff knew was that she wasn't going to give up. Not now.

Not ever.

Absently, she rubbed her shoulders against Sam's stomach. Then she picked up the report, flipped through it once more, and said, "I'll just have to go through it again."

My first and second pregnancies were fraught with medical problems. Each time, I was confined to bed rest during the last twelve weeks. My doctor said it was likely that I would be unable to carry a third baby to term. Then a friend told me about Stork Scent. I began using your product a month before my husband and I started trying to conceive and faithfully followed the directions all throughout my third pregnancy. My doctor and I were both amazed with the results! I had more energy. I barely had a day of morning sickness. The best thing, though, was that I delivered Zachary Allen Thomas at thirty-eight weeks—a happy, healthy baby boy. And I owe it all to Stork Scent.

Sincerely,
Barbara Thomas

Jenna read the fake letter over one more time and then smiled. Perfect. Just the right amount of gushing, without being too over the top. She added a photo of a newborn baby boy lying in his mother's arms that she'd plucked off the Internet earlier.

Barbara and Little Zachary. How sweet.

The Stork Scent website she had built using the templates provided by the domain registration company looked every bit as professional as other, legitimate companies she'd seen on the web. The best thing was, the templates even provided a way for her to set up an e-commerce site, meaning she could take orders and receive credit card payments online.

She had already created a brochure about Stork Scent perfume and its purported benefits and—using latex gloves so there would be no fingerprints—had addressed it to Jahia al-Sayed and dropped it off outside the main post office in Naples. Mrs. al-Sayed would get the brochure in the mail tomorrow.

She hit a button to upload the new content to her site and then put a hand to her heart in surprise when her telephone rang.

Who in the world would be calling her?

Probably some telemarketer.

She glanced at the caller ID and felt a faint stirring of unease. Instead of the usual "Unknown Name/Unknown Number" that displayed when a telemarketer called, it read, "Melman, K."

Dead men don't make telephone calls, she reminded herself as her finger hesitated over the talk button. The phone rang again and she made herself answer.

"Hello," she said.

"Hi, Jenna. It's Nicole. Nicole Solem."

Jenna's shoulders slumped with relief. "Hi. Um, what can I do for you?" she asked, wondering how the young woman had gotten her unlisted number.

"I'm sorry to bother you," Nicole began, and it became obvious to Jenna that the younger woman was crying. "I was just . . . leaving Keith's funeral. It's so hard to believe he's gone."

"I know it is," Jenna crooned soothingly, only half-listening as she began uploading content for another web-page onto the Stork Scent site—this one with scientific information to back up the product's claims.

"I wondered . . ." Nicole's voice trailed off and Jenna heard the faint sound of sniffling before she continued. "Would you mind if I stopped by? None of my friends know what it's like to lose someone like this. But you seem to understand. I know it's an imposition, but I would appreciate it. I could really use the company."

Jenna scowled at her computer screen. Yes, it was an imposition, but what could she do? If she said no, Nicole might start to wonder why she was being rude, and Jenna wasn't confident enough that her perfume plan would work to blow off a potential Plan B.

"Um, sure. Come on over," Jenna said, quickly running an eye over the room to see what she'd have to hide before she let Nicole in. The cabinet where she had been working on a method to aerosolize the anthrax would have to go into the garage, and she'd have to make certain her supplies were put away.

Holding the cordless against her ear, she walked to the sink to begin putting things away.

"Thank you so much," Nicole said. "I was hoping you'd say that. I'm right outside. I hope you don't mind, but Lillian Bryson gave me your address," she admitted sheepishly.

Jenna nearly dropped the phone in the sink.

No! She needed time to get her things hidden.

"I'll be there in just a minute. I . . . have to get dressed," Jenna said, desperately searching for a reason why she couldn't come right to the door. "I was . . . in the shower when you called."

"Oh, okay. I'll just wait out here then," Nicole said.

Jenna hung up and hurried over to the portable cabinet where she did most of her work. It was heavy, and she struggled to push it over the metal strip on the floor that separated the kitchen from the garage without having it topple over.

When that was done she raced back to the kitchen, wrapped all of her tools in a dishtowel and stuffed them into the cupboard next to the sink.

As she headed toward the front door, she glanced around the living room to see if she'd left anything suspicious lying on the coffee table or one of the white leather chairs that faced the ornamental fireplace in the center of the room. She closed the doors to every room as she passed, with the exception of the small parlor bath near the front of the house. She never used that bathroom, so she was sure it was free of clutter. And since Nicole was pregnant, it was highly likely she'd feel the need to pee at least once during her visit.

Jenna paused in the foyer and turned to give the house one final inspection before opening the front door.

Nicole Solem's blue convertible sat in the driveway, as clean and shiny as if it were still sitting on the dealer's lot. Jenna wondered absently if there was someone on Nicole's father's staff who was responsible for keeping their vehicles looking so perfect.

Probably.

"Sorry to keep you waiting," she called, and Nicole unfurled herself from where she had been leaning against the passenger side of the car.

"Oh, no. Don't apologize. I'm sorry for intruding."

As the blonde approached, Jenna saw tear tracks etched down her cheeks. She clutched a cell phone tightly to her chest, which reminded Jenna of the way Yvette had held her favorite stuffed dog whenever she'd been upset.

Jenna assumed the phone had been Keith's.

"Come on in." Jenna held open the front door and stepped back to let the younger woman pass. As Nicole stepped into the foyer, Jenna realized that she was holding a plastic grocery bag.

"I brought some wine," Nicole said, offering up the bag. "I know I shouldn't have any being pregnant and all, but I figured one small glass wouldn't hurt."

Jenna frowned. Looked like this was going to be a long visit.

Obviously noticing her expression, Nicole frowned, too. "Oh, I'm sorry. I didn't ask if you drank. You don't have to open it. I just thought . . ." At a loss for what to say, she stopped and simply waved one neatly manicured hand in the air.

"It's fine. I was just wondering if I'd gotten around to unpacking the wineglasses or not," Jenna lied. She hadn't brought anything to Naples that she didn't plan to leave here, and she'd been eating off of paper plates and drinking out of plastic cups since she moved in.

"Do you want me to help you look for them? I don't mind helping you unpack," Nicole offered.

Jenna smiled and shook her head. "No, that's all right. I'm sure we'll be fine with plain cups. Why don't you take a seat and I'll go open this up and pour us a couple of glasses."

Nicole obediently stopped near one of the leather chairs and let her purse slide to the floor. She sank down into the seat and closed her eyes, still clutching the cell phone in one hand. Jenna left her like that, continuing on into the kitchen.

She set the oversized bottle of wine on the counter and then pursed her lips. Did she even have a corkscrew?

She'd never been a big drinker, and now that she thought about it, she couldn't recall having bought a bottle of wine since coming to Naples.

She pulled open one drawer and then another.

Nothing. Not even a small paring knife she could use to try to pry the cork out with.

She forced herself not the slam the drawers shut in frustration. There had to be *something* she could use to get the damn bottle open.

Think, Jenna, think.

Hadn't she seen a small screwdriver in the garage, something that must have been left by the former tenant or the contractor who'd made the modifications she'd requested to the house before she moved in?

Jenna glanced from the entryway of the kitchen to the garage door and back. One minute. Sixty seconds was all she needed to run in, grab the screwdriver, and get back inside. She heard a creaking sound from the living room, and then silence. Nicole had probably just shifted in her seat.

Jenna made a dash for it. Unless it had been transformed into a character from some Disney movie and suddenly sprouted legs, the screwdriver should be sitting on the built-in counter to her left, about ten feet from the garage door. She pushed open the door, sprinted toward the cabinet, grabbed the tool, and ran back inside.

And stopped short in the doorway, the door open behind her and the glass cabinet in plain view, when she came face to face with Nicole Solem.

"I came in to see if you needed any help," Nicole said and then paused, cocking her head curiously before asking, "Hey, what's that?"

TWENTY-EIGHT

JENNA slowly closed the garage door behind her. What had Nicole seen? The cabinet in the garage? A stray test tube that she'd overlooked on the counter? Perhaps another piece of equipment she'd inadvertently left lying around?

Was she going to have to make a drastic change of plans? Perhaps kill Nicole right here, right now? If so, the trail back to her would be impossible to miss. The last phone call on Nicole's boyfriend's cell phone—no, make that Nicole's *dead* boyfriend's cell phone—was to Jenna's home phone. She would be the first person the police would suspect. And it wouldn't take long for them to trace Jenna Marisol back to Jenna Richardson, wife of Aaron Richardson, who had been laid off from Geon Enterprises the day he killed his twin daughters and then took his own life.

The beauty of Jenna's plan so far was that no one would even look twice at her background. A surface check of her name and social security number would reveal only that she had worked at a university in Maryland until four years ago and that she'd recently moved from Dallas to Naples, Florida. As long as there was no reason to dig any deeper, no one would suspect that she had a motive to kill Nicole Solem and her unborn child.

But if Jenna had to throw away her own future in order to get revenge for the murder of her family, then that's what she would have to do. She had enough cash in the house to book herself a flight to Mexico. From there, it would be easy enough to simply disappear.

Once Nathan Solem had been punished, it didn't matter what happened to her.

"What's what?" she asked softly and took a step toward Nicole, turning the screwdriver so that its metal end stuck out like a blade.

"This." Nicole waved toward the laptop computer Jenna had left sitting open on the table. "There's a perfume that keeps pregnant women from miscarrying? I've never heard about such a thing," she said.

Jenna let her hand drop to her side as she tried to think up a plausible lie. She decided upon a mixture of falsehood and the truth.

"Oh," she answered breezily, twisting the screwdriver into the cork. "When Jahia al-Sayed mentioned that the perfume she uses is supposed to be good for her baby, I thought it was just an old wives' tale. So I called an old friend of mine who'd had trouble keeping a baby to term. She sent me the link to this website. She miscarried three times before someone told her about this product, and of course, she was skeptical at first," Jenna added as she pulled two red plastic cups out of the cupboard and poured small amounts of wine for both Nicole and herself.

"She warned me that it was expensive, but she was so desperate to have a baby that she tried it. She's got four kids now." Jenna handed Nicole a glass and hoped the young woman wouldn't reach out and click the second browser window, which contained the program Jenna had been using to upload content to the site.

"But using perfume to keep from miscarrying? That sounds like voodoo to me," Nicole said, taking a small sip of her wine.

Jenna shrugged and nonchalantly reached out to close the top of her computer. "I know. I'm not saying that I believe in that sort of thing. There are always scams out there that target people who are desperate. It could just be a coincidence that it worked for my friend."

"Yes, that's true." Nicole said she headed back toward the living room.

They passed an hour talking about nothing before Nicole glanced at her watch, frowning slightly when she noticed the time. "I can't believe it's this late," she murmured. "I'm sorry for taking so much of your time."

When Nicole stood, Jenna noticed that she'd released her death grip on Keith's cell phone. After Aaron and the girls had died, Jenna had done the same thing—holding onto their things as if it would help her maintain a connection to them. For the first year, it had even seemed to work . . .

Jenna followed Nicole to the door and gave her a hug when that seemed like the appropriate thing to do. "You take care of yourself," she said. "You've got to think of the baby, as well as yourself."

Nicole straightened her shoulders and drew in a deep breath. "Yes. I know. You're right. You know . . ." She hesitated and then seemed to make up her mind about something. "Maybe you could write down that website address for me? I'm starting to understand how Mrs. al-Sayed must feel. When you love someone, you'll resort to just about anything not to lose them."

Jenna wondered if Nicole even realized that she had

placed one hand protectively on her womb as she spoke. Probably not.

She also wondered then whether Nicole had intentionally become pregnant as a way to bind Keith to her, or if she were simply starting to feel those first pangs of maternal love—a love so strong that one who had not borne a child herself could never understand.

Although, Jenna thought as she went to print off a copy of the page she had uploaded onto the phony website, Nicole's insight was surprisingly close to the truth. When you truly loved someone, you *would* resort to just about anything not to lose them.

TWENTY-NINE

"COME on, Keith, what were you trying to tell me?" Daphne paced the bridge of the yacht as if the pounding of her feet might help shake something loose in her brain. The banking transactions Keith had downloaded began three weeks before the party Nathan Solem had thrown and ended the day of Keith's death.

At first, Daff had thought that the beginning date of the report was significant, but then she'd checked the power company's records and discovered that the al-Sayeds had moved to Naples on that date. Or, at least, that was the date the account at the power company had been transferred into their name.

The bottom line was, if there was something suspicious in the report that Keith had given her, she couldn't find it. Even after tracing every lead back to its source.

But maybe it wasn't the report itself that was the clue.

Perhaps Keith had only downloaded the information to give Daphne somewhere to start her investigation, sensing that something was amiss, but not knowing anything concrete at the time of his death. Maybe he was getting close to something, and that's why al-Sayed had had him murdered.

Daff scratched her chin with the end of her pen. The problem was, even using all the resources at Sam's disposal, she hadn't been able to come up with anything more on al-Sayed. She needed another source, one with even better access to information than Nathan Solem and his millions could acquire.

She picked up her cell phone and hesitated with her fingers over the keys. Even now, all these years later, she knew her old boss's number by heart.

Max Raiker, head of the FBI's anti-terrorist division, was a legend in the Bureau. He was a hard-eyed perfectionist who would nail an agent to the wall if she didn't have all the facts in her case. He was also the one she'd tried to convince to let her go after her terrorist prior to 9/11.

Daphne gulped down a mouthful of water before punching in Raiker's number.

"Raiker," he answered in that same gruff, don't-give-me-any-shit voice she remembered so well.

Daff cleared her throat. "Hello. This is Daphne Donovan. I worked for you back in, um, 2000, 2001."

There was silence on the other end of the line for a moment, and Daphne found herself wiping one damp palm on the knee of her jeans. Telling herself she had nothing to be nervous about, she forced herself to sit up straight.

"Yeah, Donovan. I remember you," Raiker said.

There was something in his voice that Daphne couldn't place, but she didn't have time to analyze it now. She needed Raiker's help. "I'm down in Naples on a private case. A client of mine was murdered right after he asked me to look into something. I've hit a brick wall here and I was wondering if . . . well, if this is something better suited to the Feds. I may be in over my head here." Rule number one, if you want someone in the government to help you, pander to their ego.

Raiker just grunted.

Daphne rubbed the bridge of her nose. She should have known he wouldn't take the bait. Raiker never had been a pushover. Still, she'd push for the Bureau to take over the case as long as it meant Keith's death would be investigated the way it should.

"I think my client's death is tied to a guy named Adnan al-Sayed," Daff persisted. "He and his wife are originally from Saudi Arabia, but they've lived in the States for over a decade. They moved down to Naples less than a month ago. My client, Keith Melman, was al-Sayed's banker."

"What's that name again?" Raiker asked, sounding like he wasn't so bored all of a sudden.

"Keith Mel—"

"No. The other guy," Raiker cut her off impatiently.

"Adnan al-Sayed. He's some sort of real estate developer."

"Could you hold for a minute? I've got another call coming in."

Without waiting for her to answer, Raiker put her on hold. The line buzzed in her ear as if it had gone dead. No Muzak or chipper commercials about what the FBI could do for you played in her ear, just a little white noise to make you wonder if your caller was ever coming back.

Daphne pulled the phone away from her ear and frowned in puzzlement. What the hell had just happened here? One second, Raiker was all, "yeah, yeah, whatever," and the next it was like he'd just gotten a call from the president. Which, of course, he may very well have.

Kind of put her own case into perspective.

She drummed her fingers on the yacht's bridge as she waited for Raiker to come back on the line.

Nineteen and a half minutes later, he did.

"Look, Donovan, I know your heart's in the right place," he began, as if he were just picking up the conversation where they'd left off. He didn't apologize for leaving her on hold, nor did he acknowledge that she'd been sitting there waiting for him for nearly twenty minutes. Obviously, he had assumed that she hadn't hung up.

Arrogant asshole.

". . . but Adnan al-Sayed is not your guy. You stay away from him. Understand?"

"But he may have been involved in the murder of my client," Daphne protested.

"I'm looking at the police report right here. Keith Melman's death has been ruled a suicide by the investigating officer."

Daff blinked with surprise. How the hell had Raiker gotten his hands on Keith Melman's file from the Naples PD? And on such short notice? She shook her head to clear it. It didn't matter how Raiker had obtained the file. What mattered was that he was telling her to just let it go. Didn't he—of all people—understand that she couldn't?

"I think the detective is missing something. I think Melman's death was staged to look like a suicide. I don't believe he took his own life," she insisted.

She heard Raiker sigh. She suspected that he'd meant for her to. "Look, Donovan, I'm telling you to back off. If there's a case here, the FBI will take care of it."

Daff shook her head, but didn't say anything else. What would be the point?

"How about this, I'll make a note of your concern and be sure to let the appropriate people know," he said, as if that might appease her.

Right. The "appropriate people" being Nobody and No One.

She may be persistent, but she wasn't an idiot. Raiker wasn't going to do anything with her lead. The question was, what was *she* going to do about it?

"Donovan?" her former boss asked after a few moments of silence.

Daff grunted in response.

"I would also suggest you don't try taking matters into your own hands. I can assure you, we here at the Bureau know what we're doing."

Not always, Daff wanted to say, but forced herself to bite the words back. There was no point in antagonizing the FBI. She wasn't naïve enough to think that they couldn't make her life a living hell if they chose to.

Then, just as she was about to hang up, Raiker cleared his throat as if he had something more to say.

"By the way, I never got a chance to tell you this, but, uh . . ."

Daff raised her eyebrows. The all-powerful Max Raiker, at a loss for words?

"You were a good agent, Donovan. I was sorry to see you go."

Then the line went dead. Daphne stared blankly out the window as a pelican shot down toward the surface of the water, trying to find dinner.

Why had Raiker said that to her? Why now, after all these years?

Daff shook her head and shoved a lock of hair that had come loose from her ponytail behind her ear. It didn't matter. Raiker was probably just feeding her shit so she'd follow orders like a good little soldier.

No way was she falling into that trap again.

"Any luck?" Sam asked as he came up from below, wiping his hands on a rag.

Daff wrinkled her nose. He smelled like exhaust and had a smear of grease on his left forearm. Obviously, he'd been doing some work on the yacht's engine.

"No. I was told in no uncertain terms to mind my own business."

"Big surprise there," Sam said, absently bending down to place a kiss on her lips.

"You know, it would be so much easier if we lived in a country where you could just have someone arrested based on a hunch," Daff said and sighed exaggeratedly. She didn't really mean that. Well, mostly.

One corner of Sam's mouth quirked up in a half-smile. "So now what?" he asked, leaning back against the brass railing that ran in front of the electronics and crossing his arms over his chest.

"It would be so easy to give up," she admitted. Especially since the last time she'd pushed a case that had seemed like nothing, it had ended so tragically. She thought she'd learned her lesson, but apparently not. Here she was, ready to pick up the battle again, right where she'd left off five years ago.

"Would it?" Sam asked, all traces of amusement gone from his expression as he studied her from a few feet away.

Daff considered the question. Wouldn't it be easier to walk away from this right now? To just say she'd done everything she could have under the circumstances?

No.

Because she hadn't.

The only thing that had kept her teetering on the edge of that cliff after 9/11, the only thing that stopped her from jumping into the bottomless chasm of despair, was that she knew she'd done everything in her power to stop it. She'd tracked down every lead, had carefully built her case and organized the mounting evidence that the terrorist she'd been tracking was set on a path to destruction. If she hadn't truly believed that she'd done her best—no matter that her best hadn't been good enough—she doubted she'd be alive today.

She shook her head. "No. I can't give up," she said. "Keith needs me."

SINCE Keith's report had done nothing but lead her through five pages of dead ends, Daphne decided it was time to go back to the old-fashioned method of catching bad guys—surveillance. It wasn't high-tech and it sure as heck wasn't sexy, but it *was* a surprisingly effective technique for gathering information about what people did and with whom they did it.

Daff was often surprised at what people would do when they didn't know they were being watched.

She'd seen supposed cripples leap out of their wheelchairs and seen hardened criminals cry over beloved pets. She'd also seen a whole lot of people having a whole lot of sex in the most unexpected places.

She didn't expect to see any of that this evening, however. Sitting in the convertible in the driveway a few houses down and across from the al-Sayed's, Daff settled in as comfortably as she could in the driver's seat of her car. She didn't plan to stay here all night. Just a few hours to see if anyone came or went.

For a moment, she wished she were still with the FBI. But then she realized that it wouldn't matter. No judge would give her authorization to tap al-Sayed's phone lines or search his house on the flimsy—okay, make that non-existent—lead she was working.

Daphne crossed her arms over her chest and stared intently at the brightly lit house across the street.

"Come on," she muttered under her breath. "Screw up so I can catch you."

The house remained silent, its doors and windows shut up tightly, its occupants safely ensconced inside.

It was going to be a long night.

Daff almost wished she'd accepted Sam's offer to come with her, but she knew he would have been a distraction. She also knew he was only offering to be nice. Or maybe to get laid.

She coughed to cover her smile.

Yeah, okay. He had winked at her and asked if they could perform "surveillance" in the backseat of her car.

Daphne stifled another smile. What could she say? It was nice to be wanted.

She looked back at the street and yawned. That was another reason she hadn't let Sam come with her. He had to drive to Miami and back tomorrow to pick up some part that he needed for the yacht. He had added performing those background checks to his real job—he didn't need to be hanging out playing spy with her, too.

The most difficult part of surveillance work was trying to stay focused and alert after hours of staring at nothing. Daff found herself nodding off around 1 A.M., and it was her chin bumping against her chest that made her awaken with a start.

Or maybe it was the noise of someone rolling something down the sidewalk a few feet away.

Daphne froze.

A man wearing a pair of green shorts and a frayed gray T-shirt was coming toward her, wheeling a large black garbage can behind him. He was close enough that if he turned his head even slightly to the left, he would see her. And he'd call the police. And she'd get arrested for stalking Keith's customers probably. And this time, Sam's clout with the chief of police probably wouldn't help.

Daff held her breath, hoping the man was as unobservant as most everyone else in the world.

He let go of the trash can as if it were a bowling ball, and grinned a little to himself as it slid to the end of his driveway. Then he turned and walked back up to his house, not even once glancing in the direction of his neighbor's house.

When Daphne heard the front door slam in the otherwise silent night, she released her breath.

That had been too close.

She put her hand on the key in the ignition, intending to start the engine and slink away as quietly as possible, but stopped when she glanced across the street and saw the empty curb next to the al-Sayeds' driveway. They hadn't taken their trash out yet.

She looked up at the still-bright windows on the second floor of their house.

It appeared that the al-Sayeds were night owls.

Daphne looked back at the curb, gnawing on the inside of her cheek as she considered the thought tickling her brain. Technically, it was not illegal to steal someone's trash. Once they'd pushed it to the sidewalk, it was fair game.

Daff wasn't sure, however, if that ruling extended to going onto someone's property and removing their garbage, or if it only applied once the can had been set out where the owner of said garbage could reasonably expect it would be removed.

Since she didn't exactly have a Supreme Court justice on speed dial, she was going to have to make her own ruling. That was the beauty of being your own judge and jury—you always decided in favor of yourself.

Daff picked up her cell phone and grimaced for a second when she realized that most men would think she was crazy for what she was about to ask. Most men would tell her to give it up and go to bed.

Fortunately, Sam Bryson was not most men.

And thank God for that, Daphne thought as Sam mumbled a tired "Hello" into the phone.

If he were, he'd have ditched her by now.

Daphne felt a warm glow start to build in her chest and unconsciously rubbed a spot near her sternum, some might say near her heart. "Hey, I'm sorry to wake you," she said softly.

"That's okay. What's up?" It was amazing. He went from groggy to instantly awake at the sound of her voice.

"I need a favor. I've got to pick something up, but it won't fit in my car. I wondered if you could meet me somewhere with your truck."

Sam sounded as if he were cradling the phone between his shoulder and his ear as he answered, "Sure. Where and when?"

Good question. She didn't know this area well, but she thought she recalled that there was a convenience store nearby. She gave Sam the general location and he grunted.

"I'll be there in about five minutes," she said, then paused before continuing. "Oh, and Sam?" she asked.

"Yeah?" His keys jingled and Daff imagined him grabbing them off the nightstand next to the bed as he slipped his worn boat shoes onto his feet.

She smiled. "Would you mind stealing a garbage can on your way?"

THIRTY

JENNA logged onto the Stork Scent website as the administrator and checked the site statistics for her phony perfumery. So far, she had been the only visitor to the site. She supposed that if she were an expert on this stuff, she might be able to figure out how to interpret the statistics better and might even be able to discern the exact location of the computer used to access her site. But she was no expert. All she knew was that there was a site statistic called "Unique Users," and so far, that number was one.

Which meant neither Nicole or Jahia had taken a look at the site.

This would have been so much easier if Jenna could have figured out some other way to infect the attendees of the CEO summit. But without having access to the Solems' house, Jenna just didn't know what else to do. She could hardly hand Nicole an aerosol can filled with anthrax and ask her to spray it around during the party. She had considered simply mailing an anthrax-laden letter to the Solems but discarded the idea. If the letter was opened prior to the party, someone would surely notice the ash in the envelope and would call in the authorities. Nathan's staff had no doubt been cautioned to report anything suspicious in the days leading up to the summit. If the summit were cancelled, Jenna would be back at square one.

This plan, if it worked, would be perfect. With Jahia al-Sayed already having established the pattern of dousing herself with perfume, no one would think twice about seeing her mist herself during the kick-off event. As more anthrax spores were released into the air, they would be cycled and recycled through the Solems' air-handling system. Any woman who was pregnant would pass the infection on to the fetus. By the time the first victim showed signs of illness, the CEOs and their families would already be back in their homes. This geographic dispersion of the illness would make it even more difficult for the medical community to spot a pattern right away. If one attendee in New York came down with flu-like symptoms and so did another in L.A., no one would at first believe the two were related.

It would become evident what was happening once the attendees started dying, but by then it would already be too late.

Like an addict needing a fix, Jenna hit the button to refresh her browser. The unique user statistic still held steady at one, but Jenna didn't lose hope.

At this point, hope was all she had left.

IT would have been so much easier if the al-Sayeds had taken their trash to the curb. If they had, it would be a simple matter of stopping in front of their driveway, hauling the heavy black garbage can up into the bed of Sam's truck, replacing the barely worn receptacle with the one Sam had brought, and then driving away. The switch would be complete in less than sixty seconds.

Daphne plastered her back against the rough stucco wall as she crouched in the shadows near the architecturally acceptable dwelling that hid the al-Sayeds' garbage can from sight.

Daff slunk around the corner of the garbage's mini-home. A decorative wrought iron gate kept the trash can secured in place. She unlatched the gate and pulled it open just far enough to pull the black plastic can out.

Now came the tricky part.

A light was on in a window above and to the left of where Daff was standing. If someone was in that room, they'd easily hear the wheels of the garbage can rolling on the concrete path that led to the driveway and might come outside to check it out. But in order to avoid the noise, Daff would have to roll the garbage can into the grass, which would make her visible from the window if anyone happened to look outside.

She decided to take her chances with the path. To minimize the noise, she rolled the garbage can toward the front yard one inch at a time.

When she heard a rustling sound behind her, Daff froze. *Damn. Had she been caught?*

She looked back and sucked in her breath when she saw a face at the window, peering out. It was a man Daff had never seen before. If he turned her way, he'd see her silhouette in the darkness against the lighter concrete path.

Daff's hands clenched the handle of the garbage can. She should let go now and escape to the front of the house where Sam was waiting. But then what? She was out of clues.

So she remained motionless, slowing her breathing as she waited to see if the man at the window would raise the alarm.

Finally, the curtains at the window fell back into place.

With a shudder of relief, Daff resumed her painstaking journey toward the curb.

As she neared the street, she glanced back up at the house to make certain no one was watching from the second-story windows. Sam's truck was already creeping toward her from half a block away. He stopped near the neighbor's driveway and, without a word, slid out of the cab of the truck. The tailgate of the truck had been lowered, and Sam hopped into the bed and motioned for Daff to roll the garbage can closer. Together, they lifted the heavy receptacle into the back of the truck. Then Sam lowered an identical black garbage can to the sidewalk. The plan was that they'd leave this can on the curb to make al-Sayed think that either he'd forgotten that he'd rolled the trash out himself, or that perhaps his wife had taken care of it earlier.

While Sam secured the full garbage can so it wouldn't tip over, Daphne rolled the empty one back to the al-Sayeds' driveway. With that done, she trotted to the truck and hopped up into the cab. She strapped on her seatbelt and pulled the door toward her but didn't close it for fear that the noise of a door slamming would bring curious neighbors to their windows.

She and Sam remained silent as he smoothly put the truck into gear and glided out of the al-Sayeds' neighborhood. He stopped in the parking lot of the convenience store where her car was parked and Daff finally turned to him with an unfamiliar feeling of excitement thrumming in her stomach. She'd forgotten about this—the adrenaline rush you got from working on a case where the stakes were higher than someone ending up in divorce court or losing their job.

Over the years, she'd told herself she didn't want that rush anymore. The problem was, she had nothing to replace it, so her life had ended up feeling empty.

Of course, the high she was on now was going to fade

pretty quickly once she got down to the task of pawing through the al-Sayeds' trash. Daphne grimaced at the thought. It was an interesting exercise to delve into what others threw away, but it sure wasn't sexy.

As she pushed open the door of the truck, her mind was already focused on the supplies she needed: trash bags to line the floor; rubber gloves because no way was she touching someone else's garbage without them; an assortment of paper and plastic bags to hold anything of interest.

"Daphne?" Sam's voice pulled her back, made her turn toward him. He was watching her in the moonlight with that usual half-smile playing around his mouth, and Daff had no idea what he was thinking. Probably that she was a nutcase with some sort of garbage fetish.

"Yeah?" she asked with a half-smile of her own.

She figured he was about to ask why she'd stolen the al-Sayeds' trash or maybe suggest that she buy a can of Lysol to help cover the smell, but instead he took one hand from the steering wheel and used it to cup her cheek. Then he rendered her speechless when he said, "I think I love you."

THIRTY-ONE

DAPHNE gingerly held a banana peel between her thumb and forefinger. After turning it over to make certain nothing was sticking to it, she tossed it onto the plastic garbage bag she'd laid out on the floor of her motel room to hold the discards from the al-Sayeds' trash. So far, her discard pile was about ten times the size of the pile of items she'd kept for further inspection.

The inspection pile consisted of several empty prescription bottles, a crumpled up letter, a brochure that could be nothing more than junk mail, and a handful of shredded paper that Daff hoped she could fit together into something readable.

If she were still with the Bureau, the last item would be a snap. The FBI had a computer program that could take scanned in strips of shredded paper and digitally put them back together again. Doing it manually might take a lot more time, but it could still be done as long as the entire document had been thrown away in the same bag. Where it got tricky was when someone was smart enough to mix the documents among loads of trash. Then it became nearly impossible to reconstruct any one document.

Behind her, Sam mumbled something and kicked the sheets as if they'd offended him. Daff glanced over her shoulder at him. He would have stayed up all night to help her sort through the al-Sayeds' trash if she hadn't insisted he go to sleep. He had a full day of work ahead of him, and yet he'd still been willing to join her in this wild goose chase.

He thought he loved her? Well, she was fairly certain she felt the same way about him, especially after last night.

Daff shook her head and turned back to the dwindling pile of garbage in front of her. What an odd time to be thinking about love, sitting here amidst a stinking pile of trash, in the middle of a case leading nowhere. But the fact that Sam was here, that he hadn't balked at what she had to do, meant a lot to her. That he'd offered to help meant even more.

She ripped open the last trash bag and grimaced at the stench. Ugh. More kitchen garbage.

She glanced back at Sam to see if the smell had awakened him, but he was still sleeping with his hands curled up under his chin. He'd probably slept in worse conditions during his years in spec ops. Daff's sixteen-week training at Quantico had been no picnic, but it was nothing compared to what the SEALs went through. And, for her, the training had been the worst part. For the most part, she had spent her days in the FBI analyzing data, tracking down leads, and conducting searches. In spec ops, the brutal training was just a taste of what their lives would be like every day.

Daff shuddered as she combed through the final bag, but it didn't contain anything more interesting than the remains of last night's supper.

After covering the discard pile with several plastic bags

in an attempt to contain the smell, Daphne sat down cross-legged on the floor next to the other pile. This was it. Her only leads in Keith Melman's murder lay on the floor in front of her.

Daff sighed and picked up the brochure. The grease-smeared paper was nearly transparent in places and a corner of it was missing completely. Carefully, she unfolded it and started to read. It was from a company called Stork Scent. The first panel contained a testimonial from a woman claiming that the company's products had made it possible for her to keep her baby to term. The second and third panels were filled with a scientific explanation of how the product worked, and the brochure was signed by a Dr. Yvonne Y. Richardson. Daff turned it over. The mailing label addressed to Jahia al-Sayed had been computer generated. The return address of the company listed a post office box in Maryland, but the postmark was from here in Naples. Nothing too odd about that with those "make a million bucks mailing crap from your home" business opportunities; it didn't ring any of Daff's alarm bells that this brochure had been mailed from Naples.

The last panel of the brochure listed the various products the company offered and directed the reader to visit the company's website to place an order or find out more information.

Daphne shook her head and set the brochure aside.

A perfume that was also a pregnancy aid? What sort of gullible idiot would fall for that?

The sort who was desperate, that voice in her mind responded, and Daff conceded the point. She had no idea if Jahia al-Sayed had ever miscarried, but if she had, she might be willing to try anything to keep it from happening again. This Stork Scent perfume company could easily buy a mailing list of expectant mothers from baby stores or parenting magazines and use that list to peddle their so-called miracle product. Using someone's fears to sell a product was certainly not a revolutionary marketing method. Nor was it a crime.

Daff picked up the next letter and scanned it, only to discover that it was a thank-you note from the al-Sayeds' real estate broker.

The prescription bottles didn't tell her anything except that Adnan al-Sayed had high blood pressure and that Jahia was taking prenatal vitamins.

Nothing earth-shattering there.

Daff yawned and pushed a stray hair away from her face. This Dumpster diving was turning out to be yet another exercise in futility.

She leaned back against the foot of the bed and closed her eyes. She'd been sorting through trash for five hours now and had turned up nothing. The shredded paper was going to have to wait until she had the energy to tackle it. Right now, she needed to rest.

She peeled off the gloves and laid them next to the empty prescription bottles, then went to the bathroom to wash her hands and face before stripping down to her bra and panties and climbing into bed beside Sam. He threw a heavy arm over her waist and pulled her into him, her hips against his crotch, her shoulders against his chest.

Daff relaxed in a way she never had before, her bones seeming to melt into Sam's. The truth was, she felt safe when she was with him, as if nothing bad could happen to her when she was wrapped up in his arms.

She wondered if he ever felt the same way, if this big tough guy ever had the luxury of letting someone else take care of him and keep him safe. She had the sudden urge to wake him up and warn him that falling in love with her was an enormous mistake. Didn't he realize that she would only break his heart in the end? She wanted to tell him to walk away now, to protect himself from her.

But when Sam nudged one hairy, muscled leg between hers and mumbled something unintelligible into her hair, she knew she couldn't do it. Selfish as it was, she couldn't push him away.

The hope that maybe this time would be different was too strong. What if this really worked? What if Sam stuck around, no matter how much of a pain in the ass she sometimes was or how moody she could be? What if he really did love her, the real her?

For the first time in her life, Daff could almost imagine it—the ghostlike images of a possible future flitting just outside her grasp. What would it be like, this whole commitment-to-one-person thing? Would they live in a little three-bed/two-bath ranch house with 2.5 kids and a Labrador retriever? That life had never appealed to her, had never seemed to fit. It reminded her of the winter coat she'd been wearing when she'd first shown up on Jack Madison's doorstep, a heavy gray woolen one that was a size too small and pinched her under the arms.

But who said that had to be their future? Daff may not long for children and a dog, but the idea of buying a home, of putting down roots, was starting to appeal to her. She'd never felt that way before, never had the urge to make a life with anyone else.

She nestled back into Sam's warmth and closed her eyes as she tried to picture her future with him. Would they have the usual good-natured arguments about leaving the toilet seat down and the thermostat up? Would Sam roll his eyes about her inability to balance a checkbook? Would they draw straws to see whose turn it was to go to the grocery store or take out the trash? Or would all of these details just fall into place, leaving her to wonder why she'd resisted the idea of cohabitation for so long?

Daff didn't know about any of this, but what she did know was that for the first time in her life, she was willing to give it a try—toilet seats, thermostats, joint checking, and all.

She was just starting to drift off to sleep when she was suddenly jerked awake by what she had just been thinking. Her eyelids flew open and she stared unseeingly at the piles of trash on the floor of her room.

The joint checking account.

That was it.

She mentally ran through the five-page report Keith had printed that listed Adnan al-Sayed's banking transactions. The list had included bills, car repairs, restaurants, and a few cash withdrawals. But there had been no groceries, no housing supplies, nothing for the baby that Jahia was carrying.

Jahia and Adnan al-Sayed obviously had separate bank accounts.

What if Keith simply hadn't printed a report for Jahia's account? What if it had been e-mailed to him and was still sitting on his laptop? Perhaps Keith's killer could be traced back to Jahia and not her husband.

It was a long shot, Daff knew, but it was worth a try.

All she had to do now was get her hands on Keith's computer.

THIRTY-TWO

DAPHNE was sitting in her car outside al-Sayed's house with Keith Melman's pilfered laptop on her lap when the garage door started to rise. She hunkered down in her seat and closed the top of the computer so that her face could not be seen in the glow coming off the screen.

She'd had a busy day, what with breaking into Keith's house to steal his laptop and all, and it looked like her evening wasn't going to be any less eventful. Adnan al-Sayed was on the move.

Tailing someone in a vehicle was a real art, though most people weren't paranoid enough to ever check to see if they were being followed. Daff had a feeling that Adnan al-Sayed *was* the mistrustful type, however, so she made certain to keep her distance. That was one good thing about driving a convertible—if al-Sayed was going to travel a fair distance, she could put the top down at some point to change the look of her car. If she were still with the Bureau, they'd do a surveillance like this with several vehicles that could switch off as their target progressed on his route. As it was, Daff would have to make do with a single car. If Sam hadn't been running an errand in Miami, she might have asked him to meet her in his truck. But without him, she was on her own.

Her cell phone rang just then and she spared a brief glance down to see who it was before answering.

She couldn't help but smile. "I was just thinking about you," she said.

"Was I naked?" Sam asked, and Daff could just picture that half-grin on his face.

"You were helping me play cat and mouse," Daff replied, not really answering his question. No sense disappointing the guy.

"Ooh, I didn't know you were into costumes. When we're done with cat and mouse, can we do the pirate and his willing slave?"

Daphne grinned. "Is this where I get to make some sort of joke about booty?" she asked.

Sam's chuckle tickled her ear and made her stomach flip over even though they were separated by over a hundred miles. Man, was she in over her head here. For some reason, she wasn't too upset by that thought. Probably because she had gone into this not expecting it to last forever. Sam was just her Florida fling, someone to pass the time with while she continued to investigate her client's untimely demise. That was it.

Right. You just go on telling yourself that.

Daff cleared her throat. "Where are you?" she asked.

"I just left Miami and I'm trying to decide whether to take my chances on Highway 41 or head on up to Alligator Alley."

"Alligator Alley?" Daff asked, easing back on the accelerator as al-Sayed's Town car drifted toward a red light.

"That's the nickname for Interstate 75. I'm not sure why. The highway cuts through a lot more gator-filled swampland than the interstate does," Sam said.

"Hmm," Daff answered. As a Manhattan native, the idea of humans being preyed upon by other humans didn't make her bat an eye. The NRA's slogan was right—guns didn't kill people, *people* killed people. Where she came from, man had no natural predators except other men (and women, too, of course). So it was foreign to her that here in the United States, there were actually animals that preyed on humans. Fairly regularly, too, if the news reports were accurate.

Daff shivered despite herself. She had no idea why the thought of being blown away by a mugger didn't creep her out, but imagining being yanked into a swamp by a fourteen-foot-long man-eating alligator gave her the willies.

She grunted as Adnan al-Sayed stayed straight when she had expected him to turn left.

"Looks like I'm heading toward the interstate myself," she muttered.

"What?" Sam asked.

"I'm following al-Sayed. He's on the move. I can't imagine that he's heading out to the Everglades for a moonlight frog hunt, so I'm hoping I can finally get something that will convince the FBI to get involved."

Daff heard Sam's sharply indrawn breath and wondered if someone had cut him off or something.

"Something wrong?" she asked.

"You're killing me, Daphne," Sam said, sounding as if he were banging his head on the steering wheel.

"What are you talking about?"

Sam sighed so deeply that Daff was surprised the hair at the nape of her neck didn't stir. "You know, when I was in the Navy, I always said I'd never expect someone to be waiting at home for me, never knowing when—or even if—I'd come back. I just thought it was wrong to put someone through that."

"Yeah?" Daff said, only half-listening as she squinted up ahead in the gathering darkness, trying to make sure she didn't lose al-Sayed.

"Well I was right. It's hell going through this."

"Going through what?" Daphne asked, feeling a bit exasperated that Sam was being so vague.

"*This,*" Sam repeated, as if it explained everything. "Having to trust that you can keep yourself safe. Knowing that there's damn little I can do to protect you. Reminding myself that you are a strong, capable woman doing an important job."

"Oh," was all Daff could think of to say.

"You know, if I weren't such an enlightened guy, I might be tempted to ask you to turn your car around right now, before you put yourself in any danger."

Daff squinted into her rearview mirror as the vehicle behind her blinded her with its lights. "But you'd never do that. You respect me too much, right?"

There was a long silence on the other end of the line, and Daphne began to wonder if the call had been dropped. She didn't expect that there'd be good cell service out here, not once they got a few miles outside Naples. She'd seen the maps. I-75 passed through the upper tip of Everglades National Park and then through Big Cypress National Preserve before dumping drivers out about twenty miles north of Miami. There just wasn't enough traffic on this stretch of road to justify putting up many cell phone towers.

But after a few moments, Sam's voice came back on the line and Daff realized the call had not been dropped. Instead, it seemed that Sam had needed a minute or two to wrestle with his emotions. She wasn't certain whose side she was on and had to admit—if only to herself—to a fleeting feeling of satisfaction that was purely feminine when Sam said,

"Hell no. If I thought there was any chance you'd do it, I'd order you to turn that damn car around right now."

HE was stuck in a fucking dead zone.

A drop of sweat traced a path from his temple down the side of his face, and Sam jammed the air conditioner up a notch. He was already going ninety, which, at twenty miles over the speed limit, was par for the course in Florida.

Florida drivers fell into two opposing camps. First, there were the Snowbirds. These were the people who drove cars were big enough to house entire families. They always had a turn signal blinking as if they couldn't see the green flash on their dashboards for mile after mile. Sam thought maybe it was just their passive-aggressive way of punishing those people who blared their music so loud you could hear the words from ten cars back. Couldn't beat 'em up, so why not try to drive 'em crazy with the constant blink of the turn signal?

The second group of Florida drivers automatically added twenty miles to whatever was posted on the speed limit sign. If you were trying to keep even one car length between you and the guy in front of you, they took it as an invitation to just slip right in. Going ninety miles an hour. Then they'd slam on their brakes.

Since the first group had the attitude that as long as they were driving within twenty miles under the speed limit they were entitled to remain parked in the left lane, this meant that the members of the second group were forced to pass on the right. Or on the shoulder. Or to zip in and out of traffic so heavy that there was never more than five feet of space between vehicles. Somehow, that was always enough.

Sam had been close enough to dying in his life that he took a more laid-back attitude toward the traffic in his home state. Let everyone else play the cars-as-pinballs game. He usually stayed within ten miles of the limit, passed only when there was plenty of room to do so, and waved at the old people who left their turn signals blinking mile after mile.

But not tonight.

He looked down at his cell phone and cursed.

Still no fucking bars.

He pressed his foot on the accelerator, easing the needle up past ninety. At this speed, the slowpokes' rear bumpers came up pretty fast, so Sam kept his attention focused intently on the road.

In the "old days," even greater hazards than your fellow drivers were the gators and deer that would make their way unwittingly across the freeway in the dark. Nothing like coming upon an eight-hundred-pound alligator in your Honda Civic to make things interesting.

Fortunately, after one too many fatalities, the state sprung for miles and miles of unending chain-link fence to keep the wildlife at bay. Sam had no idea if it was someone's full-time job to maintain the fence, but he couldn't imagine a more boring job than driving back and forth along this roadway every day.

He passed a slow-moving Mercury Marquis, sliding his truck into the right lane and then zipping back to the left while praying that the driver in front of him didn't get startled by the sudden flash of headlights and slam on his brakes.

That was Sam's main reason for driving the way he did. It wasn't his own driving skills he didn't trust—it was everyone else's. You were an idiot to put your life into the hands of the guy in front of you, a guy you'd never met, never trained with, and never tested. During his years in the military, Sam had trusted his life to the guys he served with many times over, but those men had earned his trust. No way was he going to let some overconfident kid fresh out of driver's ed jerk around with *his* life.

Sam made it around the Marquis and checked his phone again.

Yes! He had a signal.

He'd told Daphne to call him if al-Sayed made any suspicious moves. And despite what he'd said about having confidence in her ability to take care of herself, he'd asked her to call with her location every ten minutes so that when they both reached the same mile marker, he could hang a completely illegal U-turn and follow her to wherever it was al-Sayed was headed.

No fucking way was he going to let Daphne handle a suspected terrorist alone.

Hell. Who was he kidding? He wouldn't want her to handle a suspected candy-store robber alone.

Sam ran a hand through his hair and grimaced. His scalp was damp with sweat. He wiped his palm on his jeans and made a note to get his air conditioner checked, ignoring the fact that before tonight, he'd never noticed a problem with it.

A flash of brake lights up ahead had him swearing again. Either there was a cop out there slowing down traffic or some skittish driver was holding people hostage in the passing lane.

Sam saw another flash of red from beside him and realized that his cell phone was blinking to indicate that a message must have come in while he was in the dead zone.

He kept one eye on the traffic in front of him as he called his voice mail and was told he had one new message. He passed mile marker 42 as he pushed the button to play the message.

"Hey Sam, it's Daff," she said unnecessarily. He recognized her voice. Sam also had the fleeting thought that she should start using her full name. Daphne was such a pretty name, whereas Daff was . . . like a joke. Sort of like the tattoo of Daffy Duck wearing a superhero cape on her ass.

Uncaring of his musings, the recording continued. "Our guy just pulled off the road in the middle of freaking nowhere. I'm about a quarter of a mile ahead and will double back on foot. I don't know who the hell al-Sayed's planning to meet out here. Maybe he just wanted to get himself some authentic alligator-skin boots."

Sam cringed at her lame attempt at humor.

"Anyway, if you get this message, I would definitely appreciate some backup. I'm guessing you frogmen had a bit more training in the swamp than we got at Quantico."

She laughed without humor and Sam scowled at his phone. Now why'd she have to say that? Like he wasn't already scared shitless that she'd get hurt out there before he could get to her.

"Oh. I'm at mile marker 52. See you soon."

The message ended and Sam started sweating again. She was still ten miles up ahead. Ten miles that seemed like an eternity as he tried to rocket past cars that suddenly seemed determined to slow him up. He'd get around one only to be forced to slam on his brakes and zip back into the other lane to avoid a collision. Someone honked at him and Sam was tempted to flip the guy off, even though he knew he deserved the reprimand.

He finally made his way out of the worst of it and floored the accelerator, praying that there were no cops around as he approached the place where he'd need to turn around. He slowed the truck just enough so it wouldn't roll over when he jerked the wheel hard to left, then slammed on the gas and roared across the grassy median. Then he tapped the brakes again and turned to merge with the oncoming traffic.

THIRTY-THREE

DAPHNE knew the exact moment when she switched from hunter to hunted.

Funny. All her earlier thinking about predators and their prey hadn't made her more cautious. Now she had no one to blame but her own stupid self for being in this predicament.

She hadn't even considered that al-Sayed might have had a second tail—either someone sent by the person he planned to meet to make certain al-Sayed came alone, or al-Sayed's own bodyguard tasked with taking up the rear just to make certain his boss wasn't being followed.

Daff crouched down in the thick brush, her booted feet sinking into the soft earth beneath her. Everything here smelled damp. Not the clean wet smell of the air after a bracing rain, but a moldy dankness that came from plants and animals that were never truly dry.

She listened intently for the sound of footsteps in the dark.

She knew she was being followed, not just because of the heavy crackle of brush she'd heard when her pursuer made a misstep and nearly lost his balance, but because of that feeling you get when you know you're being watched. She'd first felt it about five minutes after she'd found the gash in the chain-link fence near where al-Sayed had pulled off the roadway. She'd hesitated about entering the swamp—she wasn't stupid, after all—but what choice did she have?

It was obvious that whoever he was meeting had gone to great lengths to ensure their privacy. Doubtful the FBI had bugged the entire Everglades.

She stared at the thick limbs of brush and the heavy vines pressing against the fence in an attempt to escape and reclaim the strip of land that had once been theirs. Once she entered the swamp, the threat level would be magnified a thousandfold. She could accidentally stumble upon al-Sayed in the dark. Or disturb a hungry alligator. Or . . .

"Or get bitten by a mosquito and get malaria, you weenie. Stop freaking yourself out and get in there," she silently chided herself and slipped inside the gate.

It was like slipping inside a whole different world. Within five steps, the sounds of traffic had faded away, overwhelmed by the chirping of bugs and the oddly soothing belch of a frog.

She heard the faint sound of voices off to her right and cautiously struck out in that direction. And that's when she felt it, that strange sensation that someone's eyes were upon her. Daff shivered and crouched low over the spongy ground.

Slowly, she turned her head to see if she could spot whoever it was who was following her.

She saw a flash of something in the darkness and tried to leap out of the way but found herself slammed up against something hard instead. It wasn't something hard and human, but hard, inanimate, and prickly. For a second, her eyes went unfocused as her forehead made contact with the object.

When they cleared, she found herself staring at the bark of a tree while a man—at least, she guessed it was a man from the heavy feel of his body crushing her to the tree—who had to have been six inches taller and a hundred pounds heavier than her, held her immobilized. He had one hand clamped over her nose and mouth and Daff struggled to drag oxygen in through her obstructed airways. She tilted her head back in an attempt to get her nose free from his grasp, but he didn't budge.

With her chest and hips pinned against the tree by the man's bulk, her feet dangling four inches off the ground, she was rendered nearly helpless. Which really pissed her off, but there was nothing much she could do about it.

So much for thinking of herself as Super Daff.

The man had obviously come prepared for the occasion. While she struggled against him, he used his free hand to slip one end of a handcuff around her left wrist and tighten it. When he let go, Daff jerked her arm back, away from the tree. She knew exactly what this guy was trying to do, and it would be impossible for him to do it using only one hand.

She heard him grunt with pain when she finally managed to get her foot free enough to aim a solid kick at his kneecap. That's when she felt the slide of cool metal against the bare skin at her waist where her T-shirt had come untucked from her jeans. The blade of a knife pricked her flesh and Daff flinched, not from pain but from the knowledge that with one well-aimed thrust, this guy could kill her.

Human beings were such fragile creatures, really.

One sharp jab at her lungs and they would fill with blood or collapse; one slice a bit lower and her femoral artery would be severed; an upward thrust at the right spot and she'd lie there, unable to move or utter a sound as she lay dying on the floor of the swamp.

Daphne stopped struggling.

"Very good," the man whispered in her ear and Daff shuddered. He had the voice of a killer, of someone who could dispassionately take another's life in one moment and calmly order dinner in the next.

"Now, keep quiet. The men who hear you will not come to your aid if you scream. Do you understand?"

Daff nodded, her cheek rubbing against the rough bark as the man ordered her to put her wrists together on the other side of the tree. He dropped his hand from her face and she breathed in a deep breath as she did as she'd been told.

The way she figured it, if this guy wanted her dead, she'd be dead already. He must have his reasons for keeping her alive . . . for the moment at least. She was happy to cooperate if that meant she could go on breathing.

He cuffed her wrists together on the other side of the tree. Then he leaned into her, no less threatening even without the knife pressed against her flesh, and whispered, "I'll be back."

EYES had an eerie way of glowing in the moonlight. A man's eyes made him even more vulnerable in the darkness; the whites always gave him away.

These eyes, however, were yellowish-green, and they watched Sam's gliding approach with the unmoving stare of one who is confident of his position at the top of the food chain.

Sam was perfectly happy with the status quo. As long as the alligator left him alone, he'd be on his way.

Sending up a silent "thank you" that it was not yet mating season—when male alligators became more aggressive and territorial—he slid past the gator unmolested. The brackish water of the swamp was only a few inches deep in places, and Sam propelled his body along the surface by using his hands to pull himself forward. The muddy earth tried to suck him down, but he kept moving forward, always forward, toward the gash he'd seen in the fence half a mile back from where he'd pulled off the highway.

That, he was fairly certain, was where Daphne would have entered the swamp.

Sam paused when he heard the low rumble of voices up ahead, a foreign sound easily recognizable out here in the swamp. Daphne would be near, as close to the men as she could get without being spotted.

He remained motionless in the shallow water, his ears trained to listen for sounds that didn't belong. He heard the faint jingle of something metallic and frowned. He pinpointed the source of the sound, off to the east about ten yards away. He waited a moment longer, listening and watching, and saw a white flash that was clearly out of place.

Teeth were another thing that could give a man away.

Sam slowly and silently made his way toward his prey. He didn't know if Daphne had counted on there being a third man here tonight, but it was clear from the man's position that he'd been brought in to patrol the swamp during al-Sayed's meeting. If Daphne hadn't anticipated a sentry . . .

Sam closed his eyes and steadied his breathing.

No. Just focus on the job. Take the guard out of the scenario, even up the odds. Make sure there was no one else hiding in the marsh. Find Daphne. Get the hell out of here.

Step number one: incapacitate the guard.

Not as easy a task as one might expect. Sam watched the man slowly scan the area and considered his options. Killing the guy would be simple. That would certainly eliminate any danger he might pose. Unfortunately, this was not a government-sanctioned mission and U.S. law enforcement sort of frowned on random killings. Since Sam had no interest in checking out what life was like inside a prison, option number one was out.

Option number two would have to do.

Sam slipped into position and, with no drama or fanfare,

slipped up behind the goon and dropped him with a well-paced jab. He was about to drop back to the ground, but instead spun around when Daphne whispered behind him, "Well done. Now would you mind seeing if you can find his keys?"

DAPHNE Donovan was not easily impressed, but the ease with which Sam dropped the thug who had handcuffed her was a glorious sight to see. It was true—revenge really was sweet.

"Here. Put these on him," she said as Sam positioned the guy at the base of a tree. She held out the handcuffs that, until just a few moments before, had graced her own wrists.

Sam took the cuffs and slapped them on the thug's wrists. "Are there any more goons around?" he asked when he was finished.

"I don't know," Daff admitted, but no way was she going to tell Sam that she'd been taken out as soon as she'd set foot in the swamp. "But we can't leave yet. I have to find out who al-Sayed came here to meet."

She kept her gaze steady as Sam peered at her for a long moment, and she knew he was trying to decide if he should knock her unconscious like he'd done with al-Sayed's thug and drag her out here.

Finally, he gave one sharp jerk of his chin and said, "Follow me."

Daff spared a glance down at the man chained to the base of the tree. "What if he wakes up and yells for help?" she asked.

Sam crouched down and started moving toward the clearing where al-Sayed and the other man still stood.

"He won't," Sam answered, then froze.

Daphne stopped behind him, her eyes darting back and forth, searching the heavy brush for whatever he had seen.

Had al-Sayed or his cohort brought along another guard? Or had Sam been startled by one of Mother Nature's predators instead?

Sam pivoted soundlessly on his heels and pointed to his eyes and then to the ground. Daphne had no idea what he was trying to tell her. Was there something on the ground that he wanted her to see? Footprints? A snake pit? What? She stared hard at the place where he'd pointed, but saw nothing but mud and prickly marsh grass. She started to glance back up at him, to ask what he'd wanted her to see, and nearly gasped with surprise when he clapped a hand over her eyes.

O-kay.

What the hell was Sam—

"—appreciate your contribution to the cause," a man said as he crashed through the underbrush ten feet from where Daff and Sam were hiding.

"In return, I'd like to ask a favor," Adnan al-Sayed replied. Like the first man, he appeared to be making no effort at stealth. Daff wondered if that was because he hadn't suspected he'd been followed or if he simply trusted the guard that Sam had taken out to have warned him if there were any intruders.

"We do not grant favors." The man sounded angry, as if affronted that al-Sayed would even suggest such a thing.

Daff had figured out by now why Sam was covering her eyes. She touched his hand with two fingers and then pointed to the ground, indicating that she would keep her eyes down. He nodded and slowly removed his hand.

The temptation to look up, to see if she recognized the man talking to al-Sayed, was great, but Daphne had no intention of giving up their position. Instead, she stared at the mud at her feet and listened intently to the men's conversation.

"I apologize," al-Sayed immediately responded, trying to

soothe the other man's ire. "I only mean to keep my family safe. My wife and I . . . we're expecting our first child soon. We travel a lot and I . . . I only wish to keep them safe," he repeated.

Daphne frowned. What was going on here? Adnan al-Sayed had not struck her as the sort of man to pander to another. On the contrary, he had seemed hard and arrogant, certainly not the type to beg favors from someone he had just given money to. So why the hint of begging in his voice now?

The men began to move away, and Daff put her hand on Sam's thigh. If the men moved out of earshot, she would miss whatever was said next. She'd have nothing more to go on, nothing to tell the FBI.

Sam covered her hand with his own. Beneath her fingers, she felt his thigh muscle shift, as if he were preparing to move. Then the men stopped and Sam dropped back to a resting position.

"If you could only give me some hint," al-Sayed said, and Daff chanced a glance upward through the slits of her fingers. She saw al-Sayed holding one hand out in a beseeching manner to a shorter man with dark, curly hair. Both men wore business suits and expensive-looking ties, as out of place here in the swamp as a Starbucks espresso stand would be.

She dropped her gaze back to the ground and waited, holding her breath, for the other man to respond.

"I will tell you this, and this only. If you wish for your family to remain safe, keep them home on September 11."

Daphne's sharp exhale was drowned out by the sound of a frog croaking nearby. Next to her, she felt Sam tense as the implication of what had just been said hit him, too. Terrorists were planning another attack on 9/11.

Daff started to stand, to lunge for the man, to grab him in a chokehold and strangle him until he told her what was being planned, but Sam held her firmly in place. She began to struggle as the men continued toward the fence, but Sam wouldn't let her go. He wrapped his arms around her chest, holding her tightly as al-Sayed passed within two feet of the man Sam had cuffed to the tree earlier.

When al-Sayed missed a step and jerked his head around to stare intently into the darkness, Sam forced her head down so that she wouldn't be seen. Daphne wanted to shout at him to let her go, even though she knew this was for the best. Leaping out into the marsh and shouting "gotcha" wasn't exactly a smart tactical move. But it was still difficult to remain here huddling on the ground like frightened rabbits when all Daff wanted was to stand up and fight.

She would *not* sit by and let another 9/11 happen, not if there was anything she could do to stop it. Was this why Keith Melman had been murdered? Had he stumbled upon the terrorists and their plan?

Daff stopped struggling, knowing that Sam was right, that they had a better chance of uncovering the terrorist plot if they remained out of sight. At least for now.

She sank back on her heels and glared with surprise at al-Sayed's back as he continued on past the guard on the ground. Why hadn't al-Sayed raised the alarm? He had clearly seen something or his steps would not have faltered.

"I'll be right out," she heard al-Sayed call to the other man as they approached the gash in the chain-link fence.

"Is everything all right? Where is your man?" the terrorist asked.

Daff and Sam looked at each other with surprise when al-Sayed answered, "Everything is fine. He just had to . . . er, relieve himself. Feel free to leave without me. I know my way home."

THIRTY-FOUR

KEITH had obviously not been concerned about computer hackers. If he had been, he would not have used something as easy to guess as his daughter's first name and her birthday as his password. The trouble, Daff's partner Raine—a computer hacker who used her powers for good, not evil—explained, was that people needed passwords that they could remember, but the best (that is, most hacker-proof) passwords were nonsensical strings of letters, symbols, and numbers that didn't mean a thing to anyone.

But Daff was glad that Keith hadn't been worried about someone breaking into his computer. About time something went her way on this case.

She kept one eye on the al-Sayeds' house as she waited for Keith's laptop to finish its start-up routine. The wireless networking hardware automatically detected two available networks, most likely from the al-Sayeds' neighbors who were running home offices. Daff clicked on the one with the best signal and wondered how she'd survived the eighties without computers, e-mail, or even a cell phone.

As his wallpaper, Keith had chosen a photo of Nicole with his children, taken at the beach. All three were smiling, and not in that we-have-to-do-this-for-the-camera way. They actually looked happy.

Daff wondered if the kids would continue their relationship with Nicole now that their father was dead. She doubted it. Even with the best intentions, people in these types of situations drifted apart. Probably, once the kids became adults, they'd try to reconnect with Nicole in order to forge a new relationship with their half brother or sister. But it would always be awkward. Keith's death would hover over them, like a toxic cloud that filtered out the sun's rays.

Daphne shook her head at her gloomy thoughts. How like her to assume the worst. Why not envision the opposite—that Keith's children would remain close to Nicole throughout the years and would play a positive role in their sibling's life?

She'd spent her entire life expecting the worst out of people. Maybe it was time she gave herself an attitude transplant and began hoping for the best.

Daff glanced at the al-Sayeds' front door to make sure it had remained firmly shut before starting Keith's e-mail program. The laptop hummed in the quiet interior of her convertible, and Daphne turned the air conditioner up as the heat from the computer's motor warmed her thighs through the material of her jeans.

Once the e-mail program opened, she hit the Send/Receive button and waited to see if it would automatically connect to AmTrust's network. It was possible, of course, that the company's IT department had already disabled Keith's account. If that were the case, she'd only have the e-mails from up until the day of Keith's death to work from.

But, again, something was going her way. A message on the bottom right-hand corner of the program told her that it was now receiving message one of 483. That was to be expected, she supposed. Keith hadn't checked his e-mail in a week.

Fortunately, the wireless connection was good and the e-mails didn't take long to download. Daff started from the top, searching for a message that might contain a report listing Jahia al-Sayed's banking transactions.

It was surprisingly easy to find.

The e-mail had been sent from an automated system and the header included Jahia al-Sayed's name and account number. Daphne clicked on the message and then opened the attachment. The date range on the top of the report was for the last twenty-four hours. Daff assumed that there were similar reports for both Jahia and Adnan going back for the last week. Keith must have set up the reports to automatically run every morning.

"Come on, Keith, what are you trying to tell me?" Daff muttered to herself as she scanned the report. It was like following Jahia around for the past twenty-four hours. Yesterday morning at 9:14 A.M., she had placed an order totaling $38.95 through BabiesRUs.com. At 10:42, she used her debit card to pay a $14.95 bill at the Hungry Bear Café. She checked out of Publix at 11:31 with nearly fifty dollars' worth of groceries, then stopped in at Albertson's at 11:59 and spent another $19.73. She had a quiet afternoon, with no further transactions until 8:38 P.M. Daff squinted at the computer screen, trying to remember what time it had been when Adnan left the house. Had Jahia waited for her husband to leave before going online? Was her purchase related to the man Adnan had met last night?

Daphne clicked the transaction, which was blue and underlined like a standard web link. It took a few seconds for the browser to launch, but when it did, Daff was still puzzled. The link took her to a page that provided more details about the transaction. The payee was listed as Stork Scent. The amount was $95.00. There were some codes that she assumed would have meant something to Keith, but looked like gibberish to her.

Daff frowned. Stork Scent. The name sounded familiar, but she didn't recall where she'd heard it before.

Again wondering how the world had managed to revolve without the technology that was available now, Daphne clicked on the address field of the browser and typed in the company's name. As soon as the website appeared, Daff remembered where she had seen the name before. The company had sent Jahia al-Sayed a brochure in the mail and she had thrown it away.

Their advertising had obviously worked, however, because Jahia had placed an order with them last night.

But how was this related to Keith's death? Was Stork Scent a front for a terrorist group or simply a company trying to bilk money out of frightened, gullible women who would give anything to keep from miscarrying?

Daff sighed with frustration. It would be so much easier to find out if Stork Scent was legitimate if she were still with the FBI. It was times like this when she missed the Bureau and all its resources. Too bad she couldn't call her old boss again and ask for his help . . . but she knew where that would lead her. Down a long, dark corridor to nowhere.

No, she was going to have to tackle this research herself.

Good thing she had plenty of boring hours to while away sitting here watching a whole lot of nothing happening over at the al-Sayeds' house.

Daff sighed again and reached for her cell phone. The first thing she was going to do was to call the contact number listed on the website. She'd pretend to be a skeptical yet interested prospective customer and ask the company to send her additional information. Then she'd Google the company itself and all the names listed on the website and see what she could come up with. If that was a dead end, she'd go through Keith's mail and keep looking through the al-Sayeds' transactions until something turned up.

Keith had to have pointed her in this direction for a reason. She wasn't going to give up until she found out what it was.

DAPHNE Donovan had to die.

Jenna was certain she recognized the voice, but she confirmed it by comparing the phone number on the caller ID with the number she had called on Saturday to lure the private investigator to Keith Melman's house. Jenna didn't even want to guess how Ms. Donovan had found out about Stork Scent. Frankly, she had hoped the woman would still be in jail, but with the U.S.'s easy stance on crime, she supposed she shouldn't be surprised that Daphne was on the loose.

"Probably slipped someone a hundred-dollar bill in exchange for her freedom," Jenna murmured as she contemplated what to do next.

She couldn't leave Naples yet. She was too close to getting her revenge.

Jahia al-Sayed had ordered a bottle of perfume, but had not paid for rush shipping. That meant that Jenna couldn't drop off her package for another day or two yet. Besides, if she gave the perfume to Jahia before Friday, she might use it before the CEO summit began, which would only cause innocent people to lose their lives.

Jenna was going to do everything in her power to avoid that.

She planned to deliver the perfume right before Jahia left for the Solems' on Friday. If luck was on her side, Jahia would open the package and slip the perfume in her purse.

The directions stated that the perfume had to be reapplied every hour for it to be most effective. If Jahia bought this claim, then she'd want the perfume with her.

Jenna stroked the lavender box where an amethyst-colored perfume bottle was nestled. There was only enough anthrax in the atomizer to last for the first two or perhaps three sprays, but all Jenna needed for her revenge to be complete was for one dose to be released at the CEO summit. That one dose would be enough to kill eighty percent of the people who inhaled the toxin. Certainly it would kill Jahia al-Sayed, who would spray the poison directly at herself. Jenna could only hope that Nicole Solem would be affected, too.

But if Daphne Donovan somehow discovered her plan, Jenna's hopes that this would all end in two days would be crushed.

She couldn't have that.

Which meant that as much as Jenna would have liked to avoid harming innocent people, Ms. Donovan was going to have to be eliminated.

Jenna glanced down at the address the private investigator had given her a few moments before. She wasn't familiar with the street, but it would be easy enough to go online and get directions.

The heavy chair scraped the tile as Jenna pushed it away from the table and stood up. She walked over to the Sub-Zero refrigerator in the kitchen and pulled open the heavy stainless steel door. She surveyed the neatly labeled beakers for a moment before reaching in to select one.

Jenna carefully placed the sealed beaker in a padded box and closed the lid. Then she put the box into a plastic bag and sealed the top. She repeated the process with another bag. Ricin, the toxin Jenna had chosen, was a particularly nasty biological weapon, and she wasn't taking any chances.

When inhaled as a powder, ricin caused illness within eight hours and respiratory failure within thirty-six. Since the toxin acted rapidly and irreversibly, treatment was virtually impossible. Approximately five hours after Ms. Donovan inhaled the ricin, she'd begin to feel localized pain and weakness in her muscles. In another twelve hours, her temperature would rise and she would begin vomiting. Her lymph nodes would swell, followed by low blood pressure and vascular collapse. Near the end, she would begin vomiting blood.

Then, even if she sought medical treatment, she would die.

Once she inhaled the ricin, she would, in effect, already be dead. Nothing, and no one, could save her.

THIRTY-FIVE

DAPHNE grimaced as she unlocked the motel room door and inhaled the stench inside. She tugged the "Do Not Disturb" sign off the doorknob and stepped into the room. Although she and Sam had removed the bulk of the al-Sayeds' trash this morning, the place still reeked of rotting food.

Or maybe she was just imagining it.

Either way—whether the smell was real or imaginary—Daff found herself unconsciously plugging her nose as she reached over to open the window and let in some fresh air.

She knew she should still be over at the al-Sayeds', watching their every move, but the truth was, she was tired. And frustrated. Every lead she checked out dead-ended.

She'd just flopped down on the bed, her arms spread out at her sides, when her cell phone rang.

"Yeah?" she answered after briefly considering letting it go to voice mail.

"It's a beautiful night."

Daphne grimaced. "So you say."

"It is," Sam said, obviously not deterred by her grumpy attitude. "And I'm standing outside your door. If you don't open up, I'm going to be forced to break it down."

Daff lifted her head to see Sam grinning at her from the other side of the window. She knew it would be useless to try to resist. Not that she really wanted to.

She hung up the phone, pushed herself up off of the bed and crossed the room. "What can I do for you?" she asked.

Sam waggled his eyebrows suggestively. "Great question. You know, I just happen to be keeping a list."

Despite her gloom, Daphne chuckled. "Very funny."

"I thought so. Actually, though, I thought you might enjoy getting out of here for a while. There's a lot more to Naples than the yacht club and this motel."

She thought about it for all of about five seconds. "All right. I need a break, anyway."

Then, in a surprising move that Daff would later discover had saved her life, she picked up her keys, tossed them in the air, and said, "I think I'll even put the top down. Like you said, it's a beautiful night."

THIRTY-SIX

REVENGE was in the mail.

Jenna pushed open the front door of her house and smiled wryly at the thought. The package had been dropped off and marked for a 10 A.M. delivery. Jenna had paid in cash and used a bogus return address, and she had deleted the Stork Scent website last night after arriving back home from her deadly errand.

She was certain there was no way the package could be traced back to her.

She tried to ignore the doubts that nagged at her, the "what if"s that could drive a person crazy: What if Jahia al-Sayed didn't bring the perfume with her to the pool party? What if the delivery arrived too late? What if Jahia had some errand to run and missed it?

She hated knowing she was so close to achieving her goal, yet also knowing that so much of her plan depended on dumb luck. She wasn't certain she could take another day of waiting, of watching those who were responsible for her children's deaths continue living and breathing as if all were right in the world.

Jenna didn't know what she would do if it didn't end tomorrow. She couldn't live this way much longer.

With a weary sigh, she went to the kitchen to make some tea. She'd had a busy couple of days. First, she'd planted the ricin in that private investigator's car—hadn't anyone told her it wasn't safe to leave her vehicle unlocked?—and, as an added bonus, had stayed long enough to see one of Nathan Solem's employees at Ms. Donovan's door. Running on instinct, Jenna had pulled out her camera phone and snapped several pictures of the lovebirds as they engaged in a very public display of affection on the motel steps. With the investigator now certainly out of the way, Jenna didn't know if the photos might come in handy, but something had warned her to take them anyway. She'd learned to trust her instincts over the past month.

Jenna was halfway to the kitchen when she saw the red message light on her answering machine blinking. Almost no one knew here number here. Who would have left her a message?

Tentatively, as if the machine might be electrified, she reached out to press the play button.

"Hi Jenna, it's Nicole. Nicole Solem."

Jenna sank down in the chair next to the phone and clasped her hands together on her lap. In truth, she didn't trust how well things were going. If nothing else, the last few years had taught her to expect the worst. Whatever Nicole wanted, Jenna suspected it wasn't good.

"I was wondering if you'd like to come to a party tomorrow afternoon," Nicole's voice continued, oblivious to Jenna's dread. "My father's having some business associates and their families over. It should be a lot of fun. We'll have the powerboat available if you like to water ski, or if you just want to hang out by the pool, that's great, too. Anyway, you've just been so nice to me during . . . all this. I thought maybe this would be a nice way to repay you."

Jenna released the breath she'd been holding and stared at the answering machine as Nicole told Jenna to let her know if she would be attending before hanging up.

Jenna chewed on her bottom lip.

What should she do?

She wished Aaron were here so she could talk it over with him. He'd always been such a good listener. He wasn't one of those men who felt he had to solve a woman's every problem. He could just listen and offer sympathy without trying to tell her what she should do.

Jenna had always appreciated that about him.

But now she had no one to hear her out. She had to figure this out for herself.

She got up and absently walked into the kitchen to make a cup of tea. Best to think this through logically before taking any action. She had two options: accept the invitation, or decline it. If she declined, events would unfold according to her original plan. Jahia al-Sayed would receive the perfume tomorrow morning before ten o'clock. She may or may not be home when the package arrived, and there was no guarantee that she'd bring the perfume with her to the Solems' party. If she didn't, and she used the perfume later, there was no telling who the anthrax would harm. The success of Jenna's plan hinged on this one thing—that Jahia al-Sayed's fear about miscarrying was strong enough that she would open the package as soon as it arrived and immediately begin using it according to the instructions Jenna had included.

A lot of things could go wrong with this plan, but when

it had been her only option, Jenna had felt the chance of success outweighed the risk of failure.

What about now? If Jenna attended the party, she would be there in person to ensure that those she wanted harmed would get what they deserved. Nothing would be left to chance.

Only, if she chose to attend the Solems' party, she was going to have to get the perfume back. She would have to be at the al-Sayeds' house when the package arrived and would need to come up with a plan to get the deliveryman to give it to her—without being seen by the al-Sayeds and without arousing the deliveryman's suspicions.

There was no way she would attend that party if there was a chance Jahia al-Sayed was wearing her deadly perfume. Jenna didn't care about dying herself, but she could never rest in peace without knowing that those who had harmed her family were suffering. If she inhaled the anthrax, she might die before her revenge was complete. That, she could not have.

Jenna stirred her tea.

Was the risk of getting caught worth the certainty of knowing that her family's deaths had been avenged?

The answer came to her as if someone were whispering it in her ear.

Yes. She would do anything, sacrifice herself even, to ensure that justice was served. If she had the chance to know for sure that her revenge had been accomplished, she had to take it. She owed her daughters that much.

Jenna turned toward the window and squinted against the sun's heavy rays, filled with a sense of peace. A new plan had come to her, one that was even better, more perfect, than the last. And she couldn't help thinking, as she sipped her warm cup of tea, that Aaron and the girls must be looking down at her now, holding hands and smiling as they guided her toward the light.

* * *

BETWEEN last night and this morning, the Stork Scent website had disappeared.

Daphne scowled at her computer screen. Something was definitely going on here. Websites for legitimate businesses did not just disappear overnight.

This was her only lead. She was not going to just give it up without a fight.

She'd already tried to find out who owned the Stork Scent domain, but whoever had purchased it had paid extra to keep that information private. Used to be that simply typing in "whois" and the URL would give up the owner's name and address. After several years of complaints, domain registry companies had begun offering a service to hide this information.

If she were still with the Bureau, a search warrant would have taken care of that.

Daff sighed and leaned across her keyboard to grab a pen. She'd spread out all her "evidence" on the motel's tiny faux-wood desk. So far, all she had was the Stork Scent brochure and the original printout Keith had provided of Adnan al-Sayed's bank account. The other reports still lived on Keith's laptop, which was sitting on the far corner of the desk.

It sure wasn't much to go on.

She had to be missing something. Keith had pointed her to the al-Sayeds for a reason. It couldn't just be that he saw a Middle Eastern man with threatening eyes and automatically linked him to some sort of terrorist plot. Right?

No. The incident out in the swamp had to have meant something. No one would drive out to a swamp in the middle of the night unless they were trying to hide something. But why would Adnan al-Sayed meet with someone like that? If the terrorists had set up a website in order to collect money, and if Jahia al-Sayed had used her account to send them a payment, what in the hell had al-Sayed been doing skulking around in alligator country the other night?

Daff kept trying to put the pieces of the puzzle together, but they sure as hell didn't seem to fit. It was almost as if she were working with two different pictures, trying to cram the pieces of one together with pieces from the other.

But even if that were the case, there had to be something to tie one to the other. Even if Stork Scent wasn't a front for a terrorist group, it still had something to do with this whole mess. Daphne just *knew* it.

Now if only she could figure out what the connection was.

She picked up the brochure and narrowed her eyes, as if by squinting she might hone in on that one piece of information that might solve everything. It didn't help. All it did was make the letters fuzzy.

Blinking to clear her vision, Daff held the brochure up in front of her face. With nothing else to go on, she turned back to her computer and went to Google to do a search on the doctor who had written the overblown claims about the company's products.

Dr. Yvonne Richardson.

There were 768 references to that name.

This was the downside of the information age: information overload.

Daphne opened Excel and got to work. She figured that those 768 references would boil down to less than ten people. Information from different sources would be repeated—that is, five different newspapers might pick up the same story that included Dr. Richardson's name. Weeding out the duplicates would be tedious work, but that didn't deter her. Much of investigative work was tedious.

Daff actually found it comforting. She could get lost for hours tracing down some obscure lead. It was what had made her a good agent, that attention to detail . . . and her unwillingness to give up.

Before she dove into the mystery of Dr. Richardson, she got up and made herself a fresh pot of coffee. It could be hours before she was done collating the data. She'd learned long ago that caffeine was her friend.

After the rich brew was done percolating, Daff brought a steaming mug back to the table and got to work.

Two hours later, she had massaged those 768 references into eight distinct people. One was a distinguished high school teacher in Arkansas, and another was an engineer at General Motors. There was a mother of three who'd finished in the top hundred of the Boston Marathon; a young girl who had died in an apparent murder/suicide involving her father, Aaron, a few years back; a psychiatrist in New York; a woman who had invented a keychain that would store the location of a person's parked car; a chef in Seattle; and an artist renowned for her daring use of elephant dung in her works of "art."

In short, she still had nothing.

Not one of these Yvonne Richardsons appeared to be related to the perfume industry, to Stork Scent, to terrorist causes, or to the al-Sayeds.

Daff gulped down a mouthful of now-cold coffee and closed her eyes as she rubbed her forehead. What now?

She kept her eyes closed as she mentally ran through the events since Keith's death, hoping that the timeline might shake something loose.

Keith had died on Thursday, one week ago today, leaving a gift for Nicole and a note asking her to marry him. The police, obviously wanting to believe that Keith's death was a suicide, had either discovered the gift and dismissed it as being immaterial or had only given Keith's house a cursory examination and not seen the carseat at all. Daff found the gift on Friday and brought it to the Solems' attention, but they wanted even less to do with her theory that Keith was murdered than the Naples police did.

On Saturday, Nicole Solem set it up to make it look as if Daff had broken into Keith's house. That was the day Daphne had discovered the report Keith had printed out on Adnan al-Sayed's bank account. Sunday and Monday, Daff spent chasing down each transaction and ended up—as she had with everything in this case—finding nothing.

The trash run happened early Tuesday morning.

Tuesday night, Sam had saved her from being tortured by suspected terrorists and tossed into the swamp to be eaten by alligators.

Wednesday, she'd finally thought to get Keith's laptop and look into Mrs. al-Sayed's accounts, and that's when she discovered that a payment had been made to Stork Scent.

Now it was Thursday, and she was no closer to finding Keith's killer than she had been on day one. Stork Scent had mysteriously disappeared, she had no leads to follow on the man Adnan al-Sayed had met with on Tuesday night, and if she got within five hundred feet of the Solems, her ass would be back in jail so fast she'd look like Wile E. Coyote with those skid marks drawn above him as he plummeted to earth.

Daff scratched the side of her head.

Well, that little recap hadn't helped.

She had to be missing something here. But what?

She looked back at her computer screen. The Google search screen was still up. The left hand of her monitor was filled with summaries and links to information about the various Yvonne Richardsons. Lined up on the right side were businesses that had obviously paid Google to help them sell their wares. One was for Amazon.com. The listing said, "Purchase books about Yvonne Richardson here." Curious, Daff clicked the link and waited for a few seconds for the Amazon.com website to launch. When it did, Daff wasn't surprised to find that there were no books either written by or about the woman she was searching for.

She was about to hit the back button on her browser when she stopped.

Wait a second.

Amazon.com was a legitimate vendor. If Daff bought something off their website, her bank account would list the amount of the transaction as well as showing the payee as Amazon.com. If the charge went through without any problems on either end, in a few days, she'd receive a package from Amazon with the items she'd ordered. Simple online shopping at its best, right?

So, say for the sake of argument that Jahia al-Sayed believed Stork Scent was a legitimate business. She received their brochure, went to their website, and ordered herself up a miscarriage-proof bottle of perfume.

What if the company wasn't a terrorist front, but was still some sort of fraudulent business set up to separate gullible people from their money? Maybe Keith had found out about them from looking at Jahia al-Sayed's bank records and they'd found out and had him killed? Maybe it was Daphne's own racial profiling that was clouding her judgment. Perhaps Keith's death had nothing to do with terrorism after all.

It was a long shot that this train of thought would pan out, but it was the only lead she had. She had nothing to lose by chasing it down.

If nothing else, finding out whether or not a package was going to be delivered to Jahia al-Sayed from Stork Scent might give her another clue to follow.

Daff picked up the phone and called the one person she knew who could find out if a package was indeed en route to Mrs. al-Sayed—her partner in crime, Raine Robey.

"Hey Daff," Raine answered.

"Hey. Is it possible for you to tell me if there are packages out there scheduled to be delivered to a specific address?"

Raine pondered the question for approximately two-point-three seconds. "Sure. It's all out there on the Internet if you know where to look. Just give me the address."

Daff did and then grinned. "I think I love you."

"Get in line," Raine said dryly.

"Calder still after you to tie the knot?" Raine's boyfriend hadn't backed her up during a particularly ugly battle with the Bureau and she wasn't quite done making him suffer for it.

"Yeah. I gotta admit, he's starting to wear me down."

Daff's smile softened, though she was glad her partner couldn't see it. She had a reputation as a hardass to maintain. "Don't give up too easily," she said, just because she knew it was expected of her.

"You know I won't," Raine said.

In the background, Daff could hear the clacking of keys, and she wasn't surprised when Raine announced, "Okay, I'm e-mailing the tracking number to you. There's a package on its way from UPS to the address you gave me. It's scheduled to arrive tomorrow morning before ten."

Daff shook her head with amazement. She hoped she never got on Raine's bad side. That woman could track her to the ends of the earth.

"Can you find out who the sender is?" she asked without waiting for the e-mail to arrive. Raine probably knew the answer already.

"Afraid not. The label must have been handwritten and not processed through a computer, so the information isn't immediately accessible. At least not to me. It might be stored in a more secure area on UPS's intranet, but that would take me some time to get into."

"Don't bother. I'll get it off the package itself tomorrow morning," Daff said. Raine was busy on her own cases and didn't need to spend hours chasing down the rabbit hole with her. Intercepting the UPS delivery shouldn't be that difficult. Daff could make up some story about expecting the package and being a houseguest of the al-Sayeds'. In a neighborhood like theirs, stealing someone's deliveries was probably unheard of. If that didn't work, Daff would ask Raine to hack into UPS's network. But no sense risking that if she didn't have to. As good as Raine was, there was always a chance she'd get caught cybersnooping, and that wouldn't be good for Partners in Crime's business.

Daff thanked Raine and turned her attention back to her computer. She opened the e-mail Raine had sent and clicked the link to the tracking number of the package that was on its way to Jahia.

When the tracking information popped up, Daphne felt the first flutter of hope in her chest. The package had been dropped off at a UPS store here in Naples and then sent to the local processing area to await delivery—but the brochure had listed a post office box in Maryland as the company's mailing address. She could believe that the brochure may have been mailed locally, but what were the chances that a small company like that would have a fulfillment center in upscale Naples, where the cost of living had to be ten times the national average?

About zero, Daff guessed.

She didn't know what the package contained, but she was going to find out. She checked the estimated delivery time again and then leaned back and stared intently at her computer screen.

"Ten A.M.," she muttered to herself in the silence of the motel room, then added, "I'll be waiting."

THIRTY-SEVEN

DAPHNE wasn't taking any chances. She was staked out half a block from the al-Sayeds' by nine o'clock the next morning. With a yawn, she clicked the refresh button on her browser, but the estimated delivery time shown on the UPS tracking website did not change.

10:00 A.M. Another hour to sit and wait.

One of these days, she was going to take up solitaire.

Daff took a sip of the coffee she'd bought from the drive-thru Starbucks on Sunshine Parkway half an hour ago. She'd allowed herself the drink since she anticipated that this would be a relatively short surveillance. She'd worked a case once where a serial killer they'd been trailing gave his tail the slip while the agent ducked into a stairwell to relieve himself. The killer got away and the agent had ended up swallowing a bullet after the guy went on to kill two little kids the next week.

Daff understood how the guy had felt. She'd taken to wearing Depends if she knew she was going to be on a long stakeout. Knowing she could outlast her target trumped the humiliation of having to buy adult diapers.

But since the package would be delivered in an hour, she hadn't had to resort to either forgoing her morning coffee or strapping on her own personal lavatory.

Daff took another sip of her coffee as she surveyed the layout of the street. She'd positioned herself close to the mouth of the cul-de-sac, where she had a clear view of the only entrance and exit to the street. As soon as the delivery van passed her, she'd slip out of the convertible and head briskly toward the al-Sayeds' house. She'd offer to take the package from the deliveryman and would head toward the front door, as if just returning from her morning walk. If the deliveryman questioned her, she'd say she was a houseguest. And if he remained too long, she'd make a show out of patting down her pockets and pretending that she'd forgotten her key.

As long as Jahia al-Sayed remained sequestered inside, her plan would work.

And if she didn't? Well, Daff planned to leave her keys in the ignition and the car running. It was a short sprint to the convertible, so she'd just have to hope she could outrun both the deliveryman and the pregnant woman.

Daphne stretched her legs in the cramped confines of the car and the computer on her lap wobbled. Daff steadied it with one hand, and then glanced down to see that a new e-mail message had arrived.

She activated her e-mail program and chuckled when she saw that the message was from Raine. Her partner had probably been up all night hacking into UPS's intranet. Once Raine got fixated on something, there was no getting her to let go of it.

Daff snorted.

"Sounds like someone else you know," she mumbled to herself.

Yeah. Okay. So she could be a bit stubborn, too. Though she like to think of it as being tenacious.

She opened the e-mail and saw that, as she'd suspected, Raine had managed to dig up the scanned airbill attached to the package scheduled to arrive at the al-Sayeds' this morning. The handwriting was so neat and precise that Daphne wondered if the person who'd filled out the form had used a ruler to measure the width of each letter.

Whew. Talk about anal-retentive.

Daff had never seen such exact lettering. She wondered what a shrink would have to say about it. Probably that the writer was an organized control freak who couldn't stand disorder and lost it when life did not go her way.

But now was not the time for something as woo-woo as handwriting analysis, so Daff took a look instead at the information that had been so neatly printed on the form. As expected, the sender was listed as Stork Scent. The return address was a post office box in Maryland. Since UPS packages were not postmarked, the recipient would never know that the package had originated in Naples without looking at the tracking information.

The contact information was also neatly completed. Daff compared the phone number with the one from the Stork Scent brochure that was sitting on the passenger's seat and was not surprised to discover that they were the same. The contact person was listed as Dr. Yvette Richardson.

Daphne frowned. Why were alarm bells ringing in her brain? Nothing on the airbill contradicted what she already knew.

But her mind was warning her that something was wrong.

"Nice if you'd tell me what," Daff groused as she flipped over the brochure, trying to figure out what was amiss.

That's when she saw it. The medical information on the

front of the brochure had been provided by a Dr. *Yvonne* Richardson, not Yvette. Still, that mix-up didn't explain why all the muscles in her legs had tensed as adrenaline coursed through her veins. Her body had gone on full flight-or-fight alert, and Daff had no idea why.

She thought that maybe the answer would lie in the research she'd done yesterday, so she opened the Excel document she'd used to compile the information on Yvonne Richardson.

She studied the first row—the teacher in Arkansas—but found nothing. Then she checked out the GM engineer and the marathoner, but it was when she hit the fourth row that Daff's eyes widened with shock.

There it was. The information her subconscious had registered that her conscious mind had not.

Yvonne Richardson and her twin sister Yvette had been drowned by their father four years ago, right before he turned a gun on himself. It could be a coincidence, seeing these two names associated with this company, but Daff didn't think so.

With one eye on the rearview mirror, watching for the UPS van to arrive, Daff surfed to Google and typed in the name Aaron Richardson. What she found there made her certain that this was no coincidence. Aaron Richardson had indeed killed his children before committing suicide, but that wasn't what convinced Daphne that what was going on here was a lot bigger than the murder of Keith Melman and his discovery of a fraudulent perfume company.

Suddenly, it was as if the 3-D picture hidden in the puzzle had finally become clear.

Aaron Richardson had worked for pharmaceutical giant Geon—the company Nathan Solem had headed before its spiral into bankruptcy. Richardson had lost everything when the company went down and, in a fit of despair, he'd killed himself and his children. The next day, his wife, Jenna, had disappeared.

Two weeks later, rumors began to surface within the scientific community. It seemed that several stores of biological and chemical weapons—which the government claimed were only used to prepare antidotes in the case of an attack—had gone missing and no one could account for their whereabouts. And the last person to have signed these weapons out?

Aaron Richardson, of course.

So the big question was, where was Jenna Richardson . . . and what had she done with the stores of weapons that had been taken from Geon before her husband's death?

NO, it couldn't be.

Jenna's breathing stopped when she turned into the cul-de-sac and saw the red convertible idling in the driveway two houses down and across the street from Jahia al-Sayed's home.

Daphne Donovan should be dead by now. The ricin Jenna had planted in her car had been more than enough to kill her.

And yet, she was still alive.

Jenna's hands clenched the steering wheel of her nondescript sedan. Damn it. It was as if the other woman were wearing a Teflon coating. Jenna arranged for her to be arrested, but she was free the next day. Jenna poisoned her, but she miraculously cheated death.

How could that be?

Jenna clamped her teeth together. It didn't matter. Today, she would triumph. She would not let some meddling private investigator come between her and her revenge. She was too smart, too prepared for it to end now.

A small smile spread across her lips.

This wrinkle in her plans meant nothing. One short detour would take care of Daphne Donovan for good.

Nothing could stop her now.

Jenna pulled into the al-Sayeds' driveway just as the UPS delivery van turned into the cul-de-sac. Her timing was impeccable.

She stepped out of the car and met the deliveryman just as he started down the steps with a small cardboard box in his hands.

"Good morning," Jenna said. "I'm on my way to visit Mrs. al-Sayed. Would you like me to take that?"

It was as easy as that.

The man thanked her and handed her the package. Jenna turned toward the house, her smile widening as she heard the van start off down the street.

She got back into her car and automatically locked the doors as she checked the digital clock on the dashboard. The exchange had taken less than a minute.

The delivery van looped around the cul-de-sac. Jenna waited until it had passed before putting her own vehicle into reverse. Daphne Donovan stood rooted to the sidewalk near the al-Sayeds' mailbox, as if Jenna's sudden appearance had surprised her.

Jenna was certain it had.

She put the car in drive, but held her foot on the brake as she gently picked up the box on the seat next to her. Then, to taunt the other woman, she allowed herself a slow, catlike smile.

You lose, the smile said.

Daphne Donovan's eyes narrowed and Jenna let up on the brake. She didn't want to make this too easy. Sometimes, in order to catch one's prey, one must act like the hunted and not the hunter.

Jenna felt her heart expand as she sped away.

Soon, she promised herself. Soon, her babies would live again.

* * *

"IS there a Jenna Richardson attending this CEO thing?" Daphne asked, cradling her cell phone between her ear and her shoulder as she pressed on the accelerator and tore through a yellow light at the intersection.

She may not have the exact right answer here, but she was smart enough to see that missing biological weapons plus a disgruntled former–Geon employee's wife plus a meeting of the top CEOs in the country added up to a potentially explosive situation. This had to have something to do with Nathan Solem's CEO summit. Daff just knew it.

"No," Sam answered, sounding as if he were frowning. "Who's Jenna Richardson?"

Daff tapped her brakes as the woman in the tan sedan four cars in front of her slowed to take a turn.

"The wife of a former Geon employee who killed himself and his children when the company went under," Daphne said. "I don't know how this is related to Keith Melman's death, but I think she's going to use Solem's CEO summit to get revenge."

"But everyone checks out," Sam argued. "I finally got Nathan to agree to give me a list of the attendees and everyone came up clean. There's no Jenna Richardson on the list."

Daphne wiped one palm on her jeans as the steering wheel started to slip through her fingers. "Are you sure you've got everyone? I'm tailing a woman now, she might be Jenna Richardson, or she could be someone working with her. I don't know. She took the perfume that was supposed to be delivered to Jahia al-Sayed."

"What perfume?" Sam asked.

Daff waved her hand dismissively. It was too complicated to explain right now. She frowned as the sedan approached a white stucco house with green trim. The garage door was already closing as the woman in the sedan floored the accelerator. The car slid under, just before the door would have scraped the top of the vehicle.

"Look, I'm over at a house on Osprey Avenue. Could you just check out this Jenna Richardson again? She was married to a Geon employee named Aaron. They had two girls, Yvonne and Yvette. He drowned the girls and then killed himself four years ago. Jenna disappeared the next day, and it appears that she took some stolen biological weapons with her. The papers made the connection between Aaron's murder/suicide and the demise of Geon. If Richardson blames Nathan Solem for her family's death . . ." Daphne let the conclusion remain unspoken. People had certainly killed for much less.

"All right. I'll get back to you," Sam said. "You're not going in, are you? This woman could be dangerous."

"No, Sam. I'm going to sit outside and watch while some head case builds a biological weapon to kill the country's top CEOs," Daff answered dryly, then continued before Sam could argue. "The local police think I'm public enemy number one, my former boss thinks I'm a stalker, and I'm sitting here watching history repeat itself. I'm one hundred percent sure that something's going down. Right now. I felt the same way on 9/11, but I let the skeptics' doubts slow me down. What if I hadn't? What if I'd refused to listen to them? Maybe I could have prevented the attack."

"I'm not the enemy, Daphne. And neither are you," Sam said.

"I'm not going to let it happen again."

Daff was already out of her car, her pistol in one hand and her cell phone in the other. She stumbled on the sidewalk, her eyes closing briefly, when Sam answered softly, "You wouldn't be the woman I love if you did."

Those were the last words Daphne heard before the connection was dropped. She stood on the stoop, warily eyeing the unlatched front door as it creaked open in the gentle breeze coming off the Intracoastal Waterway.

THIRTY-EIGHT

JENNA sat in the garage and waited for Daphne to step inside the house. From the small screen in her hand, she watched as the redhead cautiously pushed open the front door, leading with her gun the way cops always did on TV. Slowly, she surveyed the living room, making certain it was empty before starting toward the kitchen.

Jenna smiled.

She pushed a combination of buttons on the security system's remote control. The modifications she'd made to the house before moving down to Naples had been expensive, but Jenna had suspected it might come to this.

She squinted as the bright sunshine reached her eyes when the garage door opened. She slipped on a pair of stylish purple sunglasses as she backed the car out of the garage and pressed another series of buttons.

Pausing for a moment at the end of the drive, Jenna contemplated the home she'd lived in for the past month. It was more a house than a home, really. Nowhere felt like home anymore. With her mother dead and her family all gone, Jenna had no idea where she was going to go next.

Without her plans of revenge to fuel her, Jenna wasn't quite sure what would motivate her to get out of bed every morning.

Sadly, she shook her head. Later. She'd think about that later.

For now, she had to concentrate on her plan—a plan nearly twelve months in the making.

This first part was simple. Destroy the evidence, and Daphne Donovan along with it. No problem. It was amazing what a few hundred thousand dollars would get you. Bullet-proof windows, steel-reinforced walls, a security system that could lock down the entire house with the click of a few buttons. Even more important, hidden gas lines that would ignite, burning the house—and everything in it—from inside. By the time the neighbors saw the first hint of smoke, it would already be too late. The buildup of gas inside the house would cause it to explode before the fire department had a chance to get their hoses hooked up.

Jenna patted the beach bag beside her and smiled as she pulled out of the driveway without giving the house another look.

One more hour and it would all be over.

"I'M telling you, Nathan, you need to cancel this event." Sam scowled as he paced in front of his boss in the mansion's oversized kitchen. He'd been trying to convince Nathan for the past five minutes that something very wrong was going to happen this weekend. Problem was, he wasn't able to give his boss any specifics, which didn't exactly help his cause.

"But you ran all the background checks and everything came up fine, right?"

Sam didn't stop pacing. "Yeah, but maybe I missed someone. There has to be a connection with this Jenna Richardson and someone who's attending the summit this weekend. I just don't believe this is all a coincidence."

"There's no Jenna Richardson coming. There's a Jenna Marisol, who's a friend of my daughter's, but you've met her already. She was on the yacht the other night with Nicole and the al-Sayeds. If she was plotting some sort of revenge, she could easily have gotten to me then."

Sam frowned. "Jenna Marisol? Her name wasn't on the list you gave me."

"Nicole just invited her yesterday." Nathan couldn't keep the amusement out of his voice as he continued. "No offense, Sam, but I think you spent too much time in special operations. You're seeing conspiracies where none exist. Jenna is a nice woman. She's been a good friend to Nicole during this difficult time."

"Yeah, well, that doesn't mean she's not also a killer," Sam said. He'd known plenty of seemingly nice people who were guilty of murder. Hell, for that matter, *he* was a nice guy. That didn't mean, given the right circumstances, that he wasn't capable of taking human life.

"If it makes you feel any better, then go ahead and research her," Nathan said, still sounding amused. "Our guests are starting to arrive, but I can let them know the boat won't be ready to go for another few minutes. It's not like they can't relax by the pool or on the beach for a while."

Sam nodded. Good. He'd go check out this Jenna Marisol, and then he'd call Daphne. If he wasn't certain that the danger was here at the Solems', he'd already be gone . . . and to hell with his job.

Sam hurried down the hall toward the security office. His computer was already up and running. In less than five minutes, he'd have a preliminary background check on Jenna Marisol. If it turned out that she was not connected to the Richardsons in any way, Sam didn't know what he'd do. He supposed he would have to trust the security company Nathan had hired to do their job if something *did* happen.

Sam used one hand to type Jenna Marisol's name into the computer while dialing his cell phone with the other. Daphne's phone rang four times before it flipped to voice mail. Sam left a message, but he was starting to get that worried feeling in the pit of his gut.

Why wasn't she answering her phone?

Before he could hit enter or redial his phone, the door to the security office was flung open. The doorknob bounced off the wall with an angry *thunk*. Sam looked up to find Nathan glowering at him from the doorway.

"What the hell is this?" Nathan shouted, waving a handful of papers at Sam.

Sam put his hands up in a "let's all calm down here" gesture. "I don't know. Why don't you let me see?"

Nathan flung the papers at Sam's feet. "Get out," he ordered.

Sam briefly glanced down at the mess on the floor. Some of the papers were upside down, but one clearly showed him holding Daphne, their faces close as if they were about to kiss.

"Nathan, I can explain," he said.

"You knew this woman was not welcome in my house. She's a troublemaker whose only intent was to harm my daughter. And yet you were with her. You're fired, Sam. I'll pay you your two weeks' notice because I'm a fair man, but I never want to see you—or this woman—around my family again. Do you understand?"

"Of course I do, but Nathan, you've got this all wrong. Daphne doesn't—"

"Get out," Nathan repeated, stepping aside to let two men with not-just-for-show beefy biceps into the room.

Sam knew he could take them, but what would be the point? Lance Muldoon had over twenty security guys hanging around the Solems' property. He couldn't fight them all.

He kept one hand up in a nonthreatening manner while he slowly leaned down and hit enter to start the background search on Jenna Marisol.

"Okay, calm down. I'm leaving." He started backing toward the door. "Just check this in about five minutes. If Jenna Marisol is in any way connected to Aaron Richardson, who was a Geon employee when the company went bust, call the police immediately. You got it?" Sam maintained eye contact with the security company's employees until one of them—a dark-haired guy who looked as if he realized his brain wasn't just another muscle—nodded.

"Thanks," Sam muttered. Then, fishing his keys out of his front pocket, he turned to leave, all the time thinking that this resistance was nothing compared to what Daphne must have faced on 9/11. Frankly, he was beginning to wonder how she'd managed to stay sane.

DAPHNE heard a loud click and turned toward the sound, but no one was there. She swung back around to face what had to be the garage door and reached out for the doorknob, but it refused to turn. She looked for a lock, but didn't see one. Wasn't that odd? A garage door that locked from the outside?

Daff pounded on the door in case someone was on the other side. "Open up," she yelled.

Her demand was met with silence.

Fine. There was more than one way to get through a locked door. Daff backed up a few feet and readied herself to rush the door. Typically, a well-placed kick near the lock would do it.

Only, when she jammed her booted foot against the door, it was as if she were kicking a cast-iron frying pan. The impact of it reverberated through her shin and up her thigh.

Jesus, that hurt.

Daff clutched her ankle. What the hell was that door made of? Kryptonite?

Limping, she stepped back from the door. Her second choice would have been to try to shoot out the lock, but she didn't want to chance it. If the door was reinforced, as she suspected from the shattered bones in her foot that it was, the bullet might ricochet. Better to just go around the front and try to find a window into the garage. If, indeed, that's where her suspect was still hiding.

Daff limp-walked to the front door, surprised to find it closed. She frowned. She was certain she had left it open.

She put her hand on the knob and tugged. Again, nothing happened.

Daff was beginning to feel the first fluttering of unease in her chest.

Calm down, she told herself. *You're not trapped in here.*

Maybe the doors just locked on their own, like a hotel. Of course, those locks were usually used to keep people out, not in.

Daff shrugged and reached for her phone to call Sam, but the display showed that there was no signal. Quickly glancing around the room, she saw a white telephone on a glass-topped table between two uncomfortable-looking leather and chrome chairs. She picked up the receiver and pressed the talk button, not surprised to find that it was dead.

Clearly, she had underestimated her foe.

Daphne took a deep breath as she lowered the phone back to its cradle. There had to be a way out of here.

She'd try the windows first. Even if they were locked,

glass was easy enough to break. There were no windows along the front side of the house, which Daff didn't find surprising. They'd only look out onto the street. The real beauty of the house lay in the back, with its view of the Intracoastal Waterway.

Daff walked toward a set of sliding glass doors leading from the dining room onto the patio, her eyes narrowing as she got closer to them. A slight groove had been sliced into the floor in front of the metal tracks that held the doors. Daff looked up to see that a thick sheet of Plexiglas fit tightly into a similar groove in the ceiling.

What kind of person bought a house with bulletproof glass?

Daphne stuck her head into the kitchen and found that the window over the sink had been fitted with a similar covering.

"The kind who expects trouble," Daff muttered to herself, answering her own question as she leaned back against the island separating the kitchen from the dining room. She needed a plan.

First, she'd check all the doors and windows. Then she'd try to find access to the attic. If that didn't work . . .

Daff shrugged and moved away from the counter. If that didn't work, she didn't know what the hell she'd do.

THIRTY-NINE

THE bullet hadn't even penetrated the outer layer of Plexiglas.

Daff stared at the piece of metal lodged in the material covering the sliding glass doors. Now what? She was a good shot, but not an expert. She could try aiming at the spot the first bullet had entered and pray that a second shot in the same exact spot might shatter the bulletproof glass, but she wasn't a big believer in praying.

She could also put the muzzle of her weapon over the hole she'd just made and try that, but she was afraid a bullet fired at such short range might ricochet back on her. Frankly, being gut-shot by her own hand wasn't the way Daff wanted to be taken out of this world.

She chewed on the inside of her bottom lip. There had to be a structural weakness somewhere, but she had yet to find it. The floors and walls were concrete, the doors had been reinforced with what she assumed was steel, and the windows were all covered with six-inch-thick bulletproof glass. There was no attic access that she had been able to find, and her exploratory pokes at the ceiling with a broom she'd discovered in the laundry room left her fairly certain that even the ceiling had been armored. The air-conditioning ducts were four inches by eight inches, the sewer drains were too small—not to mention disgusting—and were drilled through a foundation of solid concrete.

Bottom line: Daphne was trapped.

She'd just come to that conclusion when she heard the first pop. At first, she was too busy contemplating the swimming pool that had been cut in half by a solid wall of Plexiglas to think much about the noise.

She walked to the edge of the pool and put her hand on the bulletproof glass to steady herself. It was kind of cool, actually. If the Plexiglas were raised, you could swim from the inside of the house to the outside. The outer edge was one of those invisible lines that made it seem as if the swimming pool were part of the Intracoastal Waterway.

Unfortunately, with the Plexiglas down, she couldn't see a way to get outside. As with the sliding glass doors, the wall of plastic fit tightly into a groove that had been cut into the sides and bottom of the pool. As far as Daff could tell, there wasn't a gap to be found anywhere.

She pushed away from the glass and started to turn toward the kitchen when she saw a flash of orange out of the corner of her eye. It took several seconds for her unwilling brain to register what was happening, and when it did, Daphne's blood ran cold.

The house was on fire.

She was trapped in here and was going to die.

Trying to calm her panic, she backed out of the living room where the fire was blazing and stepped into the kitchen. She looked up when she heard another pop and shuddered when she saw the top row of cupboards burst into flame.

Wildly, she dragged her gaze across the room as the heat intensified.

She had to save herself. But how?

Her gaze stopped on the Sub-Zero refrigerator nestled between a pantry and a low set of cabinets. She glanced back at the pool, measuring the distance and the narrow space between the island and another set of cupboards. Maybe, just maybe, if she could get the fridge into the pool, she could get to the bottom and use it to shield herself from falling debris until the fire burned out.

It might not work, but it was her only hope.

Ducking to avoid the flames as the door of the upper cupboard blew out, Daff raced across the kitchen. She spread her arms and dug her fingers into the soft rubber seal between the door and the main part of the fridge, and then tugged, trying to get the Sub-Zero unwedged from its tight spot. When it barely budged, Daff stepped back and pulled open the door, hoping that she might be able to use the door as a sort of leash to drag the refrigerator behind her.

When the door opened, she expected to be hit with both the smell of food and the chill of cooled air, but was greeted only with the *whoosh* of frigid air on her heated skin. She might have been in too much of a hurry to care about the lack of leftovers, but the sight that greeted her stopped her in her tracks.

The fridge was filled with row upon row of sealed beakers, each neatly labeled in the same handwriting Daff had seen that morning on the UPS airbill.

What the—

Daff froze when she heard a tapping on the glass behind her, but she didn't turn away from the horror in the fridge.

Anthrax.

Tularemia.

Botulinum.

Ricin.

Parathion.

Biological and chemical weapons designed to disable and kill an enemy. Daff had worked antiterrorism long enough to become familiar with them all. Some of the heavy hitters like smallpox, Ebola, marburg, and plague were missing from the arsenal, but Daff's nemesis didn't need them. This particular strain of anthrax alone could kill tens of thousands of people if it got into the air or water system. And once it was out, there was nothing anyone could do. There was no antidote.

Daphne's hand fluttered to her chest as she finally turned around and saw Sam pounding on the window from outside.

She had no words for the man she had fallen in love with, nothing that would make him understand the fear that gripped her, the awful knowledge that once again she hadn't been fast enough or smart enough or determined enough to stop the unthinkable from happening.

Because they were not just dealing with a madwoman out for revenge.

They had to stop a terrorist.

SAM was not going to leave her.

Daff pressed the beaker up against the Plexiglas and pointed again to the handwritten label, but Sam just shook his head. He knew what she was trying to tell him. Get out of here. Go save everyone else and leave her to take care of herself. Or, at the very least, get out of range of whatever cell signal blocker Jenna Richardson had activated like a force field around her house and call the authorities and try to convince them of the danger.

But he wouldn't go.

Daphne watched from inside as he ran his hands along

the wall of bulletproof glass, looking for some sort of weakness.

She stepped away from the window.

What was that saying? Desperate times called for desperate measures?

She couldn't just stand here, knowing what was going to happen, and not try to do everything she could to stop it. She'd rather die than live through that guilt again.

The smoke was getting heavier now, the crackling heat of the fire growing more intense. Daff knew she didn't have much time. She had to find somewhere to put the deadly arsenal where it would be safe. If those beakers broke . . . She shivered.

No. She'd figure out something.

But first she had to convince Sam to leave. And the only way to do that was to prove to him that there was no hope for her. There was no way he'd leave her otherwise. He'd fight for her until nothing was left but her charred remains. In the meantime, everyone at that CEO summit would be exposed to Jenna Richardson's biological weapons.

Daff could not die with that on her conscience. She already had enough souls to account for. She couldn't take any more.

She crawled along the floor, pressing a wet dishtowel to her face to try to strain out the worst of the smoke.

Her gun was on the island across from the refrigerator, right where she'd left it.

Daff picked it up, ignoring the thud from across the room where Sam—seeing what she was doing—had thrown himself against the Plexiglas. Even Sam was no match for six inches of bulletproof glass.

Daphne felt her arms start to tremble as she crawled back to the sliding glass doors. Desperate, Sam picked up a lawn chair and hurled it at the glass. The door cracked on the outside, but it didn't matter. The Plexiglas was indestructible.

They stood across from one another, less than a foot apart. Daphne could see the frustration in his eyes and she understood. For people like them, not being able to save others was worse than facing their own deaths.

Daff's hand shook as she raised it and placed her palm against the sun-warmed glass. Sam hesitated, but they both knew it was too late.

He couldn't save her.

No one could.

Sam put his hand on the other side of the glass, his large palm dwarfing hers.

Daphne swallowed and didn't bother blinking back her tears. "I love you," she whispered.

Sam roared with anguish and threw himself against the window again, but the glass just shook for a second before it stilled.

"Go," Daphne said as Sam watched her from outside, his chest heaving.

He shook his head.

Daff slowly raised her gun until the barrel rested against her temple.

"Go," she said again, her finger tightening on the trigger.

Sam closed his eyes.

Daff's arm started to shake as a bead of sweat dripped down her face. She would do it if she had to.

Sam's eyes opened and he took a step back. "I love you," he mouthed.

Daphne nodded. Then, her heart breaking, she watched her lover turn and walk away.

She stared for a long moment at the empty spot where he'd stood just seconds before until a mournful groan snapped her out of her reverie. Blinking as if waking up from a trance, Daphne looked around the burning kitchen. She had perhaps five more minutes before the whole place went up in flames.

She could hear the sound of sirens in the distance, but they'd be too late. The fire had advanced too far.

All Daff could do now was try to contain the biological and chemical weapons that Jenna had stockpiled.

Working quickly, she pulled the beakers from the refrigerator and carefully set them inside the dishwasher next to the sink for safekeeping. Then, her strength fueled by a combination of determination and desperation, Daff pulled at the fridge with all her might.

After several seconds of resistance, the Sub-Zero finally gave way with a sucking *whoosh*. Daff rolled the fridge across the tile floor, giving a mighty yank when the plastic water line attached to the icemaker tried to hold her back. The connection broke when she was a foot from the edge of the swimming pool. Daff let go, and the momentum of the line breaking sent the refrigerator over the edge.

Daff jumped in after it. Initially, she'd thought she could maneuver it so the fridge sank upside down with the door open to provide her with a bubble of oxygen to breathe until the fire burned out.

But now that didn't matter. She needed a tight seal on the fridge so that even if one of the beakers broke inside, there would be a chance it might not leak. It wasn't a perfect plan, but it was the best she chould come up with. Had she found a jug of chlorine somewhere in the house during her initial inspection, she would have dropped the beakers in there. Chlorine was one of the few things that could kill bacteria such as anthrax and render them harmless. But if Jenna did keep chlorine in the house for the swimming pool, it must be out in the garage where Daphne couldn't get to it. Plan B would just have to do.

Daff shoved at the refrigerator until it filled with water and came to a rest on its back in the shallow end of the pool.

As she crawled up the steps, the heat became so intense

that she sank back down into the water. She ducked her head beneath the surface to wet her hair.

She couldn't give up now.

Daff cringed as a row of upper cabinets crashed down onto the floor, blocking her route to the dishwasher. She thought about just leaving the beakers there, but worried that the heat would get too intense and the glass might shatter. There would be a better chance that they'd stay cool underwater.

She would do this . . . or die trying.

She forced herself out of the pool and ran toward the kitchen with flames licking at her wet clothes. Halfway to the sink, another crash sounded as the bottom of a cupboard burned through and its contents dropped to the floor. Daff hunkered down, her arms over her head protectively as she crawled through the debris to the dishwasher.

She opened the door and pulled out the plastic case that held about two dozen sealed beakers. Lifting her head, Daff surveyed the path back to the pool. The floor was strewn with fallen shards of burning wood and glass. If she tripped . . .

Daff took a deep breath and straightened her shoulders.

She would make it.

Gathering her feet beneath her, she did something she hadn't done since 9/11—she closed her eyes and prayed, begging God to help her keep all those innocent people safe.

Then she made a run for it, not looking back even as a sound as loud as a thunderclap shook the house. She reached the water just as another boom rocked the foundation. Daff ignored everything but what she had to do next.

She slid into the water and carefully submerged the beakers. With her eyes open underwater, she swam toward the refrigerator and wedged the plastic holder into one of the veggie bins where it had the least wiggle room. If a piece of roof or something came crashing down into the pool, Daff didn't want the beakers to become dislodged.

The water resisted her efforts to close the refrigerator door, but Daff would not give up. Her lungs burning from the smoke-filled air she'd inhaled before diving underwater, she kept pushing until the door finally closed.

She broke the surface of the water gasping for air, gulped in another lungful, and then headed back down. Her job was not done yet.

The fridge would be safest in deeper water, where anything that might fall into the pool would be slowed by the resistance of the water. Plus, Daff wanted to get it as close to the outside wall as possible. Chances were that the concrete walls would not crumble, even in the fire, so the safest place for the refrigerator to be would be next to one of these supporting walls.

Moving it, however, was easier said than done.

As Daff surfaced again, the fridge only a few inches closer to the deep end than it had been before, she felt a change in the air. It was as if pressure were building up inside the house, a strange stillness settling in the air.

She dove down again. Whatever was going to happen would happen. In the meantime, she wasn't giving up.

When she rose to the surface once more, Daff was surprised to realize that her mind had settled into a trancelike state, as if she were in denial about what was going on around her. Instead of contemplating her own death, she found herself thinking about the people she loved. Her friends and partners, Raine Robey and Aimee Devlin, who she'd met all those years ago during their special agent training in Virginia; her brother, Brooks, who she loved with all her heart; Sam Bryson, her surprising new love who saw the best in her, while still knowing—and loving—the worst.

It was then, as pieces of plaster from the roof began collapsing around her, that Daff found the peace she'd been searching for since that awful September day in 2001.

She had always imagined that the final thoughts of those who died were of bitterness and hatred, that they focused on everyone who had failed them that day. Instead, with her own death near, she realized the opposite was true. Her heart was not filled with anger, but with gratefulness that she'd lived a good life, surrounded by those she loved.

As the force of another explosion sent a fiery beam crashing down toward her, Daphne took one final breath and dove beneath the surface of the water, knowing she was about to die, but also knowing that she had finally found forgiveness.

FORTY

DAPHNE Donovan was fucking crazy if she thought he'd just leave her here to die alone.

Sam nearly growled with frustration as he shoved his truck into reverse and lined up for another shot at the front door. Yeah, okay, he hadn't been willing to call her bluff. The complete head case he was in love with might have gone and shot herself out of sheer dumb stubbornness.

Plus, he had to admit it—she had a point. He couldn't just let this Jenna Richardson or Jenna Marisol or whatever the hell her name was get away with infecting all those innocent people. He hadn't wasted time with the local police—they would have thought he was as crazy as Daphne. Fortunately, he still had friends in the Navy, people who knew he wasn't one to see terrorists where none existed. They could pull strings that he couldn't, and get the cops to take this threat seriously.

When that was done, he'd placed another call to his pal Tony, who made short work out of digging up information on the contractor who had done the work on this house. It was obviously not your typical spec home. Someone had to have reinforced the walls and added the bulletproof windows.

That same someone had to know the house's vulnerabilities.

There had to be something—an escape hatch that only the contractor and the person who had paid for all this knew about. That person wouldn't want to take the chance that they'd be the one who got trapped inside.

So far, however, the contractor wasn't talking.

That, Sam knew, would all change in less than a minute once Tony got to the guy's house. Until then, Sam refused to just sit here and do nothing while Daphne was trapped inside.

Sam's phone rang. He rammed the truck into gear before pressing the button to answer it.

He could hear the sirens of the fire trucks approaching and knew he had to hurry. Once they arrived, they'd want to take over.

He was certain they were great guys, but Sam would fucking kill them if they got in his way.

"Bryson," he grunted as the truck bounced over a depression in the lawn. The front door was only ten feet away now.

"There's an escape hatch at the back of the house, two feet from the northwest corner and six inches up. You'll need something fairly heavy to bust up the outer sheet of plaster, but once you get through, you should be fine. That'll put you into the laundry room, between the washing machine hookup and a utility sink." Tony didn't waste any time on pleasantries . . . or on explaining how he'd managed to get this information so quickly. Which was really unnecessary. Sam had gone on enough ops with Tony to know just how persuasive he could be.

Sam slammed on the brakes just inches from the front door. No use banging up his truck any more than necessary.

Once again, he shoved the vehicle in reverse and backed out into the street, parking it where he knew he'd have easy access even after the fire trucks arrived. The way he saw it, he and Daphne were going to have to beat a hasty retreat when this was all over.

He grabbed the keys from the ignition and shoved open the door, hitting the pavement at a run. As he jumped the curb, the first fire truck stopped in front of Jenna Richardson's house. An ax hung from one side, and Sam didn't hesitate to take it. He ignored the shout behind him as he raced to the side of the house and effortlessly cleared the four-foot-high stucco fence.

His boots sank into the damp lawn on the other side as he landed heavily in the grass. Another twenty feet and he was whipping around the side of the house, the ax already pulled back for his first shot. Metal met plaster with a satisfying *thwack* and shards of white stucco went flying as Sam pulled the ax back for another hit.

As soon as the hole was large enough for him to wiggle through, Sam dropped to the ground. Searing heat and smoke billowed through the hole, but he didn't hesitate before diving through.

"Daphne!" he shouted as he pulled his feet inside.

He kept low, trying to see through the thick smoke that burned his eyes and clogged his throat. He crawled out of the laundry room and into the kitchen, where the heat was even more intense.

When he saw the devastation around him, Sam gritted his teeth and yelled Daphne's name again. This was no regular fire. How the hell could she have survived this?

He should never have let her think he was abandoning her.

Sam coughed and crawled another few feet toward the

dining room. The roar of the fire was so loud, he could barely hear his own voice as he continued calling Daphne's name.

He headed for the swimming pool, knowing that's where he would have gone during this and hoping Daphne had done the same. When he rounded the corner of the island, he saw something that made his heart drop out of his chest.

What was that floating on the surface of the pool?

Uncaring now about his own safety, Sam headed for the pool at a dead run.

JENNA pushed her sunglasses up the bridge of her nose and wistfully smiled at the children yelping and screeching with laughter in Nathan Solem's pool. Her revenge was nearly complete and she waited to feel the sense of peace she'd expected, knowing that her family's deaths would soon be avenged.

Instead, she felt restless and wondered if this, too, would be a dead end.

Would these people die, would their children suffer, and still not bring Jenna peace?

Jenna shook her head to clear away the thought. No. This had to work.

She sat up and leaned over her lounge chair to take the bottle of sunscreen from her brightly colored beach bag. She'd bought both this morning from the drugstore near her house. Before intercepting her package at Jahia al-Sayed's, she'd returned home with the sunscreen and emptied out the contents of the large plastic bottle into an even larger bowl. Carefully, she'd removed a cupful of sunscreen and washed it down the sink, replacing it with a cup of an organophosphate called parathion, which entered the bloodstream via hair follicles on the human body. Just hours after the toxin was applied, the victim would be in excruciating pain. Her eyes would become watery, and her vision would blur. She'd vomit and begin to sweat. She'd hyperventilate and lose consciousness.

If the victim lived, open sores that would not heal would appear on the body, often near the victim's genitalia. If she was pregnant, she would miscarry. Most likely, she'd die tragically young from cancer. That is, if her heart didn't stop during the initial phase of the poisoning.

All of that would come after slathering on a dollop of seemingly innocuous sunscreen.

Jenna watched the young woman beside her eye a blond girl of about four who was paddling in the shallow end of the swimming pool. With a smile, Jenna leaned forward, holding out the bottle in her hand.

"Your daughter has such beautiful skin. Better be careful she doesn't burn," she said.

The young mother turned and returned Jenna's smile. "Thank you. You can never use too much sunscreen on kids these days, can you?"

Jenna allowed herself a small laugh. "There are just so many more dangers for them than we ever thought, aren't there?" she said by way of agreement.

The woman accepted Jenna's offering without hesitation. And why should she hesitate? She was safe here, among people she assumed were just like her, people who had never felt the sting of tragedy and loss, who had never had to face the horror of coming home to find their babies drowned and their husband's blood spattered on the white walls of their bedroom.

The plastic bottle nearly slipped out of Jenna's sweat-dampened hand, but the young woman caught it. She had just squeezed a tablespoon into the palm of her hand when Jenna heard the first strain of approaching sirens.

Her eyes narrowed. Had that private investigator managed to escape and alert the authorities?

She shook her head to clear it. *Focus,* she told herself. That's what she needed to do. Focus.

All along, people had thwarted her, starting with her mother and ending with this private investigator. But no more. Jenna was through fighting. Perhaps this was how it was supposed to end, anyway. Perhaps this was what it had been driving toward all along.

With a regal tilt to her head, Jenna slipped off the lounge chair and tightened her silk pareo around her waist. Then, with a nod, she excused herself and slowly walked into the house as the sound of sirens got louder.

They might think they were going to triumph, but they were wrong. Jenna had too much at stake to stop now. She was going to get her revenge, to make it so that her family could rest in peace, even if that meant she, too, would die.

IT wasn't Daphne floating facedown on the surface of the pool, but the heavy beam that had done its best to kill her. Daff dove down and sat at the bottom of the pool, looking up, for as long as her lungs could take it. When she came up for air, she surfaced just as Sam jumped in.

Without pausing to declare her undying love or thank him for coming back for her, Daff grabbed his arm and dragged him toward the steps. Yeah, yeah, she had fallen for him and would love him forever. But for now, they had to get the hell out of here.

"You okay?" Sam asked tersely as they pulled themselves out the pool. Obviously, he felt the same about their undying declarations of love.

"Yeah."

"Follow me."

"Right behind you," Daff assured him.

They half-crawled and half-ran through the burning kitchen and into the laundry room. Sam waved at a hole under the sink, through which Daphne could see the welcoming bright light of the sun. Only, just as she was about to dive through, she stopped and grabbed a white bottle with a green label from a shelf that she must have missed on her first pass through the house.

Sam didn't bother asking what she was doing. Instead he "helped" her through the hole by shoving her down and pushing on her rear to get her to go through.

He'd thank her later, Daff thought, as she rolled away from the house and pushed up off the grass once she had her feet under her.

"Where's your truck?" she yelled, already running toward the front yard.

"Across the street. Don't stop for anything," Sam said as he caught up with her and then stopped near a stucco fence and cupped his fingers together to help her over the wall.

"My hero." Daff grinned as she placed her foot in Sam's hands and easly vaulted over the wall with Sam at her heels.

Sam just grunted. He had his keys out and in his hand as they dodged the firemen who, understandably, wanted to know what the hell was going on. Once she was inside the cab of the truck, Daff rolled down the window. "There's a fridge at the bottom of the pool that's got biological weapons in it. Don't open it without the proper gear," she shouted to the fireman nearest her, who was looking at her as if she were nuts. Still, no matter how crazy they might think she was, they'd take her threat seriously. They couldn't afford not to.

Plus, fireman lived for that kind of shit.

Daff's head hit the headrest as Sam gunned the engine. She dropped the bottle of bleach on the floor and hastened to buckle her seatbelt.

She had a feeling this was going to be a bumpy ride.

They both remained silent as Sam raced across town. For her part, Daphne didn't want to distract him. She didn't know why he was so quiet. Probably thinking up ways to punish her for threatening to shoot herself if he didn't leave her back there.

Frankly, she was glad he hadn't listened.

She heard the sirens as they neared Nathan Solem's mansion.

Daff turned to Sam then. "How do we play this?" she asked.

"I have an idea. You stay in the car and I'll take it from here," Sam suggested without taking his eyes from the road.

Daphne tried to smother a smile. This was not the time for levity.

"God, I love you," she said, unable to hold the words back.

"Yeah," Sam answered.

The truck skidded to a stop just inside the gates of the mansion, the back tires sliding on the loose gravel like in some movie.

Daff had the door open before the vehicle had come to a complete stop. She grabbed the jug of bleach from the floor and was halfway around the hood of the truck when Sam caught up with her. He stopped her with one hand on her shoulder, his brown eyes serious as they gazed into hers.

"I love you, too, Daphne. I was an idiot to think that I was just waiting to get out of the Navy to start a relationship. The truth was, I was just waiting to meet you."

Daphne raised her free hand to touch Sam's cheek. No, they didn't have time for this . . . but, then again, if these were going to be their last moments alive, they had to make time, didn't they? Because if you loved someone, and you left without telling them that, then how would they ever know how special they were?

They stood there like that for what was probably only seconds, but seemed like a lifetime. Finally, they each stepped back, knowing what had to be done and knowing it was more important than just the two of them.

Sam took the lead, threading in and out of the cars that cluttered up the circular driveway. He was heading toward the back of the house, which made sense. The cops would most likely have the front covered.

Daff was about five feet behind Sam when the door of a large black Lincoln Town Car was thrown open and a heavyset man with dark skin stepped out. Shit. It was the goon from the swamp.

Daphne zagged to dodge his grasp and didn't stop running.

"I've got this," Sam called as he executed a neat one-hundred-and-eighty-degree turn and engaged al-Sayed's thug.

Daff kept on toward the house. She could hear a commotion from the back patio, but didn't know if that's where Jenna was, or if the noise was from the people attending Nathan Solem's CEO summit.

As soon as she rounded the corner of the house, she got her answer.

Jenna Richardson, also known by her maiden name of Jenna Marisol, stood in a pool of sunshine holding a glittering purple glass bottle in her right hand. She was surrounded by uniformed officers who had their guns trained on her, but Daphne knew that wasn't the answer. If they shot her, Jenna would drop the bottle, releasing a virulent strain of anthrax into the soft breeze blowing in from off the beach.

Once the spores hit the air, there was no telling how far they would spread.

FORTY-ONE

"IT wasn't your fault, Jenna," Daphne said loudly, and all eyes turned toward her.

She had waited to speak until she was nearly to the patio, twenty feet from where Jenna was standing. She was still too far away, but she couldn't get any closer without the cops trying to stop her.

Jenna remained silent, eyeing her coldly.

"You couldn't have known what your husband was going to do," Daff continued, nudging the bottle of bleach in front of her as she tried to get closer.

"Stop right there," one of the policemen ordered.

"I'm FBI," Daphne lied. "My credentials were destroyed in a fire this morning at Mrs. Richardson's house. You can call my boss, Max Raiker, at the New York office if you need verification." Amazing how easily the words dripped from her tongue. And as Daff said them, she realized something—she missed her old job. She missed the long hours, the sudden bursts of excitement, the knowledge that what she was doing could make a difference. Yeah, so the downside was that when she fucked up, it happened in a big way. But the thing the media always missed was how much crime and terrorism the brave men and women in the CIA and FBI had prevented. Probably because when nothing happened, it didn't sell newspapers or advertising space on the nightly news.

Daff turned her attention back to Jenna and ignored the local cop. That, if nothing else, might convince him she was a Fed.

"You couldn't have known," she repeated.

Jenna shrugged, but didn't loosen her grip on the perfume bottle. "I knew he was depressed, but he refused to go to the doctor, refused to take his medication. I should have insisted."

"Doing this isn't going to solve anything," Daff cajoled, taking another step closer to Jenna and holding out her hand, silently beseeching Jenna to hand over the bioweapon.

Jenna just shook her head.

"Your husband did what he did and he alone is responsible for that act. You can't blame yourself," Daff said, thinking that maybe if she seemed empathetic, Jenna would give herself up.

Jenna tilted her chin, her slate gray eyes as dead as a shark's, and said, "I don't blame myself," she said, then waved her free hand at the crowd gathered around and watching her so intently. "I blame them."

Daff sensed that the remark was to be Jenna's parting shot, so she crouched down and grabbed the bottle of bleach at her feet. She had no idea if throwing it in the direction Jenna sprayed would be at all effective, but it was her only hope.

Only, as she straightened with the jug in her hand, a man

burst out of the crowd and tackled Jenna, their arms and legs flailing as they fell into the pool.

"HAVE your lab check out the prints that were found at Keith Melman's house the day he died. I'll bet you'll find at least one set that matches Ms. Richardson." Daphne stood off to the side of the patio where the local police were busy taking down names and statements from those who had witnessed Jenna's final meltdown.

The cop in charge—the one who had challenged Daphne earlier—had cuffed Jenna's hands behind her back and was leading her away.

"Also, be sure your team asks if anyone took anything from her today, a soda, something to eat, even a towel or . . . I don't know. Anything." Daff shrugged helplessly. The frightening thing about biological and chemical weapons was how easy they could be hidden in everyday objects. Anthrax in a perfume bottle. Botulism in a catered meal. Parathion smeared on a towel. Her weapons could be hidden anywhere.

"Excuse me? Did you say we shouldn't have taken anything from this woman?" A pretty blonde with huge brown eyes approached. She was holding a child of about three or four by the hand.

"Yes. Why? Did she give you something?" Daff asked.

"Sunscreen," the woman whispered, her large eyes going even wider. "I put it on Emily just before the police arrived."

"Do you know where the bottle is? Did Ms. Richardson leave it out here?"

The woman nodded and pointed toward a lounge chair that was covered by a thick white towel. Daff hurried over and found an economy-sized bottle of sunscreen. Using the towel to protect her from getting anything on her, she picked up the bottle and held it aloft. "Is this it?" she asked.

Again, the blonde nodded.

"Hey, can one of you get me an evidence bag? This needs to go to a lab for testing. Now." Daff glanced at the nearest cop, who ran off to get what she'd ordered. In the meantime, she had bad news for the young mother. "Get to the hospital, right now. Tell the doctor that you and your daughter have been exposed to a chemical weapon, most likely parathion."

When Daff had finished bagging the sunscreen, she turned back to find Sam watching her from a stone bench at the edge of the patio. She started in his direction, but stopped when Nathan Solem stepped in front of her.

"I owe you an apology," he said.

Daff waved him off. "Don't worry about it. I probably would have thought I was a nutcase if I were in your situation, too."

"Well, I'm sorry. I see now that you were only trying to help."

"Thank you," Daff said, figuring the best thing to do would be to accept his apology graciously.

"Do you know . . ." Nathan stopped, cleared his throat, glanced over at the sparkling water of the swimming pool. When he looked back, he couldn't quite meet Daphne's eyes. "How long will it take to find out if anything was released into the water?"

Daff knew what he was asking. Was he going to die for his heroic gesture?

She didn't know. If Jenna had managed to squeeze the atomizer after they went into the pool, it was possible that both she and Nathan would die.

With a sigh, Daphne rubbed her forehead with one hand. "I don't know, but I'm sure they'll rush the labs."

"I don't regret it," Nathan said softly, and Daff looked up to see that he was gazing at his daughter, who sat holding a toddler in her lap while the child's parents gave their statements to the police.

"I would die to protect my child's life," Nathan continued.

Daphne reached out and squeezed his arm. "I understand," she said, thinking—oddly enough—of her mother. Perhaps it was her own near-death experience today that had her thinking of things in a different, more positive light.

What if, instead of abandoning her, her mother was actually trying to do what was best for her daughter when she'd run off and left her with Jack Madison? Daff's life from that point on had gotten better. She had a stable life, a roof over her head, and a father and brother who loved her.

Maybe Mary Catherine had committed the most unselfish act of all the day she'd walked out of Daphne's life.

Or maybe it was all horseshit, and dear ol' Mom had simply not wanted to be saddled with a kid while she went off and partied her life away.

Most likely, it was a combination of the two, but for the first time in a very long time, Daff found herself wanting to believe that maybe it was more of the former than the latter.

"Ye gods, I'm turning into freaking Mary Sunshine," Daff murmured under her breath.

"What are you muttering about?" Sam came up and threw an arm around her shoulders, and Daff found herself leaning into him. God, it felt good to be held by him.

"Nothing," she answered. "What happened to al-Sayed's goon?"

Sam raised one eyebrow at her mockingly. "What do you think?"

"I think I love you," she answered with a grin. Gotta love a guy who knew how to remove the obstacles in your path.

"Good. I've always thought that would be an important trait in the woman I planned to marry."

Daphne's hand fluttered to her heart and she blinked up at Sam in a melodramatic manner. "Why, Sam Bryson, I do declare. Are you asking me to marry you?"

"As a matter of fact—"

The cop in charge interrupted before Sam could finish whatever it was he was going to say. "Ms. Donovan? I've got a Max Raiker on the phone. He says he'd like to talk to you."

Daff gulped. Shit. She was in trouble now.

After wiping her palms on her still-damp jeans, she took the phone the cop was holding out to her. "Donovan," she answered, trying to sound as if she weren't nervous. Max Raiker might not be her boss anymore, but he could put some serious hurt on her if he chose to.

She waited, half-expecting Raiker to reach through the phone line and rip her heart out through her throat.

Which was why she was so surprised when, instead, he said calmly, "You know, I always admired your tenacity. Once you got a lead, you'd never let it go. That's one of the things that made you such a fine agent."

What?

The compliment—especially coming from Max Raiker—was completely unexpected. If this damn city hadn't already wrung every last tear from her, Daff might have found herself tearing up. But the truth was she was cried out, so her former boss's praise just filled her with pride.

"Thank you, sir."

"Look, I'm busy and don't have time to beat around the bush here. I have an opening in my unit and I wondered if you wanted back in."

Daff pulled the receiver away from her ear and frowned at it. Surely she had not heard that right. Had Max Raiker really just offered her a job?

She put the phone back to her ear. "When I resigned, you told me I'd never be welcome back," she reminded him, though it probably wasn't prudent to do so.

When Raiker answered, he sounded weary. "I was angry when you left. I didn't understand how you could give up when 9/11 proved just how important the work we were doing was."

"So . . . why ask me back now?" Daff asked tentatively, not sure she wanted to know the answer.

"Let's just say I've learned some things over the last five years that have changed my perspective." Raiker let the words hang in the air for a long moment before he snapped back to full I-don't-have-time-for-your-bullshit mode. "So do you want the job or not?"

Daphne looked up at Sam, who was watching her with a questioning look on his face. A month ago, she wouldn't have even considered it. But now . . . Now she was shocked by how much the thought of being back in the game appealed to her.

She glanced around at the CEOs and their families gathered in Nathan Solem's backyard. Because of her, these people were still alive today. If she'd given up and crawled back into that dark hole she'd been living in for the past five years, they'd all be dead.

Maybe that wasn't enough to atone for failing to stop 9/11 from happening, but it was a start. How many more tragedies could she help to prevent?

None, if she kept going on as she had been, trailing cheating spouses and embezzling employees.

Daff chewed on the inside of her bottom lip. "Can I get back to you?" she asked.

"You've got twenty-four hours," Raiker said. Then the line went dead.

Slowly, Daff lowered the phone.

"Who was that?" Sam asked.

"My old boss."

"Oh? And what did he want?"

Daphne pondered how best to broach this subject. Sam was happy here in Naples, had a nice quiet life now that he was out of the Navy and didn't have to deal with terrorists and thugs every day. How would he feel about being thrown back into it, about moving to New York, where any apartment they could afford would be smaller—and much less posh—than the stateroom on Nathan Solem's yacht.

Face it. She was kidding herself. There was no way Sam would give up what he had here for that.

Daff straightened her shoulders and turned to face Sam. As much as she wanted to take the job, she couldn't ask him to sacrifice so much for her. And she wasn't going anywhere without him. She was tired of living this nomadic existence, always walking away from people before she could get too attached. She opened her mouth to tell Sam that Max had just wanted to congratulate her, but she stopped when Sam put a finger to her lips.

Daphne fell in love all over again when he bent down, smoothed a lock of hair from her face, and whispered, "I've heard New York is beautiful in the spring."

"You can't really want this," Daff protested, fighting the hope that was rising in her chest. "It will mean long hours, too much work, too much stress. You know what it's like."

Sam sighed, but didn't let her go. "Yes, I do know. It's going to be hell on me. I'm going to have to watch you leave every morning, knowing that you'll be out there. In danger. And there'll be nothing I can do to protect you. It'll be my worst nightmare."

"Then why aren't you fighting it?" Daphne asked, her eyes locked on his as if no one else in the world existed.

"Because, Daphne," Sam answered, lowering his mouth to hers. "Nobody ever said it would be easy to love a hero."

EPILOGUE

9/11/2006

"I thought I'd find you here."

Daphne Donovan didn't bother looking up from her dollar-twenty-five cup of coffee as the man slid his stocky frame into the booth next to her. Outwardly she appeared calm and unruffled—uncaring, even—despite the thought that ran through her head: *I'm so busted.* She raised the heavy porcelain cup to her lips, ignoring the heat coming through the too-hot cup and burning her fingertips as she pretended to take a sip.

Across the street, work was still going on at the former site of the World Trade towers. It would be years before construction was complete.

Daff set down her cup of coffee and leaned over to take Sam's hand. "I just thought it was fitting to come here today."

Sam nodded and squeezed her hand. He understood why she was here.

One of her first cases upon returning to the FBI had been to work with an informant—Adnan al-Sayed—who was posing as a terrorist sympathizer in order to get information about a terror cell's activities down in Florida. Today, the group was to have driven rented cargo trucks loaded with explosives over select bridges in the nation—the Howard Frankland in Tampa, the I-90 floating bridge in Seattle, the Brooklyn Bridge in Manhattan—and, at 9:11 A.M., detonate their charges, destroying the bridges along with everyone on them.

Daphne had helped uncover the plot, even though all she'd had to go on was al-Sayed's description of his contact. It had started with an oddly shaped birthmark on the man's right hand . . . and ended with nearly three dozen arrests in twenty-one states.

No one would ever know how many lives had been saved. But even if it had only been one, it was worth it. Silently, Daphne promised that she'd never walk away again. As long as they continued fighting the evil, there was still hope.

Daff took a sip of her now-cooled coffee and closed her eyes before the emotions she'd kept at bay for so long threatened to swamp her.

The gaping wound in the earth had finally begun to heal. And so had she.

THEY'RE EXPERTS IN CRIME—AND PASSION.

Dangerous Curves

by

Jacey Ford

THEY CAN BREACH THE SECURITY AT ANY BANK IN ATLANTA AND STILL BE DONE IN TIME FOR COCKTAILS.

Aimee, Daphne, and Raine are former FBI agents who have started their own security company: Partners in Crime. But when Raine's old boyfriend, Agent Calder Preston, has a job for the Partners, sparks—and bullets—begin to fly.

0-451-19685-2

Also available from

BERKLEY SENSATION

Duchess of Fifth Avenue
by Ruth Ryan Langan
The *New York Times* bestselling author of "heartwarming, emotionally involving romances"* brings the Gilded Age to life.
0-425-20889-3

The Penalty Box
by Deirdre Martin
From the *USA Today* bestselling author, a novel about a hockey heartthrob, a stubborn brainiac, and a battle of wills that just might end in love.
0-425-20890-7

The Kiss
by Elda Minger
After she finds her fiancé with another woman, Tess Sommerville packs up and takes a road trip to Las Vegas, ready to gamble—on love.
0-425-20681-5

**Library Journal*

Available wherever books are sold or at penguin.com

Also available from
BERKLEY SENSATION

Beloved Stranger
by Patricia Potter

In the second book of her Scottish trilogy, Potter tells the story of a man who has lost his past and faces an uncertain present of peril—and an impossible love.

0-425-20742-0

Awaiting the Moon
by Donna Simpson

It is said that werewolves roam the woods around Wolfram Castle, where Elizabeth Stanwycke has come to tutor the Count's neice, but her main concern is her attraction to the mysterious Count.

0-425-20849-4

Available wherever books are sold or at penguin.com